Found

Erin Kinsley is a full-time writer.
She grew up in Yorkshire and currently lives
in East Anglia.

Praise for Found:

'his is brilliant, utterly compelling, heart-wrenching
writing. I was gripped and loved it.'
Peter James

n unputdownable thriller that is also a mesmerising
stu y of a family facing their worst nightmare and realising
at it is only the beginning. The characters and events
will stay with you for a very long time.'
Elly Griffiths

gripping blend of police procedural and psychological
iller. Well-paced writing, finely drawn characters and
suspenseful plot make this novel a compulsive read.
Once started, impossible to put down!'
Minette Walters

und is one of those rare finds – a page turner that is
ally remarkable for the beauty and consideration given
o the writing. It will suck you in and take you on a
journey that stays with you.'
Jo Spain

found

erin kinsley

HEADLINE

Copyright © 2019 Erin Kinsley

The right of Erin Kinsley to be identified as the Author of
the Work has been asserted by her in accordance with the
Copyright, Designs and Patents Act 1988.

First published in 2019 by
HEADLINE PUBLISHING GROUP

1

Cataloguing in Publication Data is available from the British Library

ISBN 978 1 4722 6077 2

Typeset in Adobe Garamond by CC Book Production

Printed and bound in Great Britain by Clays Lrd, Elcograf S.p.A.

Headline's policy is to use papers that are natural, renewable and
recyclable products and made from wood grown in well-managed forests
and other controlled sources. The logging and manufacturing processes
are expected to conform to the environmental regulations
of the country of origin.

MIX
Paper from
responsible sources
FSC
www.fsc.org FSC® C104740

HEADLINE PUBLISHING GROUP
An Hachette UK Company
Carmelite House
50 Victoria Embankment
London EC4Y 0DZ

www.headline.co.uk

www.hachette.co.uk

For all those not found, and those who miss them

'It is tact that is golden, not silence.'

— *Samuel Butler*

'Out beyond ideas of wrong-doing and right-doing,
there is a field. I'll meet you there.
When the soul lies down in that grass
the world is too full to talk about.'

— *Rumi*

Your Worst Nightmare

ONE

11 October
Berkshire

There are so many ifs, and so many if onlys. If only rugby practice hadn't over-run. If only Evan hadn't gone and lost a boot. If only he'd decided to bypass the newsagent's and had caught the earlier bus, the one he missed by just twenty seconds.

If only we could all sleep soundly at night, knowing we were safe from wicked people.

The Under-Twelves First Fifteen haven't played well, and there's a match against All Saints on Saturday. Mr Griffiths likes the school teams to succeed, so he makes the boys stay an extra five minutes, practising their passing in the rain. In the changing rooms, the boys pull off their muddy boots and socks, dropping their filthy shorts and shirts on the tiled floor as they run into the showers. The water, for once, is hotter than lukewarm, and Evan and Stewie linger under the jets, bringing feeling back to their cold-reddened hands and white-numb toes. By the time they're out and dressed, the other boys are

3

gone. Mr Griffiths is in the staffroom, drinking the day's last mug of tea before he drives home.

Evan has lost a boot. Stewie doesn't help him look for it but leans impatiently against a stand of coat-pegs urging Evan to get a move on, while Evan lies down on the floor to search under the boot-racks, dirtying his trousers and his blazer. He finds the boot under someone's forgotten shorts, hangs the shorts up on a peg and stuffs the boot into his kitbag.

It's a little after five. As they head for the front doors, Stewie and Evan's voices echo in deserted corridors lined with cabinets of shields and silver trophies. In the photographs on the walls, the faces of past generations stare mutely through the glass, the bright youths of recent decades in lifelike colour, their predecessors in monochrome and sepia.

By the main entrance, Mr Prentice the caretaker is waiting to lock up, clinking an impatient rhythm on his thigh with a hoop of keys. He tells the boys to hurry up, and they do. The staff car park is all but empty, though Mr Griffiths' old Subaru is still there, as is the headmaster's Passat. The boys head down the drive towards the open gates, chattering about homework, about Xbox games and Saturday's coming match.

There's a van parked on the forecourt of the newsagent's on Belmont Avenue, and Mr Jadoon is watching a young Asian man carry cases of wine to the storeroom round the back. The boys search their pockets for coins, and Mr Jadoon leads them inside before going to stand sentinel by the CCTV monitor. Evan and Stewie dither over their choices, until Evan settles on a can of Fanta and Stewie chooses salt and vinegar crisps. By the time they reach the counter, there's another customer

4

ahead of them; when he reaches out to pay for his milk, Stewie notices his tattoo, a red-and-black snake twisting on the back of his hand. Catching him admiring his artwork, the man gives Stewie a wink as he picks up his change.

As the boys go outside, the tattooed man is walking away from them, down Ruskin Road. The boys' route is along Belmont Avenue. Evan pops the tab of his Fanta and Stewie offers him a couple of his crisps. Their schoolbags – one for sports kit, one for books – are heavy, and, since he's small for his age, Evan's slow him down. There's a bus approaching, but Evan doesn't run to catch it because he hasn't finished his drink, and the driver won't let him on unless he dumps it. No one is waiting at the stop, and the bus sails by.

When they reach the bus shelter, the boys part company casually, expecting to be talking online in a while. Stewie walks on alone towards Church Road, and home. Evan lays his bags down on the pavement.

Seven minutes later, the next bus arrives, but Evan is no longer waiting at the stop. He and his bags are gone, but his can of pop is lying on its side, seeping sticky liquid into the gutter.

Evan's mum Claire has tea ready at six o'clock, but Evan isn't home. At quarter past, more annoyed than worried, she calls Stewie, who tells her what he can – which isn't much – and Claire thanks him. As she ends the call, the first tendrils of worry tighten in her stomach. When the door slams at six-thirty, her eyes close in relief, but it isn't Evan who comes into the kitchen, but Matt. He tells her not to worry, and she starts making more calls. By seven, they're both beginning to panic, though Matt's hiding his fear with confident bluster. At eight, they ring the police. By the time they're taken seriously, it's gone eleven.

And by that time, Evan's in a very bad place indeed.

TWO

Stewie's mother Vicky switches on the bedside light and checks the time: 1.42 a.m. Someone's hammering at the front door, firing up a long-held dread of uniforms and bad news, but Paul's there in bed beside her, and Stewie and George are in their rooms. For a moment, Vicky doubts these certainties, and reaches out to touch Paul's back. His breathing changes, becoming quicker and shallower than the slow rhythms of deep sleep, and she knows he's at least half awake.

'There's someone at the door.'

She feels him tensing as he listens, but there's nothing to hear.

'You're dreaming,' he says. 'For God's sake, turn that light off.'

The hammering comes again. Now Paul's wide awake.

'Who the hell is that?' He squints towards the clock, but without his glasses, he can't read the face. 'What time is it?'

'Nearly two.' Vicky gets out of bed and puts on the pink dressing gown hanging behind the bedroom door. The room is cold; the heating won't come on for hours. As she opens the door, Paul moves to follow her. No one brings good news at this time of night, and he's thinking of his mother and father. Or maybe his brother, but wouldn't they just phone?

Vicky turns on the landing light. As she goes downstairs, the creaking of the treads seems loud. She switches on the hall light and the outside light over the front door, and through the frosted glass she sees two people. She decides to wait for Paul. The strangers at the door don't knock again, but stand and wait in silence.

Paul pulls on a pair of jeans and yesterday's T-shirt and finds his glasses. The anxiety for his mum and dad has solidified, and he comes downstairs at a run, not caring if he wakes the boys. He sees the figures at the door and glances at Vicky, who's standing back so he can be in charge. He picks up the keys from the hall table, then hesitates.

These people might be anyone.

He calls through the door.

'Who is it?'

'Police.'

Vicky's hand goes to her mouth, and Paul's head feels suddenly light. He fits the key to the lock and opens the door. The night air is dank, and the sodium-orange of the streetlights is hazy through fog. There's a car parked across the driveway, a dark-coloured Peugeot. A man and a woman are standing on the step, both wearing suits as if it were the middle of the day. The man holds up a wallet with a badge.

'Mr and Mrs Wareham?' His manner is polite, but he's not smiling. He closes the wallet in a practised movement, and slips it into his trouser pocket. 'I'm Detective Sergeant Hagen, this is DI Naylor. Can we come in?'

There's a moment's silence. Paul fears the worst; for the first time in his life, he knows what people mean by going weak at the knees. Vicky is more composed. Her mother's in a home, with severe dementia. Her passing would never warrant a visit from the police.

'What's this about?' asks Paul.

'If we could talk inside,' says Hagen.

Vicky leads the way to the living room, wishing she'd tidied round before she went to bed. Last night's wine glasses are on the coffee table, and the basket of ironing she never got to is on a chair. She picks up the basket and carries it out to the hall.

When she comes back, Naylor invites Paul and Vicky to take seats on the sofa, as if this is her house now. Naylor takes the armchair. She's the kind of woman Paul might find attractive under other circumstances, the suit jacket hiding the kind of curves he likes, dark hair pinned up in a messy French twist. Hagen helps himself to a dining chair, placing it at the centre of the room. He sits down, his legs spread, leaning forward on to his thighs, taking up space. He looks long and hard at Paul, and then at Vicky, while Paul is wishing he would just deliver the blow.

'I expect you're wondering why we're here,' says Hagen. He speaks with a Geordie burr which evokes the mean streets of Newcastle, but Hagen never denies his suburban origins. 'We apologise for disturbing you at this hour, but I'm sure you appreciate that sometimes we deal with events where time is of the essence and we have to act quickly. Unfortunately, we're involved in such an incident tonight. A young boy has gone missing.'

Paul feels a huge sense of relief, and lets go the breath he didn't realise he was holding. Not his disaster, then, but someone else's. Immediately, he feels ashamed of his selfishness.

'Who?' asks Vicky.

'Evan Ferrers.'

'Evan? Really? Oh my God.' Vicky is baffled. 'But when can he possibly . . . What's going on?'

'Evan didn't come home from school yesterday,' says Naylor. Her tone is careful, and Paul suspects the script's rehearsed. 'Mrs Ferrers thinks he was with your son yesterday afternoon. Stewie, is it?'

'Stewie, yes. He and Evan were at rugby practice. I assume they left together. They usually do.'

'Did Mrs Ferrers phone here at all?'

'Well, yes,' says Vicky. 'She said she didn't know where Evan was and asked to speak to Stewie. I don't think he was much help, but she didn't ring again, so I just assumed Evan had come home. I never thought for one moment he'd still be missing. Oh God, I should have called her, shouldn't I? Poor Claire! How is she?'

'What time did Mrs Ferrers call?'

Mentally running through the evening's banal structure, Vicky shakes her head.

'I don't know. About six, six-thirty, I suppose.'

'I wonder if we could speak to Stewie, Mrs Wareham?'

The request feels polite, but from Hagen's face, Vicky knows the politeness is all veneer.

'But it's the middle of the night,' she objects. 'He's got school tomorrow.'

Paul, Hagen and Naylor all look at her, and Vicky blushes.

'I'm sorry,' she says. 'I'll go and wake him.'

*

Stewie's dreams have taken a nightmarish turn. A stealthy sniper lies in wait for him in a network of dark rooms. As she pushes open his bedroom door, Vicky is pointlessly quiet, conditioned by years of parenting. The light from the landing forms a triangle on the carpet, acute at first, and as she opens the door wider, obtuse. It's geometry of the kind Stewie struggles with, but these days the more Paul tries to help him, the more Stewie becomes stubborn and shuts down.

His room smells unmistakably of him, a smell that's changed in recent months from the bubble-bath sweetness of little boyhood to supermarket deodorant and a base note of musk which permeates his sheets and all his clothes. The hoody and joggers he wore after school are heaped on the floor, and yesterday's uniform trousers hang from a belt-loop on a chair. There are posters on the walls – *The Walking Dead*, a Bugatti Veyron, the psychedelic masks of CamelPhat, whose music Vicky actually likes – and everywhere there's the clutter of Stewie's pastimes, DVDs and game CDs in and out of boxes, his skateboard, gloves and knee pads, the bike helmet he refuses to wear.

And in the midst of the chaos, there's Stewie, safe in this room where he should be, and Vicky believes she can imagine how Claire feels, how it would be to be standing in this doorway with Stewie missing, gone. Even the thought of it stirs her stomach, and her heart contracts as if a malicious hand has squeezed it, and her mind flashes up an image of herself, demented with grief.

She shuts the image down. Not me. Her.

The gratitude she feels is shameful, but even though she knows how base it is, the gratitude's still there.

Stewie's moving restlessly in his sleep, tormented by his

Xbox hangover. In a loud whisper, she says his name, not wanting to startle him by waking him suddenly, forgetting that often these days it's difficult to wake him at all. But something in Stewie's subconscious is anxious to escape the sniper, and in the triangle of light from the landing, she sees his eyes blinking and bright.

'Are you awake, Stewie?'

His mother's presence in his room, in the dark, signals something's going on, and Stewie sits up.

'What's the matter? Is everyone OK?'

'You need to come downstairs.' Vicky's still whispering, thinking of George. 'The police are here.' Stewie's face, half in shadow, shows he's startled, and she realises she's scared him, despite her best intentions. 'You haven't done anything wrong. They want to talk to you about Evan.'

'What about Evan?'

She hasn't thought what words to use, but actually, it doesn't matter.

'He didn't come home from school.'

'Yes, he did.' Stewie frowns. 'I saw him get on the bus.'

'Did you, Stewie?'

He considers.

'Not actually get on it.' He's climbing from the bed, wearing the look of puzzlement which was habitual to him when he was small. On his developing features, it's still endearing.

She reaches behind the door for the dressing gown he rarely wears, a present from his grandmother.

'Better put this on. The heating went off hours ago.'

For once, he puts on the dressing gown without argument.

*

12

In the kitchen, Paul's making tea, looking out as the kettle heats at the backs of the neighbours' houses. All are in darkness but one, where the downstairs lights are blazing. For a mad moment, Paul wonders if it's Evan's house, but they live two miles away. He finds the rarely used sugar bowl in the cupboard, and puts it on the tray with the best mugs, realising how much of his mother's training has rubbed off now he's confronted with authority. The kettle boils, and he makes four teas, adding milk. Finding four matching teaspoons in the cutlery drawer, he picks up the tray. *So much for me the rebel*, he thinks as he carries it through to the living room. So much for the years of student protests and sit-ins, for the baiting of the pigs. Now they're here, and he's bringing out matching teaspoons. Times change.

In the living room, he finds the seating arrangements have changed too. Stewie and Vicky are on the sofa, and Naylor and Hagen both have dining chairs. The scene looks cramped, unnatural, like a Christmas visit from distant relatives, except that Stewie and Vicky look self-consciously vulnerable in their night-clothes. Stewie is swamped by that dressing gown he never wears; it makes him look small, and Paul feels suddenly protective towards them both. Vicky's hair is a pillow-ruffled mess, and he knows when she looks in a mirror she'll be mortified, especially since the policewoman's casual up-do is designed to look smart come hell or high water, a style which could never be out of place.

He puts the tray down on the coffee table, and channelling his mother again, wonders if he ought to have brought biscuits. Stewie might have appreciated them. Then he glances at his son and realises the boy is scared. The last thing he'll be thinking of is biscuits.

'Help yourselves,' says Paul, and bypasses the armchair to sit next to Stewie on the sofa. Stewie seems to want him close, and immediately moves over to make room.

Hagen is smiling at Stewie, but his smile looks contrived as a warm-up technique, a ploy to facilitate a quick pick of Stewie's brain. Naylor takes a mug, spoons in sugar and stirs. She seems very interested in her tea and uninterested in Stewie, but Paul knows that's an act to take the pressure off his son.

Naylor lays the teaspoon back on the tray and sips her drink.

'So we just need you to tell us exactly what happened when you left school,' Hagen is saying. 'Do you know what time it was when you left?'

No chance, thinks Paul.

'Not really,' says Stewie.

'About what time do you think it was, Stewie?' puts in Naylor. 'What would you guess?'

'After rugby practice.'

'They usually finish about five,' says Vicky.

'So is that what time it was?' asks Naylor. 'You finished rugby practice at the usual sort of time?'

Stewie shrugs.

'Who takes rugby practice?' asks Hagen. 'Which teacher?'

'Mr Griffiths.'

Hagen produces a notebook and pen. He writes something down and leaves his notebook open on his knee, positioned so he's the only one who can read it.

'What did you do when you finished practice?' asks Naylor.

Painstakingly, she prises the minutiae of twenty-five minutes

14

from Stewie: the lost boot, the newsagent's and what they bought, the goodbye at the bus stop.

'Did you see anyone you know?'

'No.'

'Did anyone speak to you?'

'The shopkeeper.'

'What did he say?'

'He told us how much to pay.'

'That's all?'

Stewie nods.

'Was there anyone else in the shop?'

'There was a man with tattoos. He was bald.'

'What kind of tattoos were they? Can you describe them?'

'He had a snake on the back of his hand.'

'And on the way to the bus stop, did you see any cars you recognised? Any friends or neighbours going by?'

Stewie thinks, and shakes his head.

'Thanks, Stewie,' says Naylor. 'You've been a real help. Just one last question, for now. Did Evan seem OK to you? Was anything bothering him, any trouble at school, anything like that?'

The living room door opens, and there, blinking away sleep in his dinosaur onesie, is George. He looks around in bewilderment, then frowns at his mother.

'Mum, what's going on?'

Vicky jumps up and grabs his hand.

'Back to bed, Georgie,' she says. 'This is a grown-up thing.'

'But Stewie's here.'

'He's older than you. Excuse us.'

She leads him from the room. As they go up the stairs, George is still protesting his exclusion.

Naylor smiles at Stewie.

'So, you were telling us about Evan. Does he have any worries? Any trouble with bullies, anyone who's been picking on him, maybe?'

Paul is pleased she's using the present tense.

Stewie pulls a face and shrugs.

'I don't think so,' he says.

There seems no more to be said. From upstairs, they hear Vicky and George begin to argue.

Naylor reaches forward, picks up her mug of almost-cold tea and drinks down what's left.

Hagen puts away his notebook.

'I think that's it for now, Mr Wareham,' he says.

Naylor finds a business card, and hands it to Paul.

'We'll need Stewie to come into the station and make a statement,' she says, 'especially a description of the tattoos. We have specially trained staff to interview minors, and you can stay with him. It's all low-key, nothing to worry about, but as soon as possible, if you don't mind.'

As the police officers stand to leave, Stewie puts the question Paul didn't dare ask.

'Where's Evan? What's happened to him?'

Naylor smiles.

'I don't think he's far away,' she says. 'We've got lots of people looking for him. Try not to worry.'

Paul closes the door behind them. As he follows Stewie upstairs, the Peugeot's engine starts, and the car drives away. With the streets deserted, they hear it for a surprisingly long time.

Paul watches his son discard the despised dressing gown and

16

climb back into bed. He kisses Stewie's forehead and strokes his hair, feeling, for some reason, close to tears.

'Night night, son.'

As he's about to close the bedroom door, Stewie says, 'Dad.'

'What's up?'

'I think I should have waited with Evan to make sure he got on the bus.'

Paul hesitates.

'Don't worry about it,' he says. 'Don't go thinking anything's your fault. Probably someone gave him a lift.'

He wants to unsay the words the moment they're out. As Paul shuts Stewie into the darkness of his bedroom, both father and son are considering the same uncomfortable thought. Maybe someone did offer Evan a lift, but what if it was an offer Evan wasn't allowed to refuse?

Hagen's observing the speed limits, even though they're alone on the suburban streets. Naylor watches the needle on the speedometer, and never sees it rise above 33 mph.

She isn't keen to return to Evan's family home. The mother's distress is harrowing.

Hagen flicks on the indicator to turn right. Rules are rules, and it doesn't matter to him that it's not necessary, that there's no one to see it. The radio on the dashboard crackles and falls silent.

'So what do you think?' asks Hagen. 'If you were the betting kind, where would you be putting your money?'

Naylor glances across at him.

'Do you mean, based on my years of experience?'

'Based on past outcomes.'

17

'Decent family, no history of running away, no known problems at school. Put two and two together, I'd say we have reason to worry.'

They're turning into the Ferrerses' cul-de-sac, all post-war semis, the front gardens mostly sacrificed for block-paved parking. Outside Evan's house, the vehicles are all police-owned, but that will soon change, when the media arrive.

Hagen pulls in behind a patrol car. There's a uniformed policewoman standing under the Ferrerses' porch-light.

'Goes without saying, that stays between you and me,' says Naylor, getting out of the car.

THREE

12 October
Yorkshire

Jack Ferrers has been an early riser from being a boy, and even with most of the livestock sold and the workload not a third of what it was, old habits die hard. Jack likes to be up by five, even though this time of year there's still a good while before sunrise and there's nothing to see from the windows but the dark on the fells. In the long weeks of autumn and winter, all Jack does in the pre-dawn hours is make tea and read yesterday's paper.

The farmhouse at Ainsclough Top is three hundred years old, and cold seeps through every wall. In a while, Jack will bring in coal and light the range, so the place is warming through before Dora wakes, because Dora feels the cold these days, in a way she never used to.

Outside, Millie the border collie is restless, dragging her chain backwards and forwards across the stone-flagged yard. Probably she's scented a fox sniffing round the coop, and Jack thinks he'll let her loose a while to see it off.

But then the phone rings. It doesn't ring often, and in the quiet, it's jarring.

He folds the paper, goes out into the hall and picks up the receiver.

'Hello?'

'Dad? Is that you?'

Jack recognises Matt's voice, though it's different to normal, without its usual cheeriness.

'Don't you know what time it is?' asks Jack. 'You'll wake your mother.'

'Dad.' Matt sounds broken, tearful, and Jack knows there's going to be something bad. He closes his eyes. 'Dad, something's happened to Evan.'

Jack feels the need to sit, but there's no chair. On the side table, alongside the phone, are photographs in frames. There's one of Jack and Evan down by the beck, Evan a smiling four-year-old with sticklebacks in a jar, his grandpa's hand resting on his head. In the photo, the sun is shining. Outside, Millie begins to bark.

'Dad?'

'I'm here, son.' Overhead, he hears the creak of floorboards, Dora out of bed and coming to see who's on the phone. Jack keeps his voice low. 'Tell me what's happened.'

Matt's voice is unsteady as he tells the news. Jack senses Dora at the head of the stairs, listening, and turns his back so his face will give nothing away. He lets Matt talk, until his son has no more to say.

'What do you want us to do?' asks Jack. 'We'll come down. I'll get Bob Sturgess to keep an eye on this place.'

20

He listens to Matt give the reasons why his father should stay where he is: the house is full of police and they've been warned to expect the press.

'Whatever you think is best,' says Jack. 'Do you want to talk to your mother?'

There's silence on the line which Jack knows is Matt shaking his head. The stairs creak under Dora's feet.

'You tell her,' says Matt. 'But play it down, Dad.'

Jack has no idea how he would play such a thing down.

'We'll ring you in a couple of hours, then,' he says. 'But you let us know, the second there's any news. The very second, you hear me?'

After he hangs up, he takes a moment to compose himself.

Dora asks, 'Who on earth was that, this time of the morning?'

Jack's heart feels strange. He wonders where he's put his pills.

'Jack? Are you all right?'

'I was making tea,' he says.

She follows him through to the kitchen, tightening the belt on her dressing gown, her worn sheepskin slippers slapping on the cold tiles.

He sits down at the table, motioning her to do the same.

'That was Matt,' he says.

'Matt? What did he want? Is something wrong? You don't look well, Jack. I'll go and get your tablets.'

She moves to get up, but he places his hand over hers to

stop her. She has such small hands, not much bigger than a child's.

'Dora,' he says. 'It's not Matt, it's Evan. They think someone might have taken him.'

Her face takes on an expression he's never seen before, not in all their forty years together. If pressed to give it a name, he would say *stricken*. He tightens his hand on hers, hoping it will help her cope, hoping it will give him strength.

'What do you mean?' she asks. 'Taken him where?'

Jack shakes his head, and realises the hot pressure in his eyes is the smarting of tears. He doesn't want to cry, because it will start Dora off, and he hates it when she cries. Mostly it makes him feel awkward, but on this occasion it would speed the breaking of his heart, and it's too early yet for heartbreak. The police believe there's an excellent possibility of a good outcome, Matt said. They expect Evan to be back home soon, safe and well.

Reminding himself of this, he decides it's what he'll tell Dora.

'They don't know where he is, that's the truth of it. He didn't come home from school yesterday. He may have gotten on the wrong bus and be lost somewhere, or had an accident. They're checking the hospitals, as you'd expect.'

'Yesterday? You mean he's been gone all night?'

Jack nods. He's controlling the pressure in his eyes, but now he finds his chin is trembling.

'The police are there, at the house. Matt says it's going to be on the news.'

'What news?' Jack gives no answer. 'You mean the national news, don't you?'

22

She doesn't wait for his response but buries her face in her hands and begins to rock.

'Our boy!' she moans. 'Our poor, precious boy!'

Jack puts an arm around her back and, now she isn't looking at him, lets the tears fall. Several leave dark spots on his trousers.

'It might be nothing, love,' he says, pulling her close. He kisses the top of her head, the grey curls which used to be mahogany brown, and breathes in the smell of lemon shampoo. 'He might easily turn up yet, right as rain. There might have been a falling out, and he's packed his bags to give his mum and dad a fright.'

Dora's clinging to him in a way she hasn't done for years. There's a handkerchief embroidered with violets in the pocket of her robe. She pulls it out and blows her nose.

'What shall we do, Jack?'

Jack kisses her hair again.

'Matt says the police think if he's run away, there's a chance he might aim for here, so we're best to sit tight. He doesn't want us to go down there right away. He says they've got all on coping with the police and the reporters. Sounds like they've a house full. If he wants us, he'll let us know.'

'We should put the telly on,' says Dora. 'The news'll be on at six.'

'Matt thinks it'll upset you.'

'That boy.' Dora wipes her eyes. 'I'm tougher than he thinks.'

Jack stands.

'I'll make a fresh pot and get the fires lit,' he says. 'If Evan does turn up here, he'll doubtless be chilled to the bone. And you'd better get yourself dressed, love, and put your baking apron on. You know if he comes, the boy'll be wanting your cake.'

FOUR

'It's just routine,' says the policewoman.

She's balancing on the edge of the sofa as if she's afraid someone might catch her sitting down, an attractive girl but young and slight, not someone Matt thinks would be of any use in the face of town centre drunks or civil disobedience. But she's a good choice for keeping him and Claire confined to the lounge, if only because he thinks she'll crumble if he shouts at her.

Matt has seen overnight changes in Claire, but none so big as in himself. The calm, reasonable man he believed himself to be has been shoved aside, making way for Matt the volatile bully, who rants and yells and can pretend no respect for those trying to help him and his family. But this new persona exhausts him, his mouthy outbursts a bigger drain of energy than the worry and no sleep, and he's glad to lapse for a time into meek compliance.

What good is shouting anyway? If they have boxes to tick, let them get on with it. Overhead, men are moving about, opening wardrobes, shifting furniture. A few moments ago, he heard the catch on the loft-hatch snap back and the rattle of the ladder descending. Now there's a heavy foot on the lowest rung.

'You'd be surprised how many missing kids are found at home. Under beds, in garages and sheds. It's always the first place we look.'

The policewoman looks slightly embarrassed at the banality of what she's just said.

Claire's eyes drift to the window and the improbable scene outside, a jam of police cars and vans with satellite dishes and broadcaster logos on their sides. She's holding an empty mug, and her hand is shaking. As she places the mug on a side table, she hears the click of Evan's bedroom door opening, and sweet relief floods through her.

She starts to get to her feet, but the policewoman shakes her head sadly, and instead of Evan's soft tread, there's the sound of a hefty male in the room above.

Claire sinks back on to the sofa and feels the prick of fresh tears. As she fumbles for a tissue, a trio of polished TV presenters are laughing on the drive, and as she watches, one of them breaks away from the group, walks brazenly to the window and puts his face to the glass.

Noticing Claire's startled expression, the policewoman crosses the room.

'Let's close this, shall we?' she says, and lowers the blind.

The lounge is suddenly in twilight. The policewoman turns on a lamp.

In the attic, someone's making their way cautiously across the ceiling beams.

As if I wouldn't know if my own son were up there, thinks Matt.

'Soon be done,' says the policewoman. 'Can I get you another cup of tea?'

*

At Ashridge police station, Hagen has asked DS Dallabrida to sit in. Dallabrida has a dangerous demeanour bred in a streetwise background, enhanced by his massive gym-junkie build from protein-packing and lifting weights. It's a look which tends to encourage suspects to co-operate sooner rather than later. He closes the door behind them, still smiling at some uniform lads' banter.

He and Hagen pull chairs up to the table, and Hagen opens up his file. Dallabrida switches on the tape, declares the date and time, and names those present in the room.

Mr Griffiths has been here a while now, alone with a cup of coffee and a promise he won't be kept long. He called in, as requested, on his lunch hour, expecting to be back on the playing fields by two. He's still wearing sweats and trainers, and faced with suits, ties and close haircuts – Dallabrida's tailoring is almost suave – he feels somehow outranked.

'You do not have to say anything,' says Dallabrida. 'But it may harm your defence if you do not mention when questioned something which you later rely on in court. Anything you do say may be given in evidence. Do you wish to have a lawyer present?'

Mr Griffiths looks alarmed.

'What's going on?' he asks. 'Is all this really necessary? I've come here voluntarily. You said an informal chat.'

'We like to keep things on the level,' says Dallabrida. 'It's for your protection, more than ours. You're not likely to suffer any police brutality with the tape running, are you?'

'I hope I'm not likely to suffer police brutality anyway,' says Mr Griffiths, catching Hagen's eye. 'Not in this day and age.'

Dallabrida's smile broadens.

'Not our style, mate,' he says.

'Shall we crack on, then?' asks Hagen. 'Thanks for coming down. We wanted to talk to you, as I'm sure you know, in connection with the disappearance of Evan Ferrers. We believe you were one of the last people to see him. One of the last adult people, that is.'

'Of course.'

Hagen runs the point of his pen down the form which is the topmost piece of paper in his file.

'Can you just confirm your full name, Mr Griffiths?'

'Robert. Robert Griffiths.'

'Date of birth?'

'Twelve, seven, seventy-two.'

The tip of Hagen's pen moves back up the form. Dallabrida's smile has disappeared.

'It says here,' says Hagen, 'your full name is Quentin Robert Griffiths. Quentin. That's an unusual name.'

'My mother had delusions of grandeur on my behalf.'

'So why didn't you say your name is Quentin?'

'Would you?'

'The thing is, Mr Griffiths, you're a person of interest to us because you've been on our radar before.' He begins to sift through his papers, as if searching for the document he requires. 'Seven years ago. A complaint was made by a pupil, one David Sellers. He said you tried to touch him up in the changing rooms. Would you like to tell us about that?'

Dallabrida folds his arms. Mr Griffiths's expression is one of incredulity.

'You have to be joking!' he says. 'For Christ's sake! A person

28

of interest? It was all trumped up, all crap! You established that at the time.'

'Actually, it was before my time. So why don't you tell us what happened?'

Mr Griffiths colours.

'I'd had a bit of a fling with the boy's mother. He didn't like it when I dropped her.'

Dallabrida raises his eyebrows in exaggerated surprise.

'So do you make a habit of having relations with pupils' mothers?'

'Once or twice.'

It's difficult to say if Dallabrida is admiring or disapproving, but Hagen's face is stern.

'Some parents would take a dim view of that,' he says. 'They might be led to think you're a man without too many scruples. I've got someone out looking for David Sellers, so we'll see what he has to say when we track him down. In the meantime, I expect we could drum up another cup of coffee while you wait.'

'If you're lucky, we might even throw in a couple of Hobnobs,' says Dallabrida.

'I want a lawyer,' says Mr Griffiths.

In the classroom, Naylor is seated at the teacher's desk. The playground shouts and screams beyond the window take her back years, but there's no smell of chalk and over-boiled dinners here. Times have moved on, to whiteboards and interaction, and the sandwich she bought for lunch in the canteen earlier was grilled chicken on ciabatta.

The man coming through the doorway is dressed casually,

without the tie the headmaster insists male teaching staff should wear. His beard is blurred into several days' growth of stubble, and his crooked teeth are ugly and discoloured as a smack addict's. But he seems pleasant enough, diffident, eager to please, softly spoken.

'I hope I'm not late?' he says.

Naylor glances at her watch, and at the list of school staff she's been given.

'Mr Prentice?'

'That's right, that's me. Gary Prentice. Gareth at birth. People like to shorten it to Gary.'

'Have a seat, Mr Prentice.'

He lays a hoop of keys on the desk and sits down in front of her, smiling unselfconsciously, in spite of his teeth.

'Thanks for taking the time to talk to me.' Naylor turns to a fresh page in her notebook and writes Gary Prentice's name at the head of the sheet. 'It's just routine. We're talking to everyone on the school staff as part of our enquiries into Evan Ferrers's disappearance.'

'It's very unsettling, especially for the parents,' says Prentice. 'I don't have children myself, but I'm sure it must be a worry.'

Naylor looks at him.

'A little more than worrying, I should say.'

'I'm sorry, yes, of course. It's hard to know what word to use.'

Naylor glances at the notes she's made on her list.

'Mr Mullis tells me you haven't been caretaker here very long.'

'About six months.'

'And before that?'

'I was at a school in Guildford.'

'And you left there why?'

'I was made redundant. The school I was at merged with another, and they already had a caretaker. He had longer tenure than me, so I was out. I was lucky to find this job. Good school, nice area.'

Naylor makes a line of notes.

'Were you in school yesterday evening?'

'I was,' says Prentice. 'There's no time off for me, in term time.'

'And did you see Evan and Stewie Wareham at all?'

'I saw them on their way out. They were the last to leave. Everyone else was long gone, so I chivvied them a bit, encouraged them on their way, you know? I was waiting to lock the front doors so I could go up to the second floor and check on the cleaners.'

Naylor doesn't look up from the notes she's writing.

'They were lucky you knew they were still in the building. If everyone else was long gone.'

Now she glances up, and sees Prentice shift in his chair.

'When I say everyone, I mean the other rugby lads,' he says. 'There were a couple of members of staff still to leave. Mr Mullis always stays late, but I knew Bob Griffiths would be going soon. I was waiting for him when I heard the boys coming down the hall. Youngsters never talk quietly, do they? Anyway, if they had been locked in, it would only have cost them a few minutes. There's a button to push which activates my beeper. They'd have had to wait for me coming back downstairs, that's all.'

31

Naylor nods her understanding.

'Can you recall seeing anything unusual? People hanging around who shouldn't have been here?'

Prentice shakes his head.

'I'm sorry, no. I'm not much use to you, am I?'

'If you think of anything, you will let me know?' says Naylor.

'Of course I will,' says Prentice. 'Anything at all I can do to help.'

At 3.50 p.m., Hagen takes a call from a detective constable. He listens to what's being said, then goes to find Dallabrida, who's watching yesterday's CCTV footage from cameras in the Belmont Road area.

'Any joy?' asks Hagen, and Dallabrida shakes his head.

'Nothing so far,' he says. 'There's nothing on the bus stop itself. I'm looking for anything of interest but it's hard to know exactly what that would be.'

'Will you do me a favour?' asks Hagen. 'Will you go and tell Robert Griffiths he's free to go?'

'Has his story checked out?'

'Seems so. They tracked down David Sellers working in an optician's on the high street, and he was happy enough to confirm his accusation of assault was malicious.'

'You can ruin a man's career doing things like that,' says Dallabrida.

'Now we've done him no favours, keeping him here all afternoon,' says Hagen. 'So the sooner he's off the premises, the better.'

'What about the CCTV?'

'Come back to that when you're done with Griffiths. I'll give you a hand with it when I get back.'

'I'm on my way,' says Dallabrida.

'Is there somewhere private we can go, Mr Jadoon?' asks Hagen.

The newsagent lets out a sigh. He has the wiriness of a man who never sits, and the wariness of one who isn't trusting. His quilted jacket's fastened to the neck, and standing near the counter, Hagen understands why. Constant opening and closing of the door lets in the cold air, melding damp leaves and wet tarmac with the shop smells of newsprint and bruised apples.

'Normally, of course I would be glad to help,' says Jadoon. 'But this is my busiest time of day. Maybe you could come back later?' His eyes flicker to the CCTV monitor, where a woman out of sight from the counter is checking the price of canned spaghetti. 'The schoolkids will be in soon, and I need eyes in the back of my head. They rob me blind, and – no offence – but you and your colleagues, you do very little to help businessmen like me.'

'I'm sure you can appreciate this is an urgent matter,' says Hagen. 'A boy is missing, and we're very concerned for his safety. Isn't there someone who can help out for a few minutes?'

Jadoon mutters something in a language Hagen doesn't know, and goes to a door behind the counter. He calls out a name, and when a woman answers, beckons Hagen forward, stepping back himself to allow his wife to take his place.

In the back room, Jadoon motions Hagen to an armchair,

and sits down facing him. As Hagen takes out his notebook, Jadoon's looking round him, into the shop.

'Do you remember two boys who came in yesterday afternoon?' asks Hagen. 'Later than the usual time for the schoolkids, somewhere around five?'

Jadoon shrugs.

'I must be honest with you, it's hard for me to remember specifically. So many of them come in here, different sizes, different ages, same clothes.'

'We have a statement from the boy who was with Evan who remembers a man who was in here at the same time. Bald head, a snake tattoo on his hand. Do you remember him?'

Jadoon considers.

'Yes, I think I do. A big man. He bought milk.'

'Do you know him? Have you seen him before?'

Jadoon looks doubtful. There's a rush of noise from the shop, the chatter of the first of the schoolchildren.

'I couldn't say for sure. We get a lot of passing traffic, people who come in only once and then never again. Certainly he's not what I would call a regular.' Jadoon rises from his chair. 'I'm sorry, I have to go. My wife won't cope alone.'

'Just a couple more questions,' Hagen persists. 'Was there anyone else here at the shop yesterday afternoon, anyone else who might have seen the boys?'

'Yesterday?' Jadoon shakes his head. 'Not yesterday, no. I was here by myself.'

'We'll talk again, then, when you're not so busy.' Hagen gets to his feet. 'We'll be needing a copy of your CCTV, so please be sure the recording stays intact. I'll send someone over to pick it up.'

'The CCTV? Why?'

Hagen's eyebrows lift.

'For obvious reasons, I'd have thought, Mr Jadoon. The man with the tattoo must be on there, along with Evan Ferrers. It could be critical to the investigation. Let me give you my card. We'll be in touch to fix an appointment for you to come down to the station and make a formal statement.'

'Why a formal statement? Like I said, I don't remember very much about them, not specifically.'

'But you remember the man with the tattoos,' says Hagen. 'We'll be in touch. Thanks very much for your time.'

No news is not good news.

As far as the general public is aware, there have been no sightings of Evan, nothing to go on at all. After tea, with a subdued Stewie shut away in his room and George happily watching *Charlie and Lola*, Vicky thinks she should ring Claire. Then she changes her mind. In the fridge, the remains of last night's Pinot Grigio are well-chilled and tempting, and enough to fill a large glass. By the time she's drunk a third of the wine, she feels braver, picks up the phone and dials.

The man who answers isn't Matt. Vicky asks for Claire, and the man asks her who she is. Vicky describes herself as a friend of the family. She hears muffled voices down the line, the wind-in-microphone noises of a hand covering the receiver. Then the man takes his hand from the mouthpiece.

'She'll call you back,' he says.

The evening goes by. Vicky bathes George and puts him to bed, finishes the Pinot Grigio and opens another bottle. Paul arrives home just after nine, exhausted and full of traveller's tales of tailbacks and motorway closures. He's eaten a sandwich and doesn't want dinner, but he opens a beer, slips off his shoes and flops down on the sofa. Grabbing the remote, he skips through the channels to the second half of a football match.

'You should go and talk to Stewie,' says Vicky.

'How is he?'

'He's a bit withdrawn.' She's about to say more – how Stewie didn't eat much this evening, how he wasn't full of his usual chatter when he came home from school – but the phone rings. Paul picks it up from the sofa arm, glances at it and holds it out to Vicky. The Ferrerses' number is showing in the display.

She takes the phone from him and lets it ring. And ring. By the time she presses the answer button, the caller's gone.

She and Paul look at each other.

'I don't know what to say to her,' says Vicky. 'What can I say that won't sound inadequate?'

She presses the dial button and hears the dual tone which means there's a message. She puts the phone on speaker, so Paul can listen too.

'Hi, Vicky, it's Claire.'

And it is Claire's voice, but the confident, sometimes strident woman it belongs to has been replaced by a new Claire, who speaks hesitantly, almost timorously, with a vulnerability which brings a lump to Vicky's throat.

Claire starts with niceties – thanks for ringing, hope Stewie's OK – then stumbles over a few words Paul and Vicky can't make out.

'The thing is,' she says next, 'they've asked me to ask you if he'll do it. And you know I would never ask such a thing,

36

only things here are . . .' There's a laugh, bitter and crazy. 'Unsurprisingly, things here are not great. And I know it's a huge, huge favour, but Vicky . . . Vicky, for Evan's sake, please say yes.'

FIVE

18 October

The morning of the reconstruction – which will begin one week to the day, hour and minute of Evan's disappearance – is clear and cold. Two hours after the time she'd usually arrive at work, Claire is lying in bed, looking out at the sky. Downstairs, Matt's yelling at the Family Liaison Officer, a well-meaning man who seems content to be punchbag for them both. Tears and anger run off his back, and even the most stinging tirades on police incompetence are met with expressions of sympathy, and fresh mugs of tea.

But this morning, the Liaison Officer's really got off on the wrong foot. He's let Matt know the reconstruction won't be screened until it's shown on *Crimewatch*, five days from now.

'If that's not an admission of defeat, I don't know what is!' Matt is shouting. 'Don't think I'm going to let you lot drag your feet until Monday! I want my boy home long before then!'

Claire, too, aches to have Evan home. Her waking hours are a torment, yet sleep feels like a betrayal. What normal parent sleeps while their child is lost? She catches herself making observations on her own behaviour, quite able to distinguish

38

her rational from her irrational thoughts. She wonders if she might, in spite of herself, be losing hope. The past day or so, increasingly the possibility slithers through her mind that Evan might be dead. On that detached, removed level, she notes her biggest concern for him, dead or alive, is broadly the same: she wants him to be warm. What would be most unbearable, what she could never begin to forgive, would be if his body were left in the open, exposed to the cold, to foxes and scavenging crows.

As Matt continues to berate the Liaison Officer, Claire talks in her head to her newly discovered best friend, God. *Please God*, she prays, *let him not have suffered. And please God, let them give him a blanket, and cover my baby's face.*

It's a bad day to be out. Jack Ferrers pauses by the yard gate, wind worrying his white hair, and watches the squalls of rain blowing in over Blackmire Ridge. There's a view from here right down the lane, as far as the eye can follow it, to the beck turn.

No one is there.

He walks slowly up to the home field, his boots squelching in the mud. Birds have already stripped the berries from the scrawny hawthorn trees, sign of a hard winter to come. The ewes are sheltering along the bases of the grey stone walls, and when they hear the latch click on the gate, they raise their heads from the thin grass and run bleating towards him, following him to the tumbledown store at the field's top end. Jack hauls a sack of sugar-beet feed from the store, and tosses a couple of handfuls to the ewes before filling two buckets. He carries the buckets to the middle of the field, scattering the feed as broadly as he can. The ewes are looking well, ready for the tup in another week or two.

In the farmhouse porch, he pulls off his boots. He was generous this morning with the coal when he banked up the range, and the kitchen is warm. If the boy walks up here from the village, he'll be frozen with the cold.

One week now. The cake Dora made for Evan is going stale, but it doesn't feel right to eat it. He boils the kettle and makes a pot of tea. When he carries a cup up to Dora, he takes her a plate of biscuits, leaving Evan's cake untouched in its tin.

Claire wants to be sick.

The fear of going out there is making her feel faint, but she thinks she can cope with that; she's been living her life in a blurred light-headedness ever since Evan didn't come home.

But throwing up live on TV is something else. Maybe she should find the toilets and take care of it now.

She's left it too late. A girl wearing headphones comes through the door between them and the room where the press conference is scheduled to start. There's a blast of conversation before the door closes, and a glimpse of rows of seated people.

A lot of people. All waiting for them.

'Hold my hand,' murmurs Matt.

She wraps her fingers around his and finds him squeezing, as hard as he did the day Evan was born, a tiny, angry Evan, wrinkled and clench-fisted, screaming his fury at being forced into the world. Claire remembers the first moments of holding him in her arms, how he lit a light of purpose inside her: the only thing that mattered was loving and caring for her son.

Over the years, that light dimmed, shadowed by cravings for free time, me-time, a career and a life beyond being Evan's mum. False grails, she sees now, and fool's gold. In her life there's only one true light, and if it goes out, what's the point of carrying on?

'Are you OK?' asks Matt. His face has grown thin, and he's aged in the depths of his eyes. The confident, I've-got-this Matt she knew has disappeared, and a man she barely knows stands alongside her, waiting to be told what to do.

The policeman in charge – Chief Inspector Campbell – is relaxed as he walks towards them, wearing a smile intended to put them at ease. The pressure from Matt's hand lessens, but he doesn't let go.

'Ready?' asks Campbell, and – even though she isn't and never will be – in the face of his authority, Claire nods yes.

'You'll be fine,' says Campbell. 'I'll take all the questions. All you have to do is read out your statement. If it gets too much for you, Matt, you take over. Just remember you're doing this for Evan.'

As the door opens, Campbell leads the way, and two PR people, a man and a woman, follow behind. Matt squeezes Claire's hand again, and leads her through the door, into a dazzling starburst of camera flashes.

The PR people usher Claire and Matt into chairs. Static LED lights blaze in their eyes, obscuring the room beyond. Campbell and the PR people take their seats. A screen behind them shows a photofit of the tattooed man drawn from Stewie's description, alongside a blown-up artist's impression of the snake tattoo on his hand.

Claire moves her head, and finds beyond the lights she

can see the crowd craning for a view of her, fascinated by her devastation and despair.

Under the table, Matt's hand grasps hers.

Campbell begins to speak confidently and concisely, giving the known facts of Evan's disappearance. As he's talking, Claire notices a presenter who's been a regular on her front lawn, a face she recognises as Dale Vardy from BBC South.

And then the Chief Inspector says, 'Claire?'

Her stomach lurches. Matt lets go of her hand, as Claire feels a deep blush spread into her face.

Her statement is on the table in front of her, printed in a large font, double spaced and easy to read as a kindergarten story. The room is silent, and as she picks up the sheet of paper, her microphone broadcasts its rustle around the room.

She clears her throat. The sound of it seems everywhere.

The PR woman leans across to her and touches her arm.

'Take your time, Claire,' she says.

Claire stares out at the room.

They're here to help, she tells herself, and starts to read.

'Our son Evan . . .' Her voice sounds odd, unexpected, nothing like the voice she knows from her own head. Disconcerted, she stops.

She begins again.

'Our son Evan is a bright, kind, funny boy . . .'

The truth of these words is a punch to the heart.

'Kind and funny,' she says again, though they're not repeated in the script. 'Wherever he is, we know he just wants to come home.' The last word is unclear, hampered by the misery swelling her throat, so she says it again, more forcefully.

'Home.'

She looks out at the BBC presenter, but he's staring at his knees. Few of her audience are actually looking at her.

'Somebody, somewhere, knows where Evan is. If that's you, please, please let him go.'

There are only two more lines, but Claire abandons them to finish in her own words.

'We're begging you, just tell us where he is. Evan, my darling, we love you so much. Just hang in there. We love you.'

She stops.

There are whole seconds of silence before Campbell picks up the baton, turning to the photofit of the tattooed man.

'The man behind me is a person of interest in this investigation, and we're asking members of the public who may know him to come forward. His tattoo is very distinctive, and the message we want to get out there is if anyone's seen it, please don't hesitate, do the right thing and pick up the phone. We'll be staging a full reconstruction of Evan's abduction at five p.m. this afternoon and we'll hope to see all of you there. Any questions?'

Hands go up around the room, but Dale Vardy speaks up without waiting for Campbell to make his choice.

'Are you still treating this as a missing persons case, Chief Inspector? Realistically, what are the chances now of finding Evan alive?'

With Matt and Claire in the room, the insensitivity of his question evokes a collective intake of breath. Claire feels Matt flinch. The PR woman scowls, and her colleague looks to see who's spoken and makes a note of his name.

'We have no reason whatever at this stage to believe Evan

is not very much alive and that is how we shall continue to investigate his abduction,' says Campbell. 'We fully anticipate that this afternoon's reconstruction will bring in new information, and I have a team standing by to act on any verifiable leads to ensure he's reunited with his family in the shortest possible timeframe.'

As Campbell's speaking, Claire looks over at Vardy, and when she sees he isn't pleased, the dawning realisation hurts. These people are not Claire's allies and their interests do not align with hers and Matt's. For them, it will be a better outcome if Evan's dead; there is, after all, far more media mileage in a lonely woodland burial than a joyous welcome home. A murdered boy is a drama that can run and run: manhunt, arrest, court case, with countless cash-ins – books, biographies, documentaries – in the years to come.

What matters to these people is the story.

Campbell is summing up.

'Thank you all for coming. There are handouts by the door. Any further questions, you'll find contact details on there.'

Campbell and the PR people lead them out. Claire's legs are unsteady, and she leans on Matt for support.

'I think that went well,' says Campbell, smiling at Claire.

As the door closes behind them, the LED lights go out.

For the reconstruction, they've brought in a boy from another school. His name is Nick, and from certain angles he looks disturbingly like Evan. Stewie's finding the whole thing very strange, like a weird instance of déjà vu, but déjà vu's what it's all about. Nick's there to prod people into remembering.

They're ready to start, but they're not starting from the beginning, not what Stewie thinks of as the beginning. Stewie thinks they should start with the lost boot, because that's what made Evan miss the bus. But they say, *What's the point? There's no one to remember that, except you two. We'll take it from the moment you left the changing rooms.*

So Stewie and Nick start at the changing-room door, and head down the corridor, past the trophy cabinets and the photographs of boys who are old men now. Nick's talking about Man U, and Stewie decides he quite likes him. Then he feels guilty because it should be Evan he's with, and he sends a mental apology for being disloyal.

They reach the main entrance and go outside, passing Mr Prentice with his keys. *Exactly like you did seven days ago*, they keep saying, but it's not at all the same. That day the car park was almost empty; today there are TV cameramen, people with microphones, photographers, police. Stewie sees his mum and dad, and Evan's dad, and the headmaster Mr Mullis, and he feels self-conscious and embarrassed, and knows his face is red.

They walk down the road to the newsagent's, and from somewhere they've conjured a man who looks uncannily like the man who was buying milk, with a mocked-up tattoo just as Stewie described it. Someone hands Nick a can of Fanta and Stewie's given a packet of crisps he really doesn't feel like eating. For Evan's sake, he eats them regardless.

It isn't until they reach the bus shelter that Stewie discovers the biggest discrepancy in the reconstruction is his own state of mind. When Stewie said goodbye to Evan a week ago, his mood was light, his conscience untroubled, but as he leaves

Nick to wait alone for whatever comes next, he feels like the worst kind of traitor. Remembering his instructions, he follows the trail of his own walk home, leaden-hearted with the weight of his remorse.

SIX

24 October

'What's the news, Brad?' asks Naylor. The morning after the *Crimewatch* broadcast, Hagen looks weary, with a pallor induced by too much coffee and junk food and no fresh air. 'Isn't there a bed somewhere calling your name?'

'It's calling louder than you can possibly imagine,' says Hagen, 'but there's too much to do here. Just pour coffee into me and I'll keep going like the Duracell bunny.'

'Anything of interest?'

'Rose is correlating the data from the phone calls, so she can give you a detailed run-down, but by and large, I'd say a very good response. The big question is, will any of it produce anything useful?'

'We're back in the headlines, anyway,' says Naylor, dropping copies of the *Sun* and the *Daily Mail* on the desk. 'That never hurts, does it?'

Hagen picks up the *Mail*, where a photo of a shell-shocked Matt and a tearful Claire covers a third of the front page.

'Hey, Rachel!' Dallabrida's breezing into the office, fresh and cheerful, though Naylor knows he was manning phones last night and won't have been in bed before the small hours.

'Message from the front desk. There's a visitor wants to talk about the Ferrers case, and I think you'll want to see him. Give me a minute to get my caffeine fix, and I'll come and keep you company.'

When she enters the interview room, Naylor has to resist punching the air. She chooses the chair by the wall, and Dallabrida sits alongside her, taking his time to make himself comfortable, opening his notebook and finding a pen, all giving Naylor a few moments to study the man sitting opposite.

If he stood up he'd be tall, and he's powerfully built, stretching the seams on his leather jacket. His head is shaved smooth, and his look should be threatening, but he's relaxed and smiling at Naylor as if this situation amuses him. His right hand is on the table in front of him, and a snake tattoo is winding round his wrist.

Naylor returns his smile.

'Thanks for coming in, Mr . . .' She glances across at Dallabrida's notes, where the name is underlined. '. . . Bryant.'

'That's me, Lee Bryant. I gave my address and all that at the front desk. I've heard you've been looking for me so I thought I'd better come and make myself known, straighten things out. Seems like I've become a national celebrity in my absence.'

'I wouldn't say a celebrity,' says Naylor. 'Do you know why we want to talk to you?'

'It's about that boy who went missing, isn't it? What do they call him, Ewan?'

'Evan.'

'Evan, that's it. I was very sorry to hear about that. Is there any news?'

Naylor sidesteps the question.

'We've been looking for you for some days now, Mr Bryant. Can you explain why you haven't come forward before?'

'Dead simple, I haven't been here. I drive a truck, long distance, Europe mostly, Spain, Germany, places like that. I go all over. This past week I've been to Poland.'

'Poland?' asks Dallabrida. 'What did you take to Poland?'

'A delivery for Tesco,' says Bryant. 'Tesco's huge in Poland. Not many people know that.'

'Don't you have a partner?' asks Naylor. 'No phone calls home, no one to tell you we wanted to speak to you?'

'Not really, no,' says Bryant. 'When I go to interesting places, my missus goes with me. Our kids have all left home, so there's no reason for her to sit at home twiddling her thumbs. We go everywhere together, her and me.'

'You understand you were one of the last people to see Evan before he went missing?' asks Naylor.

'Oh yeah, I get that. I do remember them. One of them was looking at Sammy here.' He holds up his right hand, and moves his thumb and forefinger to make the snake's jaw move. 'I get a lot of comments about old Sammy. My youngest called him that. I was thinking Satan or Terminator, something really badass, but she made her choice and that was that. He looks scary but he's harmless, a bit like me. I'm happy to give a statement or whatever, though I don't know if it'll help. I just saw them in the shop, that's all.'

'We'd appreciate a statement, thank you,' says Naylor. 'If you've got time, DC Dallabrida can take it now.'

'Fine by me,' says Bryant. 'I watched the reconstruction thing on telly last night, by the way. Gave me a funny feeling to see someone who looked so much like me. But I got to tell you, you missed something out. Well, I say you missed it out. Maybe you did it on purpose. You know what you're doing, don't you? Maybe you didn't think it was important.'

Naylor and Dallabrida stare at him.

'You didn't show the van outside the shop, the one making the delivery round the back.'

When Hagen makes his return visit to the newsagent's, Dallabrida goes along for the ride.

After the morning rush and not yet lunchtime, the shop is quiet. Mr Jadoon is behind the counter, reading a copy of the *Mail*. When he sees Hagen he folds up the newspaper, but doesn't manage a welcoming smile.

'Did you see yourself on TV?' asks Hagen. 'They did a good job, don't you think?'

'My wife and I watched it, yes,' says Jadoon. 'I wasn't featured, only the shop.'

'Might be good for business,' says Dallabrida. He picks up a Boost bar, puts it down again and pats his stomach. 'Better not, eh? I have to watch my figure. Got to keep the ladies happy.'

'Can I help you with something?' asks Jadoon. 'I gave my statement as you asked. I don't have anything else to say.'

'It's about your statement we're here,' says Hagen.

'What about it?'

An elderly man pushes through the shop door, and begins to read the front pages on the newsstand.

'We can do this in private, if you'd like,' says Hagen.

The elderly man picks up a copy of the *Guardian* and

crosses to the counter to pay. He asks for twenty Sterling Superkings, and Jadoon slides open the shutter hiding his stock of cigarettes. He hands over the silver and red packet, takes payment and gives change.

'Thanks, mate,' he says, as the old man leaves.

'The thing is,' says Hagen, 'when you gave your statement, we think there may have been an omission.'

'It's an offence to make a false statement,' says Dallabrida. 'Do you want to have a quick think about anything you might have forgotten? Let us give you a clue. It's got something to do with a van.'

'A van?'

'A van that was outside your shop when Evan Ferrers and Stewart Wareham walked in.'

Jadoon drops his head.

'OK,' he says, 'OK. This way.' He leads them to the back of the shop and takes a bottle of white wine from the chiller. 'I told my wife it was a terrible idea. She has a cousin in the cash-and-carry trade. I don't know where they get it from, just that it's very cheap. It says from France on the bottle but I don't believe it comes from there.'

Hagen studies the label. It looks genuine, but many fake wines do.

'How much did you pay for this stuff?'

'One fifty a bottle. You see, it retails at seven, maybe eight ninety-nine.'

'And who was driving the van?'

'I don't know,' says Jadoon. 'I didn't know him and I didn't ask. Why would I?'

Dallabrida looks at Hagen and shakes his head.

'Do you want to tell your wife you're going out, Mr Jadoon?' asks Hagen. 'If you're going to revise your statement, there's no time like the here and now.'

SEVEN

29 November

Matt comes into the bedroom quietly, his bare feet padding on the cream carpet, navigating around the bed by the light bleeding around the edge of the door. Since that first night, the landing light's been left on, at first because there were always people in the house: investigators, liaison officers, uniformed officers to keep the press at bay, all well-meaning, all for Claire and Matt's benefit, but all strangers who invaded the sanctity and privacy of their home and left only this bedroom as a refuge from the invasion.

The press were like an army laying siege, so the curtains and blinds remained permanently closed and time went by in a perpetual evening. Claire feels they became like cave dwellers, allergic to the lost daylight, and the first few times she left the house, even in the foggy gloom of autumn, she was bewildered by the abundance of colour, accustomed as she was to the chromatic distortions of fluorescent and energy-saving lightbulbs.

Everyone is gone now. The fickle media circus left first, lured away by other dramas and disasters, rushing away to homes more recently blighted, to fresher tragedies and heartbreaks.

When the press struck camp, there was no need for the uniforms to remain, which Claire regretted, a little. Of all the people who were here, she had borne their company most easily, those world-weary men and women who handled pressure with laughter, uncovering rubies of dark humour in the rubble of once-ordinary lives.

Now the house is theirs again, the landing light stays on because neither of them sleep well, and they're often up in the night, easily disturbed by late-returning neighbours, or foxes raiding the bins, even rain on the windows, which always brings Claire back to worrying whether Evan is warm and dry.

Matt's trying not to wake her, but Claire isn't asleep. Matt's been in Evan's room, where he goes often by night, shutting himself in. Sometimes Claire can hear him sobbing through the wall, and feels the tightness in her throat and the closeness of her own tears, as much for poor Matt's pain as Evan's absence.

Thinking he hasn't disturbed her, Matt creeps into the bed, slipping under his cool side of the duvet. As quietly as he can, he sniffs away the snotty residue of his crying.

Matt suffers from cold feet. Turning over, she moves close to him, puts her warm feet over his and lays her head on his chest. He folds his arm around her shoulder, and there they lie, wide awake, welded together in their heartbreak, neither of them entirely sure they want to see another day.

Stewie has come to hate Wednesdays, Groundhog Day for the day Evan disappeared. Every lesson and every break is part of the countdown to the moment they said goodbye.

On the seventh Wednesday, George is ready early for school,

and Vicky allows him ten minutes of *SpongeBob*. George turns up the volume on the TV, and the cartoon voices of Squidward and Plankton are loud through the house.

As Stewie comes down the stairs, George is laughing. Stewie goes straight to the living room, snatches up the remote and mutes the volume.

'For fuck's sake!' he shouts. 'That does my head in!'

George is quickly on his feet, following Stewie and the remote into the kitchen.

'Mum, Mum! Stewie swore!'

Vicky is putting cherry tomatoes into George's lunch box. She looks at Stewie, surprised.

'Did you, Stewie?'

'Oh, for Christ's sake, stop hassling me! Here, snitch.' He skims the remote across the worktop in George's direction, but George isn't quick enough to catch it, and the remote drops to the floor, breaking off its back so the batteries roll loose.

'Pick that up, Stewie,' says Vicky.

'He dropped it.'

'You threw it. What's got into you? Pick that up and get yourself some breakfast. You'll be late.'

Keen to get back to *SpongeBob*, George is reassembling the remote.

'I'm not going in today,' says Stewie. 'I don't feel well.'

Vicky studies him. Stewie's pale, but he's walking and talking, and that makes him fit enough for school.

'What's wrong with you?' she asks.

'I've got a headache. I'm going back to bed.'

'Don't be ridiculous. Do you want me to do you some toast?'

'I'm not being ridiculous!' Suddenly, Stewie's yelling. 'I'll tell you what's ridiculous – expecting me to carry on like nothing's happened! Like I should just let it go that my best mate's disappeared, and you're like, that's a shame, off you go, Stewie, back to that place, day after day after day! And when I get home, nearly every day who's here but bloody Claire, wanting to talk about him, picking my brain like some weird vulture. I don't want to talk to her, OK? Why do you even let her in here? Why can't you just tell her to fuck off and leave me alone?'

'Claire needs our support, Stewie.'

'No, *I* need your support, and I need you to keep her away from me! I'm not her fucking son substitute or whatever she thinks I am and I am not going back to that school! Ever!'

There's a long silence between them, broken when Sponge-Bob's voice cuts in from the living room.

Vicky sighs.

'OK, sweetheart,' she says. 'Take the day off. We'll talk about it when Dad comes home tonight.'

EIGHT

4 January

Evan's room is a dilemma. Despite the time that he's been gone, it's barely been disturbed. In the beginning, a policeman took away his laptop to trawl its depths for undesirables, for virtual contacts who had no business being Evan's 'friends' or visits to chatrooms which exist only for dark purposes. It hasn't been returned, and its place on his cluttered desk remains a hollow. Then they bagged up his comb, the Liaison Officer explaining as Matt stared at him, pale and dismayed, that hair samples were needed to match any remains.

Apart from that, Evan's room is exactly as he left it that morning to come downstairs and eat his breakfast: two slices of toast and honey and a slug of milk from the container, for which – God forgive her – Claire told him off.

His book-bag and his rugby kit were by the door, and he picked them up before submitting to a quick kiss.

'See you later, Mum,' he said, and pulled the door shut behind him, leaving her life.

And she walked indifferent to the kitchen and finished her own breakfast, the last but one meal she ate that isn't ashes in her mouth.

See you later, Mum.

The dilemma lies in the freeze-frame of the room's abandonment: in the balled grey school sock lying by the laundry basket, in the dented pillow and the rumpled bed-sheet, in the smiling Lego fireman on the bookshelf and the Xbox controller waiting to be picked up for the next game.

How long can the room be left before she cleans it? How long before the clothes must be laundered and disposed of, the bed stripped, the Xbox and the Lego packed away?

It has to be done sometime.

Just not today.

Three months after Evan disappeared, hope is dwindling. Costs, however, continue to mount up.

When Naylor and Hagen are summoned upstairs at the end of morning briefing, they have an inkling of what's coming. They've nothing to report but depressing dead ends and trails gone cold.

Chief Inspector Martin Campbell has one of the best offices in the building, with a window and a view of the bus station, but the furniture's no better than anyone else's. Campbell sits behind his cheap desk, leaning back in his faux-leather chair. He's tried to make the place feel like home with photographs of his kids, his son grinning up at the camera from a canoe, his daughter on horseback, jumping a fence of striped poles. Hagen knows Campbell doesn't see his kids much any more, and he suspects the horse-riding and canoeing are paid for by the ex-wife's new man. That's hard to compete with, even on a chief inspector's salary.

'So what's new?' Campbell asks.

The question is rhetorical. Campbell keeps himself up to speed in case of update requests from the Chief Constable, and he already knows that Lee Bryant's trip to Poland checked out with Border Control, and that the potentially interesting *Crimewatch* leads – from Strathclyde to Dorset and the Costa Brava – all came to nothing. He knows there's a prosecution pending for Noah Jadoon and the Manchester cartel who sold him fake alcohol, and that nothing was found on Evan's computer to suggest an intention of running away. He's authorised searches of drains to recover Evan's phone, all of which came back with nothing, and undercover intelligence operatives working to discover the boy's whereabouts have drawn only blanks.

'Not much, Sir,' says Naylor.

'These armed robberies, then,' says Campbell. 'Forensics think the three of them are linked. I want you to see what you can do with them.'

'What about the Ferrers case?' asks Hagen.

'I'm going to have the incident room wound down. It can't be funded indefinitely. Resources are tight, and I don't see we're making any progress. You've just told me you don't have any new angles to pursue.'

Hagen and Naylor are silent.

'So. I know you've done your best, but there comes a time to face the facts. We all know the likelihood is that Evan's already dead, and probably died within hours of his abduction.'

'Who'll tell the parents, Sir?' asks Hagen.

'You will,' says Campbell, looking at Naylor. 'Of course, let them know our commitment to the case is unchanged. You know what to say.'

'Shall I tell them resources are tight?' asks Naylor.

The Chief Inspector seems not to have heard. He looks at Hagen.

'Let me know how you get on with intelligence on these robberies, Bradley,' he says.

Naylor's visit is short, just long enough to deliver the news that Evan's case is being de-prioritised. She uses the word *reviewed*, but Claire and Matt are not fooled.

As Claire sees her out, Naylor says, 'We'll be in touch.'

'When?' asks Claire.

Naylor wants to apologise, but that would be an acknow-ledgement of the truth.

'Take care of yourselves,' she says.

When she reaches her car she turns back to wave, but Claire has already gone back inside.

Matt's standing in the kitchen, looking out at nothing in the garden where the drooping heads of snowdrops are poking through wet grass.

Slowly, Claire goes upstairs. The door to Evan's bedroom is closed, and when she opens it she makes believe the remnants of the scent of him are hanging in the air.

The Lego fireman is still smiling on the bookshelf; the balled-up school sock is still lying on the floor.

She picks up his pillow and buries her face in it. There's nothing of him there.

With shaking hands, she begins to strip the bed.

NINE

19 March

It's the last home rugby match of the season, and the Under-Twelves are playing well. Claire knows she shouldn't be there, that she's like Banquo at this feast, but she can't help herself. She's hoping for a momentary illusion, that her mind might conjure a glimpse of him, out there on the field amongst the many bodies so similar to his. She stands under the branches of a sycamore tree in spring-green bud, out of the wind and away from the action, avoiding the other parents for their sakes. The boys have grown over the winter, and she wonders if her boy has grown, too. She closes her eyes and, in amongst the shouts and the blasts on the whistle, tries in vain to hear Evan's voice.

There's a new games master, a much younger man than Mr Griffiths, running up and down the sidelines, energetic and keen. Griffiths is gone, taken early retirement. Stewie's changed schools, had a fresh start. Other people are moving on, getting on with their lives.

If only she could do the same.

The Answer to
All Your Prayers

TEN

16 June
Ferrybridge, West Yorkshire

Roy Addesley's old van gets thirsty when it's fully laden and the fuel gauge is showing a red light, so Roy pulls into a BP filling station on the Pontefract road. He and Trevor are talking cricket, specifically Yorkshire's less-than-stellar performance against Nottinghamshire yesterday.

Trevor screws up the paper bag his sandwich came in and drops it into the footwell, amongst the other wrappings from this week's lunches.

'There's not a decent batsman amongst them,' he says. 'No wonder Nottinghamshire hammered them. They got beaten because they played absolute shite.'

Roy lines the van up alongside a pump and turns off the engine. There's the usual run-on before it dies. The van needs work.

'If they'd only got a half-decent captain, it'd help,' Trevor persists.

'You're full of it.' Roy climbs down from the cab. 'You want anything from the shop?'

'If you're buying, I'll have a Coke.'

'I'm not buying, so fetch it yourself.'

Trevor laughs, but his laughter's cut short in Roy's ears when he slams the van door. For once, it's cricketing weather – a hot June day, hottest of the year so far. Roy unscrews the filler cap, fits the nozzle into the tank, and as he's squeezing the trigger and letting the diesel run, he thinks of good things to take his mind off how much this is going to cost him. He thinks of opening the fridge at home and the first taste of a cold lager; he thinks of standing under the running shower, of washing off the plaster-dust and sweat; of sitting for a while in the garden while his missus finishes cooking his tea.

The car that pulls up behind him is an 09-plate Ford Focus in dark metallic red. Roy glances at it, and sees it's carrying two unremarkable men, the driver in late middle-age and balding, the passenger a redhead of an age to be the driver's son. The younger man appears to be angry, turning round to shout at somebody in the back. But there's no one in the back, as far as Roy can see.

He turns away to watch the pump dials. The Ford's driver takes a few litres of fuel and goes inside to pay. Finally, the nozzle clicks to say the van's tank is full. Roy hangs it up, and the pump motor switches off.

In the relative quiet, he hears noises from the car behind, prolonged pounding coming from the boot. He can hear it clearly, so what's curious to Roy is that the red-haired man in the passenger seat, the one who was angry before, seems not to hear it at all. He's just sitting there, looking at Roy. Inside the shop, the Ford's driver is handing over cash.

Roy moves a couple of steps towards the car. The petrol station isn't busy, and the other motorists filling up are out of earshot. The red-haired man is watching him, and Roy's unsure what to do. He's thinking there might be someone in the boot, but is it really his business? Maybe these two blokes are playing some kind of prank, and that's up to them. But the sun is scorching, and he wouldn't want to be sweltering under hot metal.

The car's driver comes out of the shop, and Roy decides he'll have a quick word, and waits for him to get close. But when the driver notices him, he falters and stands still. Behind him, Roy hears the Ford's passenger door open and slam shut, and the beep as the locks are activated from the key-fob. Then, to Roy's surprise, the driver walks away from him and out of the filling station, followed by his red-headed passenger, who's running to catch up.

Roy shouts after them.

'Oi! 'Scuse me, pal!' But neither man looks back. Instead, they increase their pace, and reach the road. 'Oi! Hold on a minute!'

Roy's shouting draws the attention of the other customers. From inside the shop, the staff peer at him through the window, hoping they're not going to be dealing with some nutter.

Now the two men have taken off, Roy knows something's not right. He hurries round the back of the Focus and shouts across to the cashiers.

'There's someone locked in this car! They've got someone locked in the boot! Trevor! Trevor, get out here!'

He raps his knuckles on the boot-lid.

'Hello! Are you OK?' The pounding from inside the Ford becomes frantic. 'Don't worry, pal, we'll get you out!'

Trevor moves quickly for Trevor, and comes to stand beside Roy. A young man leaves a blue Clio, and runs to join them.

'They've legged it,' he says. 'I saw which way they went. Shall I go after them?'

Roy hesitates.

'Someone should,' he says. The young man is about the same age as his son, and keen for excitement. 'But don't you go taking them on. Just see if you can work out where they're headed.'

The young man runs back to his car and drives away. A cashier appears in the shop doorway, and when Roy shouts to her to call the police, she hurries back inside and picks up a phone, talking animatedly to her colleagues.

The pounding from inside the car is becoming intermittent, as if whoever's in there is getting tired. The staff all come outside, and join Roy, Trevor and the other customers by the car's back end.

'We should jemmy it,' someone says to Trevor. 'Haven't you got a crowbar in your van?'

'Fetch the crowbar, Trevor,' says Roy. But when Trevor brings the tool, Roy's reluctant.

'It might just be some prank,' he says. 'We should wait for the police.'

'It might be a long wait,' says one of the cashiers. 'Last time we rang them, it was the best part of two hours.'

Roy calls out to whoever's in the boot.

'All right, pal. We're just going to wait for the coppers, then we'll have you out.'

The young man in the blue Clio returns, and reports that he's lost the two men, who headed down a one-way street where he couldn't follow. When a police car pulls on to the forecourt – no great speed, no blue lights – there's a round of low-key, ironic applause from the shop staff.

The police driver is bent-nosed and built like a boxer; his partner's a woman old enough to have seen it all before, several times over. The policeman accepts Roy's offer of the crowbar, while the policewoman stands, arms folded and silent, to one side.

'We didn't dare do it,' explains Roy. 'Criminal damage and all that. His mates ran off with the keys. Right pair of pricks, on a day like this. Must be like a furnace in there, mustn't it?'

The policeman hooks the crowbar under the lock, leans his weight on it and pops the boot open.

The boy inside blinks at the light. His mouth is sealed with silver duct-tape. He's very thin, and red-faced from the heat, and he's been crying. He's lying on his side, his knees bent into the only position they can be; his nails are long and dirty, and he needs a haircut and a bath. Sizes too small, his clothes don't fit him. His feet are bare, his socks knotted together to tie his wrists.

The policeman is taken aback but keeps his professional demeanour. He reaches out to remove the duct-tape from the boy's mouth, but the boy cowers away.

'Let me do it, Dave,' says the policewoman, as she steps forward. Smiling reassurance, she looks into the boy's eyes.

'Just keep still a minute, love, and I'll take this off.' She picks a corner of the tape to lift it and pulls it from his face as gently as she can. 'Are you all right, love? You look in a bit of a state. How long have you been in here? Shall I give you a hand? Just sit up slowly.' She turns to one of the cashiers. 'Fetch us a bottle of water, will you? And a pair of scissors.'

Slowly, painfully, the boy sits up.

'Take your time, love. Dave,' she says quietly to her colleague, 'I think we're going to need an ambulance. And someone from Social Services.' The policeman steps away and speaks into his radio. The cashier comes running back with scissors and water, and the policewoman carefully cuts the boy's wrists free. He rubs at the welts the bindings have left, then takes the water and drinks down the whole half-litre.

'It doesn't look very comfortable in there,' says the police-woman. 'Do you think you can stand up? Lean on me, and let's get you out.'

Stiffly, the boy swings his legs over the boot-sill, and rests his dirty feet on the rear bumper. The policewoman pulls on his arms and raises him up, and he jumps clumsily down from the boot on to the concrete standing, staggering as he lands.

'You don't look very well, sweetheart,' says the police-woman. 'Just sit yourself down there a minute, and put your head between your legs.'

The boy sits cross-legged on the concrete, hiding his face on his knees, and the policewoman crouches at his side. She puts a caring arm around his skinny shoulders. Through his shirt, she can see the nodules of his spine.

'Can you tell me your name, my love?' she asks.

'Evan,' he says. 'I'm Evan Ferrers.' He looks up at her, and the scourge of torment is in his face. 'Do you think you could ring my mum, and ask her to come and take me home?'

ELEVEN

It's something Claire feels inclined never to forgive herself, one of her life's most perfect ironies, that despite her being almost housebound and a near-recluse all this time – eight months and five days – when they come to bring her the news, she isn't home. Instead, she's meandering aimlessly around Sainsbury's, looking over the English strawberries. She picks up a punnet, and sniffs the red scent through the pierced cellophane, longing for better things, a better place, to go back in time, or forwards, anywhere but here. There's such nostalgia in the scent of strawberries – expeditions to summer fields, Evan running up and down the rows of the pick-your-own, berry stains covering his shorts. And her mother with them: her mother used to love picking strawberries. Claire feels a pang, a pain in her chest she knows is heartbreak, but for whom she isn't sure. Her mother was gone before Evan disappeared, and it's a blessing she was spared.

On the Maidenhead road the traffic's bad, and that adds twenty minutes to her journey, so she's fretting about the chilled stuff in the heat, marvelling at the same time that she can still be bothered by such trivialities as melting butter. When she turns into the cul-de-sac and sees the car, the last green shoot of hope – the one protected with such fierce care against the landslip of probability – dies.

She knows it's them, not because she recognises the car but because she's learned how they operate. There are always two, this time a woman and a man, side by side in the front seats, both in white shirts, and even though they must have heard her coming, they don't turn to look, but keep facing forwards, like automatons yet to be switched on. She knows it's them, and she knows they must have something of face-to-face importance to say, or they'd have phoned. A word comes to her mind – *remains*. Instinct tells her this is going to be about remains.

She pulls up on the driveway and turns off the engine, but she doesn't get out of the car. She's savouring these last few moments, the final moments when she isn't formally bereaved, when her son might still – an outside chance, bleak odds but odds nonetheless – come home. In the rear-view mirror she watches them climb from their car. She knows the woman; her last name's Naylor, and she always said, *Call me Rachel*, but Claire never did. The other one was here that very first night, a younger man, lean in his tight suit-trousers, walking two steps behind the woman.

She wishes Matt were here, but Matt might be anywhere. He might be coming home tonight or he might be away; these days she barely notices and doesn't really care. Over time, there have been reversals. In the early days, she clung to him, hated him to leave. Now she's glad to have an empty house: no need to cook, no reason not to collapse on the sofa with a bottle of Sauvignon Blanc and banal TV.

When the officers reach her car, there's an awkward moment

when the driver's window is closed between them and the policewoman's looking in at her expectantly. Claire thinks she would like to freeze time right here and never know what's coming next, but the scene is too ridiculous to be borne for more than seconds. She turns the key a notch in the ignition, and the dashboard lights flash on. She presses the button in the door armrest, and the window slides open.

Naylor is almost smiling, and Claire's wondering how she dare.

'How are you, Claire?' The question's unnecessary, answered in Claire's pale, unmade-up face and careless clothes. Her hand on the steering wheel is bony and blue-veined. Naylor remembers the woman she met on that first night, sleekly coiffured, her nails recently done. In the space of the next few hours, that well-groomed woman disappeared, and Naylor has never seen her since. Those once-glossy fingernails are marred with white spots, which Naylor has read is a sign of zinc deficiency. Claire has the same washed-out, malnourished sallowness as women on prison diets of white bread and margarine, the result of being institutionalised, of never breathing fresh air.

Claire thinks fleetingly about politeness and preamble but instead she asks, 'What's going on?' She's hoping Naylor will say, *Only a routine visit,* or *Just keeping in touch,* but she doesn't.

'Matt's not here?' she asks, and Claire shakes her head. 'What time will he be home?'

Claire half-remembers him saying something about Oxford, but can think of no reason why he should go there. At the time, she didn't bother to ask.

'I think he might be away tonight,' she says. 'What's this about?'

'I'll get my colleague to ring him,' says Naylor. She opens the car door for Claire. 'Shall we go inside?'

Claire puts her handbag on the hall table alongside one of the Sainsbury's carrier bags – a top-of-their-range fish pie, a bottle of New Zealand white, a packet of Mr Kipling cakes. In the end, the strawberries had seemed too emotionally charged.

'Shall we have a cup of tea?' asks Naylor, doing that thing they tend to do, taking over your house, making you feel inept, controlled and taken care of, all at the same time. 'Put the kettle on, Brad.'

The young man in the tight suit doesn't balk, but goes immediately to do as he's told, and Claire is momentarily embarrassed as she remembers the state of the kitchen, the unwashed plates she ought to have put in the dishwasher, the rubbish she should have taken out days ago, the surfaces she should have wiped down.

As Naylor ushers Claire into the lounge, she notices how things have changed. Dust has settled everywhere, and there's a stillness to the room which is unnerving. The photographs of Evan she remembers are no longer here. In their place are dirty cups and glasses, and a half-eaten sandwich going stale on a plate.

Claire doesn't apologise for the mess. In the kitchen, the young man is speaking into a phone, and she hears him saying *Mr Ferrers*, introducing himself as DS Hagen and leaving a lengthy message on Matt's switched-off phone.

'If there's any chance of Matt getting here, I'd like to talk to you both together,' says Naylor. She takes a seat in an armchair. Claire's grateful for the sofa, in case she might have to lie down. She's feeling a touch light-headed, a little shaky in her hands.

Vehemently, she shakes her head.

'Tell me now,' she says. 'You have to tell me now.'

Naylor senses the dread in Claire's voice, but with the apprehension is the desperate need to know, even though the woman's expecting the worst of all bad news. How, after all this time, could she be expecting anything else?

In the kitchen, Hagen's finishing his call.

'It's good news,' says Naylor, knowing that's only half the story. 'Evan's been found.'

'I knew it!' The grief on Claire's face is as fresh as that first night. 'Where? Where did they find him?'

'Alive, Claire. He's been found alive.'

Claire covers her face with her hands. From the kitchen comes the sound of the kettle boiling, of cupboards opening as Hagen searches for clean mugs.

'Claire?' Naylor asks gently. She leans forwards and touches Claire's knee.

Claire jumps up from the sofa and runs to the downstairs cloakroom, where Naylor can't help but hear her throwing up.

Glorious mid-summer, mid-afternoon. Curlews are wheeling and calling across the fell, and the breeze bending the cotton grass carries the peaty scent of bracken, and the bleating of the ewes and lambs in the home field. When Jack reaches the house, Dora's fallen asleep in the deckchair on the lawn, her reading glasses and newspaper folded in her lap. He thinks that he should wake her or she'll never sleep tonight, but as he's about to touch her shoulder, through the French doors he hears the phone ring.

Drowsy flies are buzzing in the hall. Out of recent habit, before he answers the phone Jack touches the photograph of himself and Evan, a talismanic gesture and a small prayer.

He picks up the receiver and says hello.

'Dad.' Jack becomes very still. Every time Matt phones, Jack fears bad news, the final snuffing of his fading hope. But this evening Matt's voice is different, lighter and brighter than it's been in a long time. 'Are you there, Dad?'

Jack clears his throat.

'Yes, I'm here,' he says, all bluff. 'You're lucky to catch me. I've only just come in.'

'You might want to sit down, Dad,' says Matt. 'I've got some news. Good news, though. Brilliant news, actually. It's Evan, Dad. Evan's been found.'

Jack isn't sure whether the buzzing he can hear is the flies, or if it's only in his ears. He looks down at the photograph by the phone, at the little boy beaming at his jar of sticklebacks, at a younger, carefree version of himself.

And he dare not ask the question that leaps to mind: dead or alive?

'They had him in a car, in Ferrybridge. Where the power station is,' Matt is saying. 'Christ knows why there. They've taken him to hospital, but they say he's fine.' There's a beat of silence between them, unwanted acknowledgement of the unlikelihood of Evan being fine. 'The police are driving Claire up, and I'm meeting her there. We just wanted you to be the first to know. Dad? Are you there, Dad?'

Warm tears are running down Jack's face.

'I'm here,' he manages to say. 'Thank God.'

'I know it's a shock, Dad. When I got the message . . . Well, to be honest I thought they were going to say something different. You'll tell Mum for me, will you?'

'She'll be beside herself,' says Jack, wiping away tears. 'She'll be absolutely over the moon. That's the best news we could ever have had, and I thank God for it. It's the answer to all our prayers. Thank God he's safe.'

'I must go,' says Matt. 'I just wanted you to know. I'll ring you from the hospital, let you know how he is.'

'You give him our best love, and a big hug from both of us.' Jack reaches out and touches the photo frame. 'And ring as soon as you can. And Matt, promise me you'll tell that boy how his grandma and grandpa missed him. Tell him his grandma's baking a cake, and we can hardly wait to see him.'

Claire is riding in the back of a police car, no siren going but blue lights flashing. They're moving pretty fast, or maybe it's that other drivers slow down when they see them in the rear-view mirror, start behaving and driving at seventy. Naylor's in the front passenger seat, next to the uniformed driver. For the first few miles, she tries to keep the conversation going, but by the time they reach the M25, they've all lapsed into silence, and Naylor has laid her head back on the rest, maybe to doze. Claire sits silent in the back, fizzing with excitement, overwhelmed with apprehension about how Evan will be, hoping for reasons she can't quite define that she'll be there before Matt, wondering how long it will take him to drive from Colchester.

Colchester. She doesn't remember him mentioning Colchester.

She wonders if Evan will recognise her, if she's changed very much, whether she'll recognise him, how much he's grown. When she spoke to him on the phone – tears in his voice, surrounded by strangers and trying to be brave – he sounded like himself but different, an Evan she fears she won't know. Out of the side window, she watches the traffic, people going about their everyday business, and marks off in her mind their northern progress. Luton, Milton Keynes, Northampton. They pass Leicester and Derby, and beyond Derby, cross the South Yorkshire border into what she's always thought of as true north: Rotherham, Doncaster. Near Doncaster, they see the first signs for Pontefract, where Evan is waiting.

Naylor hasn't spoken for a while, but now she turns round in her seat and smiles at Claire.

'Not far now,' she says. 'It'll be a big story again, when it breaks. We're going to try and get you in and out of there before that happens.'

Claire remembers how it was to be besieged, how she hated the press camped outside; then she remembers her resentment when they drifted away, when other people's dramas became more interesting. She doesn't want them back again. She looks out at the passing landscape, and wonders how her son has ended up here, in this part of the country which is unknown to her. Is this where he's been all this time? She's curious, but fearful of what he'll tell her; she wants to know, but isn't sure she can bear what he might say. Instead she focuses her mind on their reunion, on how wonderful it will be to have him home.

At Pontefract General Infirmary, they pull up at a barrier

across the entrance to a Staff Only car park. Matt's car's there, double-parked and blocking someone in, and he's at the wheel with the driver's door open, a uniformed policeman crouched beside him, chatting as if they were passing the time of day. As Claire climbs from the car, Matt gets out too, switching off his phone and slipping it into his pocket, handing his keys to the policeman in case his car has to be moved. Seeing him brings home the enormity of why they're there, and suddenly she wants to be close to him in a way she thought she never would again. Who else but he could understand how she's feeling, how it's possible to be elated and terrified at the same time? Already she wants to cry, and as he holds out his hand to her – she's surprised at that, he's not normally one for PDAs – she grasps it, and finds herself wiping away tears. When he puts his arm round her shoulder and pulls her close, she's grateful for the support.

'OK?' he asks, and she shakes her head, and he says, 'It'll be fine. Let's go get him, and take him home.'

'Will they let us?' Claire asks. 'Just like that?'

Matt doesn't answer, because he knows, as does she, that's unlikely to happen. As they walk towards the hospital building, Naylor's following close behind.

On the ward, more police are waiting, two men in plain-clothes suits incongruous amongst blue nurses' tunics and patients' dressing gowns. At the nurses' station, Naylor speaks to the sister, who pages the doctor in charge of Evan's care.

But a sixth sense has opened up in Claire, a kind of radar she didn't know she had. Leaving all of them standing at the station, she walks, then runs along the corridor. No one tries to stop her. Patients and staff stand back, out of her way.

Somehow she knows which way to go. At the end of the ward, there's a private room. On the bed lies a thin boy, his back to the door.

She'd know him anywhere. When she says his name, he turns to her with desolate eyes, and both their tears begin.

TWELVE

19 June

At Ashridge police station, the third-floor incident room has reappeared fully formed: whiteboards and monitors, keyboards and phones and the miles of cabling to go with them. The paperwork is taking over the desktops, and the waste bins are already filling up with the greasy wrappings of all-day-breakfast sandwiches. There's an undercurrent of muskiness, of male sweat held in check by deodorant, and an overtone of coffee from Ron Perdue's percolator steaming away in its corner. Hagen's got his jacket on, talking to Campbell, but it's not clear if he's just arrived, or is on his way out.

Campbell spots Naylor as she comes into the room and beckons her over. He's sitting on the corner of Hagen's desk, affecting his casual down-with-the-boys pose. His tie's off to one side, and there's a shirt button missing over his sternum. Since he's no longer married, the standard of his grooming's taken a dive.

Naylor detours via her own temporary desk, dumps her handbag, glances at a couple of messages on yellow Post-it notes but sees nothing of interest. There's a burst of laughter over by the coffee machine, and she sees Leon Dallabrida, built like a super-hero and towering over a couple of their colleagues. Dallabrida's not the brains of the outfit, but he's straight down the line and he tells some brilliant jokes. On days when it's nothing but wall-to-wall bad news, he can be relied on to come up with a real cracker and burst any bubble of incident room gloom. Naylor's sorry she's missed the gag he's just told.

'Here she is,' says Campbell, as she joins him and Hagen. 'We're just saying, we should be making arrests by now. We need Evan to look at some pictures. The photofits are ready – PR are organising national coverage on them – and the Chief's asked me to do a press conference this afternoon.'

'Don't forget to get that button stitched on,' Naylor says.

Campbell looks bewildered.

'There's one missing on your shirt,' Naylor explains. 'The Chief won't be happy if you go on the BBC with a button missing.'

Discomfited, Campbell glances down at his front, and readjusts his tie to cover the gap. Hagen's eyebrows lift almost imperceptibly, and he gives Naylor the tiniest hint of a smile.

Campbell is about to say something, but Naylor heads him off.

'Rose has a sewing kit,' she says. 'She was in the Girl Guides. She's good with things like that.'

'Do you think Evan's ready?' asks Hagen. 'Where are we on the psychological evaluations?'

'The child specialists have had a couple of meetings with him, and no surprises, he's not good,' says Naylor. 'The feedback from them is that, except for when he was first found and a short phone call with his mum, he hasn't said a single word, not even to his parents. They're calling it elective mutism. Not that uncommon following major trauma like he's been through.'

'Even so,' says Campbell. 'If you could persuade him to go through a few known offenders, that would help. What about the car? Surely there must be something from that?'

'Not as much as we hoped,' says Hagen. 'Reported stolen in the intervening. Lots of prints but no matches to anyone we know. They're checking what CCTV we've got and ANPR, but don't hold your breath.'

'So what do you think, Rachel?' asks Campbell. 'Do you think you can get the boy to have a look?'

'If he isn't talking, what's the point in putting him through that? Going through the rogues' galleries at this stage will only cause the poor kid more pain.'

'He's been gone a while, though,' says Hagen in his Geordie lilt. 'No saying who he might have bumped into on his travels, and we need that information. We've got to be proactive. It's a one hundred percent certainty they'll be on the lookout for another victim to take Evan's place.'

There's a short silence amongst them as they consider the implications of Hagen's words.

'OK,' says Naylor. 'I'll do my best.'

'Great stuff,' says Campbell. As he stands up, he looks over her shoulder. 'Where's Rose? Rose, there you are. Can I have a word?'

Campbell does a good job at the press conference. Presenting himself well is what he excels at, and he speaks with his usual authority, addressing the crowd of journalists with a suitably grave face, avoiding the stilted police-speak so many officers fall into when faced with microphones and cameras. Today two new photofit pictures are on screens behind him, images of a pair of unattractive, unremarkable men, put together from witness statements from the Ferrybridge filling station. Campbell's shirt, Naylor notices, has all its buttons in place. At the table beside him, Hagen looks hot and uncomfortable, eyes down on the notes in front of him as the cameras flash and whirr. In the front row, Naylor recognises a well-known woman presenter from ITV news, who looks older in the flesh and disturbingly thin.

The questions, when Campbell asks for them, are largely predictable.

'Chief Inspector, in the light of this development, were you too hasty before in shutting down your investigation into Evan's abduction?'

Campbell appears to consider.

'Based on the evidence we had at that time, I don't believe so, no. And it's wrong to say our investigation was shut down. Evan's case, like many others, was always subject to review if new information came to light. Which, I'm very pleased to say, is what's happening now.'

'Can you tell us how Evan's doing, Chief Inspector?'

'He's recovering at home with his family after a very difficult ordeal, and I'm sure you ladies and gentlemen will respect their need for privacy. I don't think it's appropriate or necessary for me to say more than that at present.'

As Campbell is asking the room for any final questions, Naylor feels a hand on her shoulder. A man is standing behind her, old enough to be her father but attractive in a silver fox way, wearing a hoody and jeans with old trainers.

She turns sharply to see who's touched her, meets the man's eyes and gives a broad smile.

'Bloody hell, Ron,' she says. 'Don't you know better than to sneak up behind a woman with self-defence skills? What brings you here?'

'I heard the circus was in town,' says Ron Perdue, nodding towards the front of the room where Campbell is thanking everyone for coming. 'It's a good turn-out. He'll be pleased.'

'We're all pleased,' says Naylor. 'It's a nasty case, and we need all the help we can get.'

'I've read about it,' says Perdue. 'I was wondering if you'd care to join me at the Lamb and Lion for a pie and a pint, for old times' sake.' He pats his stomach. 'As you can see, retirement is keeping me from the requisite daily calorie intake to maintain my beer gut.'

Naylor looks him up and down.

'I can see you've lost a few pounds,' she says. 'But you might have put on a suit.'

'Retirees' prerogative, to dress like a slob,' says Perdue. 'Anyway, I don't own a suit any more, except the black one I keep for funerals. I made a big bonfire and burned them all. Very therapeutic. So, are you coming, or what?'

'Bit early for lunch.'

'Call it research. You can pick my brains, and I'm buying.'

'In that case, I'm right behind you.'

On the short walk to the Lamb and Lion, Perdue and Naylor don't say much. The pub is down a narrow alley still paved with cobblestones, and the low doorways and leaded windows of the neighbouring buildings always make Naylor feel she's stepped into a Dickens novel. The illusion is short-lived. Though the outside's totally traditional, inside the pub's been given the inevitable brewery makeover to cater to their assumption of modern tastes: dove-grey walls, menus painted on blackboards, the old red-plush banquettes dumped in favour of satin-varnished pine. It's not yet twelve and the bar is quiet. Behind the pumps, a student in a low-cut T-shirt gives them a practised smile.

'What'll you have?' asks Ron.

'Orange juice and soda,' says Naylor.

'One of those,' says Perdue to the barmaid. 'And a pint of lager shandy for me.'

As the barmaid fixes the drinks, Perdue looks around.

'I preferred this place in the old days,' he says. 'Toilets out back and cigarette burns in the upholstery. It was the end of proper pubs, the smoking ban. All the interesting people you used to meet go and stand outside.'

'Why would you object to a smoking ban? You don't smoke. I remember the air in here being so thick sometimes you'd struggle to find enough oxygen to fill one lung, never mind two.'

'And are you still smoking?'

'No,' says Naylor. 'Gave up months ago. I got fed up putting all that tax into the public coffers when none of it gets spent where it should be.'

The barmaid places a tall glass in front of her, and Naylor takes a long drink.

'Very wise. Are you eating?' Perdue looks up at the black-board at the end of the bar, where the menu is written up in white chalk as if it changes every day. Perdue knows it doesn't; the only things that change are the prices, which always go up, he notices, never down. 'Steak and kidney for me, please, love,' he says to the barmaid. 'No chips, just peas.'

'No chips?' asks Naylor. 'That's a first. I'll have the same, chips and peas on mine.'

'You can afford a few chips,' says Perdue, as they make their way to a table by the window. 'You've lost a couple of pounds too.'

'You know how it is,' says Naylor, sitting down on a chair which looks more comfortable than it is. 'No time to shop, less time to cook. I end up living on sandwiches and takeaways.'

'That's a slippery slope.' Perdue takes a seat on the opposite side of the table, moving a dessert menu to make room for his glass. 'A diet like that'll give you ulcers, sooner or later. Though I have to say you look good on it. I like your hair like that, by the way. Suits you.'

Naylor smiles, and makes a show of patting her French pleat.

'Thanks,' she says. 'New hairstyle, new life. I'm moving on.'

'You ever hear anything from Tim?'

Naylor's smile slips, and the shadow of a heartache crosses her face.

'Not these days. We're not exactly top of each other's Christmas card lists, after what happened. Last I heard he was living in Cornwall. He'd love it down there, wall-to-wall surfing. Right up his alley.'

'I always wondered if you might get back together.'

Naylor shakes her head.

'No chance. Turns out he's not the forgiving kind. But I've got the flat, and I'm comfortable there. I've even got a cat for company.'

'You don't like cats.'

'This one was down on its luck, and I was feeling sentimental. We went to a sudden death, a youngish guy whose heart gave out. Turned out to be heart failure induced by so-called energy drinks. Anyway, he had this cat, a scarred old bruiser who looked like he was on his last legs, and I thought the poor thing wouldn't last long in an animal shelter. He's no trouble and it's good to have a warm body to go home to, even if it's covered in ginger fur.'

The food arrives, and while they eat, the talk's all station gossip: who's sleeping with who, who's heading for promotion, the outcomes of the cases Perdue left unresolved.

'That youth who stamped on the homeless bloke outside the Ernest Road chip shop, what happened to him?' he asks, finishing the last of his pie.

'Eighteen months,' says Naylor. 'He thought he was going to get it suspended, but with his back catalogue of offending, the judge took a different view.'

'Should have got longer. He's a vicious little bastard, that one.'

'Well, he's off our radar for now.' Naylor eats her last chip. 'And what about you, Ron? Are you finding plenty to occupy yourself, now you've hung up your spurs?'

Ron shrugs.

'I suppose. We've been away a couple of times, the Lake District, Dorset. June always wanted to go to Dorset, and I always said it was too far away if something happened.'

'So what brought you here today? Was it just coincidence that we were having the biggest bun-fight of a press conference we've had in years?'

Perdue drains his glass.

'You know me better than that,' he says. 'Fancy coffee?'

The pub is filling up. As Perdue waits at the bar to put in their order, Naylor spots a couple of the journalists from the press conference amongst the shoppers and pensioners who've wandered in for lunch. Campbell's new PA is here with a good-looking young man Naylor doesn't know. She's a pretty girl, well-dressed, not unlike Campbell's last PA, the one who got him into so much trouble. He'd have been wiser, thinks Naylor, to have hired someone older, less of a temptation. Then she looks across at Perdue and catches herself thinking how good he still looks. When it comes to chemistry between two people, what does age matter?

Perdue waits for the coffees and carries them back to the table.

'I know you have to get back to work,' he says, retaking his seat. 'A case like this with the world's eyes on you, you don't want to be caught taking long lunches.' He tears the top off a packet of sugar and pours it into his cup, reaches for a second packet but leaves it on the table. 'Old habits.'

'You should go cold turkey,' says Naylor, putting sugar in her own cup. 'They say it's the easiest way.'

'What about that old coffee-maker of mine? Is that still going?'

'Still fuelling the entire department. Working overtime most of the time. Makes a big difference, having drinkable coffee at three in the morning. That stuff from the machine gives me a headache.' She takes a sip of her Americano. 'So come on, Ron. What's your interest with Evan Ferrers?'

Perdue sighs and sits back in his chair.

'Something's been niggling at me. Probably you've thought of it already, but for me the big question is, where were they heading?'

'The filling station they called in at was on the way into Pontefract. Number plate recognition last picked them up on the M62 around Wakefield, travelling east, and we've first got them on the A61, southbound from Harrogate. Hard to say what their exact direction of travel was in Pontefract. Apparently at that filling station you can drive on to the pumps from either east or west.'

'So what's your take on it?'

'We've asked West Yorkshire to make local enquiries, check car park CCTV and see if anyone remembers the vehicle parked anywhere in the area. Problem is, of course, where did their journey originate? That part of the world is a bit sparse on cameras, so it's going to be a long, hard slog. Even if we've got an idea of the area where they started out, there are still hundreds of square miles to go at.'

'Ah, well. Now you've hit the nub of what's been niggling me.'

'What do you mean, Ron? Come on, spit it out.'

'You know me. I'm not good with technology, and you know my thoughts on putting your faith in ANPR. Did you see that story in the *Telegraph*?'

'I don't believe I've ever read a story in the *Telegraph*.'

'Maybe you should. What they were reporting was that one in twelve drivers is now taking steps to outwit the cameras. One in twelve is up to something dodgy, Rachel. Cloned number plates, altering digits and letters, all ducking and diving under the ANPR lenses. All you need's a permanent marker and you're away.

'So when I heard where the boy was found, I got out my trusty road atlas, and had a look at that neck of the woods. And you're quite right, there're thousands of places where they might have kept him. But I think you should consider a different viewpoint.'

'As in?'

'What does a tight bastard like me hate more than anything? Being ripped off at the pumps. It really bugs me, being made to pay over the odds at motorway service stations. So what do I do? Firstly, if I'm travelling on the motorways, I make sure I've got a reasonable amount of fuel before I set off. Secondly, if I do need fuel, I won't pay service-station prices. I leave the motorway and drive a couple of miles to find somewhere cheaper. Especially if I'm going to be travelling a long way. Now, if you look at the map, what do you see in the Pontefract area? Arterial routes. The M62 running east to west, and the A1 running north–south. It's a national intersection.'

Naylor drinks more of her coffee. For a few moments, neither of them speak.

'You're saying we shouldn't focus on West Yorkshire.'

'I'm suggesting you consider the possibility the driver was hard up or tight like me, and didn't want to pay top whack for a tank of fuel. So he made a detour to a cheaper filling station. I'm suggesting that it might have been anywhere, and that Pontefract is an irrelevance. That it just happened to be the place where the fuel gauge hit red. And bearing in mind what I said about not getting caught short, that by the time they reached the Pontefract area, they'd already burned a significant amount of fuel.'

Naylor looks at him.

'That's not very helpful,' she says. 'That would mean we should extend our search area massively towards every point of the compass.'

'Not quite. There's something else you want to think about. Two men with a live cargo like that, they're not going to be careless. Bet your bottom dollar they've got major concerns about falling foul of ANPR, flawed as it may be. Since you haven't found spare number plates – and bear in mind you can whip them on and off with strips of Velcro, so never rule it out – I think you should consider something else. Maybe they used more than one car.'

'That suggests some careful planning.'

'They've got a real, live boy in the boot. Wouldn't you be planning carefully?'

'So you're saying they could have been going from any-where, to anywhere?'

'It's not as bad as that,' says Perdue. 'Have a good look at the map. You've clocked them twice, so you've got a general direction of travel. My gut says don't trust the Wakefield spot, because that could be a detour. Ducking and diving, remember? They were coming from the north, no doubt about that, but don't get stuck thinking they began their journey near Harrogate. Two cars, Rachel, I guarantee it. Maybe more than two. Start there.'

'Campbell's not going to like it. He thinks we're already closing in.'

'Well, I don't think you are. Widen your search area, or I think you're going to be making a serious mistake. Remember the Yorkshire Ripper.'

'The Wearside Jack tapes.'

'Wearside Jack indeed. You think you've got a solid lead, and it takes you right up the longest blind alley of your career. Too much police time focused on that hoax cost three women their lives. Hasn't the boy given you any idea of where you should be looking?'

'He's not saying anything at all.'

'Hardly surprising. Give him time.'

'We need him to talk.' Naylor looks at her watch. 'I have to go. It's been good to see you, Ron.' She reaches for her purse, but Perdue stops her.

'My treat,' he says. 'But get your map out, Rachel, and use some logic. West Yorkshire's a red herring. I'd stake my reputation on it. Promise me you'll look into it.'

'We'll look into it,' says Naylor. 'Give June my regards.'

It's after six when Naylor leaves the office that evening. Dallabrida catches up with her as she gets into the lift, slapping a hand on the edge to force the half-closed doors to slide back. He steps in beside her, bringing his smell of Gucci aftershave and spearmint gum.

He stands legs astride like a Bob Hoskins gangster, hands folded over his crotch in a bouncer's pose, so close to her they'd be shoulder to shoulder, if Dallabrida's shoulder weren't so much higher than her own.

'I hate these things,' he says. 'Phobic, I am.' His accent's pure Essex, or maybe East End; Naylor can't tell the difference. 'I like to have someone to hold my hand.'

He has big hands, and long fingers which would make huge fists. Naylor imagines how it would feel if one of Dallabrida's hands landed on your shoulder, if it were feeling your collar.

'You could take the stairs,' she says.

The lift doors close.

'Too late,' says Dallabrida. 'I'll have to master my fears, and plunge with you all the way to the ground floor.'

Naylor almost smiles.

'How's it going, anyway?' he asks, as the lift begins to move. 'Thought we'd be bringing 'em in by now, with us having the car and everythin'. How's the boy doing?'

'Not great.' Naylor thinks she feels her phone buzz in her pocket and pulls it out, but it's wishful thinking. The screen is blank.

The lift clunks to a halt on the first floor. The doors slide open, but no one gets in.

Dallabrida leans across her and presses the Door Close button.

'These things get on my tits. You're right, I should take the stairs.' The doors close again. As the lift starts to move, he says, 'I was going to go for a drink, just a quick one at the Bell. You fancy a drink, Rachel?'

She slips the phone back into her pocket.

'Not tonight,' she says.

'Hot date, eh?' asks Dallabrida. 'Who's the lucky fella?'

'No one you know.'

The doors open on to the lobby. Dallabrida makes a show of letting Naylor step out in front of him.

'Another time then, eh?'

She looks him in the face. He's got a bullish head, his hair's shaved very close, and his nose has been broken at least once. He's not good-looking in any conventional sense, but he's got nice eyes. All the girls talk about Dallabrida's big brown eyes.

'You're not my type, Leon,' she says.

Dallabrida smiles.

''Course I am,' he says. 'I'm every woman's type, I am. Loaded with charm, like a pizza with every kind of topping. How're you fixed for tomorrow?'

'Goodnight, Leon,' says Naylor. As she walks away, she finds herself smiling. Then she checks her silent phone again, and the smile slips away.

In Waitrose, the produce shelves are depleted, and there are no avocados for the salad she was going to make. She picks up a bag of spinach and a pack of cherry tomatoes. They've lowered the chiller temperatures to compensate for the heat, and wandering between the fridges, she shivers. She puts chicken breasts and prosciutto in her basket, and picks up a bottle of Chianti from a special offer display. Then she adds a bottle of Merlot, just in case.

As she reaches her car, her phone rings. When she sees who's calling, she smiles.

'Hello you,' she says. 'How are you doing?' There's a moment of silence, long enough to tell her there's a problem. 'Where are you?'

'At the leisure centre. I've just dropped Harry off for cricket.'

'What time are you coming over?'

She can't help herself asking the question, even though instinct and experience have already told her the answer.

'It's going to be difficult tonight,' he says. 'Bridget's not very well. She's gone to bed, so I'm saddled with taxi duty.'

'For God's sake.' The bag in her hand feels suddenly heavy. Naylor presses the unlock button on her key, and the car beeps.

She pops open the boot and stows the carrier bag inside. 'You promised.'

'What could I say?' he asks. 'Come on, Rachel. Don't be like that.'

'Come on yourself,' says Naylor, and ends the call.

THIRTEEN

21 June

Jack's given Bob Sturgess a list of what needs doing, even though Bob's been farming more years than even Jack and could run Ainsclough Top with his eyes shut.

Sensing his leaving, Millie the collie presses herself against Jack's legs. He bends down and strokes her head.

'You'll ring me if there's any problems?' he says, and Bob nods his assent. 'We'll be back by Saturday at the latest.'

Dora's already waiting in the car, wearing a summer frock decorated with yellow tulips. Jack climbs in beside her and starts the engine.

'You look nice, love,' he says. 'I haven't seen that dress for a while.'

'I haven't been able to get into it for a long time,' says Dora. 'I suppose I must have lost a bit of weight. Has Bob got a key to the house?'

'House key, sheds and everywhere else. And I've told him to ring Matt's if he's any problems. He knows what he's doing. Have you got everything you need?'

'I think so.'

'And is that cake put somewhere safe?'

'I put it under your jacket to keep it out of the sun. I think it'll be all right.'

Jack takes it steady down the pitted lane, slowing down even more to make a last eyeball check on the ewes and lambs on the home field. At the bottom of the hill, two weeks without rain have reduced the stream to a trickle, though the banks are still lush with grass, and pretty with corncockles and kingcups. High clouds are beginning to encroach over Blackmire Ridge, but as they reach the road the sky ahead is clear, and Jack puts on the Yankees cap Matt brought him from America to shield his eyes from the sun's glare.

At first, it promises to be a good day for a drive, but it's high summer and a lot of kids are out of school. The roads are busy, and there's a long delay at Ripon and again just before Wetherby. By the time they get through the jam, Jack decides they'll pull into the services for a break.

He parks the old Freelander in a quiet spot and finds the cool-bag Dora has packed with lunch. Sitting with the car doors open to let in a breeze, they drink tea from a flask and eat their sandwiches seasoned with the smell of petrol fumes and the noise of fast traffic in the background: corned beef and pickle for Jack, cheese and lettuce for Dora, though she re-wraps half of hers back in the foil.

'You haven't eaten much,' says Jack. 'Do you want one of these?'

'I'm not very hungry,' says Dora. 'It's so hot.' For a long moment, she watches the motorway, the trucks and cars hurtling by. 'What if he doesn't want to see us?'

About to take another bite of his sandwich, Jack looks at her. 'What do you mean?'

'Evan. I mean Evan. With what Matt's said about him being so quiet, I wonder if we're doing the right thing, going down there.'

She turns to face him, and he sees that behind her glasses, her eyes are filled with tears.

'We didn't do anything to help him, did we? All the time he was with – whoever he was with, why didn't we try to find him? Why didn't we lock up the farm and get in this car and spend all our time looking for him? What if he asks us that, Jack? What are we going to say? And now he's come home, and we're turning up expecting him to still be our Evan, all smiles as if he'd been away to scout camp or somewhere. If he isn't pleased to see us, I shan't be a bit surprised. And if he isn't pleased to see us, it'll break my heart.'

Jack puts his sandwich on the dashboard and takes her hand.

'I won't lie, it's crossed my mind too. And to be honest, we can't expect him to be the same boy we knew. He's bound to have changed, and I'm sorry to say, not for the better. But don't you think it'll help him to know his old grandma and grandad still love him just the same? What do you think, that we shouldn't go in case he's not nice to us? After what he's been through, I should think you and I can cope with him not being very nice. We're made of tough stuff, aren't we, Mrs Ferrers, eh?'

She nods, and blows her nose on a handkerchief embroidered with primroses.

'You're right,' she says. 'Of course you're right. Not going would be far worse than going, so we'd better pack up and get on.'

*

All the way south, Dora is quiet, and Jack lets her be so. At Peterborough, they stop for tea and buttered scones, and by the time they reach the M25, it's close to rush hour. Traffic crawls. Even in his shirt-sleeves, Jack's too hot. It's time to take one of his tablets, but they're in a suitcase in the back. When they reach the turn-off to Matt's, Dora's dozing, her eyebrows pulled together, frowning as she sleeps.

It's been a while since they've been down here, not since the Christmas before Evan was taken. Last Christmas he and Dora spent alone, with a roast chicken for lunch and a bottle of wine, no tree, no decorations, no presents. There have been changes in the town – a street he used to go down is now one-way – and for a few minutes he thinks they're lost, until he sees a Tesco he remembers.

He gives Dora a gentle nudge.

'Wake up, love,' he says. 'We're nearly there.'

Dora rouses herself, looks in the sun-visor mirror, pats at her hair and freshens her lipstick. She puts her hand over Jack's on the gearstick and gives it a squeeze.

They're turning into Matt's road. The house is straight ahead.

'Ready, Mrs Ferrers?' asks Jack, and Dora nods.

'The garden's looking nice,' says Jack, even though it isn't, beyond the grass being carelessly cut.

Matt's come striding out to greet them as they pull up in the drive, and he hugs his father in a way Jack can't remember him ever doing before. It's a hug filled with relief, a survivor's hug, with a loud subtext of *Thank Christ*.

Dora thinks Claire looks unwell, though she's smiling as she kisses Dora on the cheek.

Claire leads the way into the house.

'I'll bet you're ready for a cup of tea,' she says.

'Or a cold beer,' says Matt. 'That's what I'm going to have. Dad, can I get you one?'

'By and by,' says Jack. 'There's business to attend to, first.'

The kitchen smells of frying garlic and tomatoes. There's a bottle of red wine open on the counter from which one glass is already gone.

'I'm doing spaghetti and meatballs,' says Claire. She switches on the kettle and takes mugs down from a cupboard. 'I thought we'd all like that.'

Dora has brought in nothing from the car but her handbag and the cake tin.

'I made his favourite,' she says, and looks into the lounge. 'Where is he?'

'Let's have our tea, shall we?' says Claire. 'He'll be down when he's ready. Shall I take that?' She lifts the cake tin lid. 'Ah, chocolate! I'm sure he'll love it.'

Overhead, a floorboard creaks. They settle in the lounge.

'So, any more news?' asks Jack, and Matt shakes his head and signals upwards with his eyes to denote a taboo subject.

Jack changes tack. 'How's work?'

'Oh, you know,' says Matt. 'Busy.'

'You're lucky he's here,' says Claire. 'I don't see very much of him, these days.'

'I'm doing a lot of travelling at the moment,' says Matt. 'We're trying to establish an office in Oxford.'

'And Colchester,' puts in Claire.

'Well,' says Matt. 'That's a different thing.'

The floorboards creak again. Jack catches Dora's eye.

'As long as you're busy,' says Dora. 'I worry you'll get laid off.'

'I shan't get laid off, Mum,' says Matt, with a touch of irritation. 'I've been made a director. How was your drive down?'

'Oh, we did all right,' says Jack. 'Traffic was heavy around . . .'

He stops. Through the open lounge door, he can see the stairs, and on the stairs he can see a sock-clad foot. His eyes prick with tears, but he blinks them back, and signals Dora to stay in her chair. A second foot appears, and now he can see thin fingers on the banister.

Jack's heart is beating too fast; he really should find his tablets. Standing up from his chair, he crosses to the doorway and looks up.

He sees a skinny, dishevelled Evan, pale and sad-eyed, and Jack thinks his heart will break. But he puts on a smile, and moves to the bottom of the stairs.

'Well, aren't you a sight for sore eyes, my boy,' he says. 'Come and give your old grandpa a hug.'

And Evan does.

FOURTEEN

24 June

Naylor rings the doorbell at the Ferrerses' house. The routine is familiar from all those weeks they were backwards and forwards here when Evan went missing, and now the case is back in the forefront, they'll be backwards and forwards all over again. Some things haven't changed, though the season is different. Matt's Audi isn't there, but Claire's Renault is on the drive, looking less well-cared-for than it did. When Evan disappeared, the car was brand-new. The front garden smells of British summer, wet roses and dank greenery, and in the borders, virulent dandelions have taken hold, spoiling displays of pink dianthus and poking through spikes of salvias. The small front lawn has been recently mown and is strewn with clumps of Flymo-chewed grass. As the doorbell dies away, Naylor hears the usual sounds of the suburbs: a plane high overhead, the buzz of a strimmer, traffic on the high street, and far away, a siren.

When Claire opens the door she looks different, as if she might have reached the low point of her descent and be climbing back up. There are traces of colour in her cheeks, though her hair is still careless, swept back in a corner-chemist clip. She invites Naylor in. On the hall floor, there's a black bin bag, stuffed to capacity.

'Evan's old clothes,' says Claire. 'I kept them all, and now they're too small. Time to throw them out.'

Overhead, a floorboard creaks. A door closes, and a bolt rattles home.

Claire looks at Naylor, shrugs and leads the way to the kitchen, where the air's thick with oven chips and vinegar and warm sausage-fat from a pan on the stove. She offers Naylor a seat at the table, which is covered in clutter – a laptop, unopened mail, keys, a couple of DVDs – but the place overall seems tidier, cleaner. In recovery.

'I bought him a few bits to be going on with, but it's difficult,' says Claire. 'He's lost touch with everything, what's in and what's out, doesn't know what his friends are wearing.' She's filling the kettle at the tap. 'Listen to me, talking about his friends. I don't think he'll have many of those. I expect we'll move now, have a fresh start. No bad thing, I suppose. Matt wanted to move anyway. We're notorious around here, and he hates that, being whispered about, but I always resisted.'

She switches on the kettle and takes two white mugs from the cupboard. Naylor has white mugs at home, but hers were ordered from a cheap catalogue, a job lot of crockery, four place settings, when she moved into the new flat. Claire's look like porcelain, an elegant design pleasing to the eye; they've got Habitat or John Lewis written all over them.

'Earl Grey or English Breakfast?'

'Builder's,' says Naylor. 'Milk and one, please.'

A black cat is walking down the back garden path. The view from the kitchen window is of other people's gardens, and of other houses. Claire opens the fridge to find the milk, and the fridge looks full, of vegetables and yogurt and cartons of juice.

'I had this thing,' Claire goes on, pouring milk, spooning sugar, 'that he might come home. That he might turn up here one day, and wouldn't find us. Wouldn't that have been too awful? Now I wish we had moved, so he didn't have to come back here, to being a curiosity. I don't blame him for not wanting to go out.'

'Doesn't he want to go out?'

Claire shakes her head and places Naylor's tea in front of her, still whirling from being stirred.

'I think he feels like an alien, and he can't seem to reconnect. I got him those DVDs to try and get him caught up, but I don't think he's interested.'

She finds a packet of chocolate biscuits, tips several on to a plate and puts them at the centre of the table, helping herself to one before she sits down. She dips the biscuit in her tea, and bites off the damp edge.

'I survived on chocolate biscuits while he was gone. No nutritional value but lots of calories. I'm trying to eat better now, and trying to get him to eat well too. He used to be such a fussy eater, a bit of a nightmare, really. Now he doesn't seem to care at all. The doctors say he needs to put on weight, but I can't find anything he really wants. He seems so listless, so . . .' She glances up at the ceiling. 'I don't want him to hear. The first day or two, he clung to me, like he did when he was a toddler, my little shadow. Now he just wants to be up there by himself, and I don't try too hard to persuade him down, because he feels like . . .' Her eyes fill with tears. 'He feels like someone I don't know.'

'It takes time, Claire,' says Naylor. She sips her tea, working hard to resist the chocolate biscuits. In her pocket, her phone is buzzing, but she ignores it.

'He doesn't feel safe, not even with us,' says Claire. 'He asked Matt to put a bolt on his door, and he puts a chair under the door handle when he goes in the shower. I try not to mind. If that's what he needs . . .'

'We'll get him the right help,' says Naylor. 'And when you think he might be ready, we'd like to talk to him. Not at the station or anything, somewhere he'll feel supported. We have people who are specially trained. They'll take good care of him.'

'I want to be with him when you do that.'

Naylor sighs.

'You know, Claire,' she says, 'I don't think that's a good idea.'

'Why not? I think he'll want me to be there.' Claire stops, realising Evan won't want her anywhere near. 'But if you don't think I should, I won't. I suppose you know best.'

'Can I say hello to him?'

'You can try. Upstairs, first on the left. The one with the closed door.'

Naylor knows which room it is; she spent time here, in the early days, looking for anything which would help, finding nothing. The stickers on his door are as they were: *Call of Duty*, Man U, a New York Giants pennant held on with drawing pins. She listens at the door, but there's nothing to hear.

She taps gently.

'Evan? Evan, it's Rachel Naylor, from the police. I just came to say hello.'

There's the sound of bedsprings as he moves. She waits a minute or two, but there's nothing more.

'I have to go now, but I'll be back in the next day or so. I'll see you then, OK?'

Back downstairs, Claire's waiting to show her out.

'What's he doing in there?' asks Naylor.

'Sleeping, I think,' says Claire. 'They've given him something in place of the other stuff, but he's still very tired. Apart from that, I don't know. He's not saying much.'

'Just give it time,' says Naylor, squeezing Claire's arm. 'He's been through a lot.'

Outside, as she gets into the car, Naylor looks across at the Ferrerses' house. All seems normal, but for one thing: it's broad daylight, but the curtains at Evan's windows are drawn.

FIFTEEN

27 June

'Evan?'

Rose Yazici is in the interview room as an appropriate adult. Naylor likes Rose very much – she's motherly but not mumsy, with an ability to connect with almost anyone, even Campbell. She's pretty too, dark and petite in jewel-coloured clothes and bold jewellery which reflect her Turkish heritage. Her prettiness has to be a plus with a boy Evan's age, surely? Naylor thought if anyone could get Evan to open up, it would be Rose. Turns out she was wrong.

Evan's been in here with them almost an hour now, a book of photofits and photos of known offenders open on the table, with Rose slowly turning the pages and encouraging him to take his time, see if he spots anyone he recognises. Some of the faces are the stuff of parental nightmares – ugly, dirty old bastards with a lifetime's offending behind them, obvious criminals you wouldn't let anywhere near your child. And then there are the others: respectable, even attractive-looking men, some only in their twenties, far more dangerous in Naylor's eyes than the old-timers. These younger men look friendly, trustworthy, like your next-door neighbour or your sister's boyfriend. These are men you'd talk to, be pleased to find leading a scout group or after-school club, who you'd let join you and your kids in a Happy Meal without a second thought, but you'd shudder at the appetites they were stoking while they were watching your six-year-old eat her chicken nuggets.

Naylor would never say as much to Claire Ferrers, but Evan looks terrible. He's pale and seems exhausted, as if he hasn't slept for months (though Claire says he does nothing but sleep), and he looks uncomfortable in new clothes which don't suit him, not because they're not his size but because they're not his age. He seems to be frozen in time as if he's suffering from arrested development, so if Naylor didn't know better she'd have him down as a tall-for-his-age ten-year-old. The on-trend clothes Claire has bought him – trainers and chinos and T-shirts with the right logos – look like they're from an older brother's wardrobe, and Evan looks fearful as a whipped dog, like he's expecting to take a thrashing at any moment.

'How about this one?' asks Rose. From her upside-down vantage point, Naylor recognises Danny Stokes, who's been inside some time, so she's not surprised when Evan doesn't respond. Rose turns the page again, to two faces Naylor doesn't recognise. She's watching Evan closely and sees him blink, a slight flutter in his eyelids she hasn't seen before. Hagen's noticed Evan's reaction too, and writes something in his notebook.

'Evan?' asks Naylor. 'Do you know either of these men? If you think there's even a chance you've seen either of them, please tell us.'

But Evan stays silent.

'If you can help Sergeant Naylor at all,' Rose puts in, 'it

could go a long way towards finding whoever took you. I know it's hard, but your evidence is very important. Very important indeed.'

Naylor looks down at the photographs: two white men, one clean-shaven and in his thirties, the other older, with lank hair and an unkempt beard. Which one prompted Evan's reaction?

'If you identify any of these men, I guarantee we'll keep you safe from them,' says Rose. 'They can't hurt you any more, sweetheart. We're all here to protect you.'

Evan looks at her, and there's a cynicism in his eyes it disturbs Naylor to see. He doesn't believe Rose, and why should he? If they were capable of protecting every child in their jurisdiction, he would never have been taken from that bus stop and subjected to the horrors he has yet to reveal.

Words are cheap, thinks Naylor. And who can blame poor Evan for being afraid to point the finger, when all it will do is bring the monsters back into his world?

SIXTEEN

29 June

'So, says Campbell, rubbing his hands together as if he means business, but actually looking as if he's feeling the cold. 'What have we got?'

'Just the car still,' says Hagen, 'and there's nothing from that. Not yet, anyway.'

'That beggars belief,' says Campbell. 'The boy was in the back of it, two abductors in the front, and there's nothing to go on?'

'I'm not saying there's nothing at all,' says Hagen. 'Of course there are prints and DNA. Just nothing that ties in to anyone we know.'

'The ANPR data hasn't been much help either,' says Naylor. 'We're thinking they must have switched cars shortly before we got them on the A61. But finding the car they abandoned – if there was one – is an impossibility. It could be anywhere, in a garage somewhere or under a tarpaulin. For all we know it's crushed and gone by now.'

'No soil samples, nothing like that?'

'Nothing. All that tells us is they've been sticking to city driving.'

'And what about the men themselves? How did they just vanish?'

Naylor shrugs.

'It isn't hard to do, Sir, if they split up and both found themselves a pub, sat for half an hour with a pint and called themselves a taxi. We've checked the CCTV at the rail and bus stations, nothing there. Appeals for information haven't given us anything. Most likely someone came and picked them up.'

Campbell wanders over to where the coffee machine has just brewed a fresh pot. There's an open biscuit tin which once held Scottish shortbread, recently filled by Rose with Oreos, and Campbell helps himself.

'So what's next? Rachel, how did your interview with Evan go?'

'We did our best,' says Naylor, 'but he never said a word. The closest we came to any response were a couple of photos where I thought there was something. Maybe, maybe not.'

'Worth a look though, surely, if we've nothing else? When are you bringing him back in?'

'With respect, Sir, I think we should leave it a while. He's so traumatised, it isn't ethical to keep chipping away at him. According to Claire Ferrers, he's little better than catatonic. He needs more time. Rose agrees with me.'

'I appreciate the boy's fragile,' says Campbell. 'And in an ideal world, we'd give him all the time and space he needs, but under the very pressing circumstances I think we have to push him. Bring him back in and try again. What else have you got?'

'The car's the obvious one,' says Hagen. 'We need to make sure we've exhausted everything there. And I agree we could take a look at the photos which caused a reaction, if a reaction it was. The thing is, it's impossible to say whether our photos might just have reminded him of someone. They might both be complete dead ends.'

'We only need one break though, don't we, people?' says Campbell cheerfully. He helps himself to another biscuit. 'One for the road, if no one minds. My meeting with the Chief Constable over-ran and I never got any lunch. Anyway, keep me up to date.'

The incident room door closes behind Campbell's back.

'A little pep-talk like that always makes me feel better,' says Hagen with heavy sarcasm.

'Makes it all worthwhile,' says Naylor. 'Which do you fancy, the mugshots or the car? If you've no preference, I'll take the car. I got halfway through the forensics last night before I was interrupted by a large glass of wine and an urgent need to sleep. But I've started, so I think I ought to finish.'

'Happy reading, then. I suppose that leaves me with the known offenders. Any idea who they are?'

'Not local, that's all I know. Looks like you might be clocking up some expenses.'

'Every little helps.'

'Has it struck you how none of this seems to be local, Brad?'

'In what way?'

'Everything seems to be geographically randomised, like there's a deliberate effort to keep elements apart.'

They both glance at the map of the British Isles on one of the incident room whiteboards, where the number of coloured pins denoting significant events seems to be growing.

'If I were abducting children, I'd be doing my best to make

it look randomised too,' says Hagen. 'But if we keep sticking pins in the map, maybe a pattern will emerge. Remember what Uncle Ron used to say. Nothing in these cases is ever unconnected. Find enough pointers, and we'll be able to join the dots.'

SEVENTEEN

30 June

Hagen finds the address he's looking for in the suburbs of Wolverhampton, a few hundred metres off the A449. The district he's in is called Merridale, a name which seems particularly inapt given the size of the cemetery featuring on the satnav as he makes his way through the streets of solid brick houses.

The place he's looking for is a well-kept bungalow, lace curtains at the windows and a sunroom at the front, cast-iron gates with the finials of its struts painted gold. At the edges of the block-paved drive the snapdragons and lobelia in the flowerbeds seem to be receiving reasonable care. A wooden fence separates the garden from a public footpath, where tatters of old litter have gathered at the foot of a *No Cycling* sign.

This street doesn't look like cycling territory to Hagen. The kerbsides are close-parked with vehicles, mostly cheap family motors and runabouts with the odd drug dealer's favourite amongst them, pimped Beamers and a slammed Golf.

As he parks across the bungalow's driveway, there's a view of the city centre in the distance, marked by a scatter of tower blocks and a grime-blackened church tower. The gate squeals as he pushes it open, and a hand lifts a corner of the net curtains. Naylor's taught Hagen to ignore doorbells, so he raps on the glass door, which is opened promptly by a woman he puts in her forties. She's made an attempt at urban glamour – her hair's home-dyed a shade of burgundy and her glasses are sixties-style and cherry red – but grey roots are showing through the hair dye, and there's no on-trend logo on her hoody or sweatpants. Hagen picks up the stink of cigarettes, so potent she must have just put one out.

'Yes?'

She looks quite amenable, until Hagen flips open his wallet and shows his warrant card.

'What, again?' she protests. 'Why can't you leave us alone? It's like living in an episode of *The Bill*.'

Her accent to his ears is pure Brummie, though he knows that's the same ignorance as people not knowing the difference between Geordie and Mackem or Smoggy.

'I'm looking for Robert Gillard. Is he in?'

'He's not in, no, but he's entitled to be out. Seven till seven, that's his curfew hours.'

'And you are . . .?'

'I'm Madge, his sister. Marjorie to you. What are you doing back here? We had a probation visit only last week. He's keeping to his terms and conditions. Ask the neighbours if you don't believe me.'

'Do you know where I might find him, Marjorie?'

'Do I have to tell you?'

'I can come in and wait if you'd rather.'

She gives a pantomime sigh.

'He's at the library, studying for his qualification. Why won't you people even give him a chance? He had a rotten start in life which you would know if you could be bothered to find out. We both had rotten starts, and you ought to give him breathing space to do something with his life instead of coming round here drawing attention all the time. We've Mum to think of, haven't we? It's no bloody picnic being uprooted at her age. It'll all be down to you if we have to move again.'

'I hope it won't come to that,' says Hagen. 'But with the kind of offences your brother committed, by law people have a right to know – if they choose to find out – that he might pose a danger. How do I get to the library?'

'It's a good walk, and he has to walk, doesn't he? We've no car, how could we afford a car? He hasn't a snowball in hell's chance of getting a job with his record. There's only my wage and his benefits and Mum's pension. It's no bloody picnic, I'll tell you. Straight down there to the shopping centre, it's in there. And when you find him, ask him to pick me up a packet of fags on his way home.'

The library is a light, modern building, its noticeboard splashed with posters advertising toddler story-times, knit-and-natter afternoons and a weekly board-game group, free tea and coffee, come and meet new friends.

Behind the desk a librarian in an electric wheelchair glances at Hagen before going back to her carping account of how she's been stiffed on holiday pay. On the receiving end, her colleague appears bored. In the kindergarten section, a small child sits on its mother's knee, sucking its thumb as she reads a story, both mother and child unperturbed by another child shouting for attention as he plunders the contents of a toy box.

The computer section is at the back of the room, through

a gap in the stacks between Biography and Local History. A man is sitting at a terminal, engrossed in whatever is displaying on the screen. As Hagen walks towards him, the man senses movement, and without looking up, hits a single key on the keyboard. By the time Hagen's standing behind him, the monitor's showing the front page of Betfred.

'Robert Gillard?'

'Who's asking?' Gillard folds his skinny arms across his chest. His accent's the same as his sister's but he's younger than her, dressed anonymously as she was in jeans and chain-store trainers and a grey T-shirt printed in red with the words *Why Wait?* A beige windcheater not quite old enough to be vintage – a dead man's jacket from a charity shop – is draped on the back of his chair.

Hagen flashes his warrant card, and in disgust, Gillard shakes his head. He looks up at Hagen with feral animosity in his rat-like face.

'She tell you I was here, did she? Stupid cow. She hasn't the brains to keep it shut.'

'Are you allowed to be here, Bobby? How many conditions are you breaking? Unsupervised access to a computer and close proximity to children? It doesn't look good, does it?'

'I don't think I know you, do I? You new or something?'

'I'm from out of area,' says Hagen. 'Your name's come up in regard to an investigation. Have you been out of town recently?'

'Do me a favour!' Gillard spits the words. 'How could I, when you've as good as got me chained here? I was better off inside. At least in there I didn't have them two nagging me night and day. My life's not worth living and that's the truth.'

119

'Having a flutter on the horses, are you?'

'Just a couple of quid. It passes the time. There's nothing against that in my conditions.'

'I don't suppose there is,' says Hagen. 'But with those youngsters the other side of that wall, I think it's time you took yourself home, don't you? I'll wait while you pack up.'

At the bottom of the screen, Hagen can see there are two Google windows open on the machine. Gillard hits the power button, and the computer begins to shut itself down. Pulling on his windcheater, he leads the way towards the exit, pushes open the door and lets it swing back in Hagen's face before walking away towards the shopping centre.

'Your sister wants you to take her a packet of cigarettes,' Hagen calls after him, and Gillard sticks a finger in the air.

From the information which comes through from the DVLA, Naylor learns the Focus has had three owners, all women. She studies the addresses but can see nothing there. Sevenoaks, Chelmsford, Woking. The most recent keeper – in Chelmsford – seems as good a place as any to start.

Essex is a county she doesn't know except for its trashy TV fame, and she puts her trust in the satnav as it guides her round the M25 to junction 28 and along the A12 past Brentwood. Once she's off the A12, she finds herself on the grandiosely named Essex Yeomanry Way – a bypass by another name – and from there drives into Great Baddow, a place whose origins as a pretty village are still visible despite the opportunistic development on every square metre of available space.

The house she's looking for turns out to be one of the

new-builds – a townhouse at the end of a cul-de-sac, white-rendered and with ridiculously tiny windows both upstairs and down, which could surely have made sense in an architect's mind only as a means to frustrate the neighbours' peeping. Attached to the house are two parking spaces, one of them occupied by a Hyundai hatchback with a disabled sticker on the rear windscreen.

Naylor parks in the vacant space and unlocks her phone. There are a couple of new emails, but nothing so far from Hagen in Wolverhampton. She checks her face in the rear-view mirror, applies lipstick and climbs from the car.

She doesn't use the doorbell. When doorbells don't get answered, it's impossible to know whether that's because there's no one home, or the individual she's looking for is heading out the back door as she's standing at the front, or maybe the bell is broken. Knuckles eliminate the last possibility. She raps on the glass, and immediately a dog begins to bark – a yappy terrier, her least favourite kind. Within a moment, a woman's ineffectually telling it to be quiet, but the dog's ignoring her, scratching at the door to get at the visitor. Naylor hears muttering, the rattle of keys, and a firmer order for the dog to go to its bed. Surprisingly, the barking stops as it complies. A key turns in the lock, and a chain is taken off the latch.

The woman who opens the door is enormously overweight. The journey down the hallway seems to have winded her, and she's breathing as heavily as if she'd run a mile, leaning on a stick held in a hand wearing three diamond rings, all pressing into the flesh of her fingers to such a degree, Naylor thinks they must be painful. And yet she might be attractive; she looks no more than forty, and she's made an effort with her hair and clothes, which, though voluminous, are all matched as an outfit.

Naylor holds up her ID.

'Mrs Birch? Sheila Birch? DS Rachel Naylor, Thames Valley Police. Do you mind if I have a word?'

'Police?' asks Mrs Birch. 'What's it about?'

'Just a routine enquiry. May I come in?'

Sheila Birch holds open the door, and Naylor steps inside. The house is beautifully kept, the carpets vacuumed, the paintwork freshly white, with a strong scent of lavender potpourri from a bowl on the sill of the tiny hall window.

'We can go in the lounge,' says Mrs Birch, limping and wheezing as she leads the way. 'I've put Oscar in the kitchen. He's not very good with visitors.'

'Sounds like he makes a good guard-dog.'

'He's a Jack Russell and all mouth. He doesn't even come up to my knee, and I'm not tall. I don't suppose anyone would find him very scary. Have a seat.'

Sighing with effort and breathlessness, she lowers herself into a fireside chair which appears to be of abnormally large proportions. On a side table, she has all her home comforts: the TV remote, a Samsung tablet, a mobile phone in a candy-pink case dotted with fake gems. Naylor takes a seat opposite, in a normal-sized armchair. Mrs Birch props her stick against the chair arm and looks expectantly at Naylor.

'I've a few questions, if I may, regarding a vehicle you own which was recently reported stolen. An 09-plate Ford Focus. Is that your car?'

'Well, yes and no. It's my name on the paperwork, but it's

Brian who generally drives it. I have the Hyundai which is better for my needs.'

'Brian being?'

'My husband.'

'And you've owned the car how long?'

'I should say it's about eighteen months since he bought it. Brian wanted a workhorse – as he put it – and he really rates his Fords. I preferred the newer model – I think it looks sportier, more modern – but he wasn't so keen. He thought it would leave his samples exposed if he had to leave them in the car. The model he bought has the full boot, which I suppose is more secure.'

'What samples, Mrs Birch? What does your husband do?'

'He sells compressed air, pneumatics, things like that. He's what they used to call a rep, a travelling salesman. The stuff he sells is quite specialised, so he covers a big area. He travels all over the country seeing customers.'

'And how long has he been doing that?'

'A while. Is this about Brian or the car? I'm surprised you're taking such an interest. I assumed gone was gone, and that'd be an end to it. You haven't found it, have you? Only we've started the insurance claim. I'll be disappointed to be honest if you have. I was hoping we might get something newer.'

'We have found it, yes, but that doesn't mean your insurance claim will be invalid. The car was involved in a criminal offence, so we'll be hanging on to it for a while longer yet.'

'A crime? What sort of crime?'

'I'm afraid I can't say.'

'Does that mean you've got Brian's samples? Was there anything in the boot?'

'I'm afraid not, no.'

'I expect they've sold them. Some of his stuff must be worth good money.'

Naylor is finding Mrs Birch's wheezing disconcerting, like sitting opposite a vastly oversized pug.

'Where was the car when it was stolen, Mrs Birch?'

'I don't know, exactly. I wasn't there, was I? You'd have to ask Brian. Haven't you got that information from when he reported it?'

'Where did he tell you it was?'

'He was in Hartlepool. He goes there regularly. They're doing a lot with wind farms up there and Brian's company's involved in all that.'

'And what company is that?'

Mrs Birch scowls.

'I don't see what that has to do with anything. He'll have told the police up there where it was taken from. Don't you people talk to each other? I can give you the incident number if you don't have it. I needed it for the insurance.'

'I already have that, thank you. We're just trying to establish where the car was between when it was taken and when it was found. It makes it easier for us to narrow the field of suspects. Who did you say your husband works for?'

'Petersen Hydraulics. Petersen with an "e".'

'They sound foreign.'

'Dutch.'

'And they have offices in Hartlepool as well as here in Chelmsford?'

'I don't think so. He was seeing a customer up there. But

124

I don't see why that's of interest. I just need to know where we stand with the insurance.'

'If they're an international company, don't they offer their reps company cars?'

'They do in the normal way of things. But Brian preferred to have the money instead, and sort a car out for himself. It works out better for us financially, in the long run. Anyway, he's a bit fickle with cars, always chopping and changing. He's got a couple of others he keeps at a friend's yard, old things he calls his projects. He wasn't heartbroken to see the back of this one, I don't think.'

'Did it give him trouble, then?'

'Oh no. It was always reliable. Fords, they just keep going, don't they? No, he just likes a change. He's always been that way, ever since I've known him.'

'So what's he driving now?'

'Something someone lent him as a stopgap. A Vauxhall, I think. Blue. Or is it silver?'

'If you don't mind me asking, if he's so keen on his Fords, how come you have a Hyundai?'

'It's better suited to my needs. I have it through the Motability scheme.'

Naylor nods.

'I see. I wonder if I could speak to your husband? Is he likely to be home this afternoon?'

'I'm not expecting him today, no. I don't think he'll be home before Friday.'

'Do you have a number I could contact him on?'

'I've got his mobile.'

'That would be great, thank you. And can I have your number here, just in case?'

Mrs Birch recites two numbers which Naylor notes down.

'Well, thanks for your time. I'll give you a card. Your husband's welcome to ring me if I don't get to him first.'

'What about the insurance?'

'I suggest you ring them and explain the situation. They'll tell you how to proceed. Please, don't get up. I'll see myself out.'

When she sees Naylor drive away, Sheila picks up her phone and dials.

'Hello, babe,' Brian Birch answers. 'How're you doing?'

There's noise in the background, the murmur of traffic and tyres on tarmac.

'Oh, I'm all right,' she says, and sighs. 'Tired.'

'You take it easy, lady. What're you up to today?'

'Not much. Where are you?'

'According to the sign I've just passed, I'm not too far from Rotherham.'

'What're you doing there?'

'You know me, babe. I go where the money is.'

'Will you be home soon?'

'A couple more days. Thursday or Friday.'

'I just had a visitor. She said she'll be ringing you.'

'Who's that, then?'

'A woman from the police. About the Focus.' There's a moment of silence. 'Brian? Are you there?'

'Yes, I'm here. Bad signal. What about the Focus?'

'She says they've found it, but she didn't say where. I asked her about the insurance, but she said I have to ring them to sort it out. She said they won't be giving the car back any time soon. Apparently it's been used in a crime.'

'What crime?'

'She wouldn't say. They haven't found your stuff, though. She'd come all the way from Thames Valley.'

'Thames Valley? What have they got to do with it?'

'How should I know? Anyway, she's going to ring you. She wants to know where it was taken from, though I told her you'd given them all the details when you reported it stolen. I said I thought it was Hartlepool. Was I right?'

'Thereabouts. Did you give her this number?'

'Yes.'

'I'd better get off the phone, then, hadn't I?'

'I'll ring you later, shall I?'

'You do that,' says Birch. 'Love you. Gotta go.'

He ends the call, and drives on grim-faced. Traffic news comes on the radio, with reports of hold-ups at junction 33 on the M1, in the Rotherham area.

But Birch's Vauxhall is on an urban dual carriageway where traffic is running freely, and the next exit is signposted Aylesbury. Above the road noise, something is rattling in the boot.

There's a lay-by coming up and he pulls into it. On the seat beside him there's another phone, a cheap, low-function pay-as-you-go similar to the one he's just been speaking on. Using the second phone, he dials a number from the contacts book, tapping the steering-wheel with impatience while it rings out.

'What's up?'

The voice that's answered is terse.

'We might have a problem.'

'What problem?'

'I'm expecting a call from the filth.'

A silence. Then, 'What're you talking about?'

'Sheila gave them my number. They're asking questions about the car.'

There's a sigh of relief.

'Is that all? I thought it was something serious. How can they not ask questions about the car? They're just joining the dots. Even they're not so stupid as to ignore a gift like that. Just stay calm and stick to the story. They've got nothing on you, so you give them their DNA samples and their dabs if they want them and let them eliminate you from their enquiries.'

'I'm not happy giving them DNA.'

'And if you refuse? Then they'll really show an interest.'

Birch bites his lip.

'Yeah, I suppose you're right.'

'Don't sweat it, Brian. Cross that bridge when you come to it. Maybe they won't ask. Meantime, just stick with the script.'

'Right. But what if—'

He doesn't get to finish his sentence. The man he's calling has hung up.

Naylor has a policy always to accept coffee if it's offered. People speak more freely when they're occupied with filling kettles and finding milk. But Sheila Birch disappointed, and hadn't even thought to make the offer. Now Naylor's thirsty, and she could eat something, too.

It's in her mind to pay a visit to Brian Birch's employers, Petersen's, thinking she'll get confirmation of Birch's work for them in Hartlepool. She's not expecting to learn anything which will be a great help, but she's been trained by Ron Perdue, and graduated from his No Stone Unturned school of thinking. As a member of the public who's had his car nicked, Brian Birch may be an unlikely stone, but he still needs turning over. For completeness's sake, she might as well do it while she's here.

She Googles Petersen's and gets an address from their website, then keys it into the satnav. She's a ten-minute drive away, depending on traffic. A couple of streets from the Birches' house, there's a row of shops with a boutique café in the middle. Naylor finds a place to park and dials the number Sheila Birch has given her.

The call is answered promptly.

'Hello?'

'Is that Mr Birch, Brian Birch?'

'That's me.'

'This is DI Rachel Naylor, from Thames Valley Police. I was just speaking to your wife regarding the theft of your vehicle, a red 09-plate Ford Focus.'

'Oh yes?'

'We've recovered the vehicle, Mr Birch, but as I explained to your wife, unfortunately we can't return it to you as it's been involved in a crime. I've just got a couple of questions to put to you, if you don't mind, regarding the actual loss of the vehicle.'

'Ask away.'

'Can you confirm where it was taken from? Our information says Hartlepool, is that correct?'

'Yes.'

'And you were there on business, is that right?'

'Yes.'

'And what were the circumstances of the theft, exactly?'

'I left it parked at the roadside. When I came back, it wasn't there.'

A thought occurs to Naylor.

'So how did you proceed, Mr Birch? How did you get home or to your office, wherever you were going?'

There's noise on the line, the sound in the background of an indicator flashing.

'I'm sorry, it's a bad line,' says Birch. 'Can you repeat the question?'

'I asked what you used for transport when you found the car was gone.'

'I called a taxi.'

'And he took you where?'

'The station. I got the train home. Cost me an arm and a leg, it did. I should have got the insurance to stump up for that.'

'Was that Hartlepool station?'

Naylor hears a few seconds of empty static.

'I'm sorry,' Birch says at last, 'you're breaking up again.'

'Hartlepool. Was it Hartlepool?'

'Yes, Hartlepool. Took me into Euston and I found my own way easy enough from there. Look, I'm sorry but I'm just going into a meeting. Is there anything else I can help you with?'

'No, thanks, you've been very helpful,' says Naylor. 'Thanks for your time.'

When the call's ended, Birch turns into a residential side street and finds a space to park. Picking up the phone he's just been speaking on, he copies a couple of entries from the contacts book into the second pay-as-you-go, before removing the back of the first phone and taking out the SIM.

The battery and the casing are easily separated. He tosses both into the passenger footwell, puts the car into gear and drives away.

The café's all on-trend retro, duck-egg-blue paint and artisan breads, a menu board of coffee beans from South America and the Caribbean. It's the kind of place Hagen hates, and she's glad he's not with her; he would have gone in the chip shop two doors down. But Naylor's pleased to choose from sandwich options which include hummus and green olive ciabatta. She plumps for that with tapenade and turkey, and asks them to add some chipotle mayo to make it interesting. She gets a bottle of water and a Costa Rican flat white to drink, but resists the white chocolate brownies for the sake of her waistline and her purse.

She finds an empty corner table with a good view of the street, where she can watch the comings and goings of kids in school uniform buying lunch at the chippy and the news-agent's. Some of them are young, about the age Evan was when he was taken, and too many of them seem obsessed with their phones. Naylor's all too aware of the dangers that lurk behind those screens and buttons: predators, groomers, the creeping and irrevocable loss of innocence. No wonder clued-up Silicon Valley bosses are sending their children to schools where technology is banned. When parents first gave kids phones, their main reason was for safety, but Evan's phone did nothing to save him. It disappeared and went silent only minutes after he went missing, switched off and no doubt chucked in some river or dropped down a drain.

Walking back to the car after lunch, she checks her own phone again. Still nothing from Hagen, but as she starts the engine, the phone rings. She glances at the hands-free screen on the dashboard and sees a number she knows well, unidentified by a name. She presses a button to accept the call.

'Rachel? It's me.'

She doesn't speak.

'Rachel, are you there?'

'I'm here.'

'Are you still mad at me?'

'I'm not mad at you, I'm mad at me, for being such a mug.'

'Look, I'm sorry about what happened. It was just one of those things, you know?'

'Don't tell me. I don't want to know.'

'Can we talk about it? Where are you now? I've got a couple of hours.'

'Are you serious? I should just drop everything, right now this minute? I have a job, remember?'

'Play truant. Let's both play truant.'

'And where's she? Sainsbury's?'

'She's in London. She won't be back till late.'

Naylor considers whether to say what she's got to say, whether to blow the whole thing out of the water.

'Book a hotel, then,' she says. 'Somewhere nice. And stay the night.'

'I can't stay the night,' he says. 'You know that. But I was thinking we could meet at yours. I'll bring a bottle of something you'll like.'

'So let me translate. You're too cheap to pay for a hotel, or you just don't want it on your credit card bill. What you're after is a quick shag this afternoon while your missus is away, as long as you can be back home at the usual time, smiling like nothing's going on. Well, you know what? Go screw yourself.'

When she's ended the call, she switches off the phone. There's a tightness in her stomach which might be anger and might be hurt. She doesn't think he'll call again, for which part of her is relieved and another part is close to tears. Either way, she's no appetite now for anything but a reflective drive with the music cranked up loud.

The satnav's set for Petersen's, but she soon changes that, re-setting it with the postcode of home.

By the time Hagen gets to Mansfield, it's the wrong side of lunchtime. On the through route he's following he spots Nick's Chippy, which is still busy, and, taking that as a vote of local confidence, buys fish, chips and curry sauce and eats them in the car.

There's still plenty of old back-to-back housing in the town, red-brick terraces which line backstreets looking little different to when they were built. Mansfield's foundations were in mining, and since mining got the heart kicked out of it, the town's found no way to thrive. The only businesses doing well seem to be takeaways and convenience stores.

Alan Mayhew's house is a mid-terrace which stands out from its neighbours for its lack of improvements: no double-glazed front door, no skylight in the attic, no window boxes or fake stone cladding. When Hagen knocks, a neighbour answers, throwing open her own door as if she's the one he wants.

'He's not in, duck!' She's heavy-set, a bruiser, her brash Nottinghamshire accent as thick as slurry. 'He'll not be back while three.'

'Where is he, then?' asks Hagen, and she points to the end of the street.

'The White Hart, duck,' she says. 'Every day, twelve while three.'

The pub's what the Lamb and Lion used to be before the brewery's gentrification: sticky bottle-green carpets, ugly brown tables and chairs, an indifferent landlord reading a newspaper behind the bar. Hagen pays a quick visit to the cold and draughty toilets, where there's no hot water on the basins and the hand-dryer is broken.

In the tap-room Mayhew's easy to pick out, drinking alone at a corner table holding four brown bottles and a glass. He's trimmed his beard since the booking photo was taken, but even in the gloom, Hagen sees his health has deteriorated, his skin tinted yellow with encroaching jaundice. His head sags, and his eyelids are fluttering in a half-doze.

As Hagen approaches the bar, the landlord folds his paper and rises from his stool.

'Now then, youth,' he says. 'What can I get you?'

'Nothing for me, thanks,' says Hagen. 'I was hoping for a word with Mr Mayhew.'

He nods to where Mayhew is sitting.

'Which are you, then, bailiffs or coppers?' asks the landlord. 'Not that it matters. Whichever you are, you're two hours too late. If you want to get any sense out of him, come back tomorrow.'

'Is he drunk?'

'He's one of those drinkers who's never quite drunk, but he's close enough to it. Four barley wines'll do that to a man. You ever tried a barley wine?'

'I don't think so, no,' says Hagen.

'If you've never had a barley wine, be grateful. My grandad used to reckon it was the best stuff you could use for getting a good shine on brass and I've never had reason to doubt it. And see there all the good it's done old Alan. His liver's shot but he's a creature of habit, four bottles a day, come hell or high water, with a whisky chaser or two if he's feeling flush. He says he drinks for the pain, but we could all say that in Mansfield.'

'He's in here every day?'

'Every day without fail. Mostly he's there waiting when I open up. Come closing time, I show him the door and he totters away home to sleep it off. So like I say, whatever your business is with him, you've come too late today. If you want to get any sense out of him, you'll have to come back before he's downed his first bottle tomorrow.'

EIGHTEEN

1 July

Feeling guilty for driving straight home from Chelmsford the previous day, Naylor is early for work. In the office, she notices Rose's biscuit tin is empty, and she wonders if Campbell has been hanging around again, chivvying for results. She switches on Ron's coffee maker, and as she's pouring in the water she thinks about him, deciding that she ought to get in touch.

Hagen arrives soon after her, an earplug in one ear from the phone in his pocket, so the first time she wishes him good morning he doesn't hear. She walks over to him and waves a hand in front of his face until he removes the earplug and switches off the music.

'Good morning.'

'Morning,' Hagen replies.

'I'm just making coffee, but there're no biscuits,' she says. 'Was Campbell on the rampage again yesterday?'

'I have no clue. I was late back, so I went straight home to a shower and a cold beer.'

'How did you get on?'

'Fifty-fifty,' says Hagen. 'Mayhew's alibied indefinitely by chronic alcoholism and a pub full of witnesses to his daily habits, so put a line through him. Gillard I'm not sure about.'

'You want coffee?' Naylor leads the way back to the machine, which is just finishing its perking, and Hagen follows her. She passes him an almost-clean mug, takes one for herself and pours. In the countertop fridge, there's hardly any milk.

'You have it,' says Hagen. 'I'll go black.'

Naylor smiles. There's nothing black about Hagen with his Nordic blood. In summer, his blond hair is at its fairest.

'So come on,' she says. 'What aren't you sure about?'

'From what I saw, Gillard was breaching his licence. I found him in a library, apparently indulging in a bit of online gaming. But full and free access to the internet must be out of bounds. And there were children in the library. I sent him on his way, and I think it's fair to say he wasn't happy. At the very least we should be notifying Probation. How about you?'

Naylor pulls a face. 'I think I ticked a box. I spoke to the Focus's legal owner, but she says she never drove it, that her old man used it for work. Apparently, it was nicked while he was making sales calls in Hartlepool. So I spoke to him to get his story, which sounded straightforward – a taxi and a train back down south.'

'But?'

'But what?'

'Something's niggling you.'

'It's a tiny, tiny niggle.' Naylor shows a minute gap between her finger and thumb-pad. 'So tiny, I don't even know what it is.'

'Heads up, people!'

Campbell breezes into the incident room in a white shirt

straight off the hanger from an ironing service, with an air of excitement about him which can only mean he's been speaking to the Chief Constable. Officers end calls and sign off keyboards.

Naylor notices Campbell do a quick eyeball of the biscuit tin, which Rose has only moments before refilled with short-bread fingers.

'OK, so I regret to say we're having an immediate change of priorities.' There's an undertone of a groan around the room. Naylor and Hagen's eyes meet. Campbell's upbeat attitude suggests an increase in workload, and has all the hallmarks of a paid-overtime authorisation. 'In the absence of solid leads on the Ferrers case, the CC has asked for a diversion of resources – temporary only, I'm pleased to say – on to the Foxley Wood Road shooting. It's a high-priority case as we all know, and we're looking for a quick result. There's an immediate cancellation of all non-essential leave and author-isation for paid overtime, so if you want to bank some cash for Christmas, now's your chance.'

Ian Austin – a recently married DC – is scowling.

'What about my holiday, Sir?' he asks. 'I'm booked to fly in two days' time, and my missus will start divorce proceedings if I can't go.'

'She'd be doing that anyway, if she'd any sense,' chips in Dallabrida.

'You'd better go,' says Campbell, and Austin grins. 'We don't need any more blood spilled on our patch, do we?'

It's one of Campbell's favourite gags, and they all dutifully smile.

'What about the leads we have got on the Ferrers case, Sir?'

asks Hagen. 'Can we keep someone going on those? I don't think we should just drop everything. We've got Evan booked in for another interview this afternoon.'

'That should go ahead, of course,' says Campbell. 'Naylor, you handle that with Rose.' He looks around the room. 'Anyone got anything else? If so, pass it on to Hagen. Bradley, you run with the loose ends for a couple of days, and if there's nothing new, we'll have to wind it down, at least for the time being.'

'And what if we get anything new from Evan?' asks Naylor. 'If we finally get him to open up?'

'That would put a different face on it, of course,' says Campbell. 'But if he still won't talk and we've nothing solid by the end of the week, we've other high-priority cases we need to focus on. We all know how it is. Resources are tight.'

Naylor and Rose are attempting a different line with Evan – no recording equipment, no photographs – trying to make the interview feel like a casual conversation between three people who would never in the normal run of things find themselves in the same room. The way Evan's sitting on his hands gives him a peculiar bashfulness more suited to a child half his age, and his rounded shoulders make him look as if he's cowering, which inside he most likely is. Naylor's feeling guilty for making him be here. She and Rose both know emotionally he's not fit, and without Campbell's insistence, they'd have left him sleeping in the safety of his bedroom.

Naylor begins with an apology.

'We're sorry to drag you in again, Evan. I know you don't want to be here. But the fact is, with your type of case, I'm afraid there's a very good chance that the men who took you will target other boys. We want to stop that happening, but to do that, we really need your help. Will you help us, Evan?'

Evan lifts his eyes, and Naylor sees in them his distress tangled up with mistrust and panic as if he's still a prisoner inside his own head. His lips are pressed together and his jaw's determinedly set, and Naylor knows making him break his silence will be next to impossible.

'Any little detail, Evan,' she says. 'Anything at all. Do you remember what colour the walls were painted?'

Silence.

'Was there traffic outside? Could you hear cars? Were there curtains at the windows? What colour were they?'

Silence.

'What did you have to eat? Did you have chips? Did anyone give you chocolate? What's your favourite chocolate, anyway? I'll tell you what, I love creme eggs. Can't resist them. Every year I can't wait for Christmas to be over so the creme eggs'll be in the shops.'

'My son,' says Rose. 'He loves Galaxy. If I buy any I have to hide it, or I don't get any, not a single square. What about you, Evan?'

Silence.

Rose has a pad of paper in front of her, and a wallet of felt-tip pens in attractive colours. She pushes the paper and pens across the table.

'Maybe you could draw us something, Evan. Something you remember from where you were, what the room looked like, something you could see, anything at all you can remember. You choose something and draw it for us.'

Silence.

Naylor's running out of ideas. Under the table she touches Rose's foot with her toe, hoping to prompt her into saying more.

But Rose is biding her time and doesn't react. The silence grows long, and as it lengthens, it absorbs the pressure they're all feeling and becomes more comfortable. Then Evan reaches out, draws the paper towards him and, opening up the wallet, chooses a pen with bright red ink.

Uncapping the pen, he positions the tip in the top left-hand corner of the paper and, forming the biggest letters the sheet will hold, slowly and deliberately writes a single word: NO.

He seems somehow pleased with it. Turning the page, he writes it again: NO.

The third time he writes it, he scribbles an underline, pressing so hard with the pen, he rips the paper.

NO NO NO.

Naylor stares at the torn paper and thinks what Rose asked him to do, to draw something he remembers.

'I think that's enough for today, sweetheart,' says Rose quietly.

Naylor's only too happy to agree. The guilt she was feeling has trebled, and she knows she's let Evan down. On his behalf, she should have stood up to Campbell, and never allowed this interview to take place.

NINETEEN

10 August

Claire pours the last of the Chablis into her glass. On the TV, someone on *EastEnders* is shouting at someone else, and it occurs to her she's no idea who these characters are. It isn't that she's lost track of the plot, more that she's never cared, and all it's ever been – for weeks and months – is background noise she took for company. But shouting isn't company, and even after a glass or two of wine, she's switched on enough to realise that people shouting isn't what Evan needs to hear, even at the remove of his bedroom. She has a thought, that maybe it would be nice to watch something together – something funny, or David Attenborough, or he used to enjoy *Top Gear*.

She goes to the foot of the stairs. Upstairs is silent and the landing is dark, so she switches on the light; if Evan needs the bathroom, she doesn't want him to open his door on to darkness. She thinks of calling up to him, of trying to persuade him to come down, but she knows he'll be reluctant. What, in any case, is the point? Maybe he'll come and sit with her, but he won't speak. He's living inside his head, hiding from them all, coming down for food and leaving when he's eaten. On good days, he touches her shoulder as he goes – maybe as a thank you – before heading back upstairs to shut himself away.

Has she had one glass or two? Did she open the bottle this evening as she was making Evan's tea or was it already open in the fridge? She takes a sip. The wine is unpleasant – sour and warmed to room temperature. Maybe a couple of ice cubes will make it more drinkable.

She wanders to the kitchen. Behind her, the distinctive music over the final credits begins, so it must be 8.30 p.m. Can that be right? So why is Matt not home? The kitchen clock confirms the time, and Claire is suddenly worried. The memory of the night that Evan went missing comes back to her: the slow sinking in of the undeniable truth, the hopeless wait for the ending of anxiety, the dark cloud of despair as reality was faced. Maybe Matt's been in an accident. Should she be ringing hospitals? She takes ice cubes from the freezer and drops them in her drink. Of course he's fine. There'll have been some hold-up on the roads. If he's passing Sainsbury's, he could pick up a bottle of wine. And a ready meal from their chiller cabinets, or he could bring a takeaway. They haven't had Chinese in ages. He could call in there.

But what if . . .? Does history repeat itself? Does lightning strike twice? Of course it does, every day. She dials his number, but his phone is busy, and though he's got call waiting, he doesn't take her call. In the next ten minutes, she tries twice more. Matt's number is still engaged.

Twenty minutes later he walks in the door, and it's as if he's read her mind. He's carrying a bottle of white wine, and a carrier bag from the Golden Wok.

Now he's safely home, she doesn't care enough about his lateness to nag, but what else is there to say?

'You're late.'

He puts his lips on her cheek, but holds his body away from her, seeming reluctant to be touched.

'Traffic,' he says. 'Nightmare.' He holds up the bag of takeaway. The smell is savoury, garlicky and good, and her stomach rumbles. 'I thought you wouldn't have eaten.' He puts the bottle in her hand, and she feels a flash of anger, that he thinks she can be appeased with such a humble prize. But he's right, she can be, and she is. 'Singapore noodles, king prawns with ginger and spring onions and veggie spring rolls. You go and sit. I'll bring it through.'

They eat in silence, letting Channel 4 do the talking, one of those social issues documentaries that Matt enjoys. Claire doesn't give a damn what's on; the food's tasty, and when she's finished her wine, another bottle's waiting. She may not drink more anyway. Half the comfort lies in knowing that if she wanted to, she could.

She takes a swallow and feels its acidity running down her gullet, and moments later there's the little top-up to her alcoholic buzz. Too late, she regrets it, because she realises it's the mouthful that's going to make her say something unpredictable, so unpredictable even she has no idea what it's going to be.

'Matt.' His attention broken, he looks across at her, and she realises he wasn't focused on the TV at all. The presenter rattles on, and Matt's not glancing back at him. Wherever his mind was, it wasn't with Channel 4. 'Why don't you just tell me what's going on?'

She's as surprised at the question as he is, and taken aback by her sudden knowledge that of course something's going on. If she wasn't living in a befuddled daze every evening, they'd have had this conversation long ago. All she's done with her comfort drinking is make it easy for him to take his comfort elsewhere.

'What do you mean?' Of course he would ask that, stalling for time, fishing to find out what she knows, or thinks she knows.

'Oxford, Schmoxford,' she says, and there's a slight slur in her speech. 'What's her name?'

'Don't be silly,' he says, and seems to give his attention back to the TV. Being called silly stings; her mother used to say it, and it feels patronising.

'What are you going to do?' she asks, and Matt looks uneasy. 'For Evan's sake, we need to decide. We can't stay here. We need to get him the help he needs, put him in a place where he can start to rebuild his life, maybe go back to school.'

'He's hardly ready for that.'

'I can see that, *silly*. I'm the one who's at home with him all day, remember? So what I'm asking you is, is it going to be just me and Evan, or are you coming too?'

She's expecting a quick answer, a reassurance that of course he's committed, that she and Evan are his life. Anyone would say that, wouldn't they? But instead there's silence, and she can see Matt forming sentences in his head, trying them out to see which is the best, the least painful fit.

'Listen,' he says.

And then the house phone rings.

She can see the relief on his face. He gets up to find the handset and looks at the caller display.

'It's Dad,' he says, and pushes the button to take the call. 'Hi, Dad, how are you?'

There's a long delay as Matt listens. He asks, 'What did they say?' and then Jack talks a lot more.

'I'll come tomorrow,' Matt says. 'Of course I will. No arguments. I'll set off first thing.'

There are goodbyes, and Matt puts the phone back on its stand. When he sits back down in the armchair, his face is pale.

'What was that about?' she asks.

'Bad news about Mum,' he says. 'She's had some tests done. It's cancer, cancer of the stomach. They've offered her treatment but she's saying no. I said I'd go up and try and get her to see sense.'

'I'm sorry, honey,' Claire says quietly.

'I'd better go and pack.'

He's almost out of the room when she calls him back.

'Do you think Evan might like to go?'

Matt's face registers his surprise.

'Really? I'm not sure that's a good idea.'

'Why not? I think a change of scene might do him good. He always loved it there, and what is there for him to do here? There's no school and he's no friends.'

'OK. Let's all go.'

But Claire shakes her head.

'I think you two should go without me.'

'Why?'

'I put too much pressure on him. I know I do. I must be driving him nuts, always watching him, making sure he's

146

OK. I find it so hard to give him space, and he needs space. I think it would be better to make it a father–son thing. A boys' road trip.'

'Are you sure?'

'Yes. I'll worry about him every minute, and I'll find it really hard to let him out of my sight. But I think he needs some time without me smothering him.'

Matt shrugs.

'If he wants to go, of course.'

Claire follows Matt up the stairs, and stops outside Evan's room, listening. There's nothing to hear, not even Evan's breathing, but there's a light shining under the door so she thinks he must still be awake.

She taps gently.

'Evan? Can I come in?'

In this, there's been improvement. In a few moments, the door is opened, though Evan's blocking it with his body, not allowing her in.

She tries not to mind.

'Grandpa's just rung to say Grandma's not very well,' she says. 'Dad's going to drive up in the morning and stay a night or two to see if there's anything he can do. So I was wondering if you wanted to go along for the ride.'

Evan looks at her with his sad eyes, and a flicker of something crosses his face.

Without speaking, he slowly closes the door; but before she moves away, she hears the sound of opening drawers, as Evan chooses clothes to pack for his trip.

TWENTY

11 August

On the journey north, Matt expects no conversation from Evan, but talks as if he does. He suggests Evan puts on the radio, but senses rather than sees a slight shake of his head. Matt would prefer some distraction from what's on his mind – the froth of Radio 2, a commercial station, or even, in deference to Evan, Radio 1 – but Evan seems content to look out of the car window. A few miles on the road, and Matt's finding the empty space a good place to think things over – what he'll say to his mother, the creeping worry that she may not be OK, the way things are between him and Claire, what the impact will be on Evan if they go their separate ways. While Evan was gone, life was simple. There was grief, and not much else. Now the grief for the son he's lost – the normal boy, with normal prospects – is far more complex, and the fact that life will go on means if it's to be more than the drudgery of passing days, roads must be chosen and hard decisions made. Even to be considering what he's contemplating makes Matt feel a heel.

It isn't until the pressure on his bladder starts to be uncomfortable that he realises they're totally unprepared to make this journey. Since his return, Evan has barely left the house, and then only to visit police facilities and the child psychiatrist they lined up for him to begin what they're calling his rehabilitation. Signs appear for services in three miles. Evan is still looking out of the window, hands on his knees, the fingers of his right hand tapping a rhythm which might be boredom but is more likely to be stress. Surreptitiously Matt watches the hand, thinking how it's changed – from the baby fist which used to grip his own fingers, to the toddler hand which held his crossing the road, to the boy's hand which struggled to hold his cards when they played games at Christmas. Now it's a youth's hand, long and oversized and ready to be grown into, at odds with the way Evan is mentally. He seems much younger than he was before, as if he's fallen under an enchantment reversing the path of maturation, retreating into boyishness as his body shoots up towards manhood.

'I think we'll stop for a comfort break, shall we?' Matt suggests. 'If you're hungry, we could get a bite, McDonald's or something. Only don't tell your mum.'

As soon as he's said the words, he sees his lack of tact. For all he knows, Evan was fed nothing but fast food all the time he was gone, which would make it not a treat, but a reminder. A sandwich would be safer, but in the face of Evan's apparent indifference, it seems it doesn't matter.

Matt takes the exit slip-road and slows the car. Immediately he's wondering what to do for the best: park away from the central area where it's quieter, or just find a space in the thick of things as he would do normally? His instinct is to avoid too many people, but maybe that's signalling to Evan he thinks there's an issue. He decides to be bold, and heads for the main car park.

Evan's fingers are drumming faster on his knee, and Matt doesn't blame him for being nervous. Since he was last in this kind of environment, his world view has been shattered. Maybe he and Claire should have taken him out more, done more to get him re-integrated, but there's no instruction manual for their situation, and no one's offered any practical help. *Let him take his time* is the advice they keep hearing, but how much time should that be? Should they have pushed him harder? By leaving him night and day to his own devices, have they set him up to always be a recluse?

Matt adopts an attitude he hopes Evan will take to be cool and relaxed. He takes his time to find a parking space on a row end, where the left side of the car – Evan's side – is screened by conifer hedging, and turns off the engine. Evan is looking straight ahead, at rows of vehicles and the people walking amongst them: teenagers and young children with frazzled parents, businessmen and delivery drivers, older people of Jack and Dora's generation.

'OK, buddy,' says Matt. 'Let's go.'

Praying Evan will follow his lead, he opens his door. The temptation to look back and see what Evan's doing is strong, but he resists it. *Act natural*, he's thinking, *just act natural*. He's out of the car, but Evan hasn't moved. There's a man by himself walking towards them, and Matt senses Evan's eyes on him, but the man's on his phone and passes them without even a glance.

Evan's door opens, and Matt thinks, *Thank Christ*. In a moment Evan is standing beside him – too close beside him, and the closeness provokes in Matt the urge to put an arm around Evan's shoulders.

But that would look odd and they're trying to do normal, where normal for Evan's age would be him trailing behind Matt across the car park, trying to make out they're not related.

'Stick with me, kid,' Matt says with a levity he's not feeling, and they set off for the main building, Evan almost treading on Matt's heels.

People are coming and going. Matt pulls open one of the glass doors and stands aside to let Evan go ahead of him, but Evan hangs back, so Matt goes through first with Evan too close behind.

The atrium is chaotic and hugely noisy, a dissonance of piped music, shouting children and the chatter of hundreds of people.

Evan takes hold of Matt's arm.

'First things first,' says Matt brightly, trying to keep it upbeat. 'I need to find the gents. Let's try over here.'

With Evan's arm linked through his, he feels protective. People will assume Evan has special needs, which of course he does. Taking a long way round to avoid pushing through a crowd, Matt leads his son to the toilets, and inside.

There are men using the urinal.

This is a place where men do intimate things, hidden away from the outside world. Evan tightens his grip on Matt's arm.

'We'll use the stalls, shall we?' Matt says discreetly. 'You go first. I'll guard the door.'

He senses the other men listening, and almost laughs at the irony that he may be taken for some kind of paedophile. Evan clearly likes the idea of a locked door between himself and the strangers, but he's reluctant to be parted from Matt, who touches his back, encouraging him forward. His hand there makes Evan uncomfortable. When he pulls away, it's a stab in Matt's heart.

But Evan goes into the stall, closes the door and bolts it. Matt's bladder is insisting he use the urinal, but Evan might be watching his feet under the stall door, so he handles his discomfort and stays where he is, as he's promised. He waits for Evan to flush, then waits a minute or two longer, but beyond the sound of a zip being done up, there's silence.

The pressure on Matt's bladder is becoming critical.

'Evan, buddy, are you OK?' he asks. A few moments later the bolt is slipped back and Evan appears.

'My turn,' says Matt.

Evan's eyes grow wide, and Matt sees his fear. Evan doesn't want to be alone in here.

'Tell you what,' says Matt. 'You go back in there and lock the door, I'll use the doo-dah over here. One minute max and I'll be back. OK?'

Evan bolts himself back inside the stall, where the flimsy hardboard walls must feel far safer than no walls at all.

'One minute!' calls Matt, unzipping his flies. When he's done, he taps gently at the door.

'I'm back,' he says. 'Let's go.'

Behind the hardboard walls Evan is listening, making his decision on whether it's safe for him to come out. As he's about to take the risk and slide the bolt, two men burst in, talking loudly about last night's football. They sound big and rough, the kind of men who'd easily overpower him, so he sits down on the toilet, puts his arms around himself, hugs himself into the smallest shape he can make and waits, quiet and unseen, until they're gone.

Matt takes out his phone and pretends to be engrossed in it. There's a message from Claire asking how they're getting on, and he replies with *OK* and an emoticon wearing a doubtful face.

The men leave, and several more – far less vocal – enter. Matt's preparing to knock again, but as he raises his hand, the bolt slides back and Evan appears.

He leads Evan out into the food court. The men here are diluted with women and children, and in places there are empty tables where there are no men at all.

They look around at the fast-food franchises: burgers, pizza, fish and chips.

'What do you fancy?' asks Matt. He's feeling inclined towards the fried chicken Claire never lets them eat, but Evan has other ideas. He's heading the opposite way, indisputably in the direction of McDonald's.

Claire's enjoying her first glass of the evening, but the ring of the doorbell eradicates the welcome softening of tension the Pinot Noir brings. Instantly, her mind goes to Matt and Evan, and she hurries into the hall. Through the glass panes in the door, she sees a woman's outline. Afraid it's someone from the police, she opens it.

She doesn't know the woman, and she doesn't look like police: too young, too colourfully dressed. Even plain-clothes police like Naylor seem to stick to navy-blue and black, occasionally grey. This girl's in green with flashes of yellow, and her kitten-heeled shoes are yellow to match.

Her smile's a salesperson's smile, showing all her white teeth but going nowhere near her eyes. There's an expensive handbag slung over her shoulder – *Mulberry?* wonders Claire – and some kind of notebook under her arm.

'Mrs Ferrers?' she asks.

Claire is still sober enough to be cautious, and she could deny who she is and be believed. The woman on the doorstep has seen photos of Claire from when Evan was taken, and the Claire she's seeing now looks nothing like those pictures. She looks more like an older relative, and without too much imagination she could be taken for her own mother.

'Who's asking?'

'I am,' says the young woman, with what she's hoping is cheeky charm. 'I'm Annabelle, from the Fletcher magazine group. You're probably familiar with some of the titles we publish. We mostly do women's interest, coffee break stuff, lots of celebrities and true stories. It is Claire, isn't it? Would you mind if I come in?'

In her mind, Claire runs an inventory of the state of the housekeeping. There's laundry in various conditions in the kitchen and utility – waiting for washing, waiting for drying, waiting for ironing, waiting to be put away – and even though it would be dinner-time in a normally functioning household, she's yet to tackle the dishes left over from breakfast. The carpets need vacuuming, the bathrooms need cleaning and the kitchen floor needs a mop. Without thinking about it in any detail, there's enough to keep her going an entire weekend.

She takes up a position which blocks the door, stopping Annabelle from seeing into the hallway.

'What is it you want?' she asks.

'Just a little chat, really,' says Annabelle. She lays her head on one side, another charming gesture which might work on some men. 'We think our readers would be really interested in your story, in the feel-good aspects of it. You know, your son back home with you, how you feel about that, how it is to be a family again.'

Entirely of their own accord, Claire's eyebrows lift.

'Are you serious?' she asks.

Annabelle misses the incredulity in her tone.

'Readers would love to hear how it's been,' she says. 'There'd be a fee of some kind, of course.'

Claire reflects on how it's been: her silent son, her absent husband, the sense of everything still as irreparably broken as it ever was.

She produces her own version of Annabelle's insincere smile.

'I don't mean to be rude,' she says, 'but why don't you just fuck off?'

Late afternoon, and the motorways have been left far behind. They're passing through open country glorious with summer, where sheep are grazing amongst the upland bracken, and rivers sparkle in valleys where wildflowers colour their banks.

This tranquil beauty is balm for the soul, and Matt realises he's missed it. Evan seems to be enjoying the scenery. Maybe he's missed it, too.

At the turn for Ainsclough Top, the stream where Evan used to fish runs under a bridge. Matt slows the car, allowing Evan a view of the clear water where wild cresses flourish.

'I expect you could find time to come down here with your net while we're here, see what you can catch.'

Immediately Matt regrets saying it, thinking Evan's far too old now for such childish things. Evan's solemn face doesn't move, but as they turn up the track towards the farm, he looks back over his shoulder, and his eyes, it seems to Matt, are on the stream.

Jack's waiting, smiling, at the door. As they get out of the car, Matt looks for signs of worry in his face, but there's nothing to see. Evan walks straight up to his grandpa, gives him the briefest of hugs and goes inside the house.

'How's Mum?' asks Matt, and Jack shrugs.

'She's all right,' he says. 'At least she says she is. Stubborn as ever. Let's talk about it later. We don't want to upset the boy.'

In the living room, Dora's sitting on the sofa, a book of word-search puzzles on her lap. To her obvious pleasure, Evan is sitting beside her, holding her hand.

Matt crosses to her and kisses her cheek. Her face is undeniably thinner, and the bones at the base of her throat are prominent.

'How are you doing, you old attention-seeker?' he asks. 'You look pretty well to me.'

'I'm all right,' she says. 'A bit tired. Just feeling my age, aren't I, love?' She squeezes Evan's hand. 'I'm hoping you might help me a bit with these puzzles, and I'm sorry to say your grandpa's threatening to cook tea.'

The ghost of a smile touches Evan's eyes and the corners of his mouth.

'I shall make a good job of it, too,' says Jack, mock-indignantly. 'Sausages, chips and beans, and maybe an egg if you're lucky. And I'm commandeering your dad to peel potatoes. Dora, my love, you'll be ready for a cup of tea, and

156

Evan, you'll be wanting something cold. But you stay where you are and look after your grandma. I'll get your dad to bring it through.'

Outside the open kitchen window, the perfume of the honeysuckle which clings to the old stone wall mingles with the smell of straw from the barn, and the sharp, familiar stink of sheep. The window looks on to the rose garden, where Dora planted the first bushes just after Matt was born. Over the years, she's nurtured it to an immaculately cared-for Eden, and Matt's troubled to see some of the blooms have browning petals, while others are dead and dried. On the path, the secateurs lying in a trug are spotted with the beginnings of rust.

Matt pops the cap off a bottle of Sam Smith's.

'You want one?'

He takes another from the fridge, and hands it to his father. A red kite is wheeling over Blackmire Ridge, in a sky that's still bright as midday.

'So,' says Matt. 'Tell me.'

Jack takes a drink of his beer.

'It's been a bad week,' he says. 'Here, start on these potatoes. I blame myself for letting it get this far.'

Matt hunts for a peeler in the drawer, which is a confusion of his mother's lifetime collection of cooking implements: knives and graters, wooden spoons, spatulas and whisks.

'What do you mean, "this far"? What's the story?'

'The signs were there, the lack of appetite, the weight loss. But we were wrapped up in other things, weren't we? We were worrying about Evan.' As Jack's talking, he's laying sausages in a pan, big, fat Cumbrian sausages from the village butcher.

He turns on a hotplate on the old stove and puts the frying pan on the heat. 'Then she was sick, and said it was nothing. She was sick again, and I caught her taking pills for the pain in her stomach. Turns out it's been going on a while.'

'How long is a while?'

'A year. Maybe longer.'

Matt lays the peeler on the table. He looks distressed.

'Bloody hell, Dad. A year? Why didn't she say?'

'She thought we all had enough on our plates. Which of course we did, but now it looks like we've got two plates instead of one. We got the scan results yesterday. That's why I rang you. I didn't want to burden you until we were sure.'

'What's the prognosis?'

Jack stares out of the window. He lowers his chin to his chest.

'Don't ask me that, son,' he says. 'Let's take it one day at a time.'

Dora, Matt notices, eats very little – a few slices of sausage, a spoonful of baked beans, a piece of dry toast Jack has made her instead of chips.

Evan has cleared his plate, and instead of disappearing, has stayed to watch a DVD Jack has found.

'*Only Fools and Horses?*' asks Matt. 'Bit retro, isn't it?'

'There's nothing wrong with retro,' says Jack. 'Some things stand the test of time.'

The comedy takes Matt back to boyhood, to the age where Evan is now. Evan's holding Dora's hand, and as he watches the screen, he begins to smile, a cautious, hesitant smile, as if he's trying on something that used to be a comfortable fit, as if he's rediscovered something precious but isn't sure it's meant for him. The gags come thick and fast, and Matt finds himself smiling too. Jack loads up another episode, a Christmas special. Matt has seen it several times and remembers it well, but it still entertains.

And at the high spot, in the famous moment when Del Boy, fancying his chances with a couple of girls, loses his cool falling through a gap in the bar, a miracle occurs.

Evan laughs.

'Your grandma thought you should have your dad's old room,' says Jack, following Evan up the creaking stairs. 'There's a better view from there. Your dad's seen it often enough, so she's put him in the guest room.' Upstairs the house shows its considerable age, low ceilings and bowed walls, black beams and latched doors. 'You're handy for the bathroom there, too. There's plenty of hot water if you want a shower, but that's it for the mod cons, I'm afraid. No telly up here. You know me and your grandma. We like to live in the Stone Age.'

Evan pushes open the door at the end of the landing. It's a small room with a window looking out across the home field and the grazing sheep. In an apple tree whose branches almost touch the windowpanes, a blackbird is singing evensong, melodious and clear.

A single bed made with line-dried linen is pushed against the wall, a hand-knitted patchwork blanket in the crazily bright colours Dora loves folded at its foot. On the bedside table there's a lamp and a stack of books: a tattered *Beano* annual, a collection of Spike Milligan's poems, Barry Hines's

A Kestrel for a Knave, an outdated encyclopaedia of amazing facts, a new magazine of word-search puzzles with a pen. On the dressing table are three white roses in a vase.

Jack points to the roses.

'I told your grandma young men don't appreciate flowers, but she goes her own way, as you well know. Unpack your things if you like, make yourself at home. The top drawer of that chest is empty. The rest of it's full of your dad's stuff which I reckon should have gone in the bin years ago, but that's your grandma again. So. I'll leave you to it. Sweet dreams, son.'

In the distant past, he would have kissed Evan goodnight. Under normal circumstances, Evan would be beyond that now, well into those early teenage years of self-conscious separation. But Evan looks small, slightly bewildered and alone, and the urge to put an arm round him is strong.

Jack resists. As he reaches the top of the stairs, he hears the knock of wood on wood as Evan props a chair against the door, barricading himself in and sealing out the world.

Dora has gone to bed. Jack goes to the sideboard and takes a bottle of Glenfiddich and two of the best lead crystal glasses from the cupboard.

He holds up the bottle to Matt, who nods his head.

'What's this?' he says. 'Christmas come early?'

'I've fallen out with Christmas.' Jack pours a generous measure into each glass. 'It never came last year, and it looks like it might not this year either. Cheers.'

They clink glasses, and Jack sinks into an armchair.

'What do you think to Evan?' asks Matt, and Jack shakes his head.

'I don't know, son, I really don't know. Something inside him's switched off.'

'Hardly surprising, is it?' There's repressed rage in Matt's voice. 'What's happened to him, what he's been through . . . I have to stop myself thinking about it. If I think about it, it makes me so angry I could kill someone.'

Jack swills the whisky in his glass. 'Maybe he feels the same.'

'I worry that his life is slipping by. He's missed so much already – school, of course, and friendships. All those things we wanted for him, gone. How will he ever catch up? Sometimes I think his life is ruined forever. Is he destined just to stay in that dark place where he is now? Will he ever come back from there? What happens if he doesn't?'

'Is he still seeing that counsellor?'

Matt sighs. They had kept all their appointments, ushering Evan into the waiting room of a converted Victorian gentleman's residence, sitting on the hard chairs, flicking through back copies of dog-eared magazines while a mahogany-cased clock ticked in the hallway. The place was drab, dark, unappealing, but Evan submitted quietly, as he seems to submit to pretty much everything, these days. When she called him through to her office, Dr Mellor was soft-spoken and kind, the sort of woman you'd want for a favourite aunt, unsexy, unthreatening, the epitome of a human being you'd trust.

Matt had imagined with some unease the kind of things Evan and Dr Mellor might discuss, mentally squirming at the possible involvement of anatomically correct dolls and explicit diagrams. A part of him had been irrationally jealous, thinking his son was confiding in a stranger what he wouldn't say to him, even though, God knew, the last thing on earth he wanted to hear was what Evan had to say. To know the facts would be unbearable; only to imagine them allowed a level of denial, an element of soft-focus which kept the pain in check. Certain knowledge of his son's suffering would mean those responsible would have to die. Which wasn't a problem, necessarily. If Matt spent the rest of his life in jail, honour would be satisfied, and it would be appropriate payback for his not having protected Evan in the first place.

But there had been no discussions, explicit or otherwise.

'They canned it after three sessions,' he says to Jack. 'He wouldn't speak to her any more than he'll talk to us.'

After the last session, while Claire led a sad, silent Evan out to the car, Matt had taken the opportunity to talk to Dr Mellor and express his most pressing concerns.

'He seems younger than when he left us,' he said. 'Like some kind of Peter Pan.'

Dr Mellor had nodded wisely, as if what Matt was saying made sense to her. 'That's hardly surprising. Subconsciously, he's retreated into childhood, to a time where he felt safe.'

'So what can we do about it?'

Dr Mellor shook her head. 'At the moment, your only option is to wait.'

How long the wait would be – weeks, months or years – she wasn't prepared to guess. The day before Evan's next scheduled appointment, she rang and said she thought it better to put the counselling on hold, postpone it until Evan was further down the road to recovery.

'Claire was pretty pissed off, considering the shrink was supposed to *be* the road to recovery,' says Matt. 'She thinks they've abandoned us.'

'And what do you think?'

'I think he's better left alone for a while, to let him try and get his head in some sort of order.'

'So he still hasn't given a statement?'

'Not a chance. What gets me is, if the police had got anyone in their sights, or were close to arresting anybody or even had the slightest idea where to look, they'd have him down there every day, asking him questions. My worry is, the longer he stays silent, the harder it'll be to break the habit.' He takes a drink of the warming whisky. 'I don't know, Dad. I just want our old Evan. Do you ever wish you could turn the clock back?'

'Just lately, all the time,' says Jack. 'But if wishes were horses . . .'

'. . . Beggars would ride. It's a stupid saying.'

'And how's Claire?'

'As you saw her. Drinking too much, but that's rich, coming from me.'

'You want another?'

'Best not. I don't want a thick head in the morning.'

'Have a small one with me,' says Jack, getting up to fetch the bottle. 'You wouldn't want to leave your old dad drinking alone.'

TWENTY-ONE

13 August

It's been a busy week. On Saturday, glad of a lie-in, Naylor stays in bed till after eleven, until her usually placid ginger cat decides it's waited too long to be fed and wakes her by jumping on the bed. She's hungry too and would love a proper breakfast. As usual, though, there's very little in the fridge.

After a long, hot shower, she puts on jeans and a T-shirt, flip-flops and sunglasses, and heads out. At Waitrose, the car park's busy, and she has a long walk to the store. Passing one of the trolley return stations, she catches sight of a familiar face, unloading bags into the back of a car.

He's looking good in casual clothes. Sensing he's being watched, he looks across and smiles, and she's smiling back, until she sees there's someone else in the picture: a pretty blonde climbing into the front seat of Dallabrida's white Audi.

He gives her a wave, and Naylor does the same. As she sees him drive away, there's something in her heart which might be disappointment.

Evan is outside in the barn, sitting high up on the straw bales, from where the view's down the farm track to the stream. He likes it there: the clean, country smell of it, the prickle of the dry corn stalks on the back of his legs, the tickle of the breeze blowing through the door. In the garden, he can see his dad dead-heading roses, cutting clumsily at the bushes, not taking dainty care like Grandma. Grandma's sitting in a director's chair keeping an eye on Dad, but she's not saying anything, which Evan thinks must be hard. Though he can't see it, he can hear a bird calling overhead, a harsh cry Grandpa's told him is a bird of prey, a red kite. And having a sudden wish to see it, Evan climbs down from his eyrie, and wanders out from the barn's shadows, into the sunshine on the home field.

'You've got sheep-muck on your shoes,' says Jack, as Evan enters the kitchen a while later. 'Don't be traipsing it through the house. Take them off on the mat, or your grandma'll be having a fit and blaming me. Haven't you brought your wellies?'

Evan looks at him, but doesn't speak.

'I don't see how you can be on the farm without proper footwear,' says Jack. 'Your dad's having a run to the shops in a while for a few bits and bobs. Shall we ask him to pop into Hooper's and see what they've got that might fit you?'

Evan shrugs, but his expression is on the pleased side of neutral.

'What size do you think you are?' Jack makes a performance of studying Evan's feet. 'An eight or nine, I'd say. We'll ask him to get nines, then you've something to grow into. Now go and use the outside tap, and get those shoes cleaned up.'

*

Dora appears to be dozing, but she's not asleep, she's listening to the bees amongst the roses. She knows someone's approaching from the rattle of a cup on its saucer and the light chink of a teaspoon on china.

Matt touches her shoulder very lightly, and she opens her eyes.

'Mum? I brought you a cup of tea.'

She smiles.

'That's very nice, dear. Come and sit down.'

Matt puts the tea down on the cast-iron table, and fetches another canvas chair from the shed where Dora keeps her gardening clutter, rakes, hoes, trowels and shears.

As he sits he says, 'I should have brought you a biscuit. I bought Jaffa Cakes. Evan likes those.'

'Me too,' says Dora, 'but I don't want one just now.'

'How are you feeling?' Matt's attention, like Dora's, seems focused on a stem of red roses, where the bees are crawling in the innermost petals.

'I'm all right,' she says.

'Dad says they've put you on painkillers.'

'They're a double-edged sword. They do a good job, but they make me so sleepy. And I don't want to be sleeping. Not the way things are.'

Matt takes a deep breath before he speaks.

'Why won't you have the op, Mum? You're breaking Dad's heart. And mine.'

The tears he's wanted to avoid are suddenly there, and he wipes his eyes with the back of his hand.

'Oh, sweetheart. Please don't.'

'How can I not?' he asks. 'You wouldn't be very pleased if I didn't give a damn.'

166

'I suppose I wouldn't.'

'So why? If there's a good chance . . . You know.'

'If there's a good chance of what? The truth is I'm just an old coward, and I can't bear the thought of all that cutting and stitching and all that uncomfortableness, and then they want me to take all those drugs. And there's no guarantee any of it will work. Shall I tell you a little story? You won't remember Josie Makepeace, but I've known her for years. Stalwart of the WI, involved in everything, that was Josie. Heart and soul of any party. Well, last year she was diagnosed with something nasty. I don't know where it was exactly – ovaries maybe, somewhere in the down-below. You wouldn't have known it to look at her. She didn't look ill. Only in her fifties, and she looked the picture of health. But she signed up for all the treatment, the surgery, the chemo, radiotherapy, everything they'd got. Within a fortnight, she looked a different woman, so ill and grey. And you know what? After her second lot of chemo, she had a stroke. Three days in a coma and she was gone, like that! So if a young woman like her couldn't stand the treatment, what chance for an old bird like me? I've thought about it long and hard – and it's been harder than you could ever imagine – and I've decided I would far, far rather let nature take its course, and spend what time I've got here, with your father and you and everyone, than in some hospital being sick and losing my hair. The choice is between quality of life and quantity, and I think I'd prefer quality. Can you understand?' She reaches out and takes his hand, squeezing it hard. 'You are so, so precious to me, Matty. I haven't said it enough. We're a bit stick-in-the-mud about our emotions, aren't we? I've loved you in the fiercest way since the moment you were born. But none of us live forever. I hope I shall see Christmas, in fact I'm determined I shall. Last year was so miserable for everyone, and I want us all to have a happy Christmas this year. And I shall rest easier, if I see Evan on the road to recovery. I think he seems a little better.'

'Do you?'

'A little. Maybe he's caught the sun. He looked so pale when we first saw him.'

'He hates to go outdoors at home. He seems to like it well enough here, though.'

'No people. No threats.'

'I suppose so. I think he had a settled night, no nightmares. I didn't hear him, anyway, but then I slept like a log. Probably the influence of Dad's Glenfiddich.'

'He'd be glad to have someone to share it. I'm not much for drinking, at the moment. You know, Evan could stay with us for a few days if you like, see how he gets on. It might take the pressure off you and Claire.'

'What pressure?'

Dora pats her son's hand.

'I'm not a fool, Matty. I see what I see. For Evan's sake, you should try and work things out. You've been through a lot together, and Evan needs you both.'

Matt sighs. A honey bee takes off from one red bloom and migrates to another, pure white.

'I'm afraid that ship may already have sailed.'

'You might be surprised. Things are different now he's home.'

'Not as different as they should be.'

'So what about Evan? Do you think he might want to stay?'

'I don't know. I'll ask him.'

'You'd better ask Claire first, see how she feels about it.'

'I'm sure she'll say it's whatever Evan wants.'

'I think so too. And your father would be over the moon.'

TWENTY-TWO

14 August

Jack's still keeping up old habits, up and about before dawn, even though he's barely slept for worrying about Dora. She seems to be sleeping too well, dozing at every opportunity, falling into deep slumber as soon as she lies down at night, dispensing with her lifetime's habit of reading a chapter of her library book. The books are piled up now on the ottoman at the end of the bed. They're due for return in a couple of days, and Dora hasn't read a single one. Jack tells himself it's the drugs that are making her sleep so much, and there's no doubt the opiates do induce drowsiness. In optimistic moments, he believes she's sleeping herself a cure, shutting down non-essential functions so her body can focus on fighting the enemy within. In pessimistic moods – which he tries to keep at bay – he can't help feeling that her body's winding down, that his Dora is being pushed aside and undermined by the invading armies of her disease.

He's made tea, but there's no newspaper to go with it. There have been no papers in the house since his family made the headlines. He's seen first-hand the price people pay to give them a story, and how a few words of newsprint don't tell even the beginning of the narrative as it actually is. Misery, despair, grief, hope. Column inches touch none of those things, and they're the only things which count.

As he's drinking his first cup and thinking about going outside, he hears the latch on the kitchen door. He turns round from his view down the valley – all mist and promise for a perfect summer's day – and sees Evan, dressed in his jeans and a hoody, his hair dishevelled from sleep.

Jack smiles.

'Now then, youngster. You're up early! Are you having a cup of tea?'

Evan shakes his head. He wanders to the fridge, finds a carton of orange juice and fills a glass. He drinks half, and goes to stand by his grandfather's chair, so his view of the valley is the same as Jack's. With Evan so close, Jack's somehow afraid to startle him, as if the boy's a nervous, wild thing which will take flight at the slightest movement.

'Since you're up, you can come and help me,' he says. 'We'll go and let the poultry out, and have a look in on the sheep. What do you say? But you'll have to put your wellies on. Your grandmother'll have a fit if you bring more muck in on your shoes.'

Outside, in the apricot light, Jack leads the way across the yard. Millie's lying outside her kennel, still half-asleep, but when Jack unfastens her from her chain, she's all wagging tail and excitement, running at Jack, and then, to his obvious pleasure, to Evan, who strokes her head. In the barn, Jack lifts the lid of a corn-bin, and shovels out a couple of scoops into an empty sack as Millie darts back and forth along the barn's back wall sniffing for rats.

Jack hands the sack to Evan, and they head for the home field, Millie running ahead as excited as if she's never done this before, bounding over the wall while Jack unfastens the gate and leads Evan across the grass to the rickety shed where he keeps the chickens. Undoing the latch, he fastens back the door, and the birds come tumbling out, squawking and complaining.

Jack points to an empty feeder.

'Corn in there,' he says, and Evan tips it in, smiling as the chickens squabble to get to it. 'You'd think they hadn't been fed for a week. Your next job is to fetch them some water with that bucket by the sheep trough. That's very important for them in this hot weather. Thirsty birds give no eggs. When that's done, we'll have a look how many they've laid. You see what's in the coop, and then we'll check the field. Every day's an Easter egg hunt with these girls, but we'd better find a few, or there'll be nothing much for breakfast.'

When they go back inside, Matt is in the kitchen, making a fresh pot of tea.

'Here we are,' says Jack. 'Eight of the finest. Show your dad, Evan.' Evan reaches into the front pocket of his hoody and one at a time, brings out the eggs they have found, ivory white and buff brown. 'He's got a nose for them. I only found three yesterday. If that's fresh tea, I'll have a cup, and I'll take one up to your mother. She should be awake by now.'

Evan sits down at the table and begins to play with the eggs, lining them up by size, rolling them as if to understand their physics.

'How shall we cook them?' asks Jack. 'The world's our

oyster. Scrambled, boiled, poached or fried?' He's on his way to the fridge to get milk for the tea, and without thinking, he reaches out and ruffles Evan's hair.

But Evan doesn't seem to mind.

Dora is still sleeping. Jack places a flowered cup with a single digestive biscuit in its saucer on the bedside table, and opens the curtains. The room floods with the brilliance of summer light, and Dora stirs. Jack crosses to the bed and bends down to kiss her forehead.

'Rise and shine, sleeping beauty.'

Dora opens her eyes, but he doesn't see the smile he usually gets when she wakes. Instead, she's frowning, and under the blankets he can see her hand move to her stomach.

'Are you all right, my darling?'

'I've got a bit of a pain,' she says. 'Do you think you could pass my pills?'

Awkwardly, she sits up, leaning forward so Jack can put an extra pillow at her back. The blister-pack of medication is on the dressing table, and he presses out two, passing them to Dora with a glass of water.

'It's a beautiful day,' he says. 'Evan and I have been collecting eggs.'

'That's nice,' she says, and swallows the tablets. 'Any luck?'

'We found eight. So it's eggs for breakfast. Scrambled or boiled?'

Dora smiles.

'I think I'll stick to toast,' she says. 'How did he seem?'

'He seems to be relaxing, but I didn't get a peep out of him. Maybe he needs a little nudge.'

'Oh, Jack, don't be impatient. He'll come round when he's ready.'

'Maybe. Shall I leave you to get dressed?'

'You can leave me to drink my tea, and I'll get up, by and by. But I feel like being lazy this morning. I might read for a little while.'

'If you're tired, my love, just stay where you are. Would you like marmalade on your toast?'

'A dab of honey would be lovely. And Jack, don't you be thinking about putting any pressure on that boy.'

'Don't worry,' says Jack. 'I won't.'

TWENTY-THREE

15 August

On the journey south, Matt is thoughtful. Claire has agreed Evan should stay with Jack and Dora a few more days, but without him, the vacancy in the passenger seat feels pronounced, and there's a part of Matt which aches with the loss of his son almost as if he were still missing, which in truth he is. It's been weeks, and he feels all his attempts to reconnect with Evan have been useless. He isn't so naive as to expect Evan ever again to be the sunny, happy boy who was taken away, but he's dared to hope some of the old Evan might re-emerge, that there might be flashes of him, moments, minutes, hours of the son he lost.

But there's been little evidence of it so far, and Matt's ashamed to admit even to himself that leaving Evan on the farm will be a few days of respite he didn't even realise he needed.

He doesn't rush to get home. He thinks he knows what he'll find, and the prospect's not one he relishes. He picks up dinner for himself from the Chinese takeaway three streets away: Singapore noodles, chilli beef, salt and pepper chicken wings. He doesn't buy anything for Claire. Left to her own devices, she will have used the summer's evening as an excuse to open the wine extra early: a glass in the garden in the sunshine, she'll tell herself, and before very long the glass will have been a bottle, and she'll be pretty much out cold.

As he pulls up in the driveway, the day is finally drawing to its close in a dusk where the city-bound traffic is no more than a background hum. After the farm, the air smells distinctly of suburbia: fresh cut grass on next door's lawn, charring meat on a barbecue, warm tarmac. He turns off the engine, and for a few moments stays where he is, looking at the house which is supposed to be his home. He used to love this house, was proud of it, felt glad to be here at the end of the day. Now he doesn't feel he belongs here, and he's briefly overwhelmed at the unfairness of how their lives have turned out, of how much has been taken from them by the stealing of Evan.

Yet what choice does he have but to go inside to his miserable wife? How can he blame her for what she feels? But the weight of her grief drags him down. He's tried to be strong for them both, but the burden is too heavy alone and she can't or won't help him carry it. In spite of himself, he resents that.

He climbs slowly from the car. Putting his key in the lock, he turns it and opens the door.

It's not what he's expecting. The house smells different, like the old, pre-loss days, and he tries to identify what's fighting with the garlic and frying oil coming from his bag of takeaway. There's floor cleaner, and Windolene, and the woollen smell of carpets after vacuuming. And on top of that there's cooking, something with chicken and mushrooms.

From recent habit, he looks for Claire first in the lounge,

thinking she'll be lying on the sofa, the unwatched TV showing *Emmerdale* or *Corrie*. But the TV's silent, and the sofa has the plumped-cushion look of not even having been sat on. On the windowsill, there's a vase of fresh flowers.

Fresh flowers?

'Hello!' He finds her in the kitchen, stirring a pan on the hob and smiling. Things have been put away – the sink is empty of unwashed plates and mugs – and the worktops have been wiped down. A window is open on to the back garden, letting in the scents of the summer evening. What's missing is a wine bottle, and an always-full glass.

In Claire's tired eyes there's a hint of sparkle, a trace of the woman he married.

He puts his Chinese food on the counter.

'Hey.' He gestures at the cleaned-up kitchen. 'What's going on?'

'Elves,' she says. 'They came while I was sleeping.'

'Looks good. What are you making?'

'Some super-speedy Jamie Oliver thing. Speedy when he does it, anyway. But it looks like you brought your own.'

'I'd rather have home cooking.' Through his shirt, he squeezes a handful of the belly fat this unwanted Just Eat, chips-with-everything new life has forced on him.

She seems embarrassed, a little self-conscious.

'You can ask me if you want.'

'Ask you what?'

She gives him a look.

'OK, I'll ask. Where's the wine?'

'I thought I'd have a night off. Actually it's my third night off. Since you and Evan went.'

He's surprised. There hasn't been a night Claire hasn't been drinking since – he can't remember when.

'How come?' He crosses to the stove, lifts the lid on a pan. 'Couscous? You're scaring me.'

'I've had an epiphany,' she says. 'And I'm hungry. Let's eat and I'll tell you.'

She reaches into drawers and cupboards for plates and cutlery, actions that used to be routine but it hasn't been this way for a long, long time. Pushed to say when they last ate together properly, Claire couldn't begin to guess. Christmas, maybe, although even then she can't remember that she ate much; most of her calories were in a glass. She spoons couscous and chicken on to two plates, and adds generous portions of green beans.

Matt's peering over her shoulder, crunching on a prawn cracker.

'Are those actual vegetables?' he asks. 'Fresh vegetables?'

'Yes, they are. You'd better eat them up, or there'll be no pudding.'

'Is there pudding?'

'Chocolate tart.'

'You've been baking?'

'I haven't gone that far. Courtesy of Mr Sainsbury. Shall we eat at the table?'

Matt raises his eyebrows. These days, it's all eating on knees, TV on. He's been thinking of football or a Sky box set, but he's intrigued to know what's going on in Claire's mind.

The food is good. Claire hasn't lost her touch.

'Very nice,' he says.

'Thank Jamie Oliver.'

He puts down his fork and touches her hand.

'I'm not thanking him. I'm thanking you.'

Claire puts down her own fork.

'Can I tell you something terrible?' she says. 'About me?'

He looks into her face and sees all the changes there, the new lines, the dark circles under her eyes, the dryness of her lips, the hollows where there was a healthy plumpness. The prettiness he fell in love with is all but gone, and his wife appears decades older than she did before Evan's abduction. Whatever happens between them now, whether this marriage sinks or swims, in this moment he feels her pain and aches for her, for them both.

'What could be terrible about you?' he asks.

'I need to tell you something, even though you might hate me for it.'

'I promise I won't hate you.'

'Don't make promises you can't keep.'

'Try me.'

He picks up his fork and spears a piece of chicken, chewing as she gathers her thoughts.

'When Evan was taken, I thought I'd die of misery.' She's not looking at him any more but out of the window on to the summer garden, as if she can see there the past she's remembering. 'Every day was torture. The only reason I didn't kill myself was the faint hope that he'd come back, even though I'd begun to accept he wouldn't, towards the end. I didn't have any hope left and then, miraculously, there he was. Our boy. My son, back from the presumed dead.'

Matt nods.

'It was a massive shock,' he says.

'A good shock,' she says. 'The very best you could hope for, in the beginning. And I wasn't stupid enough to think things would ever be like they were. I never expected that. Even though I hate to think about it, he must have suffered. He must have suffered terribly.' Her eyes are wet with tears. 'I know the kind of thing that must have gone on, and that makes me so very, very angry, I want to find those men and kill them, kill them in the most horrible way possible, with knives and burning and anything else I can think of. I want them to suffer the way they made him suffer. That's one reason for the wine. It makes me sleep, and takes the edge off all that anger.'

Matt's appetite is suddenly gone. He recognises the rage she feels; as his car eats up the miles of his daily drive, he's regularly planned murderous, bloody assaults on his son's captors, slow deaths and vengeful tortures.

'That's understandable,' he says. 'No one would blame you for that. We can plot revenge together, pool our ideas.'

She manages a teary smile.

'Maybe. But that's not why you'll hate me.' She draws a deep breath. 'When Evan was first home, I was patient. I tried to understand the silence, the bolted door, and I tried to cope with the rejection, but all the while a voice was nagging in me, a resentful voice asking why he wouldn't trust me. Why he wouldn't trust us. We're his mum and dad, and he doesn't trust us. And you can say all those things about how damaged he is and I know it isn't logical or even beginning to be fair, but there came a day – I couldn't say when, exactly – when I needed some acknowledgement, some gesture of affection, just a hug or kiss to say, *I know you're there, Mum*. But that's never come. He seems so lost, so shut down, that I doubt that he's ever coming back. And so I started thinking I don't have a son any more. He's alive but that's all he is. He's like some kind of hungry ghost, a shell of what he was, and he'll never have any affection for us ever again, because that's what those men have taken. We have Evan's body, but they've eaten his soul, and he's never coming back. And so I thought – and this is the really bad part – I thought if we didn't have Evan, if Evan is going to be a ghost for the rest of his life, haunting us from up there in his room, I thought I don't have a son any more and I want a son, so I thought we should start trying for a baby. A replacement for the son we didn't get back.'

It's not what Matt's expecting. Despite his protestations of an open mind, he's shocked.

'A baby? Really? Sweetheart, I don't think . . .'

She holds up a hand to stop him.

'I don't think that now. I thought it for a couple of weeks. Then I thought with the way you and I have been . . . I mean, it's a long time since you and I thought about each other in that way, and I'm not exactly an enticing prospect, am I? And I realised how shallow I was being and how crazy it was to even think about giving up on Evan, because that's what I was thinking about doing, just abandoning him to his twilight world and saying, well, that son didn't work out too well, so I'll give it another go. I was putting my grief ahead of his well-being. I was being needy, when my needs pale into insignificance, into non-existence when you think about his needs. So I thought again, and I thought I wasn't being much of a mother, was I, being pissed by four every afternoon and spark out on the sofa by seven. What boy could resist spending time with a mother like that? So in the spirit of being the change you want to see and in the interests of my liver, I've turned over a new leaf. Back to the old days of domestic efficiency and home comforts.'

Matt smiles.

'I'm pleased to hear it.'

'I just think it's time we pointed the Ferrers family ship back in the direction of normal. You and me, at least. Especially me. Even if Evan can't join us for the time being, I want there to be a home for him to come back to when he's ready. There was a moment when I was watching *EastEnders* and there was a punch-up, all the usual shouting and violence, and it was like I could see myself from above, lying on the sofa, half-drunk in my don't-care clothes with my don't-care hair, just a mess. And I thought, the old me would never have done this, drinking from tea-time, watching soaps until I fell into a coma. The old me was busy and sociable and involved, and I thought how could I expect to find the old Evan when he'd come home to new me all raddled and slovenly and sprawled on the sofa? What right did I have to expect him to recover if I haven't put a foot on that road myself? I want to set an example. None of us can be the same, I know that, but I want to be someone he wants to spend time with, someone who looks strong and together and capable. Someone who looks and acts like the mum he remembers, not this sad thing I am now.'

He feels the tightness in his throat which presages tears, a feeling with which he's become far too familiar. Leaning forward, he puts his arm round Claire's shoulder, where he finds more bones than there used to be. While he's been growing

182

portly on his on-the-road diet, she's been getting skinny on Chablis and Pinot Noir.

She leans into him in a way she hasn't since he doesn't know when, and hides her face in his shirt, in his end-of-the-day smell of stale aftershave and sweat.

'I can't say I'm not struggling,' she says. 'I'd kill for a glass of white.'

'Three days,' he says. 'I'm proud of you.'

'I made myself a chart,' she says. 'Look.' Standing up, she opens a cupboard door, where there's a ragged piece of paper stuck up with Sellotape, two columns with the days of the week and next to two of them, a tick. 'I'll get my third tick at bedtime.'

'That's my girl,' he says.

'It's hard. But every time I think about heading for the fridge, I think how much harder it's been for Evan. Infinitely, immeasurably harder. I should have stopped the minute he came home. I don't know why I didn't.'

'Because you weren't ready,' says Matt. 'But if you're ready now, I'm really, really pleased.'

He squeezes her shoulder and gives her a peck on the cheek. They continue to eat, and Matt feels the beginning of a lightness in his heart he hasn't felt in too long.

'He seemed better at the farm,' he says. 'Not happy, but more relaxed. Did you mind me leaving him there?'

'I'm worried about him, but it's not about me. Not if it's better for him. Why do you think he's more relaxed there?'

Matt shrugs.

'The wide open spaces, maybe. He can see there's no one coming to get him. I get the impression he daren't go outside here, and who can blame him? In the middle of a field, there's no threat.'

'We should have thought of that.'

'Maybe. But if he won't talk to us, there's no knowing what he's thinking. Don't be so hard on yourself. There's no textbook or manual for this situation. We're all just groping in the dark.'

'I'll come with you to fetch him back,' says Claire. 'Or maybe I could pick him up.'

When their plates are empty, Matt stands to carry them to the sink. He has his back to her when Claire says, 'Matt.'

He senses by the hesitation in her voice, by the softness of her tone – as if she's reached out for his hand, though it's been a long time since she's done that – that something's coming, something he realises in that moment he's been expecting. He wants to look at her, to judge from her expression what she's thinking, but he's afraid his own face might give something away. Better keep it light, non-committal.

'That's me.'

'There's something else I want to say. I feel I've already lost my son, for the time being at least, and I'd be devastated if I lost you, too. I'm not losing you, am I?'

He turns on the hot tap, and doesn't look round as he rinses the plates, so she doesn't see the slight blush colouring his cheeks. He thinks of Dora's words, her insistence that he and Claire should work things out. When he turns to her, he's smiling.

'Of course not. Why would you think that? We're a team, you and me, always have been.'

She's watching him earnestly, and her eyes are travelling

over his face, reading his features for clues, figuring out if he's telling the truth.

He keeps his eyes steady and maintains the smile, then shuts it down in case it's gone on too long, not sure he's prepared for the scrutiny of this newly sober Claire.

'What do you think,' he says, 'that after all this, I'd give up on us? You know me better than that, don't you? Didn't you mention pudding? I'm ready for something sweet. How about cutting us a piece of that chocolate tart?'

TWENTY-FOUR

16 August

'Look what I've got.'

Evan's on the sofa next to Dora, helping her with word-search puzzles. He's sitting very close but not quite touching her, his knees drawn up and wrapped round with his arms as he used to do when a very small boy. Dora is holding back, letting Evan do most of the work. When he finds a word, she hands him the pen to draw a line through it, and when he's drawn his line, he hands the pen back.

Jack's holding a fishing net on a bamboo pole, and a large pickle jar.

'Well,' says Dora, 'where on earth did you find those?'

'In your shed. There's treasure beyond measure in there.'

'I should have a clear-out, shouldn't I?'

'I'm glad you haven't. It's been too long since I've been fishing, and you know what they say, you're never too old to do the things you love. What do you say, Evan? Are you going to keep me company?'

Evan looks at Dora, as if he's reluctant to leave her.

'You go on, love,' she says. 'I'll have a little nap. You can help me finish this one when you come back.'

186

The photo of Jack and young Evan with his jar of stickle-backs is still by the phone. As they walk by it, the picture they would make now would be very different. There are physical differences, of course – Evan isn't smiling, and he's getting closer to matching his grandfather's height – but there's a delightful simplicity in the photo which has been wiped away, smashed like a mallet taken to fine porcelain. It's Jack's hope that maybe something remains amongst the shards of what's been broken, a pearl left undamaged, ready to be found.

As they walk down the track, Evan's feet are hot in his wellingtons. Millie's trotting at their heels, breaking away from time to time to sniff what she finds interesting in the verges. The day is warm again, the long grass and cow parsley growing against the grey-stoned walls ruffled by a breeze which blows Evan's hair into his eyes.

Jack notices Evan's hair is getting long as Evan pushes it back behind his ears, and it occurs to him that someone must have been cutting his hair while he was gone. Before he was taken, there were trips to the barber's every four weeks, just Evan and Matt on Saturday mornings, Evan in the chair first while Matt read a magazine, then Evan given a comic while Matt took his turn. Who cut his hair when he was away from them? Was it a woman or a man? Was it done kindly and with care? Such a minor thing raises questions it's not his place to ask, and he pushes the thought away, not truly wanting to know. What concerns them is Evan's care now. He'll ask Dora to find her scissors and have a go, if Evan will allow it.

There are crickets singing in the grass, and overhead a

skylark's risen, singing its heart out. Jack points up at it, and Evan follows his finger, straining to see the tiny spot in the sky.

'See that? She's a crafty bird. We've startled her and got too close to her nest, so now she's creating a distraction. She's over there, so you know the one place you won't find her nest is directly below her. Over there, or over there maybe. But she's drawing our attention from her little ones with that beautiful song, and here we are, looking and listening. That's quite a trick Mother Nature gave her, isn't it?'

At the bridge, the sun's warm on their backs. The stream's tumbling over pebbles, rippling the weeds rooted in the water, and tall trees cast shade over the banks, where the grass is lush and stippled with motley-coloured flowers. Where boulders have formed a calm pool a dragonfly hovers, its turquoise body wafting on diaphanous wings.

'It's a while since we've done this,' says Jack. 'Where do you think looks like a good spot?'

Evan makes for the pool. The sun on the water makes it hard to see, but somewhere under the surface there is movement.

Jack nods encouragement.

'I think you're right. That's where I'd be starting. Mind you keep your shadow behind you. We don't want to let them know we're here.'

Evan slips the net into the water and slides it cautiously along the bottom. When he brings it up, as water dribbles back into the pool the mesh glitters, mimicking the wriggling of a fish.

But there's nothing there.

'Unlucky,' says Jack. 'Have another go.'

Evan tries again, and again, and again. Jack crouches beside him, peering into the water, as absorbed as Evan is in the task. The skylark has stopped singing. There's just an old man, his grandson and the soothing babble of the stream.

A vehicle's coming down the road, slowing as it draws close to the farm entrance. They hear the crunch of gravel under tyres and music on a radio before the engine is switched off. The music stops and a door slams.

A young man appears, wearing the shorts and red shirt of Post Office uniform. He's bringing letters, but rather than slipping them into the old mailbox nailed to the gatepost, he wanders the few paces to join Evan and Jack.

'Morning,' he says cheerfully.

'Morning, Ben,' says Jack. 'It's a beautiful day. I don't think you've met my grandson, Evan.'

Ben nods a hello.

'It's glorious,' he says, 'and too nice to be at work. I'd far rather be doing what you're doing. Have you caught anything?'

'Not yet,' says Jack, 'but we will.'

'I used to love fishing,' says Ben. 'I should get my rods out, next time I have a day off.'

'Not so easy to make time for it when there's a baby in the house,' says Jack. 'How's he doing, anyway?'

Ben grins.

'He's champion, absolutely champion. Except for all those nappies. I'm not so keen on them. Look, I reckon there's one down there, under that rock.'

The three of them peer at the water, and Evan directs his net. When he brings it up, there's a fish struggling in the bottom, the spines on its back stuck in the mesh.

Jack hands Evan the pickle jar, and Evan extricates the fish from the net. When it's swimming in the jar, he holds it up for them all to see. And smiles.

'Look at that, I brought you a bit of luck,' says Ben. 'You have to be careful with them, as I remember. They're not called sticklebacks for nothing. Anyway, much as I should prefer to stay, I'd better get on.'

As Ben drives away, Evan places the pickle jar in the shade.

'We've still got it,' says Jack, all smiles. 'We haven't lost that old magic. He's a lovely lad, Ben, a lovely lad.'

For a little while, Evan fishes in silence.

'You know, people like Ben, they make you think, don't they?' says Jack, as if he's been considering the matter. 'You and I know too well there are bad people in this world – some very bad people – but I can look back from my great age, and if I think about it – really think about it – I can count the number of really bad people I've run across on the fingers of one hand. I'm not saying everyone's perfect, because they're not, and I'm not saying ordinary people don't sometimes do things they shouldn't be proud of. But people who are bad through and through – downright wrong 'uns who'd be better locked up with the key thrown away – the fact is, you don't run across many of them at all. When you meet somebody new, the chances are astronomically higher they'll be a cheerful sort like Ben. Now then, look down there. If you play your cards right I reckon you might get two together.'

There are roadworks on Oakland Way, and Naylor's been stuck at the temporary traffic lights for almost fifteen minutes. Some idiot has set them up wrong, so the main flow of traffic from Byron Road is only getting seconds to pass through.

When her phone rings, she's expecting a call from Hagen. She doesn't even glance at the caller display before pushing 'answer' on the dashboard.

'Hello?'

'Is that DS Naylor?' A woman's voice, a voice she knows. 'It's Claire Ferrers.'

'Claire! Hi, how are you?' She wasn't expecting this and doesn't have her story ready. She hasn't spoken to Claire or Matt in probably too long.

'I'm OK.'

'And how's Evan?'

'Evan's away at the moment. He's staying with his grand-parents in Yorkshire. I think the peace and quiet does him good.'

'I can see it would. You must miss him, though.'

'I got used to missing him while he was gone. At least I know where he is.' Is there a reproach in there? Naylor dismisses the thought as the product of her guilty conscience.

'So, what can I do for you?'

'I was just wondering, we haven't heard from you in a while, and I was wondering . . . Well, you know. Whether there have been developments, whatever you call them. I'm sorry, developments sounds a bit Sherlock Holmes.'

There have been developments at Ashridge, but Naylor doesn't want to tell Claire what they are – that they all relate to other cases, and the resources they piled into Evan's case have been re-assigned elsewhere.

'To be honest, there's not much to report.' That much, at

least, is true. 'I've been looking into leads from the car, and DS Hagen's pursuing another line of enquiry relating to some photographs of known offenders Evan reviewed.' *But that was six weeks ago*, she thinks. *Since then we've done next to nothing on Evan's case, thanks to staff shortages and Campbell's ever-changing priorities.*

'Did he identify someone, then?' asks Claire. 'I didn't know that.'

'Not exactly,' says Naylor. 'We're just playing hunches and making routine enquiries. No stone unturned.'

'So nothing to report?'

'I'm afraid not. But we only need one good lead, and the dominoes will fall. In the meantime, what do you think about us trying to talk to Evan again? Do you think there's any chance?'

Claire sighs.

'Not unless things have changed in the last couple of days. He's still said barely a word.'

'Do you want to have another go with the psychiatrist? Or I could ask Rose to get in touch, see if he'll respond to her. She's got a bit of a magic touch in difficult cases.'

'Maybe,' says Claire vaguely. 'I was just thinking if there were any chance of arrests being made, Evan might feel better. If they weren't still out there, he might begin to feel safe.'

'That's an excellent suggestion, if only we could deliver. Believe me, Claire, we're doing our absolute best.' The lights change again, and Naylor moves slowly forward. 'As soon as we have anything, you'll be the first to know. And let me know if you think Rose can help.'

Finally moving and heading home, Naylor thinks about

Claire, about how different she is from the woman she first met, about the effect this crime has had on the whole family. They need results so they can move on, and the constant reallocation of resources isn't fair. How can there be results when they have no manpower?

A Tesco juggernaut pulls up two cars behind her at a roundabout, and Naylor looks at the driver in her rear-view mirror, wondering if she might see Lee Bryant at the wheel.

When she found Bryant in the interview room, she thought they were home and dry.

Something's got to be done. Something which could cost her job if Campbell finds out.

To hell with it.

She reaches for the dashboard phone, and puts in a call to Ron.

Rain. Evan's watching the storm from his bedroom window, counting the seconds between the flashes of forked lightning over Blackmire Ridge and the crashes of thunder which follow. Count slowly, Grandpa said. One thousand, two thousand . . . Each second is a mile in distance from the heart of the storm, which makes the storm very close indeed, right over the house, right over his bedroom. Grandma's roses are taking a battering, and the oak trees in the copse on the opposite hillside, even they are bending in the wind.

The hills are becoming familiar. He likes to look out at them. At home, he doesn't like looking out; there are too many people about, and he doesn't want to be seen. But here, there's nothing between him and the oak trees except the home field and the stream, and then just open, empty space.

If he wanted to, he could take the chair away from his door, walk out of the house and into the landscape, and he could walk as far as those trees. No one would bother him. No one would stop him.

Evan feels something shifting in his shoulders and his back. The muscles are looser, more relaxed.

It's true. No one would stop him. He can come and go as he pleases.

He's free.

TWENTY-FIVE

18 August

'How are you doing, Ron?'

Naylor hands Ron Perdue his pint and, sitting down next to him, takes a sip of her orange-and-soda. The beer garden is all lawns and picnic tables, with an overhanging willow tree which almost manages to create a sense of country riverside. The only thing spoiling the illusion is the stink of diesel and the sound of heavy traffic from the road on the other side of the high wooden fence.

Ron is looking good, in Italian-style twill shorts and a polo shirt, deck shoes on his feet.

'I'm doing all right. Just wondering to what I owe this honour.'

'You're looking very brown. You been away?'

'Only as far as the bottom of the garden. She's got me re-landscaping. So much for retirement, eh?' He raises his pint to her. 'Cheers. Whereas you, I have to say, have all the unhealthy colour of a copper doing too much overtime. You need to get out more, and I mean that literally. Get more sunshine and vitamin D, or you'll be getting rickets.'

'I take my daily vitamins,' says Naylor, defensively. 'I don't look that bad, do I?'

She's made all the effort she's had time for: shower and shampoo, tracksuit bottoms, a vest top and canvas slip-ons. The other women in the beer garden are in summer cottons, pretty dresses and golden tans, real or fake. Most are wearing make-up, and Naylor wishes she'd spent ten minutes more getting ready, but that would have made her later than she already was, and Ron gets very snippy about people being late.

Ron smiles.

'You always look good, Naylor. But you look tired. Goes with the territory, I know.'

'You're just feeling smug, now you're looking at a future of long lie-ins. Did June mind me borrowing you?'

'As she says, that depends why you're borrowing me. She says hello, by the way.'

'Say hello back. And the reason I'm borrowing you is for a good cause.'

Ron looks at her over the top of his glass.

'Namely?'

'Evan Ferrers.'

'Ah. I did wonder.'

A family group enters the garden, a young woman holding a thumb-sucking toddler by the hand, her partner with a protective hand on the tiny newborn strapped to his chest. The woman is glowing with something Naylor can't name. The toddler is making a big thing of climbing on to a bench, and the partner is unstrapping the baby from his chest, cradling its head like it's the most precious thing on earth.

Ron follows her glance.

'I see people like that and it just makes me realise how often we fail,' says Naylor. 'Fail to keep people safe, I mean.'

'On the balance of probabilities, they'll get through life just fine,' says Ron. 'You know the statistics.'

'We all know the statistics. I don't suppose they'd impress Claire Ferrers.'

Ron shakes his head.

'No, I don't suppose they would. Why don't you tell me what's going on?'

'It's what's not going on. We were all ticking along, following – by and large – Uncle Ron's golden rules for a successful investigation. No stone unturned. You taught us well. But we've been pulled off it for the second time. Stones have been left face down in the mud.'

Ron sighs. The young woman is now cradling the baby, while the toddler's becoming engrossed in a colouring book. The partner is walking purposefully into the pub, smiling in anticipation of a cold drink.

''Twas ever thus,' says Ron. 'Staff shortages have been a fact of policing since the year dot. I know you don't rate Campbell, but don't shoot the messenger. I don't suppose it sits any easier with him than it does with you. If you want to complain about it, write to your MP.'

'I was thinking of taking more effective steps than that.'

'Like what?'

'Like drafting in a support team on the quiet.'

Ron's eyebrows lift.

'Come on, Ron, it's nothing major. Nothing illicit involved. Just the kind of enquiries anyone could make, if they'd a mind to. If they had the training to ask questions without getting anyone's back up.'

'I feel the need for a bag of crisps,' says Ron, standing up. 'You want one?'

'Peanuts, please.'

Ron returns and throws two bags of Walker's on the table. 'No peanuts,' he says. 'Cheese and onion or prawn cocktail.' Naylor grabs the prawn cocktail. Ron opens the cheese and onion.

'The way I see it,' he says, 'is this. I don't mind dabbling on the perimeters, looking at a few maps, applying my little grey cells from the comfort of my own sofa. But out there on the streets, that's a different matter.'

'OK, I get that,' says Naylor, dipping into her crisps. 'But I had a call from Claire Ferrers asking how we were getting on, and I felt so guilty. I didn't have the guts to say we didn't get a quick result – again – so we've moved on to something else, something where we might get to put a tick in the "solved" box. And it doesn't feel right to me. Evan's abduction was the most serious type of crime, and we're letting it slide by. We might be coppers, Ron, but there has to be some leeway. Under current circumstances, we can't play by every rule.'

'I like rules,' says Ron. 'If more people lived by them, we wouldn't be in this mess.'

'But we are in this mess. We're in a mess where Evan Ferrers has been abducted and abused and would without question have been murdered but for a massive stroke of luck, and nobody's even been interviewed for it, let alone convicted. What kind of message does that send out? If we don't get you in the early stages, you're golden, you've got away? That's not policing, Ron, that's anarchy.'

Ron's finished his crisps. He folds up the packet and sticks it between two slats of the table top.

'If I thought anyone was doing what you're suggesting on my watch, I'd have had them transferred out so fast their feet wouldn't have touched the floor. And if Campbell finds out we're having this conversation, he'll go ballistic, and he'd have the right to do so. You're undermining his authority. He's told you to drop it, and he'll take the public flak for that. It's why he earns more than you do.'

'He might take the flak, but he's not taking the phone calls. He's not the one Claire Ferrers's ringing for updates that aren't there.'

Ron looks her in the eyes.

'OK, hit me,' he says. 'What were you thinking?'

'I was looking at one of the previous owners of the car Evan was found in, the Ford Focus. Sheila Birch. She hadn't been the main driver of the vehicle. That was down to her husband, Brian. There was something there that gave me a feeling. You know how sometimes things just feel a bit off? It niggled me for days, and then it came to me. His story was, after the car was taken, he got a train back down south. Hartlepool into Euston, he said. And that didn't sound quite right, so I had a look on Google, and sure enough trains from Hartlepool go mostly into King's Cross. OK, that could've been misremembering or a slip of the tongue or maybe he took some obscure route, travelled via Blackpool or Leicester or Aberystwyth. It's not a solid lead, I know, and it may be nothing, but I just think it's worth a closer look, where exactly the car was taken from and what he was doing in Hartlepool. No stone unturned, right? This is a guy who doesn't want a company car. Who on earth turns down a company car for an 09-plate Ford?'

Ron frowns.

'Who indeed? That's an interesting one. So where are we talking about? Don't tell me you're wanting me to go all the way to County Durham?'

Naylor shakes her head.

'Not as far as that. This guy's offices are in Chelmsford. I didn't have time to visit while I was there but they might know something about his background. I'd really appreciate it, especially as there's nothing in it for you. It's not as if I can even offer you expenses.'

'I've been to Chelmsford once or twice, but only to the prison. Haven't they got some gardens there, a stately home?'

'I've no idea.'

'I drove past signs to it, and I thought June might like to visit. I'll run it by her, and I'll let you know. And if I'm considering doing you this massive, illicit favour, I think you should be buying me another pint.'

Leaning on the sill of his bedroom window, Evan watches the Freelander drive slowly up the track, rocking as the tyres find the potholes. He's been alone for several hours, but alone is what he prefers to be, though some company is becoming tolerable to him now. He's OK with Grandma and Grandpa in their slow, bumbling ways, he can spend time with his dad, and his mum's all right if she isn't being over-attentively fussy. He remembers his mum before –

pretty, super-efficient Mum when she was always so busy she barely had time for him, but that was then. He hasn't seen that mum in a long time. Mum now is nervous, anxious and worried about him, even though she doesn't say so. She's always giving him things he hasn't asked for – crisps, chocolate, cans of pop, new stuff to wear. Evan's happy to eat the crisps and chocolate and drink the pop, but he doesn't care what he wears. It's luxury just to have clothes that are clean and his size and his own, the same way it's luxury to be able to get clean, to have a bath or shower when he likes, with hot water and shower gel or Grandpa's old-fashioned soap, and towels to dry himself with that smell of fresh air from the washing-line. When he was . . .

He stops the thoughts of then, there, that place using a trick he's invented to shut them down. Closing his eyes, he empties his head of everything but a staircase, a silver spiral fantasy of a staircase leading upwards, like one you might find in one of those computer games like *Elvenar* or *World of Warcraft*, a stairway between worlds. And in his mind he slowly climbs, counting the steps as he goes up, up, up towards blue sky where birds are flying, plump Disney cartoon bluebirds which smile and chirp as they fly around him, and land, in his mind, on his shoulders and his head. When he reaches the high top of the staircase there's a stone platform surrounded by a wall overgrown with ivy, a sky-borne platform like the turret of a fairytale castle, and that's where Evan stops and counts the birds. It's like the way Mum used to tell him to count sheep when he couldn't sleep, and he'd picture fluffy lambs jumping in a field. Now he counts bluebirds until the fear has diminished, and he feels it's safe to open his eyes.

He feels his bedroom here is like that imagined sanctuary, high up and isolated with a view of birds. Not so many birds, and they're not bluebirds, but swallows, jackdaws, crows, sparrows, kites and kestrels. Grandpa's been teaching him how to tell the difference between them all, even from far off, and Evan's read *A Kestrel for a Knave*, about Billy Casper – a youth about his own age – who found and trained a bird of prey. If Evan could do that, nothing would make him happier. What a great thing it would be, to have a wild creature as a companion, to set the bird free and have it come back to you . . .

The Freelander pulls up in front of the house. For a while nothing happens, and Evan can see Grandma and Grandpa sitting in the front seats, looking out, not speaking, watching swallows dip and loop over the rose garden. Then Grandpa reaches over, puts his arm round Grandma's shoulder and kisses the top of her head, a gesture so affectionate Evan feels a lump rise in his throat.

Grandpa gets out of the car and walks round it to open the door for Grandma. He holds out his hand to her as she gets out, and they walk slowly into the house arm in arm, Grandma making them stop to admire one of her rose bushes which is bowing under blush-pink blooms. Once they're in the house, Evan can hear the sound of the kettle boiling and the rattle of teacups, familiar noises he finds comforting. In a few minutes he hears the stairs creak, footsteps on the landing and a light knock at his door.

'Are you there, young man?'

Grandpa's voice.

Evan leaves the window and crosses to the door, where he lifts away the chair under the handle. A part of him remains cautious, and he opens the door just a crack at first, keeping his foot against it in case of the unexpected or the unwelcome, needing to be sure it is Grandpa, and that Grandpa is alone.

Jack's there with Evan's favourite mug – gold-rimmed with an airborne Spitfire – filled with sweet, milky tea, and on a flowered side-plate, a buttered cherry scone.

'Permission to board, Captain,' he says, and Evan smiles and gives a mock salute and steps back to let him pass, but he's unable to resist looking up and down the landing to check for unwanted visitors. He closes the door against intruders who aren't there.

Jack puts the tea and scone down on the bedside table.

'Your grandma thought you'd like a bit of something,' he says, sitting down on the bed. 'Just to put you on until teatime. She'll no doubt be thinking you might starve between now and then. Women, eh?' He pats the bed beside him, encouraging Evan to sit, but Evan's wary. Instead, he sits down on the chair at the door.

A look crosses Jack's face which Evan can't quite read: weariness, sadness, despair. He glances at Evan, and musters a smile.

'I'm tired, old lad,' he says. 'Nearly all day in that hospital, and a long drive there and back. It's a good job you didn't come with us. You'd have climbed the walls with boredom, all that waiting about. Anyway.' The smile is gone. 'There's something I have to say to you, man to man, and I wish to

God I didn't have to say it, because God knows you've had enough to cope with in your short life without having any more troubles piled on you. But that's life sometimes, my boy. Bad things come together.' Evan's expression is startled. 'It's about your grandma, Evan. You and I knew she wasn't very well, didn't we? We've known that for a while. But the truth is the doctor has told us today that she may not be with us very much longer. Grandma reckons she'll be here for Christmas but odds are that won't be the case. So what I want to say to you is this. You know you've been everyone's priority, don't you, your mum's and your dad's and mine and your grandma's. Of course you have. You're precious to us all, more precious than you'll ever know. But just for a short while – not too short, though, I most sincerely hope – your grandma needs us, and I need you to be a help to me. If you can be fully responsible for some of the work here, then I can have more time to look after your grandma, give her the care she needs so she can be home as long as possible. She wants to be at home, of course. It's a lot to ask of you, I know, after what you've been through, and never think you're anything but top of my list. Do you understand me? Can we be a team, for your grandma's sake? You'll have to be out and about a bit more, and I know that sometimes makes you uncomfortable. I don't want you to be uncomfortable, but it's a state of emergency, isn't it? A real state of emergency.'

Jack looks at Evan, and Evan sees desolation in his grandfather's eyes. Silently he rises from his chair to sit down next to Jack, and takes the old man's hand in his youthful own.

As Grandpa says, it's a state of emergency, and that changes the rules. He knows it's time to speak, but when he opens his lips, it's as if his throat has closed through lack of use, and he can't put the words together.

Instead, he squeezes his grandfather's hand, and when Jack returns the pressure, he knows he's understood that Evan's answer is *Yes*.

TWENTY-SIX

21 August

Ron's left June at the RHS gardens at Hyde Hall with a promise to be back in time to meet up for lunch. He's not anticipating problems: a short drive to Petersen's, and a casual enquiry at reception as to whether his old mate Brian Birch might be around. Beyond that, the plan is less concrete, but he's got the confidence born of years of experience to know he can carry it off. And there's a maverick freedom in being outside the framework, not being bound by the rules: no warrant card, no traceability. Ron never did any undercover policing, but he's worked with men and women who have, and they all say the same. You can get away with so much more if no one knows who you are. Anonymity rules. If he finds anything of interest, he'll pass it on to Naylor, and she can get herself over here and ask the same questions on an official basis. Job done.

As it turns out, the job is done much quicker than he expects.

The satnav leads him on to an industrial estate, one of those places populated by small businesses you've never heard of, all doing essential, niche jobs not enough people need doing to ever make it big. Widget grinders and laundry services, motor factors and skip hire. And companies like Petersen's, compressed air and hydraulics specialists. Not everybody's everyday supplier.

And it would seem it's possible to be too niche.

When the satnav shows the chequered flag to tell Ron he's reached his destination, he stops the car. He's in the heart of the estate, surrounded by low brick buildings with a few cars and vans on their forecourts and very little, apparently, going on. What should be Petersen's building is between an electrical supplies place and a company specialising in tile adhesives, but there are no cars on its forecourt and no lights on inside.

He parks right in front of the door and gets out of the car. There's mesh on the windows, a collection of rubbish and blown leaves around the doorstep and a piece of wood over the letter box to stop the delivery of mail. The only sign Petersen's were ever here is the nameplate by the door which no one's bothered to take down, a stylised image of a wind turbine and a strap-line reading *Pneumatic Technology Solutions*.

Ron looks around. At a road junction about a hundred metres away, there's a breakfast and burger van. He walks over to it.

Seeing Ron approach, the guy sitting behind the counter folds his copy of the *Mirror* and stands up, wiping his hands on his chef's trousers.

'All right, mate,' he says. 'What can I getcha?'

'Just a tea,' says Ron. 'Milk and one.'

'Milk and sugar's at the end of the counter.'

As the man pours hot water on to a tea bag in a polystyrene cup, Ron fishes in his pocket for change.

'You been doing this job long?' he asks.

'Couple of years.'

'Little goldmine, this set-up, I should think, in a spot like this. Captive clientele. No McDonald's or KFC to bother you.'

'I do all right.'

The man hands Ron his tea, and Ron gives him a two-pound coin.

'Keep the change.' At the end of the counter, he fishes out the tea bag and adds a splash of milk. As he's tearing open a sachet of sugar, he says, 'Actually, I was hoping to find a mate of mine I haven't seen in a while. He used to work for Petersen's down the road there, but looks like they've closed down or moved on.' He points to Petersen's old building. 'You don't know anyone who used to work there, do you?'

The man shakes his head.

'Nah, mate,' he says, sitting down and picking up his newspaper. 'Like I say, I've had this pitch a couple of years, and there's never been anyone in that place while I've been here.'

Ron stirs his tea.

'You got a lid for this?' he asks, and the man hands him one. 'Looks like I'll have to look for my mate elsewhere. Thanks for the tea.'

Back in his car, Ron sips his brew and stares thoughtfully at what was once Petersen's UK office. Seems Naylor's hunch was right about those stones still lying in the mud. The pity is, she didn't turn this one over sooner.

'Let me show you how this works,' says Jack, and he moves along the bonnet of the old Land Rover he uses for running the sheep so Evan can squeeze in beside him. The sun is hot, and Evan's glad to be in the bonnet's shade. 'This is called a distributor cap, and these leads here are where the sparks come from to fire the engine. So when this old girl is running a bit rough, the first thing to try is to do what I'm doing here, and just tickle the ends up with a bit of sandpaper. If you had a matchbox in your pocket, you could use that. We just need to make the ends nice and shiny again, like this.' He shows Evan what he's doing, then hands the sandpaper to him so he can have a go. 'Not too much elbow grease. Just enough to get them nice and clean. That's it.'

When all the points are done, Jack re-connects them and checks everything looks sound.

'Right then. You jump in the driver's seat, and when I shout, you fire her up.'

Evan beams, and runs to get in. Jack follows, and leans inside to check that the Land Rover's in neutral.

'Wait till I give you the thumbs up,' he says.

Jack takes up his position under the bonnet, and when he gives the signal, Evan solemnly turns the key. The engine fires, running less roughly than it usually does.

Jack gives another thumbs up and drops the bonnet down.

'You've done a good job there,' he says to Evan. 'You'll make a decent mechanic, one day. Shall we take her for a spin, make sure she's OK?'

Evan seems uncertain.

'Go on, shift over,' says Jack, and Evan clambers over the gearstick, into the passenger seat. 'Let's go and see what we can find.'

Jack drives them down the pot-holed lane. As they pass

over the stream, he stops, and from their respective windows they peer down into the water, looking for fish.

'They're hard to spot when the sun's on the water,' he says. 'But we know they're in there, don't we?'

He follows the lane in the direction of the village, but before they reach it, he takes a turn up an even narrower lane, where the frothy heads of cow parsley brush the Land Rover's sides. Evan's looking out over dry-stone walls into meadows alight with yellow buttercups, at doe-eyed cows swishing away flies as they chew the grass. In the corner of one field, there's a ramshackle barn where rampant nettles are growing through the blades of an abandoned plough.

They pass a sign announcing a village where Evan hasn't been before, which turns out to be not much more than a well-kept green with a duck pond, surrounded by a scattering of grey stone houses and cottages. One of the cottages has been converted into a post office, and Jack parks outside.

'This place here,' he says, 'is a bit off the beaten track, but it holds a closely guarded secret. This little place just happens to sell the best ice-cream in all England. Come on, I'll show you.'

He climbs out of the Land Rover. Evan doesn't follow, so Jack walks round and opens his door.

'Come on, lad. It's just one old lady and a bad-tempered cat.'

Reluctantly, Evan gets out, and follows Jack as far as the post office door.

Inside, the woman behind the counter might be older than Jack, but she's not dressing her age. Her hair's tied in a ponytail reaching below her waist, and her clothes are sixties hippy: purple cords, big hoop earrings, a crocheted jacket in rainbow colours. She should look odd, eccentric, but somehow on her the style looks cool.

'Afternoon, Mona,' says Jack.

Mona gives him a big smile.

'Hello, stranger.' Evan hears an American accent. 'What blows you into town?'

'The quest for some of your ice-cream. This young man is my grandson. Evan, Mona, Mona, Evan.'

'Pleased to make your acquaintance,' says Mona.

'We've just been doing some repairs on the old bus.'

'What, more repairs? Buy something newer, Jack.'

Jack shakes his head.

'There's plenty of mileage in her yet. But it's been hot work, so I thought what better way to cool us down than a couple of scoops of your famous ice-cream. Come in, Evan, and choose what you'd like.'

He holds out his hand to encourage Evan inside the shop, and Evan takes a tentative step in the direction of the freezer, where the tubs of ice-cream are on display.

'All hand-made,' says Mona. 'All from our own herd, and all natural flavourings. What takes your fancy, Evan? Strawberry, chocolate, vanilla, rhubarb and ginger . . .'

'That's for me,' says Jack. 'A double scoop. Evan, what are you having?'

Evan ventures a couple of steps closer, and peers down at the display. He points at the chocolate. When he doesn't speak, Mona gives Jack a quizzical look.

'He's a man of few words, is Evan,' says Jack, touching his grandson on the shoulder. 'I expect he'd be wanting a Flake in that, if you have one.'

As Mona and Jack talk – the vagaries of the parish council, vandalism of a phone booth, the upcoming agricultural show – Evan carries his ice-cream outside. It's sweet and rich; the sunshine is warm and welcome. Intrigued by a mallard with ducklings on the pond, he wanders over there, and takes a seat on a waterside bench.

Jack and Mona watch him through the post office window.

'Poor, poor boy,' says Mona. 'I can't imagine how you're all coping.'

'One day at a time,' says Jack. 'Like re-acclimatising a beaten dog. We're trying to teach him not everyone is bad, lead him back to the view of the world he used to have.'

'That's a long road, after what he's been through.'

'It's a very long road, and progress is slow. But he is making progress, and he's our boy, so whatever it takes, we're more than glad to do it.'

At home that evening, Ron opens up the Google browser on his laptop and types in 'Petersen's Chelmsford'.

There's a website.

He clicks on it, and a professional-looking page fills the screen, with a logo and the same strap-line he's seen on the doorplate: *Pneumatic Technology Solutions*. There's a picture of a wind farm and another of some kind of machined metal part whose use Ron couldn't begin to guess, and a few lines about Petersen's being established in Holland in the 1960s and now being at the forefront of wind-farm technologies.

On the menu across the top are four buttons. Ron clicks on them, one by one. The Products page is empty. So is Current Projects. On the Gallery page, there's a single line of text asking the reader to use the Contact page to view it. The Contact page appears to be live, though there's no phone number, only a form to submit his own details.

Thoughtfully, Ron considers. He opens a new page on his browser and makes another Google search: Petersen's pneumatic.

A very different website appears, the website of a major international organisation, fully loaded with lists of satisfied clients, pictures of smart office buildings and men in high-vis jackets supervising installations. The Products pages are many, filled with obscure and expensive precision-engineered parts. The Contact page has phone numbers, an email address, and social media buttons – Facebook, Twitter, a couple of platforms Ron's never heard of – inviting clicks. The About Us page opens with the short paragraph Ron has seen on the other, somewhat truncated site, but goes on at considerably more length about government contracts and presence in other countries. There's a list of Petersen's worldwide offices. Chelmsford isn't on it.

June calls to him from the kitchen that dinner's ready. Ron shuts down the browser and closes the laptop lid. But as they're eating dinner, he tells June what he's found, and as he's telling her, she suggests what he's already thought to himself: that he should try and get in touch with the creator of the dummy website via the Contact Us page.

'Use a fake name,' she says. 'Set up a new email address, Yahoo or Hotmail, one of those junk kind.'

But Ron's reluctant, thinking he's getting too involved.

'Well, pass it on to Rachel, then, if you don't want to do it,' says June. 'Then it's official.'

When the table's cleared and the dishwasher's loaded, Ron returns to his laptop and watches it power up. Opening a Google window, he re-loads the dummy website. It looks harmless enough, but why is it there? He clicks on Contact Us, and for a few minutes stares at the empty fields asking for his details. Resisting with difficulty the temptation to fill them in, he does the sensible thing, and dials Naylor's number.

Dora's sleeping deeply, almost comatose from the opiates prescribed for her pain, but Jack's wide awake in the dark, thinking over the future, trying to picture it without Dora, trying to persuade himself he can cope with her loss.

When the shouting begins, it doesn't trouble him; he knows how to deal with it. Climbing from the bed, he moves quietly to the bedroom door, feeling his way carefully in the dark, anxious not to disturb Dora or put any worry on her.

The landing light is on. It's always been left on since Evan arrived, for times such as this, in case light can be any help to him with his night terrors. They don't come every night; sometimes days go by now without them suffering broken sleep. Claire has left medication for if it gets too bad, but Jack has his own method which everyone prefers to the drugs – especially Evan, who hates the morning-after feeling from the tablets, the spaced-out weirdness and tiredness which lasts all day and (far worse) reminds him of that place.

Outside Evan's door, Jack listens. There's momentary quiet, and it's possible the nightmare's passed and Evan's fallen back into dreamless sleep. If there's a chance he might be sleeping peacefully, Jack doesn't want to disturb him. But listening with an ear pressed to the door, he can hear mumbling, a low, disturbing murmur of *no no no no no,* the soundtrack of some terrible memory his grandson shouldn't have. Jack's heard it many times before but still it gives him chills. The mumbling subsides, and there's a silence; then a shout which makes him jump, and he knows it's time to act before the yelling starts in earnest.

He and Evan have a pact: no barricaded doors by night. Jack won the battle for access by arguing the house's age and the dangers of fire. Turning the handle cautiously, he opens the door a crack. Startling Evan is to be avoided at all costs. In the early days, Matt made this mistake, and Evan flew at him and punched him in the face.

He opens the door further. Evan is subsiding back into mumbling, and this is a good time to begin. Slipping through the door, Jack grabs the book he needs from the nightstand, sits down in the chair and by the light from the landing, begins to read aloud.

'*Biggles leaned out of the cockpit of his Vandal amphibian aeroplane, pushed up his goggles, and peered ahead anxiously.*'

'Grandpa?' Evan's voice is drowsy. Jack can see his eyes reflecting the light.

'I'm here, son,' says Jack. 'It's just you and me.'

Evan's eyes close, and Jack reads on, an entire paragraph before the import of what has happened hits him. In these dark watches of the night where time seems suspended, the exchange was entirely natural.

Evan spoke to him. Evan actually spoke to him. Jack's lost his place on the page, and it takes him a few moments to find his last sentence and regain his rhythm. But then he reads on, page after page until Evan's breathing is even and Jack's certain he's immersed in peaceful sleep.

Back in his own room, Dora hasn't stirred. His side of the bed is cold, and he presses up against her, trying to push away the thought that she won't always be there.

TWENTY-SEVEN

22 August

As Hagen enters the office the next morning, his earphones are in, so he doesn't hear Naylor call his name. He's wanting to hear the end of the track he's listening to, and by the time it's finished and the earphones are out, Naylor's standing right next to him.

'Morning,' says Naylor, and Hagen jumps. 'Anyone could whack you over the head and rob you when you've got those things in. Doesn't it worry you, when you're walking down the street, that you're a target?'

Hagen grins.

'I don't do much walking,' he says. 'Everywhere I go, I dance.'

Naylor narrows her eyes.

'You're in a very good mood,' she says. 'What's going on?'

'I met the girl of my dreams,' says Hagen. 'Well, she was last night, anyway.'

'Forget her for now,' says Naylor. 'I've got a job for you, a nice little desk job. Come and look at this.'

Hagen follows her to her desk, where she pulls up the Petersen's dummy website on her monitor. She had a good look at it last night following her phone conversation with Ron, but if she's going to try and reel anyone in, she wants to do it from an official computer.

'Brian Birch, last official owner of our red Ford Focus and alleged employee of Petersen's pneumatics.' She clicks on a couple of the menu buttons. 'See? Next to nothing there. To be honest, I'm not optimistic this will take us anywhere. Chances are all Brian Birch is guilty of is deceiving his wife, for reasons which will likely turn out to be entirely personal. If he's lost his job and daren't tell her, he won't be the first or the last. But I want you to have a good look at him. No stone unturned.'

'You've been talking to Ron.'

'Here's your starter for ten, address and mobile number.' She gives him a piece of paper. 'See if he's got any form, anything at all. If there are parking tickets, I want to know where they were issued. Bank statements, definitely have a look at those. His wife thinks he works somewhere he doesn't, so I'm interested in sources of income. Put in a request for credit card info as well, and phone records. Social media maybe, though he may not be the Facebook type.'

'With respect,' says Hagen, 'I'm happy to do all that, but isn't this one for the white-collar guys?'

'It would be if they had any resources, but they're more strapped than we are. So roll your sleeves up and see what you can find.'

'What about the website? Should I try and make contact?'

Thinking of entrapment protocols, Naylor hesitates.

'Yes, why not? But don't use anything official, not yet. Campbell says I'm supposed to be leaving this alone, so I can't authorise it, but you've probably got all kinds of random email addresses you could use. Or if you haven't, set one up. Use your imagination. And for God's sake leave the earphones out. I'm starting to think you're antisocial.'

Hagen spends a few minutes setting up a new Yahoo email address, picking a jokey username, verifying it via his mobile, setting up an email notification on his phone. Opening the Contact page on the fake website, he tries to come up with a name halfway between believable and dubious, the kind any bloke might pick to register on a porn site. He comes up with Mick Rutter and keys it in below the new email address. When he comes to the 'Message' field he's stuck, and settles on *I'm interested in your products and price list.*

Suitably generic, he thinks, and presses Send.

Ron has got the bit between his teeth. Naylor's given him the remaining two addresses the DVLA supplied as previous owners of the Ford Focus, and the first is an address in Sevenoaks where traffic's terrible and there's nowhere to park. Figuring people are out at work, Ron takes a risk on blocking a driveway, and still has a three-minute walk to where he needs to go.

The address is an old Edwardian house, long ago converted into flats. There's a scrubby garden out front where what was once a lawn is now overgrown with weeds, and a For Sale sign which looks like it might have been there quite a while. The curtains at the ground-floor windows are floaty, orange and drawn, which immediately makes Ron think it's occupied by someone with some kind of habit.

The intercom at the door has a dent in it as if someone might have gone at it with a claw-hammer. There are buzzers for five flats, but only three of them have names, and none of them is the name he wants: Jennifer Lambert.

He presses one of the buzzers anyway, and waits. There's no answer, so he tries a second.

There's crackling, and a voice that sounds very far away says, 'Yes?'

It's hard to tell if it's a man or a woman.

'Can you let me in?' says Ron.

'Who is it?'

There's a short silence in which Ron doesn't reply.

'Fuck off then,' says the voice.

Ron presses a third buzzer. Moments later, he sees the orange curtain move, and stands back so whoever's looking has a clear view of him and can see he's respectable. He gives a casual wave.

The curtain drops, and the intercom buzzes. Ron moves fast to open the door before he misses his chance.

Inside the hallway, the decor is as he'd expect: shabby, drab, depressing. Someone's left a bicycle at the bottom of the stairs which makes it difficult to move. From somewhere upstairs there's a smell of curry.

A door on his left opens. The man standing there is again what Ron might have predicted: long hair, funny slogan T-shirt, five days' stubble, bad teeth.

'Can I help you, mate?' he says, in a way which suggests helping Ron is the last thing on his mind.

'I hope so,' says Ron. 'I'm looking for a lady called Jennifer Lambert, Flat Four. You know her?'

'What's she done, then?'

'I'm just asking if you know her.'

The man gives a slow, lupine smile.

'Don't give me that. You're a copper. It's written all over you. Not the type for trouble, I didn't think she was. I know 'em all, I do, I see 'em come and I see 'em go. But she's been gone a while, 'as Jen.'

'Any idea where to?'

'She met up with some South African, went to live with him over there. He was a doctor or something, as I remember. That was the last I heard. She said she'd send a postcard, but she never did. Anything I can help you with?'

'I don't think so,' says Ron, opening the front door to let himself out. 'But thanks anyway.'

The drive from Sevenoaks to Woking takes longer than it should, but once Ron hits the A3, progress improves. As he's driving, he calls Naylor and tells her he's found one more dead end.

'Not going too well, is it?' says Naylor. 'Still, you never know. No stone unturned.'

The address in Woking is a terraced house whose front garden has been bricked over for parking. There's a car parked there now, a bright orange Mini Cooper. As he climbs from his own car, the traffic lights at the end of the road turn green. The waiting traffic moves on and the road falls into a brief hiatus, quiet enough to hear the shouts from a school playing field a couple of streets away.

It was Ron who taught Naylor to be suspicious of doorbells. He knocks, and waits, and in a minute or so a woman answers, a woman pretty good for her age, fit-looking in tracksuit bottoms and a high-vis Lycra top. Her cheeks are pink, as if she might just have been running.

'Yes?'

Ron gives a bright, non-threatening smile.

'I wonder if you might be able to help me,' he says. 'I'm looking for a lady by the name of Lindsey Stockman.'

'That's me.'

'I'm sorry to disturb you. Is it Miss Stockman or Mrs?'

'Neither.'

'I'm sorry to disturb you, Ms Stockman, but I'm hoping you might be able to help me with a problem. It's about a car you used to own.'

'Really? What car?'

'A red Ford Focus.'

Lindsey Stockman thinks.

'Yes, we had one of those, but not for very long. I like something a bit smaller, like my Mini. Why do you think I can help you with anything?'

'I've got an insurance issue,' says Ron. 'I'm trying to prove it's a long-standing problem. Did you have any problems with it while you owned it?'

'What sort of problems?'

'Brakes. Anything in that department?'

Lindsey shakes her head.

'Not that I'm aware of. My other half drove it more than me. It was in my name but it was his car really. I'm sorry, I don't think I can help you. If you don't mind, I'm just getting ready for work.'

'If I could just ask you,' says Ron. 'I don't suppose you can remember who you sold it to?'

222

She shakes her head again.

'It was nothing to do with me. What I know about cars you could write on a postage stamp. He put it on eBay after he set his heart on a nice little Alfa. If you want to know who bought it you'd have to ask the DVLA.' A thought seems to strike her, and her eyes narrow. 'How did you get this address, anyway?'

'Off the log book,' lies Ron. 'I just wondered if you might have sold it to a friend, anything like that.'

Lindsey shakes her head.

'I've no idea who he sold it to.'

'Can I have a word with him? Maybe he'll remember.'

'He and I aren't together any more,' says Lindsey. 'I'm sorry, I have to go.'

Ron rings Naylor on his way home.

'I'm sorry, kiddo,' he says. 'I did my best, but I don't think there's anything there.'

Naylor sighs.

'Thanks for trying, anyway. At least there are two less stones in the mud.'

As she hangs up, the office is quiet. Hagen has left a note on his desk asking her to give him a call. She looks across the room at the whiteboards and the map they've been using to log activity.

There are a few spare pins to the side of the map, and Naylor chooses a red one and a green one. She sticks the green one in the heart of Sevenoaks to mark Ron's visit there, and one on the outskirts of Woking as a visible record of his conversation with Lindsey Stockman.

Standing back, she considers the map. No matter how she looks at it, there's no pattern to be seen, no connections to be made. But as Ron always used to say, one small piece of intelligence can make all the dominoes fall.

Back at her desk, Naylor puts in a call to Hagen, and reports the disappointing news that Ron appears to have come away with empty hands.

Since the last hospital visit, Ainsclough Top has become a place of much activity. There are regular visitors – palliative care nurses, carers and the local GP – interspersed with Dora's many friends and family, some of whom she hasn't seen for years and have travelled great distances to be here. They are welcomed with laughter, hugs and tears.

Evan might have struggled with this influx, except that most of the visitors are women, and all without exception are kind. They respect his wish not to interact with them directly, accepting his silent presence at mealtimes, since Jack has always gently insisted Evan eat downstairs at the table.

And in truth, he's leaving behind the disquieting, almost spectral Evan who came back to them. The Evan who sits down to meals, though quiet, takes some interest in those around him, listening to conversations even if he doesn't join them, sometimes smiling at jokes and trying to make himself useful in the fetching and carrying of the endless stream of plates and dishes, tea and cakes. If the comings and goings of people gets too much, he seeks sanctuary in the barn, where one of the feral cats that stalk the rodents there has had a litter of kittens. Evan's found a vantage point overlooking the cosy nest the mother-cat has made in the straw, and is happy to lie quietly on the bales, observing them from above.

Claire has been spending much time at the farm too, with Matt as a regular visitor. The change of air has benefited her in some ways – a light tan has lifted the paleness from her face, and she's put on a little weight from eating properly. With people to cook for, the effort seems worthwhile. Life might be looking brighter, except that Dora's decline casts a shadow over them all.

On a rare afternoon when there are no visitors, Claire goes to find Evan in the barn. Seeing her approaching, he puts a finger to his lips to stop her speaking, and beckons her over to his observation point. Claire scrambles over the heavy bales, the dust of the sweet-smelling straw tickling her nose, reminding her of Sunday morning riding lessons in the days of her childhood when she was pony-mad.

She smiles at Evan, and he smiles back.

He points down to the nest.

'Oh, aren't they gorgeous!' whispers Claire, and Evan finds himself regretful that he can't talk to her about the kittens. He wants to tell her the names he's given them, about when their eyes opened and about the poor, tiny one that died, how he removed it while the mother-cat was away hunting and buried it in the garden.

She asks how many there are, then answers her own question by making a count.

'Are there seven, or eight? I'm trying to count the heads, but they're so wriggly, aren't they?' She lapses into silence, enjoying alongside Evan the antics of the newborns.

'I have to go,' she says at last. 'There are some things for

Grandma I have to pick up from the doctor's, and we need something for dinner.'

He nods that he understands and watches as she leaves, before giving his attention back to the kittens. He hears his mother's car drive away, and then immerses himself in the mewling from the nest and the calling of the swallows overhead.

TWENTY-EIGHT

29 August

Hagen's been occupied with other things – while most of the team is working on the Foxley Wood Road shooting, he's fielding everything else, and there seems to be a constant stream of claims on his attention, requests for him to make phone calls and visits, tie up loose ends and chase lines of enquiry no one else can spare the time to deal with.

When Dallabrida drops a hefty brown envelope on his desk, Hagen is on the phone, on hold for a forensic pathology lab he's been asked to call. The data requests he filed the previous week are all but forgotten.

'Here you are,' says Dallabrida. 'I saw this with your name on it downstairs. No need to thank me for my kindness. My usual fee's a pint.'

Hagen looks down at the envelope and frowns. That's definitely his name on the front.

'Cheers, mate,' he calls after Dallabrida's retreating back, and Dallabrida raises his hand.

With the phone still to his ear, Hagen breaks the seal on the envelope and pulls out a couple of the sheets it contains. Bank account data for Brian William Birch.

For a moment, the name rings no bells. Then he recalls the Ferrers case, and Naylor's request for this information. There's a voice in his ear at last from the pathology lab. Hagen pushes the papers back inside the envelope and gives his attention to the woman who's finally taken his call.

It's getting late when Hagen remembers the envelope. The office is quieter, winding down; the day's been hot, and he's been looking forward to a cool beer on his way home. But his conscience pricks him over the Ferrers case – he's the only one doing any work on it at all now, as far as he knows – and so he decides he'll give it ten minutes before he leaves.

What did Naylor say to him? Look for sources of income. He pulls the sheaf of papers from the envelope, finding a lot of paper covering two years' worth of transactions.

The top sheets are statements from a joint NatWest account – Brian William Birch and Sheila Marie Birch – and unsurprisingly there are hundreds of transactions representing the minutiae of everyday life. In the debits he sees payments, among many others, to Asda, Costa Coffee, Total petrol, Domino's Pizza, the National Lottery and Pets at Home. There are ATM withdrawals within the Chelmsford area and the usual utilities – Essex and Suffolk Water, British Gas – credit card payments and store-card bills. In the credits there are far fewer entries, mainly returns to stores and refunds, making it look as if Mrs Birch might be a keen shopper who loses interest in her purchases very quickly, and unshops on a regular basis. A sign, maybe, of a woman with too much time on her hands. What's funding those purchases – apart from the credit cards – is what appear, without close scrutiny, to be regular credits from a company payroll, identical amounts month on month with *Petersen Pneumatics Plc* in the payee reference field.

Hagen grabs a yellow highlighter pen and marks a couple of these entries. Placing the sheets from the joint account to one side, he moves on to the next account, a NatWest current account in Brian Birch's name only. For this account, there are only a couple of sheets, listing a few cash deposits – not huge amounts, but all four figures – and regular monthly payments made via standing order to his joint account with Sheila on the 28th of the month. The amounts of the payments tally exactly with what appear to be payroll credits in the joint account.

Hagen highlights these corresponding entries and stares at the sheets in front of him. Brian Birch is faking his salary. Why would he do that? In Hagen's experience, the most common reason for that kind of deception is embarrassment over a job loss. Quite possibly, as Naylor suggested, Birch has been made redundant and daren't tell his wife. But if he's been made redundant and is no longer an employee of Petersen's, who is he working for? He searches for the current balance on Birch's personal account, and finds it a little over £8,000. That's not someone who's hurting for money – Hagen wishes his own account were only half as healthy – but it's all coming from cash, and that's a red flag. Generous deposits in cash are, as often as not, at least marginally suspect, signalling funds from a range of activities from tax evasion and illegal dumping of waste to drugs-peddling and people-trafficking. Where's Birch on that spectrum? However he's been making his daily bread, for some reason he doesn't want his wife or the tax man to know about it.

There's more in the envelope, statements from a Lloyds savings account. What catches Hagen's eye first about this account is the amount of money it holds. Brian Birch has over £30,000 in savings. That's not unusual for the man in the street – a legacy, a house sale or even a lottery win would cover it easily – but Birch's money hasn't come from any of those sources. Like his personal current account, this money has come from cash, a string of deposits that have begun to add up to a significant amount. For a man who seems to be unemployed, Brian Birch is on a very nice little earner.

There's one thing outstanding. Hagen picks up the phone and dials the tech guys on the second floor. The girl who answers sounds flustered and weary.

Hagen states his name and his business.

'Relating to a mobile phone owned by a Brian William Birch,' he says. 'We were looking for whatever you've got on that from June thirtieth onwards.'

She's gone a while, hunting through the completed requests, and he's expecting her to say he can come up and pick up the sheets. The kind of records he's asking for commonly run into hundreds of calls.

'Two inbound calls from Chelmsford, Essex on the thirtieth,' she says, at last. 'Phone switched off in the Aylesbury area the same day.'

There's silence.

'Is that it?' asks Hagen.

'That's it.'

'It's never been switched on again?'

'Nope. Not so far.'

'OK,' says Hagen slowly. 'Thanks very much for your help.'

TWENTY-NINE

30 August

Hagen's back at his desk early the next morning, pulling out the envelope with Brian Birch's bank statements and glancing over them, re-confirming what he found last night. He needs to alert Naylor to what he's uncovered, but in the meantime, he's feeling inspired to do some digging in other areas.

He pulls up Naylor's notes on the theft of the car. There's a crime number from Cleveland Police and the basics of the incident: a red Ford Focus and its registration number, reported stolen from outside a Costcutter on Chatham Road, Hartlepool, at 18.43 on the 16th of June.

A prickle of intuition runs down Hagen's spine. Something about the timing isn't right. It takes him only moments to check, and he doesn't even need to go through their own database to do so. News reports from Google confirm Evan Ferrers was found in the back of that Focus on 16 June, but the first reports are timed before 5 p.m. They'd been making the assumption Birch reported the car stolen before Evan was found, because that's the way it usually is. Car reported stolen, car turns up days later in some kind of criminal use.

But Birch's car must have been missing for at least a few

hours before he picked up the phone. Why would that be the case?

When Naylor comes in, Hagen gives her the full run-down: the cash deposits in Birch's accounts, the switched-off phone, the mismatch on the stolen car timing.

'Great work, Brad,' she says. 'If we can get the guys who nicked it on CCTV, we might get an ID and start to really put things together. The bad news is, I think you should go up there.'

'To Hartlepool? No worries. My nan lives near there. She'll be pleased to see me.'

'It's a long drive. You'd better take the train, or you'll be gone for days. I'll talk to Campbell and tell him what's going on so he can authorise it. Make contact with Cleveland before you go, tell them you want to look at any CCTV footage they can get hold of for that location on that date, and see if they can dig out details on the call reporting the vehicle stolen. Allelujah, we might be making progress here at last.'

Cleveland Police Headquarters is an anomaly of a building, a modern, red-brick fortress amongst the vintage buildings of old Hartlepool – the Masonic Hall (now a tea-room and wedding venue), the Town Hall theatre, the Engineers' Club and Snooker Room. Hagen announces his business and signs in, and waits in the reception area only a few minutes before a plain-clothes officer about his own age comes to greet him.

'DC Alex Heron,' he says. 'Pleased to meet you.'

'Pleasure,' says Hagen, and here amongst friends, already his accent is lapsing further into its north-eastern origins.

'We'll take the stairs,' says Heron, leading the way. 'You'd wait all day for the lift.'

They pick up coffee from a machine, and in an open-plan office almost identical to the one he's left in Berkshire, Hagen pulls up a chair to Heron's desk.

'So, you know what I'm after,' he says. 'This is all connected to the Ferrers case, the abduction.'

Heron shakes his head.

'A bad business,' he says. 'The sooner someone's doing time for it, the better.' He has a copy of the original report of the Focus theft and places it in front of Hagen. 'The theft was reported online.'

Hagen glances over the printout. Birch gave his full name and his address in Chelmsford. The phone number he provided is a mobile, the same one that's since gone dead.

Heron opens up Google Maps and finds the location of the reported theft: Chatham Road.

'It's an interesting one, this. Bearing in mind the seriousness of the offence, we've done you a favour and pulled in what CCTV we can find, which has come from some interesting sources. What line did you say the car's owner is in?'

'Pneumatics,' says Hagen. 'Allegedly. Offshore wind farms, stuff like that.'

'See, if your man was interested in wind turbines, he'd need to be down the coast a-ways, down at Redcar. The only offshore wind farm plans they had for around Hartlepool got turned down last year. Which makes you wonder why your man was parked up on Chatham Road, in an inland residential area. So we got CCTV from the Costcutter where he says he was and from another place of possible interest.'

Heron zooms in on the Google map, grabs the tiny figure to switch to Street View, and lands it on Chatham Road. The screen changes from a map to 360-degree-view photographs and the outside of the Costcutter. With a few twists of his mouse, he's refocused on another building further down the street.

Hagen stares.

'A children's centre.'

'Run by the council, mostly for the benefit of children under five.'

'Well, what the hell.'

'Begs the question again, what was your man doing parked up near there?'

'Have you looked at the footage?'

'Not yet. Thought I'd leave that to you. There's an office you can use down the hall.'

Hagen starts with the images from the Costcutter, quickly finding the date and time Birch reported the car stolen and working back from there. He goes back an hour, two hours, three. In seven hours of footage, there's no sign at all of the red Ford Focus.

He switches to the footage from the children's centre, scrolling backwards through the hours from late morning to the middle of the night, watching in the daylight hours a parade of parents and pregnant women with small children and babies. Sticking with this one in case there has been, after all, a mix-up with the dates, he backtracks all the way to the previous morning, then goes back to the Costcutter footage and does the same with that. Up and down Chatham

Road for forty-eight hours, there's no sign at all of a red Ford Focus.

Brian Birch's report of his car being stolen appears to be false.

Hagen takes out his phone and texts Naylor the outline of what he's found, and he's about to put away his phone when he sees an unfamiliar icon on the screen. With a jolt, he realises there's email in his new account, the one set up for non-existent Mick Rutter as bait for the fake Petersen's website. He clicks the link and opens up the message.

It's from a generic-sounding address – *info@petersens.org* – and it's short. *We have a range of products to suit a variety of tastes. Prices vary according to requirements. Please supply a phone number and a convenient time for us to call and discuss your needs.* There's no signature and no attachments, but it's a reply. Whatever the status of the website, the *Contact Us* link is live. Now all they have to do is find out who's on the other end.

Hagen forwards the email to Naylor without adding anything to it and texts her again.

Like Naylor said, progress at last.

THIRTY

4 September

It's a while since Naylor's been on shift this early, but this is an operation she couldn't bear to miss. Hagen's done the driving and she's dozed some of the way, but she's still grateful when he pulls into a twenty-four-hour petrol station and comes out with hot coffee. He offers her a chocolate croissant, but she declines.

'Too early for me.'

'It's never too early for breakfast,' says Hagen.

He eats his croissant and hers as they drive the last half-mile, and finds a place to park behind an unmarked police van.

Twenty minutes before first light, the birds are singing, pitting themselves against the background of traffic already running on the A12. She and Hagen join the group from the Essex force gathered in a residents' parking area around the corner from Pentland View. They're talking quietly but are fired up and raring to go. The operation's commander is young and keen, checking one last time everyone knows where they should be, making it clear to Naylor and Hagen they're bringing up the rear.

At ten to the hour, the signal's given, and the team heads for the property, the tramp of boots heavy on the air. When they reach the house, those designated to cover the rear melt away, and Hagen and Naylor find a safe spot behind a neighbour's car.

There are lights on in the house, and that makes the commander wary. He'd rather deal with a target still asleep.

The officer with the big red door key – the locker-room name for the battering ram – moves into position, and the commander raises his hand, glancing round to be sure everyone's ready. Talking quietly into the microphone clipped to his flak vest, he receives confirmation they're all set round the back.

He drops his hand and hammers on the door.

'Police!'

The big red door key goes into play, pounding against the door to break the lock. A woman's voice starts shrieking inside the house, and as the big red door key persists, the shrieking turns to shouting. In a couple of neighbouring houses, lights come on.

When the door slams back, men rush through it, pushing past Sheila Birch who's wailing in the hallway.

'What are you doing? What are you doing?'

The men disregard her, taking the stairs two at a time to check the bedrooms, striding into the downstairs rooms. There's a thundering of feet overhead, and the shifting of the hatch as they check the attic space.

'Target not found!'

Sheila's face is red with rage and trauma.

'What are you *doing*!' she yells. 'If you're looking for Brian, he isn't here!'

By the time Naylor gets to her, Sheila's sitting on her chair, dabbing at tears. Naylor offers her a glass of water, but Sheila declines.

'Where is he, Sheila?' asks Naylor.

'Spain. And that's where I'm going.'

The claim makes sense; she's decked out for travelling, fully made up despite the early hour, dressed in a bright skirt and jacket which couldn't be anything but holiday wear. If further proof is needed, there's a large suitcase and a carry-on bag in the hall.

The commander makes his initial report.

'We haven't recovered any electronics yet, no laptops or phones, and there's not much stuff in the wardrobes either,' he says. 'Looks like your man's done a runner. By the way, there's a taxi outside says he's got a booking.'

'That's my taxi,' says Sheila, struggling to stand up. 'All of you, out. I've got a plane to catch.'

'Tell him he's not needed,' Naylor says to the commander.

'Of course he's needed,' Sheila objects. 'Tell him to hang on, I'm getting my stuff.'

'Sorry, Sheila, no airport for you today,' says Naylor. 'We need you to tell us where we can find Brian.'

'I've told you, he's in Spain.'

'What's he doing over there?'

'He's told me not to talk to you, so I'm saying nothing more. And if I miss my flight, I'll be wanting compensation, same as for the door, for the damage you've done there. That just wasn't necessary, all that drama. If you'd just knocked and waited, I would have let you in.'

239

*

The early morning's taking its toll, and by the time they're back at Ashridge Naylor's dog-tired, running on the sugary fuel provided by the peanut butter Krispy Kreme doughnuts Hagen picked up en route. When she asks him why he chose the peanut butter, he tells her they have valuable protein.

Campbell's pleased to see them because he's expecting a good result. When they tell him Birch has slipped the net, he slams both hands on his desk.

'Goddammit! Did the wife have anything to say?'

'Soon as we put her in the interview room, she went no comment,' Hagen tells him. 'Obviously Birch told her how to play it. Without a reason to hold her we had to let her go, but she's been left in no doubt her holiday's cancelled.'

'Maybe it was less of a holiday and more of a permanent move,' Naylor adds. 'She wouldn't even tell us what she's done with the dog.'

'You wonder what he told her about why we might come to visit,' Campbell says.

'Probably he fed her some line about embezzlement,' suggests Hagen. 'People see that as a nice, respectable crime.'

'We've come away empty-handed all round,' says Naylor. 'And Birch did a first-class job of clearing his tracks. Nothing's left we might get a trace on, not even a recent photograph we might have circulated. So all we can do now is get in touch with Border Control and the airlines, see if we can find out when he left and where he went with a view to extradition, if he can be tracked in Spain. That's an almighty task, given we've no idea where he's been since I spoke to him when he was in Aylesbury. He might have been gone for weeks by now.

When you think about how many flights there are to Spain on a daily basis, and from how many airports, even I would say that's an expensive job.'

'You'd have to include the sea ports too,' says Hagen. 'And we don't even know what car he'd be driving.'

Campbell sighs.

'It's a massive job, I agree,' he says, 'and we can't do it with existing resources. I'll have a word upstairs. But we're not quite empty-handed. Let me cheer you up with some good news, and tell you that we've had a result from digital forensics on the email received via the fake website. They've pulled an address for the computer which sent it. Dallabrida's got the details, but rather improbably it seems to have originated in a library in Wolverhampton.'

THIRTY-ONE

6 September

Bobby Gillard is smiling.

Hagen's not delighted to be back in Wolverhampton, but Naylor's kept his spirits up, persuading him Gillard's the key to Evan's case.

'Here's the thing, Bobby,' says Naylor. She leans forward across the desk, and Gillard slouches further back in his chair. The duty solicitor's sitting beside him, a diminutive woman who looks far too delicate to be spending time with low-lifes like him. Naylor's met her kind before. Undoubtedly, she's tougher than she looks. 'Library records show that at the time this email was sent, you were the only person signed in to use the computers, the only person issued with a password. You signed in with that password, so we've got you at the keyboard.'

From her file, she takes out two sheets of paper and slides them across the table, one to Gillard, one to the solicitor. The solicitor reads what's on the sheet. Gillard doesn't even glance at it.

'For the recording,' says Naylor, 'I have handed Mr Gillard and his advocate a copy of an email sent from the email address *info@petersens.org*. The text of the email is as follows. *We have a range of products to suit a variety of tastes. Prices vary according to requirements. Please supply a phone number and a convenient time for us to call and discuss your needs.* Would you like to tell us what products and tastes you're referring to there, Bobby?'

Bobby's foot-tapping becomes faster, but his smile grows.

'No comment,' he says.

'Can I ask,' says the solicitor, running the point of her pen along the sender line of the email, 'whose is this email address? With who was my client corresponding?'

Naylor turns to Hagen, who raises his chin.

'Is that relevant?' he asks.

'I think you know it is,' says the solicitor curtly. 'If this is a private email – and even if it isn't – I think what we see here is a possible case of entrapment.'

Bobby Gillard grins.

In the canteen, the coffee looks awful. Naylor chooses tea.

Hagen looks dejected, showing no interest in the cherry cake Naylor's bought him as he over-stirs his grey latte.

'Don't worry about it,' says Naylor. 'The library computer's gone to forensics, and I don't doubt for one second there's stuff on there Bobby Gillard doesn't want us to see. When we find it, his feet won't touch the ground. Go directly to jail, do not pass Go, do not collect two hundred pounds.'

'I made a rookie error,' says Hagen. 'When I got the initial response, I should have ignored it, and sent another from an official account.'

'And made a possible entrapment official? What difference

would that have made? It doesn't matter, Brad. Admissible or not, it's flushed Gillard out of the undergrowth. We'll be able to see where his online travels have taken him, and that's bound to throw up something new. Really, don't worry about it.'

'What if he does a runner, and disappears like Brian Birch?'

'He hasn't got the resources, unless he's had a big win on the horses, and he didn't look much like a winner to me. The only choice he's got is to sit at home and wait for the knock on the door.'

Hagen remembers Gillard's words about the misery of his home life.

'Maybe it'll come as a relief to him,' he says.

In the two weeks since their visit to Wolverhampton, Naylor knows all they've done is chase their own tails. The knowledge that Evan Ferrers's case has stalled again is tough on them all.

'So you've nothing new?' asks Campbell, at the weekly case review.

'Apart from Gillard being back inside, no,' says Naylor. 'That was a good result.'

'How have your approaches to the family been taken?'

Naylor shakes her head.

'No joy at all there,' she says. 'Evan's making progress, but he's still not speaking.'

'The Petersen's website's been taken down,' says Hagen. 'Which suggests that if Gillard was one administrator, there's at least one more still out there. We should be going after them.'

'And how will you do that, Bradley?' asks Campbell.

Hagen and Naylor are silent.

'I'm afraid the time has come,' says Campbell. 'Unless and until we receive new information, I want you to keep your main focus on your other cases.'

Somebody Else's Child

THIRTY-TWO

13 October

Jack never meant to fall asleep, but he's had so little rest this past couple of weeks. He lay down next to Dora just to hold her hand for a while, but the comfort of that feeling with the softness of the pillows was a seductive combination. How long has he been asleep? He doesn't know. Probably not long, as the sun's still high, and the shadows in the bedroom look no different to what they did when he lay down.

What's woken him is the shaking of the bed: not just the play of springs as Dora turns on to her back, but a full-on, bone-rattling shaking. Drowsy and disoriented, he looks around for the source, and finds it in Dora herself. Everything about her is trembling; her eyelids are fluttering over the whites of her eyes, her back is rigid and arched and she's drooling mucous liquid from the corner of her mouth.

In panic, Jack runs around the bed, stands over her and tries to hold her down, thinking he can somehow force her out of the fit, shouting her name to snap her out of it. *It can't go on long*, he thinks, but the spasms won't let her go, and he begins to think of stories of people choking on tongues and vomit and of the recovery position. He's seen pictures of it and rolls her on her side, all the while calling her name, praying he can break through the wall of the seizure and bring her back. When he thinks she's in the right position, he takes the pen from her book of word-search puzzles and jams it in her mouth, doing his best to anchor her tongue flat.

This is an emergency, and Jack won't leave her. At the bedroom door, he listens to hear who's downstairs.

'Claire! Claire! Are you there?'

His shouts fall into silence, so he runs to the bedroom window and throws it open. The red roses in Dora's favourite vase are past their best, their petals scattered on the sill. On the bed, Dora is momentarily still, so still Jack fears that she's dead. When she begins to shake again, it's almost a relief.

'Claire! Claire!' His voice sounds loud across the yard, but Claire's car isn't there.

Evan appears from the barn and looks up at his grandfather, his face showing his concern.

'Evan! Evan, your grandma needs an ambulance. Go and ring them, son! Ring 999, and tell them where to come.'

Evan's still looking up at him, hesitating.

'Just do it!' Jack orders in desperation, and Evan runs away round the house and in through the kitchen door.

Upstairs Jack is crying, pressing Dora's trembling hand to his lips. In the hall where the photo of him and Evan stands near the phone, Evan picks up the receiver and dials 999. When the operator answers, Evan's voice is clear and loud.

'We need an ambulance quickly,' he says. 'My grandma's very ill.'

THIRTY-THREE

15 October

'Where's Dad? Dad?' Thinking Jack must be in the bedroom, Matt calls up the stairs but there's no reply. He puts his head round the lounge door and glances into the dining room. Jack isn't there.

'He can't be outside, surely?' he asks. 'It's pouring out there.'

Evan is sitting at the kitchen table, an empty milk glass and a plate with a few cake crumbs by his elbow, engrossed in a Manga version of *The Count of Monte Cristo* he found at the library.

'Evan, do you know where Grandpa is? He and I need to get going. The registry office closes at four.'

Evan looks up from his reading and around the kitchen, as if surprised Jack isn't there. He shrugs, closes his book and leaves the kitchen to go upstairs.

The door to the bedroom Jack shared with Dora for forty-three years is closed. Evan taps on it, and pushes it gently open. The bed is neatly made, but Jack isn't there. Evan checks the bathroom, but there's no one there either. He goes back downstairs.

'No sign?' asks Matt, and Evan shakes his head. 'Any idea where he might be?'

In reply, Evan takes a waterproof coat down from the rack and slips on his wellingtons.

Outside, the rain's what Grandpa calls stair-rods, hammering down from dark clouds where thunder rumbles, bouncing off the yard and running in rivulets down the lane. A muddy puddle has already formed under the gate to the home field. The air smells of lightning's sulphur and dank earth, and of the yellow leaves fallen from the hawthorn trees decaying in the grass.

His vision hampered by the huge hood on his jacket, Evan makes his way to the field gate, pulls back the latch and slips through the smallest opening he can, checking the gate is properly shut behind him as Grandpa has taught him. Hearing the click of the latch, a few sheep raise their heads from grazing and gaze at him, indifferent to his presence and to the rain, though most are pressed together in the shelter of the wall.

The field slopes upwards, and it's towards the top end Evan's heading, head down against the rain and the blasts of wind that have carried it in, towards one of the twisted hawthorn trees, and three stones set in the wall to form a stile.

Jack's there, sitting on the second step of the stile in only his shirt-sleeves, facing the view he frequently tells Evan is the best in all England, of the undulating dales and distant farmsteads, of sky that goes on forever. This is the place, he's told Evan, where he asked Grandma to marry him, and this is the place he's chosen to come when his grief is too much to bear.

When Evan reaches him, the view is obscured. The valleys

are hidden by mist and rain, and the sky's oppressive with the burgeoning clouds. Jack's face is wet from the rain dripping from his hair, but his eyes are red, and Evan knows some of the wetness is from tears.

He says nothing, but taps Jack's feet so he'll move them along the stile's bottom step and give him a place to sit. Wondering how he can offer comfort, he reaches for his grandfather's hand.

For a while they sit in silence in the rain, Evan watching how shiny the water makes the spots of lichen on the wall, Jack looking into the distance for hope he can't see.

Eventually Jack says, 'I suppose your dad's looking for me,' and Evan nods.

'I'm being silly,' says Jack. 'We have to go and record your grandma's death, make it official. But I have the feeling that until that's done, she might come back. Once they've put it in their book, there's no denying it. Dora Violet Ferrers, née Hodgson, will be no more.'

They sit a few minutes longer, and as Evan feels the truth of this sinking in, he squeezes Jack's hand tighter.

'I expect you'll stay at home, shall you, and look after your mum?' asks Jack, and Evan nods. 'Maybe your dad and I could find something good to eat in town, cheer us all up. How about some eclairs?'

Evan shakes his head. 'Eccles cakes.'

'Eccles cakes it is.' With his free hand, Jack wipes the water from his face, and climbs down from the stile. 'I shall catch my death of cold, being out here underdressed. That's what your grandma would say, isn't it?'

Evan doesn't answer, but as they walk together back across

the field, he keeps his grandpa's hand in his, trying through his fingers to send Jack as much of his own body warmth as he can, anxious Jack shouldn't catch his death of cold.

The loss of two dear people would be too much to bear.

THIRTY-FOUR

22 October

In the churchyard, the late days of autumn have robbed the trees, stripping the bronze from the horse chestnuts, the gold from the sycamores and beech. In the tower of the ancient stone church a single bell begins to toll, as Dora's coffin is carried between the crooked headstones towards the studded oak door.

The church is full. Every available seat on the polished black pews is occupied, and there are mourners standing under the medieval stained-glass windows with their scenes of saints' blessings and the rising of the dead. Jack, Matt, Claire and Evan take their reserved places at the front and the first hymn begins, the wheezy old organ always a few notes ahead of the congregation.

As the congregation sits, the vicar ascends to the pulpit and talks about Dora, about where she was born, about her sisters and her schooldays, about how all those years ago she and Jack met and fell in love. There's another hymn – 'I Vow to Thee My Country', because Dora loved the tune – and then Matt's called to read his mother's eulogy. He looks handsome and smart in his black suit, and as he walks straight-backed and solemn to the pulpit steps, Jack thinks how proud of him Dora would be.

In the end it's not the vicar's reminiscences which fell Jack's resolve not to make a fool of himself, but the realisation that his Dora's lying there in a box, unable to see or hear her son at her side. He pulls a white handkerchief from the pocket of his jacket.

Matt's hands are trembling, and as he begins to read his speech, his voice is breaking. Somehow the words come out, telling of an idyllic childhood, of help with homework and picnics by the sea and of his gratitude for all the years of diligent care.

Then he speaks of sponge cakes and splendid roses, and the one thing that defined Dora beyond all else.

'Without any doubt,' he says, 'my mother was the kindest woman who ever walked this earth.'

And Jack weeps.

Misery loves company. With Dora gone, the misery is more Jack's than Evan's, but Evan's preference for silence suits Jack's grief while his presence and need for care prevent Jack from sliding from shock and despair into suicidal depression.

In fact Evan has been a godsend, dealing capably with most of the mundane tasks relating to the farm, prodding Jack into action when he can't cope by himself to shift bales and sacks of feed. The season's growing cold, and overnight frosts have already glazed the puddles on the yard, transforming the meadows to silvery white. It won't be long before the first snowfall, and Christmas will soon be looming, when Jack knows Dora's loss will be even harder to bear.

Evan's got a new interest. After meeting Jack's distant neighbour, Helen Trewitt, he's been with Claire to visit her hives, and now spends a good part of his evenings reading books on keeping bees. Come spring, Jack's promised to think about getting a hive to see how Evan gets on.

But spring's many weeks away. In the long evenings, while Evan reads, Jack sits, sipping whisky until he slips into a doze. When Evan's bored of reading, he turns on the TV, watching cheerful vintage sitcoms and wildlife documentaries, marvelling at the wonders of the animal kingdom in places he's no wish ever to go.

THIRTY-FIVE

8 December

''Ere, Rachel!' Dallabrida's left his side of the office where he's been holding court with a handful of his mates, and he's heading for the exit via Naylor's desk. 'I bet you look good in sequins! What you wearing for this do?'

Naylor doesn't look away from her monitor, where she's perusing a list of assaults, trying to make a connection in a trio of rapes. There's a small tinsel Christmas tree on the counter near the coffee machine and glittery foil decorations have been draped round the walls, but with the kind of crimes the team are investigating, the festive spirit seems both irrelevant and lacking.

'Haven't given it a moment's thought,' she says, though that isn't true. On her last day off, she took herself shopping to buy a new dress for the occasion, a clinging red stunner featuring – as it happens – a lot of sequins. It was a momentary aberration, way out of her comfort zone, and she's thinking about returning it and finding something more decorous. Anyway, she hates the office party – this year, dinner and a DJ at an Italian eatery – and she's thinking she'll be leaving as soon as coffee's served.

'I'll be there in me best bib and tucker,' says Dallabrida. He's standing close to her and she can smell that Gucci aftershave, a scent she's beginning to think she rather likes. 'Play your cards right, I might even buy you a drink. You're a champagne lady, I bet.'

Naylor looks up at him. It's true what they say. He does have beautiful eyes.

'A glass of Chablis will do me,' she says. 'And what do you mean, bib and tucker? Sounds like a pair of overalls.'

Dallabrida laughs. 'Me, in overalls? That'll be the day! Nah, I'll be in me tuxedo and cummerbund, the works! You won't recognise me, girl, I tell you, you won't know me! So come on, are there going to be sequins, or what?'

Naylor smiles.

'If I answer that, it takes away the element of surprise,' she says, 'and you know your best friend in this line of work is the element of surprise.'

Dallabrida laughs again.

'You crack me up, you do. Anyway, I can't stand round here all day nattering, even if I might like to. Some of us got work to do.'

And with a wave, he's gone.

Though she doesn't expect it, he's rattled her concentration. For some reason she now thinks she should make an effort, maybe get her nails done and book a blow-dry.

She's taking out her phone to make the call when it rings. Ron Perdue.

'Hi, Ron,' she says. 'How's tricks?'

'Not so bad. Me and June were just indulging in that favourite pastime of the idle retired, watching the lunchtime news.'

'All right for some.'

'I don't know why we bother. It's nothing but misfortune and corrupt politicians lying through their teeth, as always. But there's just been an item on there I think you should know about. How's the Ferrers case going?'

Naylor sits up in her chair.

'Stalled. Why?'

'Well, I'm ringing you because it's a long way off your patch, and I think it'll take a while before anyone makes a connection, if there is one. And it may not be connected, but it struck me there were some distinct similarities and that you could do with jumping on it while it's red-hot.'

'What are you talking about, Ron? What's going on?'

'Looks like the same MO to me, similar age, a bus stop not far from a school. Better get Googling, Naylor, Middlewich, Cheshire. There's been another snatch.'

Déjà vu, again. Though it's still weeks away, on the Ferrerses' cul-de-sac Christmas appears to be in full swing, with sparkling trees in every window and the house-fronts festooned with LED lights and cheery Santas, waiting to be lit up when dusk falls. Even the Ferrers house seems to be in on the mood, with a wreath of holly and silver ribbon hanging on the door.

Major progress from last year, thinks Naylor. Christmas last year, they were looking at a life of never seeing Evan again.

Hagen knocks at the door, and it's opened promptly by Claire – a different Claire again, still on her way up but definitely getting there: hair nicely cut, better clothes. She smiles uncertainly when she sees them on the doorstep.

'Hello, Mrs Ferrers,' says Hagen. 'I'm sure you remember us, DS Hagen, DI Naylor.'

'Of course,' says Claire. 'Come in.'

Naylor's pleased to see the house looking better, too. There's the smell of winter spices – cinnamon and cloves – from a reed diffuser, and the place looks clean and cared for, like it did the first night they arrived. That seems a long time ago.

Claire offers them coffee, which she and Hagen accept. While the kettle's boiling, Naylor feels the need to apologise.

'I know it's been a while,' she says. 'We've no excuse to offer really, except the trail went cold and we'd nowhere else to go. And with the pressure of other work . . .'

'I understand that,' says Claire, spooning coffee into her smart white mugs. 'Of course I know budgets are tight. But those men who took Evan are dangerous, and they're a risk to everyone until they're caught. Aren't they?'

Hagen looks at his shoes and clears his throat.

'Yes, they are,' he says. 'To be honest, that's why we're here. I don't want to beat about the bush. Another young boy has been snatched.'

Claire freezes with the spoon halfway between cup and coffee jar, her eyes wide with shock.

'You're kidding,' she says. 'Another boy's gone? From Evan's school?'

'Sadly we're very far from kidding,' says Naylor. 'But he's not from this area. There's been an incident in Cheshire. You may have seen it on the news. We've been in touch with Cheshire police and there are some distinct similarities, so we're pretty sure the two cases are related. So we're here to speak to Evan,

261

to see if he can help us help this other boy. I don't need to tell you how desperate his parents are feeling.'

Coffee forgotten, Claire lays the spoon down on the counter. She shakes her head and covers her mouth with her hand.

'My God, those poor, poor people. This is terrible. How awful. How can it have happened again?'

Naylor and Hagen have no response. With no dedicated resources assigned to Evan's case and no leads from Bobby Gillard – who has persisted with his *no comment* stance – a repeat of the offence was almost inevitable, though it's in no one's interests for them to say so. They need Claire to believe or be persuaded there's a good chance now of a breakthrough, because without her co-operation, they'll never gain Evan's help. And Evan's help is absolutely essential if the new victim is to be rescued alive.

To that end, Hagen opens the leather folder he's carrying and brings out a photo, a school-uniform pose of a boy in a blue blazer, dark hair freshly barbered, a grin over slightly crooked teeth giving an air of character and cheekiness.

'This is him,' says Hagen, and Claire's eyes fill with tears. 'Liam Keslake, aged eleven.'

'Just like Evan,' breathes Claire. 'He looks so young.'

'Just like Evan. On his own at a bus stop, there one moment, vanished the next.'

'The thing is, Claire,' says Naylor, 'we're really hoping this may be enough to persuade Evan to talk to us, to give us that statement. It's been several months. How's he been doing?'

'Better,' says Claire. 'He's been doing better, but he's not right, he's not normal. He acts like a boy half his age. He lives in his own world, and he's content there, finding his way. If you go making him remember, how can it not set him back?'

Claire's right, of course, and Hagen and Naylor know it.

'We have people who are specially trained,' says Hagen. 'They tread very carefully. They'd take it at a pace comfortable for him.'

'I don't believe you,' says Claire. 'You need information, and you need it as quickly as possible. If that means riding roughshod over Evan, I think that's what you'll do.'

'Don't you think Evan will want to help, when he knows what's happened?'

Claire shrugs.

'You'd have to ask him that.'

'Can we speak to him?'

'He isn't here.'

This is a blow Naylor and Hagen aren't expecting.

'Where is he?' asks Hagen.

'He's staying with his grandfather, up in Yorkshire. He feels safe up there, and he's company for my father-in-law. My mother-in-law died recently, and my father-in-law's taken it hard. They suit each other pretty well, two damaged souls, shut away from the world. I've been up there a fair bit myself, so you're lucky to find me here, to be honest. I come back for Matt's sake. It's hardly fair on him, is it, always coming home to an empty house? But to be frank I really wouldn't be happy about you intruding on Evan, and I don't think Matt would be either.'

'Claire, I understand one hundred percent where you're coming from,' says Naylor. 'And we can't force you to do anything, we can't force Evan to help. But we would really appreciate it if you'd talk it over with Matt, see what he thinks, and maybe talk to Evan. For Liam's sake, for his family's sake. You could be key in getting to him before too much damage is done.'

'The damage is already done by now, though, isn't it?' says Claire. 'Now it's degrees of damage he might never come back from. Like Evan.'

Naylor is on the point of telling the whole truth, of telling Claire something she hasn't said before. Too much experience in cases of this kind suggests that when Evan was found, chances are he was hours away from a shallow grave, lost forever on wasteland or bleak moorland. The problem paedophile rings have with their victims is perpetual: children grow older and grow up, and no longer suit their abusers' tastes.

But Claire's been through enough, and if she hasn't thought of it herself, she doesn't need to know.

'Please, Claire,' says Naylor, and she places a contact card on the counter. 'Please talk to Matt, talk to Evan, and ring me. The sooner the better, if you don't mind.'

Back in the car, Hagen throws the folder on the back seat and starts the engine.

'That could have gone better,' he says.

'You think so? It could have been a lot worse. She might have slammed the door in our faces, and I'd have understood that. We haven't exactly been heroes in this case.'

'Not so far.' Hagen pulls away from the kerb. 'But this is a long way from over. This is another chance, another bite at the cherry.'

'We all need to stay positive, but I don't think that's how

the Keslakes would look at it, Brad,' says Naylor, and Hagen has to agree she's right.

When the phone rings, Evan is on the sofa eating his fish fingers, watching a nature programme about grizzly bears in Yellowstone National Park. Jack is in the kitchen, dumping the uneaten remains of his own meal in the bin. He's ready for a whisky, but won't allow himself to open the bottle before the clock shows 7 p.m.

It's cold at the foot of the stairs. Maybe the whole house is colder than it should be. His and Dora's battle over the central heating thermostat was a running gag between them, her turning it up, him grumblingly turning it down. The place feels chilled, and before he takes the call, he turns it up a few degrees and blows a kiss for her into the air.

'Dad? It's me.'

Jack's pleased to hear Matt's voice. Matt will indulge him in his grief, giving him a chance to reminisce, to talk about Dora, which if the truth be known, in his hurting heart of hearts is, at the moment, all he wants to do.

'How are you doing, Dad?'

'Oh, I'm all right,' says Jack, and as he says the words, tears prick his eyes. 'Soldiering on. What else can you do? I was going through a few things this afternoon, having a bit of a clear-out, but I didn't get very far. Everything I thought I should throw out, I ended up putting back in its place. Just like your mother would have done.'

'It's early days,' says Matt. 'Don't go worrying about that yet. You and I can do a bit when we come up for Christmas.'

At the prospect of Christmas, Jack sighs.

'She didn't make it, did she, bless her. It'll be a strange do without her.'

'Yes, it will. But for Evan's sake . . .'

'Oh, yes, for Evan's sake,' says Jack. 'I expect he'll want a tree.'

'We'll bring a tree. We'll bring turkey, pudding, the lot. All you have to do is sit and drink your Glenfiddich and wear a party hat. You can do that, Dad, for Mum's sake. Listen, can Evan hear what you're saying?'

'He's watching telly. I'm out in the hall.'

'Have you seen the news today?'

'We don't watch the news. You know that.'

'Well, first of all please make sure you don't, not in front of Evan. Something's happened. We've had the police round. They came to see Claire this afternoon.'

'Have they got the bastards?'

'I only wish they had. Actually, it's the opposite. Another boy's been taken.' Jack takes a deep breath and decides to sit down. 'Are you there, Dad?'

'I'm here. That's very bad news.'

'They think it's the same gang or ring or whatever they call themselves. The same ones who took Evan.'

'God help him. How old?'

'Eleven.'

Jack shakes his head.

'And does this unfortunate young man have a name?'

'Liam.'

'If I ever get near them, they'll wish they'd never been born.'

'The thing is, Dad, the police want to talk to Evan. Hardly surprising, really. They want to see if he knows anything that can help them. He must know something, after all. He might know plenty, if only he'd talk.'

'He says enough, these days,' says Jack, 'enough to get by. There's too much chatter in the world anyway, if you ask me.'

'Claire and I talked, and we think we should try and help, as one family to another. If there'd been anything anyone could have done to help us, we'd have been desperate for them to do it. We just think it wouldn't be fair to say no, for Liam's sake. For his parents' and grandparents' sake. What do you think?'

Jack considers, and as he's thinking, he believes he hears a footfall on the stairs, on the second step from the top which always creaks. He turns and looks up to the landing. No one is there.

But it makes him think of Dora and what she would say. She'd try and help, without the slightest hesitation.

'If you agree then I'll agree, but it isn't down to us, is it? It's up to Evan.'

'We think you could persuade him. We think he'll listen to you.'

'And if he says yes? Have we got to come hiking down there? I don't believe I'm up to driving all that way, not the way I've been feeling. My ticker hasn't been good. The doctor's given me some new pills.'

'They'd come up there, Dad. And either me or Claire would come too. You won't have to drive anywhere.'

Jack sighs.

'All right, I'll do my best. As long as I'm not to blame if he refuses.'

'No one's to blame for anything,' says Matt, 'except those bastards. Look on the bright side, we might see them in court yet.'

'We should see them swinging from the highest branches of the tallest tree in the land,' says Jack, 'but of course that'll never happen.'

'Never say never,' says Matt, and he laughs a laugh with little mirth. 'Will you let us know how it goes?'

'Aye, I'll keep you posted.'

Jack hangs up the phone and glances at his watch. Close on seven. A decision must be made: Glenfiddich first, or talk to Evan. The Glenfiddich should be deferred. The music on the closing credits of the nature programme is just beginning and now would be a good time, before Evan's absorbed in something else. Once Evan has focused on something these days, it can be difficult to snap him out of it. When he enters the world of grizzly bears or whales or dolphins, he seems to join the creatures there, and slip away.

He considers the thermostat and decides to leave the heating turned up till bedtime. As he heads for the lounge, he feels that strange fluttering in his heart, a palpitation his new tablets are supposed to have stopped. He stands still, waiting for it to pass, but the fluttering continues and tickles his throat, making him cough. A minute goes by, and the palpitation passes, but just when he thinks it's settled down, there's a stabbing pain in his chest which takes his breath away. It hurts, but only briefly, there and gone in a flash so he can tell himself it was nothing. Did he take his pills at lunchtime? Maybe he forgot. He should be using that special box of Dora's with the compartments for a week's worth of

268

pills, Monday through Sunday, morning, noon and night, if he could only find the motivation to sort it out.

He's so tired. As he enters the lounge, Evan shifts some of his bee books out of the way, and pats the sofa next to him for Jack to come and join him rather than sitting in his big armchair. Jack's glad to sit down, and decides he'll do the smart thing – the thing Dora would tell him to do – and skip the whisky tonight. Evan's offering him the TV remote, asking him to choose something to watch, but when Jack takes it, he switches off the set.

'I've got a better idea than telly,' he says. 'First of all, you and I have to have a bit of a chat. And after that, I think it's time we had a re-match at draughts. I seem to remember last time we played, you won, and I want a chance to reclaim my laurels. What do you say?'

Evan smiles, nods, and is going to jump up from the sofa to fetch the draught board. Jack touches his arm to stop him.

'Not so fast, ace,' he says. 'That was your dad on the phone. I'm going to tell you something now which might upset you, but much as we might not like it, sometimes upsetting things come knocking at the door. Like losing your grandma. We'd have done anything to stop that but there wasn't anything to be done. What's happened, happened, and we have to do our best and get on. Like the business when you were gone from us.'

He feels Evan stiffen, his muscles tense, and knows he might be about to run from the room.

'You must listen to me, son. There's something we have to talk about and it can't wait until we're entirely ready to face it because the world doesn't work like that. It's here and it's urgent, not for us – if it were down to me it would never be mentioned, ever, you know that – but because someone else is involved now and I think we should try and help them. But before we talk about what your dad said, you and I are going to set some ground rules, because the world might be coming looking for us but that doesn't mean to say it has to come here. This place is a special place, wouldn't you say, and I see no reason why we should let anyone in who we don't love or like or want here. Only nice people are welcome. And I'm not saying the police aren't nice people, but they deal with bad people, and we don't want anyone here either who's got any connection to anyone bad. So you and I can agree where our boundaries are. And I say, we make the stream at the bottom of the lane there our frontier. No one we don't want here crosses that. Everywhere this side of that line – this house and the barn and our fields – is sanctuary. Do you know what I mean by sanctuary?'

Evan shakes his head.

'It means a place where you can't be touched, somewhere protected by an invisible shield. This is our land. One day I hope it'll be your dad's and yours to look after, the same as my dad – your great-grandad – looked after it before me. So picture it with a great, high imaginary wall down by the stream, and that's how it's going to be. OK?'

Evan nods uncertainly.

'The thing is, son, those men who took you, they've taken someone else. A boy called Liam.'

Instantly, Evan curls into the smallest ball he can make. With both hands, he covers his face, then covers his ears instead and squeezes his eyes shut.

'Evan, you must listen to me. The police need your help to find him. You know things that could help him, could bring him home much faster than . . .' He thinks of Dora's words when Evan was found, her dismay at their negligence in not spending all their time between his leaving and returning in searching for him, in not dedicating themselves to that quest. Ever since she said that, Jack has felt the same. Why did they do nothing? Why did they rely on the authorities? 'Well, faster than you came back to us.'

Evan is crying, and Jack finds it hard to bear. He pulls Evan's hands from his ears, and hugs him close.

'I know, I know. Sssh now, ssh. There's another thing about this place of ours I forgot to say, and that is that it breeds Ferrers men who are brave as lions. When something has to be faced, we tackle it square on. Don't we, old man? Don't we? If I could do this for you, you know I would, and your dad and your mum and your grandma would have done too, but only you can do this. What they need to know is locked away in your funny old brain-box.' He taps Evan on the head. 'It's all locked away in there, and it's time for some of it to come out. They'll be nice people who'll want to talk to you, but they won't be coming here. They'll have a special place where you'll go, a safe place, and I wouldn't doubt for one second they'll be supplying all the chocolate digestives you can eat. But we have to think of that boy Liam. If we don't try and help him and help his mum and dad get him home safe, then are we good people? I think if we don't help him, we might come one day to regret it. Do you want some time to think about it?'

Tucked away under his grandpa's arm, Evan nods.

'All right then. You be having a little think and you let me know what you decide. Now, are you ready to take on your mighty grandpa at that game?'

Evan shakes his head.

'We'll save that for another time then, shall we? Is there something good to watch on the old goggle-box?'

Evan doesn't move, so Jack takes the controller and finds an episode of *Dad's Army* they've watched a couple of times before, vintage humour from an era Jack remembers well but which seems distant and out of reach, as remote in time as the dated clothes and set furnishings and even the characters. *Do people like that still exist? Did they ever? Was it a more innocent time, really?* he wonders. *Weren't the same horrors out there that are out there now?*

Evan isn't really watching; Jack can tell because he isn't laughing at the gags. Twenty minutes later, Evan reaches for the controller and mutes the sound.

There's silence between them. Then Evan says, 'I will help Liam.'

Briefly Jack closes his eyes, picturing all the drama to come, more disturbance in an already too-disturbed young life.

'That's my boy,' he says. 'My brave boy. You're doing the right thing.'

Evan says nothing else but stands and leaves him, and Jack hears him padding up the stairs in his Star Wars socks, and the creaking as he reaches the second step from the top.

That night, in the small hours, Jack hears Evan shout, in the torment of his first nightmare in several weeks. Maybe they should leave him be, let him put it all behind him. But there's

272

another boy out there, another Evan, and how could they live with themselves if they did nothing to help?

In the panic of his dream, Evan shouts again. Jack climbs from his bed and puts on his dressing gown and slippers. Opening Evan's door as quietly as he can, he finds *Biggles Delivers the Goods* on the nightstand and, by the light seeping in from the landing, begins to read.

THIRTY-SIX

10 December

From the third floor, the view from Campbell's office window is of a typical British December: wet roads in cold rain, sky a persistent, drab grey, bright, twinkling lights forcing a mood of manic festivity and panic shopping. Campbell's got all his official Christmas cards arranged on his desk, tasteful snowy scenes with generic greetings from various organisations – the Prison Officers' Association, branches of the Courts and Tribunals Service, Victim Support – and scrawled signatures with no messages. As far as Naylor can see, there isn't a personal card among them.

Campbell must be expecting a long meeting, since he's asked her and Hagen to sit down, but Naylor sees no reason it shouldn't be quick. Campbell's got a short 'to do' list by his left arm. Naylor can't read his handwriting upside down, but the items he's completed have been crossed out using a ruler.

Campbell sits back in his chair.

'So, give me some good news.'

'Liam's abduction has prompted the Ferrers family to encourage Evan to talk to us,' says Naylor. 'Of course we're hoping something will come out of that.'

'I hope so too,' says Campbell. 'How are you going to proceed?'

'We've requested a room at Harrogate station as being the nearest place to where Evan's staying with viable facilities. We might have interviewed him at home but he doesn't want that. We're thinking Rose should go with me rather than relying on North Yorks to provide someone. Women only, of course, and Evan's met me and Rose before. The fewer new faces he sees, the better.'

'Sounds good,' says Campbell. 'When will you meet?'

'We're planning to travel up this afternoon, just as soon as Rose can confirm childcare arrangements, with a view to seeing Evan tomorrow morning, as early as we can. Obviously Cheshire are pushing us to get on with it but it's not an easy situation. As we understand it, Evan's still very fragile. If we go too fast, he might clam up on us again.'

'Rose knows what she's doing,' says Campbell.

'With respect, Sir, she didn't get far last time,' says Hagen. 'I think we need to stay mindful that Evan's been highly traumatised and he may never open up, or not before we're collecting our pensions, anyway. Maybe you could advise Cheshire that we're doubtful of a result through this interview and suggest they pursue every other avenue they've got as aggressively as possible.'

'I'm sure they're already doing that. But we can hardly blame them for keeping their fingers crossed, can we?'

'As long as there's no reliance,' says Hagen. 'That's all I'm saying. The other thing to bear in mind is that the family's not exactly overwhelmed with what we did for them. Evan was only recovered by a happy accident, so I can't say I blame them. If he reacts badly, I can see them pulling the plug. We've had no resources on this case for months. Now it's all hands to the pumps again. It just feels like we're fire-fighting all the time, instead of taking a methodical approach which might have got a result.'

'I'll be sure to pass your comments on to the Chief Constable, Bradley,' says Campbell, 'but you're not saying anything I don't already know. Just do your best. And let's hope Rose and Rachel come back from Yorkshire with something we can use.'

'Is that your strategy for a fast-track promotion?' Naylor asks Hagen as they walk down the stairs. 'Telling him he's mishandling our caseload?'

'It wants saying,' says Hagen. 'How can we work like this, dropping investigations and picking them up again at a moment's notice? We need to be methodical, organised. If he'd left us on the case, we might have had a result by now and Liam Keslake might never have been taken.'

'And all those cases we've looked at in the interim would still be waiting to be assigned,' says Naylor. 'I get what you're saying, of course I do. We'll just have to make sure we use this breakthrough to nail these bastards, for all our sakes.'

THIRTY-SEVEN

11 December

Rose guides Evan into a room in the Vulnerable Witness Suite where Naylor is already waiting. The room's without windows, but it's pleasant and warm, with plush, comfortable chairs and a coffee table, and soft pink walls. There's a picture of purple heather in bloom on open moorlands and a TV on a stand with video recording equipment, but there's no intention to video anything today. The sound recording equipment is unobtrusive, and there are biscuits on the table – though no chocolate digestives – along with a can of Coke and bottled water. Naylor has brought in coffee for her and Rose. The room smells of it as Evan enters.

The three chairs are arranged with equal spacing round the table: no obvious divide.

'Come in, Evan,' Rose is saying. 'Have a seat, sweetheart.'

Naylor doesn't stand up, but turns in her chair and smiles. Evan looks much better than when she last saw him – he's put on weight and grown a little, and the anaemic pallor she remembers in his face has become a healthy pinkness, probably due in part to his embarrassment in this situation. He's better dressed too, in clothes that fit, and yet there's still something unnatural about him. Naylor knows he's twelve, but if you saw him in the street you'd take him for an oversized nine- or ten-year-old. Most kids his age want to dress older, growing up too fast. Evan seems the opposite, wearing clothes which are too young. And there's something else: he doesn't have a phone. What kid these days isn't always on a phone? But Evan's hands are empty.

'Hi, Evan,' she says. 'It's nice to see you again.'

Evan doesn't reply, but sits down next to her, Rose taking the third chair.

'You remember Rachel, I expect,' she says. 'She was with us when we spoke a few months ago.'

Very briefly, Evan looks at Naylor, before his eyes return to a spot on the floor.

'I want to start by saying thank you for coming to meet us,' says Rose. 'I think you're already aware of the reason we want to talk to you, but before we get to that I just want to emphasise that you're free to go at any time. Your mum's waiting downstairs, ready to whisk you away as soon as we're finished. But we're hoping you'll stay with us for a little while at least.'

There's no reaction from Evan, except that his foot is tapping rapidly on the floor. He looks so keyed up, so uptight, Naylor won't be surprised if he makes a run for the door. Somehow they have to secure him in place, get him settled down.

She lifts the cover of the file that's on the table. Rose won't approve of what she's about to do, but she hopes she'll understand the rationale behind it.

She slides a copy of Liam Keslake's photo under Evan's

nose. Evan glances at it, then whips his head away, as if taking a sudden interest in the picture of moorland heather. But Naylor sees his eyes come back to it. Then they're back on the floor.

'When those men took you, Evan,' says Naylor quietly, 'one of the first things we did to try and find you was to put your picture everywhere we could. Newspapers, TV, magazines, everywhere we could think of. Thousands and thousands of people saw your picture, so if they got even a glimpse of you, they'd call us. This picture is of Liam, and I'm very sorry to say we believe he's in the same place you were, not very long ago. That's why we're asking you again to talk to us about that place, difficult though we know it is for you to remember. Because you can do a good thing by talking to us, Evan. You might be the key to finding Liam, and to finding the men who hurt you, and if we can find them, we can punish them, and put them in jail for a very, very long time.'

She waits, and Rose waits with her. Evan doesn't speak.

'Please, Evan,' says Rose. 'Please help us. Please help Liam.'

The silence goes on, and on. Naylor is about to shake her head and signal to Rose that they should give up.

But then Evan speaks.

'I want to help Liam,' he says. 'But I can't.'

Rose meets Naylor's eyes, signalling her to keep quiet.

'Why do you say that, Evan?' she asks.

'Because if I tell you anything, my mum will know and my dad will know. They'll know what happened. And my grandpa.'

Tears are running down Evan's face. Rose passes him a box of tissues.

'Is that what's worrying you, Evan, your mum and dad knowing?'

Evan nods. 'Mostly.'

'Is that why you've been so quiet?'

He nods again.

There's a lump in Naylor's throat, stemming from her pity and compassion for this boy in his embarrassment, and she tries to imagine how she'd have felt at his age, with the threat of revelation of the details of the abuse hanging over her.

'You were afraid if you spoke to them, they'd ask you about it?'

He nods.

'Oh, sweetheart.' Naylor can tell that, like her, Rose is aching to put her arm round Evan, but distance must be maintained.

'That won't happen,' she says. 'We give you our word that nothing you say to us – nothing, not one word – will be discussed with your mum, or your dad, or your grandpa or anyone else who knows you. You won't have to show your face in court and you won't set eyes on those men. And when we catch them, I'll make sure your mum and dad come nowhere near the court while your case is being heard. They'll know nothing you don't choose to tell them, and if you choose for them to know absolutely nothing, then that's how it'll be. You'll be anonymous to everyone except us and the judge. How does that sound?'

Evan blows his nose.

'Could you agree to work like that, Evan?' Rose persists. 'I'm sure your mum and dad will understand. I've got kids and I know if any of them felt like you do, I would absolutely respect their wishes. Any mum and dad would. So if we talk to your mum and get her agreement, will you talk to us then?'

Evan looks at her and nods his head. *Yes*.

'I'll go and have a word with her,' says Naylor.

Claire is sitting on a hard, lime-green sofa facing a window with a view of leafless trees and melancholy sky, asking herself how their lives ever came to this. The feelings she has – of unwanted disconnection, of loss of control, of fearfulness, of deep, aching love – she's experienced before, though at a much lower pitch. She cried on Evan's first day of kindergarten, and again when he had his first sleepover, on his first trip to scout camp and when he started his last school, which in relative terms was only a short while ago, but as things have turned out, was in another life. What came after that, while he was really gone, was wholly different. That was wailing, primal grief, which put anything she's feeling today into telescopic perspective. What is it they ask in hospitals? The pain scale, one to ten. Today she'd give an eight or nine. The grief while he was gone, in the low twenties.

Now here they are, Evan's first day in the Vulnerable Witness Suite. She's fighting the instinct to run to that room, to barge in and grab her son's hand and haul him out of there, and tell those women with him to send apologies to the Keslakes but they must get through it as best they can, as she and Matt did. Evan's been through enough, God knows. He doesn't deserve to be reliving it.

He might say that for himself. He might still refuse them. But just as she's hoping that's what he'll do, the swing doors to the reception area where she's waiting open, and Naylor's walking towards her.

Evan's only been in there ten minutes. He must be refusing to speak.

Naylor gives her a smile that's a long way from her usual efficient, put-you-at-ease, I'm-in-charge professional greeting. This smile is diffident, uncertain, the same smile of empathic sympathy undertakers wear. She sits down next to Claire, slanting herself towards her, and in an unprecedented move, gives Claire's hand a squeeze.

'Are you OK?' she asks.

'Not really,' says Claire.

'There's good news,' says Naylor, and Claire thinks what's good news for Naylor is probably bad news for her, and she's right. 'He will talk to us, but only on condition . . . I'm sorry, Claire.'

'On what condition?'

'Only on condition that you and Matt stay well away from all this. He's told us why he hasn't been speaking.'

Claire has never asked herself why Evan stopped speaking. She's assumed it was down to some manifestation of shock, an understandable reaction to a horrific situation, like in the French Revolution when Marie Antoinette's hair turned white before they chopped off her head.

'This may be hard to hear,' Naylor goes on, 'but he thought the only way to stop you asking about what he went through was to keep silent. He's desperately, deeply ashamed about the abuse. It's not an uncommon reaction. But he doesn't want you to know what happened to him.'

Claire bursts into tears.

As she scrabbles in her handbag for tissues, Naylor puts a hand on her shoulder.

'I'm sorry, Claire. I'm so sorry to put you all through this. But if we're to have a chance of catching these men, this may be the only way.'

Claire dabs her eyes and blows her nose.

'What's he said, exactly?'

'He wants to know that you won't get to hear anything he has to say. That means you staying away from the trial – assuming we get that far – and not asking him anything about our meetings with him.'

'He wants to exclude us.'

'He wants to protect you, and himself. He's afraid if you get to know what he's been made to do, you'll love him less.'

Claire begins to cry again.

'That's not possible. Please tell him that's not possible.'

'I will,' says Naylor. 'And I have to say, I think his approach is the right one. Trust me. Some things it really is better not to know. What he wants from you is acceptance of his need to keep this private, between him and us.'

Claire wipes her eyes again.

'I don't know what Matt will say. All he talks about is our day in court. He wants to know who did it. He wants to kill them.'

'Better he's not there, then. But I have to ask you to trust us to guide Evan through this process, to take a step back. To just be his mum and dad and leave the crime and punishment to us. Can I tell him you'll do that? I know how hard it is, Claire. I really do.'

'Is that what he wants?'

'It's what he needs.'

'There's no choice, then, is there? OK.'

Naylor pats Claire's shoulder.

'Thank you. So on that basis, we're going to talk to him now. Probably not too long. We'll be taking it at his pace, and if he becomes at all distressed, we'll stop. Why don't you go and find yourself a cup of coffee in the cafeteria, and plan to be back here in an hour or so? The latte's not bad if that's your thing. I've got your mobile. If we need anything, I'll give you a call.'

When Naylor leaves her, Claire visits the sanitised toilets and splashes cold water on her face. She doesn't want Evan to know she's been crying, but with a lipstick top-up and a line of eye pencil she doesn't look bad. No one interrupts her while she's in there, so she thinks it would be a good place to have a private conversation with Matt.

When he picks up, she can hear noise in the background, the hiss of a coffee machine, a cashier's voice asking for money.

'It's me,' she says. 'Can you talk?'

'I'm in Costa. I've been thinking about you both. How's it going?'

She gives him a précis of her conversation with Naylor. When she stops talking, Matt doesn't speak.

'What do you think?' she presses him.

'I get it,' he says, and then with the phone held away from his mouth, he says *Thank you* to the barista. 'I get what he wants and I get why, but we'll be so in the dark.'

In the dark.

As soon as the words are said, they resonate with them both, how appropriate they are for the place their son has been.

'Maybe they're right,' says Claire. 'We're not the people to bring him back. They know what they're doing, and we've just been floundering.'

'I don't know about that.' She hears him take a gulp of his coffee. 'I think he's doing OK, considering where he's been.'

'I worry this will set him back, making him relive it.'

'Or maybe it'll help him come to terms with it. A bit of therapy. And anyway, if he gets set back, we'll just bring him forward again.'

'I wish you were here.'

'So do I,' says Matt. 'Will you ring me later, let me know how he is?'

'Of course.'

'We can do this, you know. We got him back, and that's all that matters.'

A few short months ago, Claire would have questioned that. Now, she thinks he's right.

'I'd better go,' she says. 'I'll talk to you later.'

'Love you,' says Matt.

Jack's taken advantage of Evan's rare absence to pay a visit to Helen Trewitt, his bee-keeping neighbour. He takes the Freelander to the bottom of the Trewitts' lane, but finding the gate closed, he parks up on the rough ground, and sets off to walk up to the house. The day is bright, biting cold, and Jack feels every breath of frigid air deep in his lungs. A third of the way up the track, he stops to rest, telling himself it's to get a look at Andrew Trewitt's Blackface ram. A few paces further on, he feels the need to stop again, fighting against a rising feeling of nausea. The track's somehow grown in length since he was last here – how is that possible? – but only months ago he ran up here like a young man. By the time he reaches the farmyard, he's feeling very unwell, fighting for breath and his heart-rate unsteady.

Pulling himself together as best he can, he knocks at the farmhouse door.

'Jack! Come in!' Helen's always welcoming, but she takes one look at Jack and makes him sit down.

'Are you all right?' she asks. 'I'll make a cup of tea.'

'A glass of water,' says Jack, hunting in his pockets for his tablets and inhaler, but he's left them in the glove-box of the Freelander.

'Tea's good for everything,' says Helen, and she finds fruit-cake to up Jack's blood sugar. 'I don't know why you didn't drive up. At our age, who wants to be slogging up that track? How are you anyway, Jack? How are you getting on?'

'I miss her,' he says, repressing the pricking tears, as he seems to do constantly these days. 'It isn't easy, not easy at all. But I'm soldiering on, for Evan's sake.'

'He's a worthwhile project, that boy.' Helen pours tea and cuts the fruitcake. A cat lying on the windowsill above the Aga gets up from its blanket, turns round and settles back to sleep. 'He's a credit to you, Jack, he really is.'

Jack tells her about the police intervention and how he fears a backward step.

'I wouldn't be too worried,' says Helen. 'It had to come sometime. They were always going to need some kind of statement, and it might do him good to actually talk about it. It's not good to keep things bottled up.'

Jack doesn't agree, though he doesn't say so. He has no wish to know what Evan went through.

'Anyway, we're thinking about Christmas now,' he says, 'and I've been wondering what to get the lad. Thanks to you he's very taken with the idea of bees, so I thought I might get him one of those outfits, you know, the white overalls and the mask.'

Helen laughs.

'A bee-suit. That's a very good idea.'

'It is if you'd agree to tutor him a bit before we get a hive. Bees are well outside my remit. Would you take him under your wing, Helen, show him the ropes?'

'It'd be my pleasure,' says Helen.

'And where would I get one of these bee-suits? I don't suppose you've one to fit him?'

''Fraid not. But you could get one off the internet.'

Jack waves a dismissive hand.

'We don't have anything to do with technology at our house. Dora and I, we're . . . At least, I'm too old a dog to learn that new trick. I could ask Matt, I suppose.'

'Would you like me to get one for you?'

Jack smiles.

'Mrs Trewitt, you're a godsend. If you wouldn't mind, that would be champion. I'll leave you some cash to pay for it.'

Helen laughs.

'Pay me when it arrives. And would you like me to wrap it for you?'

Jack smiles again.

'You read my mind. Dora always did all the wrapping and labelling. To be honest, I wouldn't know where to start.'

'You're an old dinosaur, the same as Andrew,' says Helen. 'He can lamb two hundred ewes, but reckons he couldn't wrap a box of chocolates.'

'It's the male temperament.'

'It's laziness. But under the circumstances, you deserve a break. I'll give you a ring when it arrives.'

Jack finds the going easier on the way back down, but still takes it steady. In this direction, the view's spread before him, familiar yet unique in its changeability. Isn't that what Dora used to say, never the same view twice? And it's true: the light, the colours, the sky mean that though there are constants in the land and its features – the walls, the valleys, the track-ways – everything else is always changing, an eternal dance of infinite variety.

Close to the gate, he looks across the valley towards the gritstone edge at Ainsclough Top. It's a bleak spot from here, a castle on its hill, a bastion as he described it to Evan, and he wonders about him and how he's getting on. Then he thinks how empty the house will feel when he arrives back there, how there'll be no one in the kitchen to make him a cup of tea or hear how he got on with Helen.

Maybe he shouldn't go home quite yet. Maybe he should drive into town and buy a paper. Maybe he'll find something for Evan there, a little treat to welcome him back. So, climbing into the car, he turns it round, but instead of heading up his own lane, he stays on the road, leaving Ainsclough Top to its own brooding isolation.

The lanes are dark and slushy with the remains of winter's first snow, which melts on contact with the roadside puddles and is too wet to make an impact on the tarmac. Claire wonders if Evan's sleeping, but he's still and quiet much of the time these days, and stillness and silence are indicators of nothing.

The headlamps light familiar landmarks. A stand of trees too large to be a copse but not quite big enough to be a wood – which Evan knows is a perfect place to look for owls – looms up out of the dusk, just before the lopsided milestone Jack says has been there three hundred years, its guidance – *Harrogate 27 miles* – barely readable for its covering of moss.

Beyond the milestone, Claire makes the turn across the stream, on to the track up to the house, and Evan stirs, sits up and looks about him, as if he feels it's safe to come back to life.

Jack's been dozing on the sofa, and the fire's burned low. Rousing himself when he sees the headlights on the wall and hears the crunch of stones under tyres, he crosses to the hearth, chooses a couple of good-sized logs and drops them on the embers. The dry bark pops and crackles, and smoke begins to rise. He closes the curtains and, making his way into the kitchen, turns on the light.

'We brought fish and chips, Grandpa!'

Evan's laying the paper-wrapped parcel on the table, and heading to the cupboard for plates.

Jack smiles.

'Did you now? And what kind of fish have you brought for yourself? Not those sausagey ones, I hope?'

'Mum said I could have three.'

'Well, your mother's madly irresponsible.'

He resists the strong urge to ask about how the day's gone or make any reference to it at all, except for a slight raising of the eyebrows in Claire's direction. She signals with a slight nod of the head, *OK*, but she's marvelling at Evan, at how now he's home – for this surely is his home, now – he's a different child to the one he is in the outside world.

Evan's loading up the plates, pouring mushy peas on to his own.

'I'm watching you,' says Jack. 'Don't you be snaffling my chips!'

They eat at the kitchen table, Evan dousing his food in vinegar and dipping his chips in ketchup.

'You never used to like vinegar,' says Claire.

'It's Grandpa's fault,' says Evan. 'He puts vinegar on everything.'

'Apple cider vinegar's very good for you,' says Jack. 'And very good for livestock too, as I've shown you.'

'Is Sarson's made from apples, then?' asks Claire. 'I didn't know that.'

'Not Sarson's, no,' Jack admits. 'Sarson's is made of stronger stuff, to put hairs on your chest.'

'I don't think Mum wants hairs on her chest,' says Evan.

'I really don't,' Claire agrees.

Jack winks at Evan, and adds a dash more vinegar to his plate.

'I went shopping this afternoon,' he says. 'I bought you a present.'

Evan's eyes light up.

'What is it?'

'When you've finished your tea, you can go in the parlour and have a look.'

But Evan won't wait; he jumps down from the table and runs to the lounge.

In front of the window there's a Christmas tree, of modest size, but scenting the room with pine, and on the floor in front of it, a box of decorations, another of lights.

Jack and Claire hear him yelp his delight.

'It's just a few baubles,' says Jack. 'I didn't feel inclined to be blundering about in the loft. Dora's got quite a collection up there, as you know, but I thought we'd leave those till next year.' Claire feels for him, respecting the rawness of his grief, the difficulties of the approaching season, and she's relieved he hasn't taken himself up into the attic with no one to help. 'I'm afraid we'll be busy this evening. I'm sorry, Claire. You must be tired.'

'I really don't mind,' she says. 'A little weariness I can cope with. But you look tired yourself. Are you all right?'

'Oh, yes, don't worry about me,' Jack says. 'I haven't been sleeping so well, these last few nights. But now this business is behind us for today, maybe we can relax. Evan! Come back in here and finish your tea!'

As they're walking into the incident room, Hagen's rallying the troops.

'Gather round, people! We need to come up with an action plan fast!'

The team don't need asking twice. They're keen to hear the news from Harrogate, whether there's been any breakthrough after Evan's interview.

'Someone ring upstairs and tell Mr Campbell's PA he might want to join us,' says Hagen.

As Dallabrida makes the call, Naylor dumps her handbag and phone on her desk, and finds pens for writing on the whiteboard.

The team's pulling up chairs, making seats out of desktops. In a couple of minutes Campbell comes hurrying in, and the loud chatter in the room becomes more stilted. Campbell perches on the corner of a table and folds his arms, trying to look relaxed. Dallabrida finds himself a seat near the front, and gives Naylor a wink as he sits down.

'So,' says Naylor, 'good news and bad news. The very good news is, Rose did a first-class job in persuading Evan to finally speak to us.' A murmur goes round the room. 'Obviously he's still in a fragile state, but to have anything at all from him is a major step forward. The less good news is that what he could give us was very limited. From the moment of the snatch he was given drugs – given how he says they made him feel, we're guessing Diazepam or something of that nature to gain compliance – but that's affected his memory and his perception of his surroundings. So what there is is minimal.'

She uncaps a red whiteboard pen.

'I'm afraid I won't need much room to write down what we've got. He was kept mainly in one room, with very restricted access to a bathroom. All he knows about where he was is that it was on a high floor of some building, he thinks a block of flats. A room with a view, as it turns out, because on the few occasions he could look out, he could see a river with two bridges which we're hoping might narrow it down.'

'So you've no idea even what town he was in?' asks Hagen.

'Not so far, no,' says Naylor. 'So that'll be Job One for someone – Brad, I'm looking at you – to come up with a list of towns that might fit the bill and print off some pictures of the bridges, see if he can identify which ones match his view.'

'Does he know how far he was driven from where he was snatched?' asks Campbell.

'Not really,' says Naylor. 'A long way, he says, but anywhere would feel a long way in the boot of a car.'

'Colour of car?'

'Maybe light blue or silver.'

'Make?'

'No idea.'

'Direction of travel? North, south?'

'Doesn't know, except there was a long stretch of motorway.'

'What about his abusers?'

'Several men were regular visitors. We had him look at some photos but we got no hits. All white, one with red hair. He describes them all as old, but to a boy his age that could mean anything over twenty-five.'

'So the redhead could be the one who was at the petrol station?'

'Very likely.'

'Names?'

'He says they used what sounded like code names, not their real names.'

'So what you're saying is, all we've got is a flat overlooking a river?'

'And two bridges.'

'That's it?'

'That's it for now. But we're hoping now he's not actively repressing it, there'll be plenty more coming back to him.'

THIRTY-EIGHT

12 December

Hagen's booked a conference room for the meeting, and connected a laptop to a screen up front, projecting a blank Google search screen with several windows open behind it. Campbell, Hagen and Rose are already seated round the table, set for the long haul with coffee and biscuits, notepads and pens and an old-school *Road Atlas of Britain* Campbell's fetched from his car.

When Naylor arrives, she's out of breath from hurrying, her hair damp from running through the rain.

'Sorry,' she says. 'I was talking to Cheshire. In a nutshell, they've nothing new to report and they're desperate for us to come up with something from this. The press is all over them. The *Sun*'s running a piece on their Chief Constable's alleged crazy budgeting priorities. Apparently he authorised hundreds of thousands to be spent on a crack-down on speeding last year, and they're questioning why that money wasn't spent on catching paedophiles. Unfortunately for him, there might be a case to answer.'

'Let's get started then, shall we?' says Campbell, leaning forward to take a biscuit. 'Bradley, why don't you kick off by showing us what you've found?'

'Well,' says Hagen, 'all I did really was Google every way I could think of for twin bridges over rivers. I restricted it to UK cities and major towns because the high-rise view excludes everything else, on the principle you don't get high-rises outside urban areas. Here, for example.'

He clicks on the tab for one of the open windows. The screen fills with an attractive image of two bridges over a wide river.

'This is the Tamar Bridge in Plymouth, alongside the Royal Albert rail bridge, running between Cornwall and Devon. I think we should rule this out for two reasons. First, the settlements with a view of the bridges are mostly full of private houses and in no way fit Evan's description of the place he was held. No sign of high-rises anywhere. Also, if you look here, you can see a third stone-built bridge just up-river, so I think if this were the place, Evan would have mentioned three bridges, not two. And it's not a conclusive point but Plymouth's a heck of a way from Pontefract.'

Campbell is nodding.

'That's not it. Are we all agreed? Let's move on.'

Hagen opens up another tab. The landscape on this photograph is more urban, and again shows two bridges running over a wide stretch of water.

'Rochester in Kent, a road and a railway bridge crossing the Medway. You can see in this area here, there are blocks of flats which might fit the description.'

'Kent,' says Naylor. 'It's near London, and not too far from the abduction site. That's a big tick for me.'

'Those blocks of flats, though,' says Rose. 'They're low-rise rather than high-rise. I got the impression from Evan he was on a really high floor.'

'He didn't really know, though, did he?' Hagen puts in. 'I say this one's a possibility.'

'I agree,' says Campbell. 'How many of these possibles are there, Bradley?'

Hagen glances at his notes.

'Seven in total, Sir. But I think good possibilities, maybe three or four.'

'Carry on, then,' Campbell says.

There's a lengthy discussion on Manchester, where two or even three sites look like possibilities.

'Plus it's not far from where Liam was taken,' Hagen says.

'That's a daunting prospect,' says Rose. 'Just look at all those flats.'

'Doesn't that make it all the more probable?' asks Naylor. 'Sadly for us.'

'It's in,' says Campbell. 'We'll make use of Greater Manchester intelligence. Next.'

A new picture appears on the screen.

'Sunderland,' Hagen says. 'Same set-up as Rochester, a road and a rail bridge running parallel. And plenty of high-rises to go at.'

'Yep,' says Campbell. 'Next.'

'Newcastle,' says Hagen. 'Same again. The good news is with this one, the bridge has that distinctive green arch, which Evan's likely to remember.'

'Got it,' says Campbell. 'Next.'

'This is the last one,' says Hagen. 'Glasgow. I've put this one in as an aerial view, because to my mind it's like London. There may be too many bridges. If you could see bridges, chances are you'd see more than two.'

Naylor looks sceptical.

'I'm not sure. If you were in those flats down the bottom there, you might only see one, but from those on the far bank, you'd see . . . It's impossible to say without going there and taking in the view. I think it has to be in.'

'So where does that leave us?' Rose asks.

'We've got five possibles,' Hagen says. 'Glasgow, Manchester, Sunderland, Newcastle and Rochester.'

'I love the way you say Newcastle,' Rose smiles. 'New*cas*tle.'

'There has to be a plan,' Hagen says. 'We don't have the resources to go charging off to all points of the compass on the off-chance we'll find the right room with the right view.'

'Too right,' says Campbell.

'We have to narrow it down,' Naylor says. 'I think the only way to proceed is to print off a montage of all of these places from as many angles as we can find and run them by Evan. Even if he only rules a couple out, it'll be something.'

'Just pray he rules out Manchester and Glasgow,' says Hagen, 'though I have a horrible feeling those are the ones that he'll leave in.'

'God help us then,' says Campbell.

'I think I should go back up there and talk to him again,' Rose says. 'If I go armed with photos, there's a good chance he might help us nail down a location. It's a question of coaxing him to remember but without pressing him too hard.'

'Any more you can get from him will be a bonus,' says Naylor, 'and a level of certainty on the location would be phenomenal. But I'm not sure we can rely on the quality of the pictures we've got here. No offence, Brad. They're from the wrong angles, not at all how Evan would have seen the bridges.

We need something better. Might it be worth contacting local councils, Chambers of Commerce, planners, rail operators, anyone we can think of, to see if they can help with publicity shots, stuff like that?'

'Great idea,' says Hagen. 'Pity we haven't got time to get people out there with drones. We need a portfolio for each place, with the bridges from every possible angle. Rachel, why don't you and Rose take a town each, and maybe we can requisition someone to do another. I'll do two since I had a head start.'

'A vote of thanks is due to you, Bradley, for your hard work on this one so far,' says Campbell. 'And let's make this our priority, so Rose has got something useful and solid to take with her by the time she has to leave.'

THIRTY-NINE

15 December

A few days before Christmas. In the red light of the Christmas tree and the fire, Evan, Jack and Claire are watching a programme about bygone children's television, a countdown of the most popular programmes from the last fifty years.

Jack remembers most of them well, and Claire remembers many. For both of them, it's enjoyable nostalgia, and Evan's amused by the bright and imaginative characters he's never met before, and incredulous at the sometimes poor quality of the animations and the occasional oddness of what passed in his mother and grandpa's days as youthful entertainment.

They pass through many well-remembered theme tunes – *Andy Pandy, Captain Pugwash, Tales of the Riverbank, Noggin the Nog* – until a piece of familiar, cheerful music fills the room.

'Oh, I used to love this!' says Claire. 'Every tea-time, just before the news.'

On the screen there's a little girl puppet with a bow in her hair, and a shaggy-coated dog zipping about. Moments later, they're joined by a purple-faced puppet on a spring, and a slow-moving rabbit whose eyes droop as if he's been smoking dope.

'*The Magic Roundabout*,' the announcer is saying, 'was one of the most popular children's programmes ever to hit Britain's screens. With its zany mix of loveable characters – including Dougal the dog and Florence, Mr Rusty the organ grinder, Brian the snail and jack-in-the-box Zebedee with his nightly sign-off – viewers were entertained . . .'

Evan reaches out and touches his mother's arm.

Claire looks at him.

'Evan? Are you OK?'

His face appears frozen, as if he's glimpsed something which has scared him very badly.

'What is it, sweetheart?'

Evan says nothing, but seems to have lost all interest in the TV. He picks up one of his bee books and opens it on his knee, but Claire can tell he isn't seeing the page.

The programme runs on, and Evan never turns the page of his book, never jumps up to throw more logs on the fire.

When the programme ends, Claire feigns a brightness she isn't feeling.

'Shall I make some hot chocolate?' she asks, but Jack prefers his whisky and Evan shakes his head. 'Well, I want some,' she says, and goes to the kitchen, but as she's finding a mug and milk, she hears the lounge door open, and a few moments later, the creak of the second stair from the top, as Evan retreats in silence to his room.

FORTY

17 December

Claire manages a smile as Rose leads Evan away, back into the cocooned rooms of the Vulnerable Witness Suite, trying to find the *he'll be fine* optimism she relied on in his early primary school days, not finding it in this non-parallel situation. Back then, there were other mums to call, plenty to occupy her mind. Now she sits down on the lime-green sofa and tries not to be resentful, not to think how, as Evan's in here, other women's children are preparing for Christmas, rehearsing school plays, shopping with friends. Living normal lives. She thinks back to the days when Evan was small, to the excitement of Christmas Eve, to hanging stockings and putting out reindeer food, the shrieks and laughter on opening presents, the delight he took in looking out of the window for Santa Claus.

Times change.

Times do change. This time last year, Evan appeared to be lost to them forever, and life seemed a burden in every way. Now she's living again for her son, at a time when his friends – boys like Stewie – are cutting the ties. She and Evan are bound together more tightly than ever, and she must try and encourage him back into a world he's no wish to rejoin.

She has her cross to bear, but it's surely much lighter than it was before he came back, and looked at from some angles, it's no burden at all. This Christmas, that dreadful weight has passed over, to a family named Keslake she hopes never to meet.

Better by far to be sitting on this sofa than to be Mrs Keslake, weeping and desperate to know where her son is. Looking at it that way, Claire's glad to be here, appreciating that there are far, far worse places she might be.

The room's the same as last time – same soft chairs, same biscuits on the table, same picture on the wall – but the woman with Rose is different, a quietly smiling woman from Social Services whose name Evan can't recall.

'Thanks for coming back, Evan,' says Rose. 'Sit down wherever you like. Have you been OK since we talked?'

Evan nods. Rose thinks he looks a little pale, as if he might not have slept well.

'All we want to ask you to do today is have a look at some photographs.'

Evan stiffens, and Rose knows he's thinking of the offender portfolio, a nightmare gallery of men who'd trouble anyone's dreams.

'They're pictures of bridges today, Evan. We've tried to narrow down the town where you might have been held. With the description you gave us, we've come up with some possibilities. Even if you can't tell us for sure that we're on the right track, if you can say that some definitely aren't the place, that's a help in itself. What I'm saying is, a no is as useful as a yes. So will you have a look?'

Evan nods again. He's retreated into silence, and that troubles her, since it's likely to be their interview that's set him back. At the same time, she's a realist, and knows that can't be helped. Getting to Liam Keslake is the number one driver now.

They've all done their best to find high-quality photos from every possible angle. She agreed to take Manchester, and since they're the ones she's most familiar with, she decides to show them first.

She lays out six pictures of bridges, some over the canal, some over the river. Evan seems willing to co-operate and leans forward to get a good look, but she can see from his expression there's no recognition there.

He shakes his head.

Next, the Tyne Bridge in Newcastle with the High Level Bridge behind. There's actually a third bridge in between them, but from many angles you wouldn't know. There are four photos of these bridges, and Evan studies them for a while.

'Might it be these, Evan?' asks Rose.

'I don't know,' says Evan. 'Maybe. I'm not sure.'

'We'll leave this town in as a possibility, then.'

She moves on to Glasgow, but he rejects the pictures out of hand.

'That's not it. The river didn't look like that.'

Knowing Campbell will be pleased to have both Manchester and Glasgow in the reject pile, Rose moves on.

Sunderland. Again, he considers for a while.

'Maybe.'

'OK. This place?'

She shows him pictures of Rochester. She has to admit, she's finding this tricky herself. One bridge looks very much like another after a while, and the rivers they cross look almost identical.

He shakes his head.

'I don't know.'

'But it could be?'

'Yes.'

'Thanks, Evan. That's very helpful, very helpful indeed. Is there anything you'd like to ask me or tell me, anything you might have remembered since we last talked?'

She's expecting the standard answer – no – and so is taken aback when he says, 'Yes.'

'Oh. Great. What is it? What would you like to tell us?'

'I watched a programme,' he says hesitantly. 'It was about kids' TV, old-fashioned stuff from years ago. The characters on this one programme . . . I recognised the names, like they'd pinched them to use as code names or avatars or something. They thought using them was funny. I suppose they did it so we wouldn't know who they really were, if we ever got out.'

There's a prickling on the back of Rose's neck.

'What was the programme, Evan?'

'Something about a roundabout. It had this really annoying music.'

She frowns, casting her mind back to childhood.

'One called himself Mr Rusty, the one with red hair,' says Evan. 'There was Dylan and Florence.'

'*The Magic Roundabout*,' says Rose. 'They called themselves characters from *The Magic Roundabout*.'

'I didn't get it at first,' says Evan. 'But they kept saying the names on this programme, and I realised what was going on.'

304

'That's fantastic, Evan,' says Rose. 'I'll pass that on to the team. Thank you.'

He looks down at the table.

'Will it help you find Liam?' he asks, quietly. 'That's why I told you.'

'I hope so, sweetheart,' says Rose. 'Everything you tell us – like the bridges and the names just now – is a piece in a jigsaw. And the more pieces we have in that jigsaw, the clearer the picture becomes.'

He nods his understanding.

'There're some other things.'

Beside her, the woman from Social Services leans forward to speak, but Rose forbids her with her hand.

Evan's foot begins to tap the floor, and he starts looking around the room, doubtful if he should go on.

'This place is safe, Evan,' says Rose. 'Whatever you say is secret between us, until you say it's not.'

Evan's remembering what Jack said to him, about lion-hearted Ferrers men.

He thinks about leaving school that day, for the last time ever, when he was in the final few minutes of normal life, unaware of the fact, so unprepared.

He finds a blur of a memory, him and Stewie crossing the school playing field, sharing a Kit-Kat. No, that wasn't the right day; the day he's remembering was warm and sunny and they weren't wearing their blazers. They were heading home for tea, chicken nuggets or whatever. Home like it used to be, a cosy, welcoming place, when he still believed in the existence of safe havens.

The day he was taken, the memories are distorted. Sepia

305

photographs of smiling boys, silver cups with purple ribbons, the school smells of changing rooms and the canteen. The shock of a hand over his mouth, the terror and the crying. Those memories are a giant stain, a spill of darkness which wiped out everything before.

He closes his eyes, remembering the blackness of that first confinement. When he opens them, he focuses on the picture of the purple heather, making himself think of the peaty scent of the moors in August bloom.

'They put in me in different cars,' he says. 'They kept changing cars and sometimes the driver. One of them had tattoos.'

'What kind of tattoos?'

'I couldn't see very well. It was really dark by then. I saw them on his neck when he gave me a drink. I drank it and then they made me get back in the boot. I was really cold and shivering. Sometimes I could hear music on the radio, and sometimes I could hear them talking, but only bits.'

The woman from Social Services looks close to tears.

'Is there anything you can remember them saying from that day they took you?' asks Rose. 'Anything about where you were going?'

Evan looks down at the table, thinking.

'Only strange things. I think they must have given me drugs in the drink. One of them was talking about someone who'd bought a spider. I don't like spiders. It made me think there might be spiders in the boot.'

Rose shudders.

'I don't like spiders either. You've done really, really well, Evan. Shall we finish for today?'

'Will you let me know when you find Liam?' Evan asks.

'I'll let you know personally,' Rose promises.

As she's gathering up her folder, she recalls something which struck her.

'When you were talking about the names – Mr Rusty and Brian – you said *we*, Evan. *So we wouldn't know.* Are you saying you weren't alone in this place?'

Evan doesn't want to be misleading.

'I don't know,' he says. 'I never saw any other children. It could have been next door, or in the room above. It was just that sometimes, I thought I could hear a girl crying.'

As they drive away from Harrogate police station, Claire represses all the questions she'd like to ask, which are essentially no more than social niceties – how did you get on, are you OK? Those are questions none of them must ask, which she, in one way, welcomes, since she certainly wants no details of the conversations in that room. And she appreciates it's a relief to Evan to know that once he's left the police station, the subject isn't coming back, at least not today. Not until the phone rings again with another request for him to attend.

She's feeling the pressure easing off, an end-of-term lightness of no immediate obligations.

'What shall we do now?' she asks. 'Shall we go and get something to eat? And how about some Christmas shopping? You could get something for Dad and Grandpa.'

It's a long shot. Evan's still uncomfortable in public places, but to her surprise, he shrugs OK. She finds parking on Montpellier Hill, and as they walk together across the park, she notices he's not clinging to her as much as he usually does when they're out, maybe because he can see across the open grassy space who's close by and make his own assessment of threats, unsurprisingly finding none in an elderly couple and a woman walking a pair of dachshunds.

The dachshunds make him smile. As they cross the road to Bettys Tea Rooms, she feels Evan draw closer, seeking protection from the strangers they're passing on the pavement. But still, Harrogate's not like down south with its overcrowded supermarkets, its bustling high streets and dense traffic. There's no need here to get too close to anyone he might want to avoid, and there's plenty of space to step away from anyone who might remind him of people he's trying to forget.

As Claire's hoped, the tea room is an oasis of gentility, like opening a door into another time, a time she can't herself remember of good manners and polite hospitality. Above all, it feels confidently, unthreateningly safe, a storybook place where nothing worse could possibly happen than that you might spill tea on one of the starched tablecloths. The air is sweet with chocolate and mince pie spices, and she senses Evan relax and dare to take a step away from her, putting an almost normal distance between them.

A waitress dressed in a high-necked blouse and white apron leads them to a table. Evan orders hot chocolate and – loving the name – a Fat Rascal scone. Claire chooses Ceylon Blue Sapphire tea and a slice of lemon curd torte. Their table has a view of the road along the edge of the park, and as they eat and drink, the woman with the dachshunds passes by.

'I'd like a dog like that,' says Evan, and it strikes Claire that in that throw-away remark there's an aspiration, an im- agining of a future for himself she wouldn't have seen in him six months ago. She sees, too, that he's relishing his food, spooning up whipped cream and chocolate flakes from his tall glass of chocolate, carefully buttering each piece of his giant scone, rather than shovelling it in unaware as he did when he first came back. Food then was no more than fuel to him, a matter of survival, something to be consumed as fast as possible in case there was no more where it came from, with the thought surely constantly hanging over him that any meal might be his last.

Suddenly, she feels the magnitude of her gratitude for being here with him. If she dared, she'd reach across the table and touch his adolescent, long-fingered hand, which she notices is starting to resemble Jack's hands, a little reddened from all weathers, a little calloused from hefting feed-sacks and forking hay and straw. A country boy's hand. But she daren't touch him; there's something still about him – and maybe always will be – of wariness, of distance. Any contact is on his terms, to be instigated by him. It's a privilege that he sometimes feels safe enough to touch her shoulder or her arm.

As she's paying the bill, Evan beckons her to the counter display of glorious confection, and points to the Fat Rascals.

'Grandpa,' he says.

The counter assistant bags one up, and gives it to Evan to take home.

They wander companionably along wide streets with the open space of the park to one side, looking into shop windows which are marvels of seasonal magic: twinkling lights, gold baubles and glitzy tinsels, ribbon-wrapped parcels, fairies, reindeer and elves.

Evan stops at the window of a gentlemen's outfitters, where there's a display of ties in bold and interesting patterns. Claire lets him take his time to choose one for Matt, and offers him money so he can pay. He's reluctant to go alone to the till, and she doesn't force him but leaves him by the door while she goes herself, turning round two or three times to make sure he's still there. When she does so, she finds him looking back at her for reassurance, holding his bag from Bettys, a picture of innocence whose innocence is lost.

Along the street, there's a toy shop. Evan wants to go in, and wanders for a while among the displays, picking up toy cars and wooden puzzles, scanning the shelves of games, checking out the latest Lego, pulling out books whose titles intrigue him. Maybe he's moving on here, too; Claire notices the books he's looking at are young adult, more zombie and science fiction than Biggles, but when she offers to buy him one, he declines.

Instead, he leads the way upstairs, to a room filled with jigsaws.

'Grandpa might like one of these,' he says, and Claire agrees. A jigsaw might be good for all of them – companionable, quiet, absorbing. Healing.

'Which one do you think?'

Evan is drawn to a cartoon picture of a summery farm, with chickens sitting on a broken-down tractor, a sheepdog that looks like Millie failing to round up a fluffy flock of escaping sheep, a red-faced farmer being chased by a snorting bull.

He points to the farmer.

'That looks like Grandpa,' he says, and Claire laughs.

'It does a bit,' she says, 'but don't tell him so.'

From the toy shop they go on to buy wrapping paper, mince pies and some toffee for Matt.

As they wander back to the car, Claire's all but forgotten the reason they came to Harrogate, but she suspects that, despite his good humour, Evan has not.

FORTY-ONE

18 December

'So,' says Campbell to the team gathered in front of him. 'Let's put our heads together and see what we've got. Rose, can you update us on what Evan said about the bridges and let's take it from there?'

Rose stands up.

'Cautiously good news,' she says. 'Evan ruled out two of the most troublesome possible locations, Manchester and Glasgow.'

'That's a great relief,' says Campbell. 'Trying to nail down a riverside flat in Manchester or Glasgow would have been a logistical nightmare. So where does that leave us?'

Rose glances down at her notes. 'We've still got Newcastle, Sunderland and Rochester. There were a couple of other things. He remembers being given a drink and feeling confused afterwards, so that may be how any narcotics were administered. On the original snatch, he recalls a man with tattoos, and overhearing a conversation about spiders.'

'Spiders?' Naylor frowns. 'Sounds like the drugs kicking in.'

'There's one very troubling thing he said, I'm afraid. Evan believes there was another child being held alongside him.'

'Oh crap,' says Hagen.

'He thought he could hear a child crying,' Rose goes on. 'Probably a girl. It could, as he says, have been in another flat, but we can't rule out the possibility that we have other victims in the location.'

'Wherever it turns out to be,' says Dallabrida.

'Absolutely,' says Rose. 'And one last thing I think you'll find interesting. He had his memory jogged by something on TV the other day – which is a good thing in itself, because it suggests he's letting his memories come back. I don't know how useful this might be at this stage, but he says the men in the flat used nicknames for themselves. Characters from *The Magic Roundabout*.'

There's laughter as those old enough to remember recall the programme and do impressions.

'You know what,' says Dallabrida, 'there's an actual Magic Roundabout in Swindon. That's what they call it. I've been round it, and it's a soddin' nightmare, traffic coming at you from all sides.'

'Is that true, Leon?' asks Naylor.

Dallabrida winks.

'Would I lie to you?' he says.

But Campbell is frowning.

'Just a thought,' he says. 'Bit of a wild card. If there's a Magic Roundabout in Swindon, might there be one in Newcastle, or Rochester or Sunderland?'

Hagen picks up his phone and opens a browser.

'I think that would be too good to be true,' says Naylor. 'Found anything, Brad?'

There's a look of surprise on Hagen's face. He holds up the search results.

'A bus route,' he says. 'Sunderland used to have a Magic Roundabout bus route.'

There's silence.

'Sunderland?' asks Naylor. 'A Magic Roundabout bus route in Sunderland?'

'Yes,' says Hagen, reading from the screen. 'It went all round the town and along the river, apparently, for the shoppers.'

'Well, I'll be damned,' says Campbell. 'I'm surprised you didn't know that, Bradley, coming as you do from that part of the world.'

'I'm from Gateshead, Sir,' says Hagen evenly. 'It's a different place, like Windsor is different from Reading.'

But Campbell isn't listening.

'Let's get to it, people,' he says. 'I think we just got our next lead.'

As Naylor puts the key in her door after her visit to the hairdresser's, her phone begins to ring. Laden down with shopping, she hurries to open the door, drops her bags on the hall floor and digs her phone out of her coat pocket.

'Hello, Ron.'

'Merry Christmas.'

'You're being a bit previous. It's days away yet.' She glances in the hall mirror at her freshly blow-dried hair, all silky curls and with a level of shininess she could never hope to emulate herself, and decides it looks pretty good. 'Though the festivities begin tonight, call-outs permitting. Big night out at Alfonso's. Bet you wish you were joining us, don't you?'

Ron laughs.

'Not really. I remember last year some pillock spilled a pint of raspberry cider or some such horror in my lap and I spent the rest of the evening feeling like I was wearing a wet nappy. Alfonso's wife lent me a hair-dryer but it didn't help much. And then there was an hour-long wait for a taxi in the pissing rain. But you go ahead, enjoy yourself.'

Naylor smiles.

'Thanks. I'm sure I will.'

'Who's your date, Rach?'

'I haven't really got one.'

'Not a certain senior officer from Traffic, I hope?'

Naylor feels a deep blush rise up her neck and cheeks.

'What d'you mean?'

'Don't you mean *who* do I mean? You know who I mean. Stop wasting your time there, for pity's sake. He's got form. You're not the first and you won't be the last.'

'How do you know about that?'

'Aha. Uncle Ron's network of spies runs right through that building. I didn't climb the slippery pole without knowing who's shagging who.'

'Bastard. Anyway, that's long over. I told him where to go over the summer, so your info's not as current as you'd like to think.'

'How do you know? Betcha I can put the name of the man you'll be leaving with tonight in a sealed envelope right now and I'd be right.'

'You do that, then. I'm not planning on leaving with anyone.'

'We'll see. Anyway, to be truthful I wasn't calling to find

315

out who you'll be kissing under the mistletoe. I was wondering how the Ferrers case was going, whether the Keslake abduction has given you any kind of leg-up.'

Naylor sighs.

'We're getting close. Evan's talking at last and we think he was taken to Sunderland, so obviously there's massive activity up there. But it's hard to know what's reliable witness statement and what's distorted by his being under the influence of the drugs they were giving him. He's mentioned tattoos, buying spiders, *The Magic Roundabout*. At least we've got plenty to go at. The bad news is, he thinks he wasn't alone, that there may have been a girl there with him. Ron? Are you still there?'

'I'm here,' says Ron thoughtfully. 'That's ringing a bell, somehow.'

'What is?'

'A distant, forgotten bell,' says Ron. 'But it'll come back to me.'

'So go and lie down in a dark and silent room until you remember.'

'I'll do better than that. I'll spend half an hour having a wade through my notes. You never know what I might find in there. Well, I'd better let you get on. No doubt you'll be stepping into a fragrant bubble bath with a glass of fizz to get you in the party mood. Shame I can't join you.'

'Cheeky.'

'Seriously, have a great time. Let your hair down. And I'm putting that name in the envelope now.'

'Waste of a good envelope,' says Naylor.

*

The bar at Alfonso's is packed with people Naylor barely recognises as those she shares an office with day-to-day. She's glad she kept the red dress; she feels good in it, and it's pulling one or two glances as she makes her way to where Rose is talking to Hagen and a crowd of others from the department. All of them look smart, relaxed, normal, just punters on a night out, a regular office party. Hagen puts a glass of wine in her hand, and as she takes the first sip, she hears a blast of laughter from a group near the door. Dallabrida's first joke of the night.

Dinner, as it turns out, isn't bad – essentially beef in red wine but with Italianate touches, breadsticks and pasta, curly endive in the salad and tiramisu at the end. By the time coffee's served, Naylor's enjoying herself, and in a moment of lucidity, she realises why. Last year, she'd spent half the evening in the toilets, obsessively checking her phone for a message from *him*. This year, she's free of that compulsion. Anyone she might be interested in is in this room.

People begin to drift back to the bar, and the DJ fires up. The music's loud and upbeat, and with the laughter and the alcohol they've already drunk, she and Rose are thinking they might order more prosecco. Naylor bends down to find her bag and hunt for cash. When she resurfaces, someone's standing by her chair.

'Looking good, Miss Rachel,' says Dallabrida. 'Red is most definitely your colour.'

Naylor finds herself smiling. Dallabrida's looking pretty good himself, decked out as he promised in a tuxedo with all the works.

'Nice threads,' she says, pointing to his jacket.

'I've got me dancin' shoes on an' all,' he says. 'You fancy comin' with me for a test drive?'

As Naylor steps with Dallabrida on to the dance floor, Ron Perdue carries a large glass of Merlot into his study, sits down at his laptop and opens up the file of notes he made on the Ferrers enquiry.

It's all in here, everything on the red Ford Focus and the places he visited.

Where did he go first? Sevenoaks, on the trail of Jennifer Lambert, to those grubby flats with the addict on the ground floor.

He reads through the notes he made. There isn't much, just a mention of a South African doctor and Ms Lambert's probable emigration, and his observation that he thought she was unconnected to the enquiry, a turned-over stone with nothing underneath.

Woking. He remembers the address when he sees it written down, and he's noted the registration number of an orange Mini Cooper. Attention to detail: it's a bad habit he's no intention ever of breaking. There was a school nearby; he remembers hearing the noise.

Lindsey Stockman. She'd asked what his interest was in the car.

And there it is, exactly the little detail he's looking for.

FORTY-TWO

21 December

Naylor's phone rings as she's driving to work, sitting in traffic at the Cauldwell roundabout, hearing Slade on the radio for the thousandth time this week.

'Good morning, Mr Perdue,' she says. 'How's tricks?'

She edges the car forward a couple of feet. The dashboard clock is showing a time which is getting close to her being late.

'How's tricks yourself? Did you have a good time Saturday night?'

Naylor smiles.

'As a matter of fact, I did.'

'And Sunday morning?'

'Way outside your area of interest, Ron.'

Ron laughs.

'Do you want me to open the envelope?'

'Did you really do that?'

'The name inside begins with L.'

'What makes you say that?'

'Right or wrong?'

'As one of our clients might say under caution, no comment.'

'I'll take that as a yes, then. He'd be good for you. Maybe he was already.'

'Moving on.'

'As you wish. While you were out heating up the dance floor, I was having a look through my old notes, and I came across something that could be interesting. That address I went to in Woking, a previous owner of the Focus.' Naylor hears a pause as he refers to his notes. 'Lindsey Stockman.'

'You said you thought she was clean.'

'At the time, I did. Maybe she still is. But she mentioned a car her ex-partner bought when he got rid of the Ford.'

A gap in the traffic has opened up in front of Naylor. Concentrating on what Ron's saying makes her slow to drive into it, prompting a beeping horn behind.

'What sort of car?'

'An Alfa Romeo.'

'And?'

'Maybe an Alfa Romeo Spider? Nippy little sports car, used to be many a middle-aged bloke's wet dream?'

'Bloody hell. Evan's spider could be a car.'

'Could be, maybe. Could be nothing of interest, but if I were you, I'd be having an official word with Lindsey Stockman. Rule it in, or rule it out. No stone unturned.'

Naylor's thinking.

'How am I going to bring it to the table, though? If Campbell finds out I asked you to go there, he'll go mad.'

'You're forgetting our old friend, the anonymous tip-off.'

'Who'd tip us off about that, though?'

'That's the beauty of anonymous tip-offs, Rachel. You don't

get to know who's made them, nor do you have to put a name to them.'

There's a short silence.

'You know what I'm going to ask you to do, don't you?'

Ron sighs.

'Ring it in, I suppose.'

'It would make my life a hell of a lot easier.'

'Do you want me to supply her full address?'

'It would save time if you did. And time is of the essence.'

'The things I do for you.'

'It's not for me, Ron, except in the way of saving my job. It's for Liam, and Evan, and for whoever might be next.'

'OK, I'll do it. But I'll be driving to a secret location and using an untraceable phone.'

'You've got a burn phone?'

'Haven't you?'

'Ron Perdue,' says Naylor, finally getting her slot to cross the roundabout, 'there's a lot more to you than meets the eye.'

'I sincerely hope so,' says Ron.

In the incident room, they're studying a satellite view of Sunderland. The most prominent feature by far is the river, an undulating muddy snake until it reaches the dockside and the surprising blue of the sea.

Hagen uses a mouse to focus on the double bridge carrying both traffic and the railway lines. With the bends in the river, the good news is there's a relatively short stretch of the banks from where you'd see the bridges. And on those banks, there are very few buildings where there are flats with river views.

'Looks like here or here,' says Naylor. 'University halls of residence, or this building here, the Echo building. It was supposed to be Sunderland's best address when it was built, but by all accounts it's a bit ropey these days.'

'I don't think it's likely to be the halls of residence,' says Hagen. 'Too much turnover and in the hands surely of the university admissions office.'

'I agree,' says Naylor. 'The only problem is, the Echo building's huge. There must be over a hundred flats in there. We have to find a way to narrow it down.'

The situation seems ridiculous, but also fun. Naylor assumes a serious expression, and speed-dials a number on her phone. Across the office, she hears Dallabrida's absurd but funny ringtone – a tannoy announcement, *Will the man with the twelve-inch penis please pick up your phone?* – and watches him discreetly as he pulls the phone from his pocket and glances at the screen. When he sees who's calling, he turns his back to her.

'Hey, beautiful,' he says.

'Hey, handsome,' says Naylor. 'How's tricks?'

'I'm doing OK. Just thinking about grabbing lunch.'

'Lucky you. Me and Hagen have bagged ourselves a ride out to Woking.'

'Is this your way of telling me you're breaking our date for this evening?'

'Not breaking it so much as letting you know there's a possibility I might be late.'

'How late?'

'You should know better than to ask anyone who works in this office a question like that.'

'You're right,' says Dallabrida. 'I should, and I do. How would it be if you came to mine when you're finished and we'll order a takeaway?'

'Tempting. Indian or Chinese?'

'Your choice.'

'Will there be wine?'

'Red or white, madam?'

'How could I resist? I'll call you when I'm on my way.'

Lindsey Stockman appears harassed. Her blond hair is falling out of the clip holding it off her face, and as she opens the door, she glances behind her, as if she's reluctantly abandoned something requiring her urgent attention. The hall walls are strung with clumsily made paper chains, red and green links marked by small, gluey fingers. In a room behind her, an episode of *Justin's House* is playing very loudly.

Naylor holds up her warrant card, and Lindsey peers at it, then looks directly at Naylor.

'Police?' she asks. 'I think you might have got the wrong house.'

The singalong music on the TV is annoying. Lindsey turns round and shouts down the hall – 'Izzy! Turn that down!' – but the volume stays the same.

Naylor introduces herself and Hagen.

'Are you Lindsey Stockman?'

'Yes.'

'May we come in for a moment?'

Lindsey hesitates before standing back to allow them to pass. Pointing the way to an untidy kitchen, she dives into the next-door room, and moments later, *Justin's House* is reduced to barely audible background noise, drowned out by the whining complaints of a young girl and boy.

Lindsey closes the door on the children and joins Naylor and Hagen in the kitchen. She doesn't ask them to sit, but in any case the stools at the breakfast bar are laden with discarded coats and a pink backpack embellished with unicorns. On one of the worktops, bags of shopping are waiting to be unpacked, and there's a mess of chocolatey crumbs and purple foil around an opened pack of Mini Rolls.

'Kids,' says Lindsey. 'I don't know why I bothered. So. What's this about?'

'We won't take much of your time,' says Naylor. 'We'd like to ask you a few questions about a car you used to own.'

'Let me guess,' says Lindsey. 'The Ford Focus.'

Hagen gives Naylor a sideways glance.

'That's right,' he says. 'What made you think that?'

'I had a man asking questions about it a while back, something about the brakes. Is he all right? Has there been an accident? I told him, the brakes were fine while we had it.'

'There hasn't been an accident, no,' says Naylor. 'You sold that car, I assume?'

'My ex sold it, yes. Nothing to do with me, and before you ask, I don't know who he sold it to.'

'We can find that out through the DVLA. Can you tell me what car he bought after that?'

Lindsey frowns.

'An Alfa Romeo. What's that got to do with anything?'

'What model?'

'A Spider, bright red. A beautiful car that was, a pleasure to drive. It's the only thing about him I miss.'

Hagen's pulling out his notebook.

'Can we just get some details from you, Lindsey? What's your ex's name?'

'Gary,' says Lindsey. 'Officially Gareth. Last name is Prentice, with a "c".'

Hagen hasn't made any connection, and he's writing down the name without thinking. But Naylor's memory has thrown up an image: the reconstruction following Evan's disappearance, and the caretaker standing by the school doors, telling Evan and Stewie to get a move on, as he rattles a bunch of keys.

'Gary Prentice is your ex?' she asks.

Picking up something in her tone, Hagen looks at her.

'Yes,' says Lindsey. 'This isn't about Gary, is it?'

'Should it be?' asks Naylor.

Lindsey moves to check the lounge door is still closed.

'Would you like a coffee?' she asks. 'I was just going to have one.'

'Thanks,' says Hagen. 'Milk and two.'

'Just milk for me,' says Naylor. 'Do you know where Gary's working now?'

Lindsey's filling the kettle and finding clean mugs.

'I've no idea. Our split wasn't too friendly and we haven't kept in touch. This is about him, isn't it?'

'I'll be as honest as I can with you,' says Naylor. 'When we knocked on your door, this wasn't about Gary, but it might be now. How did you two meet?'

Lindsey pours boiling water on to instant coffee and takes milk from the fridge.

'He was caretaker at the school where I work, Woodrow Primary in Guildford.'

A flicker of understanding crosses Hagen's face. Lindsey adds sugar to Hagen's coffee and hands both him and Naylor a mug.

'How long were you together?'

'Not long, maybe about six months. Looking back on it, he was a rebound for me. My husband had just left me, and I was feeling pretty low. Gary's attention was flattering. If I'd been a bit more myself, I don't think it would ever have got past a one-night stand.' She takes a sip of her coffee. 'When we fell out, it was pretty much over anyway. He never wanted to do anything except spend time on his laptop – eBay, Auto Trader. That's what he told me, anyway.'

'What did you fall out about?' asks Hagen.

Lindsey takes a deep breath.

'I caught him taking pictures of Izzy. Not naked, nothing like that. But he'd got her in her bedroom wearing my lipstick and one of my silk scarves, and he was encouraging her to do these poses, what I suppose you'd call coquettish. Something about it made me feel sick, but when I challenged him he got really angry. He said I was deranged, that he loved the kids and they were just having a bit of fun playing supermodels, but I felt I couldn't trust him any more. You read so many horror stories, don't you? It was over for me, after that. A couple of days later I told him to pack his bags and off he went.'

'What happened to the pictures he took?'

Lindsey's hands go to her face. 'I don't know. Oh my God. You don't think . . . If he's done anything with those pictures, I'll kill him.'

'Are you aware of the Evan Ferrers case?' asks Naylor. 'An abduction, late last year?'

Lindsey nods.

'I heard about that, yes. A boy taken on his way home from school.' She stares at Naylor. 'Not Gary's school? Was he working there? You know, after the incident with Izzy, I thought about reporting him, but I didn't because I thought it was just me. Tigress mummy, over-protective, you know? He must have passed all the DBS checks to be working in schools, mustn't he?' Naylor's eyebrows rise. 'Oh my God. I did the right thing getting him out of here, didn't I?'

'You absolutely did,' says Naylor. 'I just hope for the children's sake you did it soon enough.'

'Now that's what I call a result,' says Hagen, as they walk back to the car. 'If Prentice is still caretaker at Evan's school, he'll be easy enough to track down. I'll put a call in and get someone to bring him in.'

He presses the button on his key fob to unlock the car doors.

'This fella asking questions about the car a while back,' he goes on, climbing into the driver's seat, 'and us here on an anonymous tip-off. I don't suppose our anonymous tipster by any chance goes by the name of Ron?'

'I've no idea what you're talking about, Bradley,' says Naylor.

FORTY-THREE

22 December

In the interview room, Gary Prentice has adopted a bored expression which doesn't quite hide the spark of arrogance in his eyes. His solicitor is a dour, middle-aged man who's glanced at his watch once already, and clearly doesn't expect to be here very long.

Naylor settles in her chair next to Hagen, who's unnecessarily rearranging papers in his file. Prentice settles back in his chair, extending his legs in front of him so his feet touch hers. It's a power-grab on his part, taking up more space, but Naylor doesn't care. She folds her feet under her chair and gives Prentice a warm-up smile.

'Could you do the honours, Brad?' she says.

Hagen presses the buttons on the recorder, and they wait for the red lights to be steady and the beeping to stop before he recites the preliminary words – who's in the room, and the standard caution.

'We have a few questions for you, Gary,' he says. 'But before we start on those, we want to let you know we've been over at your house having a good look round, and we brought away a few things for closer examination. Laptop, phone, stuff like that.'

Naylor and Hagen watch Prentice's face, where the bored expression suddenly looks hard work and the spark of arrogance has gone.

'You had no right to do that! That's an infringement of my civil liberties!'

The solicitor shakes his head to let Prentice know he's wrong.

'Actually, it's all above board. We've a warrant all nicely signed and official,' says Hagen. 'Your girlfriend was a bit upset, I'm afraid. It isn't nice having people tramping all over your home, I realise that. But we believe the trouble was worthwhile.'

'We have some guys upstairs who really know what they're doing,' says Naylor. 'Everybody thinks when you press the delete button and empty the recycle bin, all that embarrassing stuff on your tablet or your laptop you never want anyone to see has vanished, like a magic trick. But those guys upstairs in forensics are really good at bringing files back from the dead. Stuff you've downloaded, especially. There are little bits of data that get right down into the innards of your computer – down into the sewers, you might say – and that's where those guys go fishing. And they're going fishing on your laptop, Gary. I wonder what they'll find?'

Prentice is silent.

'I'm curious too,' says Hagen. 'I'm wondering what'll get snagged on their lines. Do you want to tell us what's down there?'

'No comment.'

Hagen smiles a wide smile.

'This is no time for no comment, Gary. We've been talking

329

to your ex, Lindsey Stockman. You remember Lindsey, of course. According to her, you lived together for a period of time at the address where she's still living in Woking. That would be, we assume, while you were employed – as you told us in your original statement – at a school in Guildford. Woking to Guildford, that's an easy enough commute.'

Prentice doesn't speak.

'While you were living there, she confirms you and she owned a red Ford Focus, registered in her name but bought and sold through your eBay account. Is that right, Gary? And that's of great interest to us, because that car is the very one which had Evan Ferrers locked in the boot. What're the chances, eh? You right there on the day Evan goes missing, almost the last person to see him before he's snatched, and here you are again, a one-time owner of the car he was found in.'

The solicitor is paying close attention, making lengthy notes on a pad of paper.

'There's more,' Hagen continues. 'While Evan was locked in a car boot, being taken – well, maybe you can tell us where he was being taken? No? Anyway, while he was being driven away from his home and family, he overheard a conversation, two men talking about someone buying a Spider. I think you owned a Spider, didn't you, Gary? Maybe you still do. That's not conclusive by itself, but it's certainly a coincidence some might say connects you to those men. Put it all together and I'd say it's a good thing you've got legal representation.'

Prentice glances across at his lawyer, whose attention seems all on his notes.

'So this is where you start talking to us and volunteering information,' says Naylor. 'Do you know someone called

Brian? Brian Birch? We're giving you an opportunity here to save your own skin. Only to an extent, of course. You know you'll be going down for a stretch. But that stretch could be much shorter, if you'll help us out. We'll get a result with or without help from you, so this is a short-term offer only. Talk to us about Evan Ferrers and Liam Keslake, and we'll persuade the judge to look favourably on you when it's time for sentencing. I should say, while you're considering your options, that we'll be making the same offer to Brian when we catch up with him, and only one of you can benefit. There might be a decent reduction in the offing, but it's you or him. So what you have to ask yourself is, when we make Brian that same offer, will he refuse it to save your skin?'

Prentice's response is almost immediate.

'I want to speak to my lawyer in private,' he says.

FORTY-FOUR

23 December

Tuesday morning, and everyone's in so early, by 8 a.m., the coffee machine is on its second refill. Naylor's trying to make good use of her time, going through some of the statements on a new incident where a businessman and his family were robbed at gunpoint. It's a serious case – shotguns, violence and three traumatised children – and it should be getting her full attention, but her mind's on what she hopes is happening in Sunderland.

A few minutes after nine, Campbell walks into the office, sharp-suited and overloaded with aftershave. For once, he doesn't have to call for attention. All eyes are on him, and a hush falls on the room.

'OK, listen up,' he says, unnecessarily. 'I've just got off the phone with Northumbria, and I'm pleased to report a fantastic result from there.'

Naylor's surprised to notice she has butterflies in her stomach, and finds herself willing Campbell to say what she wants to hear.

Campbell glances at his page of notes.

'Acting on information received from Gareth – known

as Gary – Prentice, forced entry was made at an address in Sunderland early this morning. Two children – two children, ladies and gentlemen – were removed from the scene, one female, aged approximately six years old, identity not yet established – an interpreter is being sought – and one male aged eleven, who gave his name as Liam Keslake.'

A cheer goes up around the office. Naylor turns to Hagen, who's grinning, and Hagen gives her a double thumbs up. From across the room, a smiling Dallabrida gives her a wink.

'Furthermore,' goes on Campbell, when they settle back down, 'two arrests were made at the location and a further two have subsequently been made at addresses in Lancashire and Essex. Four men remain in custody to be charged with a range of offences. They are . . .' He looks again at his notes. 'Brian William Birch, Daniel Kawcznski, Neil Alexander Roper and Peter Clive Sewell. I've been asked to pass on thanks from both Northumbria and the Chief Constable to everyone who's played a part in what I think we can call a highly successful operation, which will of course be front and centre in the press when the news breaks. So, well done everyone. Great result.'

When Campbell's gone, the air of celebration remains, but as Naylor approaches Hagen, her delight at Liam being found is tainted by the feeling that the path they followed to make the arrests was too long and too slow.

She sees the same in Hagen's face.

'Is it a great result?' she asks.

Hagen shrugs.

'We did our best,' he says. 'And they got Liam out.'

'We might have got to Brian Birch earlier, if Border Control had been able to confirm in a timely manner he never went to Spain. That was a clever plan, shipping his missus over there as a decoy.'

'How could we have proved he hadn't left the UK?' asks Hagen. 'We couldn't have known he wasn't there until we found him here. We didn't drop any balls, Rachel. We just juggle so many of them, it isn't humanly possible to keep all of them in the air. If we'd been allowed to stay dedicated to this case, chances are we'd have got a faster result. Don't beat yourself up over it. Just think how happy Mr and Mrs Keslake are at this moment.'

Naylor recalls giving Claire Ferrers the news Evan had been found, the car journey to Pontefract, the way Claire ran down the hospital corridor to find her son, and knows Hagen is right. Better late than never.

'Someone had better call Mr and Mrs Ferrers,' she says. 'It'll be great news for them.'

'I hope so,' says Hagen. 'Maybe we should let them enjoy their Christmas first.'

Naylor understands his diffidence. There's no doubt Claire and Matt will be relieved Evan's tormentors are finally behind bars. But their arrests bring the prospect of courts and prosecutions, and proceedings which may cause as much stress to Evan as they will to those sitting in the dock.

FORTY-FIVE

25 December

Christmas morning, 6.30 a.m. Sitting in his chair with its view out of the window, Jack has drunk a pot of tea, but has no appetite this morning for his toast and marmalade. The blackness from outside seems oppressive, but there's no prospect yet of sunrise lightening the sky.

He's thinking about Christmas mornings of days gone by: boyhood days, the almost sleepless Christmas Eves and the unbearable excitement of the weight of a full Christmas stocking on the end of his bed, the thrill of a new bike or sledge under the tree. He's been remembering too his first Christmas with Dora, when he bought her an engagement ring that cost him a month's wages. In later years, that ring looked as cheap as it was, a tiny chip of a solitaire she needed a magnifying glass to see. As time went by, he bought her better jewellery, but the first ring he bought her never left her finger.

Now she's wearing it in her grave.

He feels that pain again in his chest. It's come and gone more regularly these past few days, a crushing, aching pressure which makes his fingers tingle and numbs his shoulder. If he sits still, it will shortly pass, and when it passes, he'll go and find his tablets and his inhaler.

The kitchen door opens, and Evan is there, looking small in his dressing gown – though Claire's recently bought him new slippers to replace his outgrown old ones – and carrying a pair of Christmas stockings.

Something gives a cruel stab to Jack's heart, sharp enough to take his breath away, and he feels his face lose colour. Even so, he finds a smile for Evan.

'Here he is,' he says, with a cheerfulness he's pressed even to fake. 'Merry Christmas!'

'Merry Christmas, Grandpa.' Evan holds up one of the stockings. 'Father Christmas left this for you. I thought we could open them together.'

Jack smiles, and the stabbing in his heart fades.

'Father Christmas brought me a stocking? Well, that is a surprise! I don't suppose I've had a stocking in fifty years! I wonder where he found the stuff to fill a stocking for an old man like me?'

'Harrogate, mainly,' says Evan. 'Shall we open them in here?'

'I'll tell you what, since it's Christmas, you run through to the front room and light the fire. Let's have it warm like your mother likes it, though the rest of us will be boiled to death like Christmas puddings. And then we'll go and sit nice and comfortable on the sofa, and see what we've got.'

Evan leaves him, and Jack takes advantage of the hiatus to force himself from his chair. His tablets and inhaler are in the drawer, and the hit from the inhaler brings almost instant relief, making him wonder why he lets himself get so miserable with unnecessary pain. Downing the maximum dose of tablets, he puts the kettle on to make more tea.

In the lounge, Evan's beaming with excitement.

'Look at all the presents, Grandpa!' he says, and it's true there are plenty, put there by Matt when they'd all gone to bed. With the fire going and the tree lit, the room's festive, but he'll miss the little niceties from Dora, the chocolate brazils and merino wool socks and the Marks and Spencer's vests he's always worn.

Evan's waiting expectantly on the sofa, the first of the brightly wrapped gifts from his stocking in his lap.

Jack sits down next to him.

'Come on, then,' he says, and takes out his first parcel. It's a thoughtful gift, but fuel for his heartbreak: like Dora always used to buy him, a box of chocolate brazils.

Boxing Day has been and gone, and in the squalls and gales of mid-winter, Ainsclough Top is bleak. There's snow on Blackmire Ridge which looks like it might be there till spring, and the old house will miss the cheering fairy lights and tinsel of another Christmas past.

Claire is sad to be leaving. Matt's business commitments have called him back to the office, and Claire wants to spend time with him at home, but she will miss Evan badly. She'll miss Jack too, and the farm; she's come to love the peace of its isolation almost as much as Evan does, and the gentle routine of its unhurried days is soothing to her soul. She's found time for things she never thought she'd enjoy – baking and reading – and she's dared to have a go at knitting with some of Dora's old yarn.

She's put one of her bags in the car boot, and she's hurrying back to the kitchen through the driving rain when the phone rings. Jack's sitting on the sofa, and it seems a shame to make him get up, so she answers it herself.

'Is that Claire? I'm glad I've found you. It's Rose Yazici here, from Ashridge police station. How are you doing?'

'I'm fine,' says Claire. She remembers Rose: the pretty one who looked after Evan when he was interviewed at Harrogate. 'You just caught me. I'm heading back south today. We've all been up here for Christmas. I think Matt's feeling it, coming home to an empty house every night, so I think it's time I did my wifely duty.'

'I'm glad you've had a good break,' says Rose. 'Recharged your batteries. I'm afraid you're going to need to be at peak resilience.'

Claire's heart sinks.

'Why?'

'It's good news, in many ways. I'd have come to talk to you in person, only we don't have the budget to keep making the trip.'

'I don't mind,' says Claire. 'Please, just tell me what's going on.'

'We've had a breakthrough in Evan's case. We've made some arrests.'

Claire sits down heavily on the stairs.

'You're kidding me. After all this time.'

'We haven't gone public yet because the operation's ongoing and there are more suspects out there we don't want to abscond. And of course we want you to know before it's in the press. There's even better news. We've found Liam Keslake.'

338

'Oh my God.' Tears fill Claire's eyes. 'Is he OK?'

'I wouldn't want to say that, not to you. You know better than anyone that there are degrees of OK. But he's alive, and going back home to his family as soon as the doctors give permission. Not only that, we've rescued another child, a girl who isn't known to us. We think she may be from Eastern Europe, but at the moment she's too traumatised to speak.'

'So where was this? Where did you find them?'

'In the north-east, in Sunderland. Please tell Evan we wouldn't have found them without his help. He was very brave and very unselfish to help us with those interviews. I know he didn't want to, and how difficult it was for him. So please thank him from everyone, especially Liam's family.'

'I will.'

'The thing is,' says Rose, 'we're going to need him again. There'll be a trial, of course, and we'll need Evan to give evidence. It won't be for a few months yet. There's plenty of time to get him ready emotionally.'

'It can't be avoided?'

'I'm afraid not. But it will be video testimony. He won't have to see his abductors.'

'How many were there?' Claire has asked the question before she realises she doesn't want to know, and Evan doesn't want her to know. 'No, don't tell me. What do you think we should do about Evan seeing the news? Do you think it would be good for him?'

'If he asks, then let him,' says Rose. 'Remember you gave him your word you'd take no interest. I would just leave the news alone. Watch something more cheerful instead.'

It isn't until Claire hangs up that she notices Evan at the top of the stairs, standing in the shadows, listening.

She smiles up at him.

'Hi, sweetie,' she says. 'That was Rose, from the police. Do you want to know what she said? It was quite important.' She pats the step beside her as encouragement, and Evan comes down and sits beside her. 'They've got them, Evan. They've got the men who took you.'

She isn't prepared for Evan's reaction, the burying of his head on her shoulder, the racking sobs and the way he clings to her. She puts her arms around him and pulls him close. The lounge door opens, and Jack appears. When he sees Evan crying, he looks concerned.

'They arrested them in Sunderland,' she says to Jack. Then she looks down at Evan, only now understanding the threat that he's felt, the fear that they might come for him to silence him. 'They can't get you now, sweetheart. They're all locked away. And they found Liam. Liam's fine' – though she knows this is a lie – 'and there was a little girl there too. Rose says it was thanks to you and what you told them in Harrogate that they found them. She says thank you from Liam's mum and dad.'

Jack's thinking of returning nightmares.

'I think you should stay,' he says. 'It's quite a shock for this young man.'

'It's a shock for us all,' says Claire. 'I'd better ring your dad and let him know.'

'And I think we should have a little celebration,' says Jack. 'A cup of tea, and chocolate digestives all round.'

*

Jack's right about the nightmares. A while after midnight, Evan shouts in his sleep, but Jack's so tired, he doesn't hear him.

But Claire hears. Pulling on her dressing gown and slipping on the fluffy rabbit slippers Evan gave her for Christmas, she makes her way to his room, and as Jack has advised her, opens the door as quietly as she can.

The books Evan had in his Christmas stocking are on the bedside table, and one has a bookmark in it about halfway through. But instead of the book he's currently reading, she hunts to the bottom of the stack, for a ragged old copy of *Winnie the Pooh*, and by the light seeping through the doorway, she finds the page she wants.

Evan is troubled and restless in his sleep, but Claire sits at his bedside and begins quietly to read.

'I don't feel very much like Pooh today,' said Pooh.
'There there,' said Piglet. 'I'll bring you tea and honey until you do.'

FORTY-SIX

3 January

In the mirror, there's no trace of the vital, fit, good-looking man Jack used to be. Instead, he's been replaced by someone barely recognisable, an old man with flabby biceps in a baggy vest. He's lost weight in his face, and there are blue bags under his eyes which make him look as if he hasn't slept in months. And he hasn't slept in months, not the long hours of deep slumber he used to fall into the moment the light was out, with Dora beside him in the best place in the world, his own bed in his own house. Sleep these days is erratic, demanding his surrender at odds hours of the day so he has no choice, wherever he is, but to find a place to make himself comfortable and close his eyes. Yet when he most feels the need for it – in the lonely night with the place beside him empty – sleep is elusive and refuses to take him, so what used to be the world's best place is nothing more now than a reminder of all his world is lacking.

Wetting his face, he rubs shaving cream into the short stubble on his jaw. He makes the first swathe with the razor, then rinses the soap and whiskers from the razor in the basin and makes a second cut.

The pain which hits him is astonishing in its severity and suddenness, as if he's suffered a violent sledgehammer blow to the chest. Without knowing how he got there, he finds himself on his knees, leaning on the toilet seat with one arm, holding himself with the other, as if doing so will help reduce the pain. He's going to be sick, but doesn't want to be, as being sick's incompatible with lying down. He lies down now – his body compels him – as his mind is urgently weighing the possibility that this might be it, whatever it becomes. Yet there's a remnant of instinct crying out, a glimmer of hope that he might survive, if he can get help. It's that instinct which makes him struggle to shout – though the best he can manage is more of a groan – and realise if there's to be help, he must let them in. Before the black descends, with everything that's in him he reaches up and turns the key to unlock the bathroom door.

What Jack remembers next is a view of the basin pedestal and his face on the bath-mat; the pressure of the door in his back, and someone calling his name; two men in green suits, and a yellow mask over his face; a needle in his arm, and the lessening of pain; being manhandled into a chair, and a skewed view of the pictures on the landing walls; Evan's tearful face, and the worry written on Claire's; the slam of the ambulance doors.

Beyond that, nothing.

Even though he feels like death, tender and sore inside and weighed down with a tiredness that makes it an effort to raise a cup of water to his lips, Jack's cheered to see their faces. Matt's hiding his concern behind a smile full of relief. Claire just looks pleased to see him, and Evan's beaming and proud to be carrying gifts – black seedless grapes, a James Patterson paperback and a copy of *Farmers Weekly*.

Evan's intrigued by the environment, the mechanics of the automatic bed, the table-on-wheels with its jug of water, the drip and needle arrangement in the back of Jack's bruised hand.

Claire's finding chairs as Matt sits down on the bed.

'How are you feeling, Dad?'

Jack wants to lie and say he's fine, but he's feeling so unwell it's too much effort.

'Better than I did when I was lying on that bathroom floor. I thought my time had come.'

'We brought you these,' says Evan, and lays the presents on the over-bed table. 'I wanted to get you a Mars Bar, but Mum says you're probably not supposed to have chocolate for a while.'

'What have they said to you?' asks Matt. 'What have they done?'

'Angioplasty.' Even though Jack should be feeling better, his breathing still feels difficult, as if something heavy is weighing on his chest. 'Some sort of stent. They should have done it years ago. Might have avoided all this drama if they had.'

'When are you coming home, Grandpa?' asks Evan.

'I don't know, son,' says Jack, and as he says it he's suddenly homesick, for the simple pleasures of his old armchair and a hot cup of tea, for the view across the valley and the bleating of the sheep, for cold air that smells of rain and grass, and for Millie running ahead of him across the yard. He misses it all, and feels a sudden, devastating sense of loss as if it might be lost to him for good, and he wants to cry.

But he doesn't want to make a fool of himself.

'Pull up a chair, youngster,' he says, 'and help yourself to some of those grapes.'

'Don't you want them?' asks Evan, but he's already pulled half a dozen from their stalks and is popping them in his mouth. 'Do you want me to read to you? We brought a book in case you do.'

Jack thinks of the nights he's read to Evan, whether Evan in his sleep heard him or not, and it strikes him how, sometimes, life takes odd turns.

'I found nine eggs this morning when I went to feed the chickens. I fed the sheep too. I think one of them is lame, but I couldn't catch her by myself to see the problem.'

'Your dad will help you, won't you?' Jack looks at Matt as he speaks, and Matt frowns, sensing his father is talking about more than rounding up sheep. He gives Jack's hand a squeeze, and is surprised when Jack replies with pressure of his own, a tight grip which leaves his knuckles white. 'You must all help each other. That's what families do.'

Sensing Jack's uneasy mood, Claire tries to change the subject.

'Would anyone like coffee? I saw a machine just outside the ward.'

'Hot chocolate,' says Evan, without hesitation.

'I'll have one, yes,' says Matt. 'Dad?'

Jack shakes his head.

'Evan, you come and help me carry them,' says Claire. 'I can't carry three.'

Jack watches them until they disappear past the nurses' station.

'You will look after him, won't you?' he asks. 'He's got a tough time coming up. You'll have to take care of him while it's going through the courts.'

'Don't be daft, Dad. You're just feeling a bit down after the operation. They fill you full of drugs and you don't know whether you're coming or going. You'll be home to look after him yourself in a couple of days.'

Jack doesn't answer. On the monitor above his head, the line showing the rhythm of his heart is steady as it should be, but Jack can't shake a sense of dread, that the regular rhythm is no more than a diversion, and that an enormous change is waiting in the wings.

That night, alone in the dark, Jack can't sleep, probably because he isn't alone at all. Even from the luxury of a bay to himself he can sense other bodies nearby, occasionally hearing their snuffling and snoring. It isn't truly dark either, with fluorescent light leaking from the nurses' station, where from time to time the night shift gathers to chat and keep the patients awake.

But despite physical evidence to the contrary, Jack feels alone, and he senses the darkness deepening. He decides to keep his eyes closed so as not to see it, but with them closed he senses something else, someone standing watching him from the end of the bed.

He opens his eyes. No one is there, but the sense that someone's close by won't go away.

'Dora?'

He glances up at the machine tracking his heart – all the lines look normal – and closes his eyes again against the light he doesn't want.

As soon as his eyes close, he senses again that someone is there, alongside the bed now, almost touching his face. Maybe one of the nurses has come to take his blood pressure, and he waits to hear her speak, but no one tries to wake him. Lying perfectly still, he listens, but if someone is there, their breathing is silent. After a while, he finds he doesn't mind them being there. He's finally easing into sleep, tempting himself to drift off by replaying memories he loves: the first lambs of spring running on the home field; Dora on their wedding day; the day Matt first rode a bike; happy young Evan and himself hand in hand, carrying their fishing net down to the stream.

When the pain hits, it's a harder blow even than in the bathroom, an explosion in his chest which takes away his breath and numbs his arms. There's a moment he knows he should press his red button, but the thought of doing so is transitory and floats away.

Dora. His last thought is the certainty that it's Dora waiting at his bedside, and he's grateful that she's there. Her presence soothes his strong objection that his time has come too soon.

2.43 a.m., and at Ainsclough Top the phone is ringing, heralding bad news, just as it was the night Evan was lost. Befuddled with sleep, Matt hurries down the stairs and grabs the receiver before the caller rings off. As he listens to what the nurse is saying, he's looking at the photograph of Jack and Evan, his younger, fitter father and his happy, smiling son.

'I'm very sorry,' says the nurse. 'It was totally unexpected. There must have been another problem we weren't aware of.'

Matt is in a daze.

'What do we do now?' he says. The question is rhetorical,

a reflection on the abyss of the future, but the nurse answers with practical details on undertakers and morgues.

Matt understands none of it. When he puts the phone down, Claire's standing beside him. She puts her arms round him, and Matt begins to cry.

FORTY-SEVEN

9 January

In the days following Jack's death, some difficult decisions must be made. Matt and Claire are suddenly the owners of two properties, the Berkshire house where their life has been, and Ainsclough Top, where Evan is happier – as is Claire, now.

Matt and Claire are sitting in the kitchen, drinking tea and looking out on the view Jack loved, the view Matt grew up with. The rain has turned to sleet, and there's already a covering of white on the home field. Evan is in the lounge, staring at the scattered pieces of an Airfix model, seeming to lack interest in any pastime at all.

'I can't just quit,' says Matt. 'We have a mortgage to pay, remember?'

'Not for much longer,' says Claire. 'Whichever house we sell, there'll be no more mortgage. Evan doesn't want to live in that house again, and I don't care about it either. It would get snapped up. Close to motorway links, good school catchment area. All the reasons we bought it will sell it again.'

'And then what?'

'We'll live here.'

Matt's cup is at his lips. Over its rim, he raises his eyebrows in incredulity.

'Look at this place,' says Claire. 'Matt, it's gorgeous.'

Matt laughs.

'It's old and draughty and bitter cold. Set one foot outside now and it'll freeze your extremities.'

'But Evan doesn't mind that. He loves being outside. He's flourishing here.'

Matt lowers his voice.

'He's not flourishing, Claire. He's reclusive. He has no friends and no prospect of any. He's got the body of a young man and the emotional age of an eight-year-old.'

'That's a defence,' says Claire. 'It's the plaster on the wound while it heals. One day that plaster's coming off, and there'll be a new Evan underneath. In his own time, when he's ready.'

'I wish I shared your optimism.'

'What's the alternative, anyway? If he never moves on, where else can he be safe but here? What's your suggestion, that we move to Maidstone or Bracknell or Slough, where he'll stand out like a sore thumb? I know what you're thinking, Matt. You're thinking you don't want to give up your company car and your designated parking place and your smart office and your seat at that big table in the boardroom.'

'I don't see what's bad about that. I worked hard for those things.'

'I know you did, and I'm not criticising you for that. But in case you hadn't noticed, something bad happened to us, and that changes everything. Our ambitions don't count any more. The only thing that counts is doing what we can for our son, the same way as we would have done if he'd lost a leg or suffered catastrophic brain injuries. He's crippled, Matt. The only thing is, we can't see the damage. But we owe him our support until he doesn't need it any more. Please, think about alternatives.'

'What alternatives?'

'There are other jobs, Matt. Other companies. Couldn't you try looking for a job near here? You know it's what your dad would have suggested.'

'It's just not what I see as my future. Our future. We like the urban life.'

'We used to. Things are different now. Please.'

She reaches out across the table, offering her hand. He hesitates, and then takes it.

'I'll think about it,' he says.

As the second hymn ends, the vicar beckons Evan from the front pew. Outside, the day is bitter, bright and blue; inside the church, the cold of centuries accumulated in the stone floor is numbing Claire's feet. There's the scent of white lilies, beeswax polish and, from the prayer books and embroidered hassocks, the mustiness of damp. Except for a throat-clearing cough, the rows of mourners behind them are silent. As he walks to the lectern, Evan's new black shoes sound loud.

He's getting taller, filling out, and in his suit, shirt and tie, Claire thinks anyone would take him for a normal young man on his way to adulthood. And any normal young man would be nervous at the prospect of what Evan's about to do. For Evan, it's the equivalent of a difficult assault on Everest, and Claire feels so proud she could cry.

Painstakingly printing in his childish handwriting, Evan's

copied out on to card what he intends to read. He, Matt and Claire have written the words together during an evening of reminiscence, Evan eating chocolate digestives in Jack's honour, Matt and Claire toasting him in Glenfiddich.

Evan props the card up on the lectern.

Claire's afraid for him. She's afraid he won't be able to speak, more afraid he'll look a fool. The silence grows long. Flushed with embarrassment, Evan glances down at his card and clears his throat.

Beyond that, the silence grows longer.

Claire's thinking about going to rescue him, standing up to stand beside him, when Evan finally speaks in a voice that's clear and strong.

'My grandpa was a man who loved the land. He loved the fells in summer and the frosty fields in winter. He loved to watch the fish swim in the beck and hear the skylarks sing. He loved his sheep and he loved Millie, his dog. He loved my dad and mum and he loved his friends and everybody here. He loved my grandma very much indeed.'

Chin trembling, he falters, unable to read any more of what he has written until he has wiped away tears with the back of his hand. Claire can hardly bear to look at him and see the misery of his grief. Matt's head is bowed.

But Evan carries on, and says his final words.

'My grandpa loved me, and I loved him. I miss you, Grandpa.'

FORTY-EIGHT

31 May
Crown Court Trial, Day 1

'We have to stop meeting like this,' says Ron. 'People will talk.'

The Lamb and Lion is quiet, in its usual Monday lunchtime dip. Naylor is already sitting at a window table, though there's no view to the outside through the thick glass in the leaded panes, only half-hearted, watered-down daylight which doesn't reflect the brightness of the warm day outside.

'Let them talk,' she says. 'It never bothered us before. Nice tan, by the way. Don't tell me you've got the sun-bed habit?'

'Not in the way you mean,' says Ron, taking off his jacket and hanging it on the back of a chair. 'We've had a couple of weeks away. Malaga, very nice. Didn't want to come home.'

'We all have to come home.'

'Maybe,' says Ron. 'You want another drink?'

'I'm all right with this, thanks.' Naylor points to her orange juice and soda.

While Ron's at the bar ordering his pint and their food – steak and kidney as always for himself, regardless of the weather, a chicken Caesar salad for Naylor – she's thinking he's changed, and trying to put her finger on exactly what's different. Straight after his retirement, anyone would still have picked him out as a copper. He hadn't lost the tension everyone at the job seems to carry, even on downtime, with the permanently overhanging threat of the ringing phone, regardless of whether you were in Malaga or Margate; the buzzing in the brain, *did I think of this, what if we did that*. All that seems to be leaving him at last. Looking at him now, he's a regular bloke, as likely to be taken for an ex-accountant as a retired detective. It's taken him a while, but it seems as if Ron might have actually, mentally, retired.

As he sits down, she sees it in his face. The old Ron had that skill of keeping one eye on the room, ninety percent focused on whoever he was with, ten percent aware of his surroundings, who was coming in, who was going out. For the first time since she's known him, he seems properly relaxed.

'Bottoms up.' He raises his pint, and they chink glasses. 'So. How's it going?'

'First day of the trial today. Nothing to report yet, of course, just the usual legal arguments, all the jury stuff. You know how it goes. It's going to be a long one. The whole case will keep the CPS in business for years to come.'

'How many did you hoover up in the end?'

'The network we've uncovered so far includes thirteen men, some more involved than others. There's been a massive amount of work tracking them down, mainly via internet history and phone records, and we've shut down a number of sites on the dark web. Very nasty stuff. Let's not go there.

Gary Prentice has already pleaded guilty but will only do two years, thanks to information he provided. But he'll go on the sex offenders' register and that's worth something too. Thanks to you, Ron.'

'That's a fantastic result, Rachel. I was merely following your direction. Congratulations.' Ron raises his pint to toast her.

'It gets me down sometimes, to be truthful,' she says. 'No matter how many of the bad guys we take out, there'll always be more tomorrow.'

'Why can't people just behave themselves, eh?' asks Ron.

'Exactly.'

'Ah, the problem of all mankind, right through history. Sounds to me like you're at that point where you have to abandon your ideas of saving the world and accept you can only do so much. Keep focused on your successes.'

'Is that what you did, Ron?'

He takes another sip of his pint.

'Sometimes. When June reminded me. The wisdom is hers, not mine.'

A young waiter arrives with their food. Ron's pie smells deliciously savoury, and Naylor briefly regrets her healthy choice, but there's a holiday bikini to be considered, in a few weeks' time.

'Cracking,' says Ron, picking up his knife and fork. 'Wherever you go in the world, you can't beat British pub food.' He reaches for the vinegar bottle and shakes it over his chips. 'How are those two boys doing, Evan and Liam?'

Quietly in the background, a song Naylor knows well but can't name begins on the sound system. The lyrics seem sadly apropos, speaking of a return to childhood's innocence.

Without a large dose of amnesia, for Evan and Liam that must be an impossible goal.

And yet . . .

'Liam I don't know about,' she says. 'He's not officially our case. But I've seen a fair bit of Evan, and I have to say I think he's finding his way. His own way, at least. He isn't hanging out with his mates down the skate-park or anything, and the parents are still concerned that he's stuck in his own little time warp, that he's suffering from arrested development. And maybe he is, but maybe that's OK. If he wants to stay a youngster for a couple of years – or even for the rest of his life – does it matter? Isn't there a bit of Peter Pan in all of us that would rather not grow up? Given a choice, I'd love to spend my time building tree-houses. He's not shut away in a dark room taking way too many drugs and hooked on video games, which is what a lot of people would call normal, these days. He's making the best of the terrible, awful hand life dealt him, and I think we can all learn from that.'

Ron smiles.

'Very philosophical.'

'We have to keep learning. Life's a shark pool. If sharks stop swimming, they die. If we stop learning, we sink.'

'And what shark's eating you today, Inspector?'

'Oh, I don't know.' Not really hungry, she lays down her fork. 'The way it was all handled – which wasn't exactly badly, but we made some mistakes – I'm not proud of that. Those mistakes weren't far off being fatal errors. It's all reactive, changing priorities every five minutes, so there's never enough time to do a thorough job. But while we were being transferred on to other cases – which I admit were important, it wasn't

356

like we moved on to handbag-snatching or sheep-rustling – Evan was still lost, still waiting to be found. And we weren't looking.'

Ron studies her.

'You didn't know that. You and I know that he was likely to be dead within days, maybe within hours of the snatch. People like Campbell and the Chief make difficult decisions. That's why they make the big money. You only have to do as you're told. They're the ones doing the telling, and those are tough calls they make.'

'I know. But if you hadn't got involved and done a bit of the legwork, we might never have made that connection to Prentice, and those thirteen would still be out there now.'

'We broke the rules. It paid dividends. We were lucky.'

'We have to play by rules. Those we're hunting don't.'

Ron picks up one of his chips with his fingers and holds it out to Naylor.

'Carbohydrate and fat deficiency,' he says. 'Bad for your mental well-being. Have a chip.'

Smiling, she takes it.

'You're the guys in white hats,' says Ron. 'Never an easy job, especially when you're facing a sea of black Stetsons. If you've had enough, give it all up and go and work at Primark. But I don't think you're going to do that.'

'Too right. I'm too pig-headed to give up. But you didn't come here to listen to me whinge about how the job's not perfect. It's hardly news to you, is it? What about you, Ron? I have to say you're looking good. Malaga suits you.'

'It's funny you should say that. Are we having pudding, by the way? I've a taste for some sticky toffee cheesecake. June and I are thinking it's time we did a bit of travelling. She's persuaded me to buy a camper van.'

'A camper van? Rocket Ron Perdue, one-time legend of the high-speed chase, in a camper van?'

Ron looks embarrassed.

'I know,' he says. 'Not quite my thing, you'd be thinking. But to be honest, I feel ready for life in the old farts' lane. We're going to head across to France, then just bumble about a bit, see where the road takes us. Down to Italy, if we get that far. Good food, maybe a bottle or two of wine, maybe even a case or two.'

'Sounds brilliant. But what if we need your undercover assistance or an anonymous tip-off?'

Ron shakes his head.

'Not this side of September. But you never know, come winter, I might be available for hire. And I come cheap, these days. A pie and a pint, and I'm all yours.'

'I'm glad to hear it.'

'And what about you, Rachel? I trust you're going to make good use of your precious leave this year? No repetition of last year when you had two weeks home alone in your flat?'

'As a matter of fact, I am going away this year.' Naylor gives Ron a big smile. 'Two weeks on the Costa Blanca, just outside Alicante. I can't wait.'

'And will you be travelling alone?'

She smiles again.

'Not exactly.'

Ron reaches into his trouser pocket and pulls out an envelope.

'Remember at Christmas, I put a name in here?'

Naylor looks surprised.

'I thought you were joking about that.'

'I did it as a little test for myself, and now I'd like to find out for certain if I'm right. I reckon that I have in here the name of your travelling companion.' He tears open the flap, takes out a slip of paper and shows her the name written on it. Leon Dallabrida.

Naylor laughs.

'How did you do that?'

'By my amazing powers of deduction. Well, more observation, actually. He had a thing for you for a long time. It's just that you were a bit slow on the uptake.'

'I had other fish to fry.'

'Rotten, dead, stinking fish. Leon's a good man, a heart of gold.' He picks up the remains of his pint and raises his glass. 'Happy holidays.'

Naylor chinks her glass to his.

'Happy travels. Drive safely.'

'Sometimes you need a break,' says Ron. 'But make sure you both come home ready to get stuck back into the fight.'

FORTY-NINE

28 June

Crown Court Trial, Day 21

Ron's not taking the kind of interest in the Ferrers trial he would have a year ago. There's too much to do readying the van, chrome to be polished, crockery to be bought, maps and ferry schedules to be pored over.

It's been a while since he's caught the Six O'Clock News, but he's sat down for ten minutes while June is putting the finishing touches to dinner. The credits roll, and there it is in the headlines, lead item on the BBC, a summary of the abduction and Evan's miraculous return, and now the lengthy sentences handed down from the trial.

A set of mugshots flashes up on the screen. Four unremarkable-looking men with no apparent links between them, dissimilar ages, dissimilar backgrounds: Brian Birch, a middle-aged engineer from Essex; Daniel Kawcznski, a good-looking young man, a care-home assistant from Bolton; Peter Clive Sewell, a red-headed Scot, most recently working as a gas fitter; and Neil Roper, clinically obese and unemployed, a one-time IT specialist from Letchworth.

Nothing to link them but their predatory appetites.

Ron switches off the TV. In the kitchen, June's spooning food on to their plates. Ron takes a bottle of sparkling wine from the fridge and holds it up for her approval.

'This time tomorrow, we shall be far away from all this,' he says. 'And I think that warrants a bit of a celebration.'

Sunlight on Water

July

Much of what they owned in Berkshire didn't seem right for their new lives. A small removal van carried personal possessions and little more: clothes, jewellery, books, the washing machine to replace Dora's antiquated model, their beds and the TV.

There are a couple of boxes from Evan's bedroom too, books, games and posters, the contents of his desk, and he's been upstairs a while, sorting through it all. When he comes downstairs, he's carrying a photograph mounted on card.

'Look what I found,' he says.

Claire is at the kitchen table, working on her laptop, surrounded by jars of preserves. She makes no pretence at being capable of making jams and chutneys, but there's talent amongst the women in the village, and Claire's making it her mission to form and promote a co-operative and get their produce into stores. Amongst the jars there's one of pale-gold honey, harvested by Evan (with help from Helen Trewitt) from his first hive.

'What is it, kiddo?'

Evan lays the photograph on the table. Taken in his third

year of primary school, it shows his whole class, five rows of grinning children in blue uniforms and Miss Robbins looking disgruntled on the end. There's Evan, near the front, with a tooth missing, sitting between Stewie and Andrew Duffy, another friend from those long ago days.

Where are they all now? wonders Claire.

'I've been thinking about it a while,' says Evan, 'and I've decided I want to go back to school.'

When Matt comes home from work – a new job he finds he enjoys, despite a loss of status and an inferior car – Claire tells him the good news.

But Matt is sceptical.

'He's two years behind, at least,' he says. 'I can't see how it could work. He'll soon be fourteen, for heaven's sake. How could we put him in a class of eleven-year-olds?'

'There must be private schools, a special school who'd take him.'

Matt's taken a cut in salary and feels the need – justified or not – to be careful with money.

'And how much would that cost?'

'Does it really matter?' Claire asks. 'There's plenty from the house sale, and there's his victims of crime compensation. What better use could there be for it than that?'

'We could think about a tutor. Maybe that's the way to go.'

'I don't think it's the education he's wanting, especially,' Claire says. 'I think he's ready to make new friends.'

'He might hate it once he gets there,' says Matt.

'Nothing ventured, nothing gained,' says Claire.

*

At the weekend, Matt and Evan walk down to the churchyard to visit Jack and Dora's grave. Evan's picked wildflowers Jack always loved, and Matt's cut a few of the best roses from Dora's garden. The churchyard is peaceful, undisturbed except for a breeze in the beech trees and the cooing of belfry pigeons.

Matt picks a few blown leaves from the earth still mounded on the grave, and touches the newly placed headstone like a talisman. Evan's taking his time placing the flowers in the vase.

'So,' says Matt, 'your mum says you want to go back to school. Have you really thought about it?'

'Grandpa thought it was a good idea. He used to say I should, one day.'

'You could have a tutor at home, you know. Someone who comes to the house.'

Evan shakes his head, and places a white rose beside a stem of musk mallow.

'I'd like to try a proper school. See if I can make some friends.'

'If you think you'd enjoy it, I think that's a great idea.'

'Have you made friends in your new job?' Evan's question is heartfelt, and Matt feels touched.

'I think so. It's not something you can hurry. But there are some people I get on really well with, yes.'

'So it hasn't been all bad, moving up here?'

Matt considers. The air smells fresh, and not of diesel and fast food. When he drives home in the evenings, there's no traffic. Best of all, he has much more free time. Family time.

'No, it hasn't been all bad,' he says. 'In fact, it's not been bad at all.'

September

Claire's waiting for the bus. Through the open kitchen window she can see down to the road where it joins the track up to the house, and every school day, the wait is difficult, a reminder of the day he didn't come home. Every time she sees the bus pull up, she feels relief.

It's a day of Indian summer but the kitchen smells of autumn, of the fading leaves on the honeysuckle which climbs the house's old stone walls and of the blackberries she's picked to make a pie. She's thinking of tea on the terrace, because outside is always Evan's preference. He's drawn to meadows and woodlands and uplands, regardless of the weather. In that, he's like his grandfather.

The mini-bus pulls up at last, and Evan climbs down, gawky and slightly awkward in his school uniform. Usually, there's only Evan who gets off here, but today, there's someone else.

Evan is bringing home a girl.

Down at the stream, there's sunlight on the water, sparkling on the ripples.

Evan beckons to the girl, and leads her along the grassy bank to the pool where sticklebacks hide under the stones.

'Look,' he says, 'down there.'

She crouches beside him, and for a while watches with him the silver slivers cutting through the weeds.

'Come and meet my mum,' he says.

As they walk up the track, Evan takes the girl's hand. She isn't beautiful, but her face is kind.

Watching from the window, Claire sees them laugh, and feels a weight she didn't know was there lift from her heart.

Evan is reaching the end of his journey home. In his own way, he will be fine.

A honey-bee lands on the last of the roses, and Claire smiles.

ACKNOWLEDGEMENTS

Found would never have been completed without help from the Society of Authors, whose generous grant bought me much-needed time and space to write.

I offer a huge thank you to my editor Toby Jones, whose insights and molecular-level dissection inspired me to hone and polish the manuscript he first read into the book I hoped it could be.

In developing the police investigation, I mercilessly picked the brain of ex-Det Sgt Terry Parry, whose patient and thorough responses on the technicalities of contemporary detective work have been invaluable. Thanks, Tel.

To all my advance readers, thanks for your time and critiques, and a special thank you to Ken Fishwick, who went the extra mile (and then some) to check and re-check the timings throughout the novel.

Much of the book was written in the calm Norfolk oasis provided by Ann & Andy Allenby – thanks for the peace and quiet.

As always, thank you to my lovely agent Christopher Little, who found *Found* a perfect home.

And last but never least, thanks for everything to Andy, who's there through thick and thin.

Thank you all.